The Second
Continental War

(revised edition)

A Novel by
Deron Rennick

Dedication

To my grandmother, Margaret Macpherson-Villeneuve, who, during the Great Depression, and at only thirteen years of age, had to appear before a judge in North Bay, Ontario and convince him she was mature enough to quit school and raise her four younger brothers and sisters because both of their parents had died. She did it too. Wow! I love and miss you, Nanny. Yours truly was the Greatest Generation.

Deron

TABLE OF CONTENTS

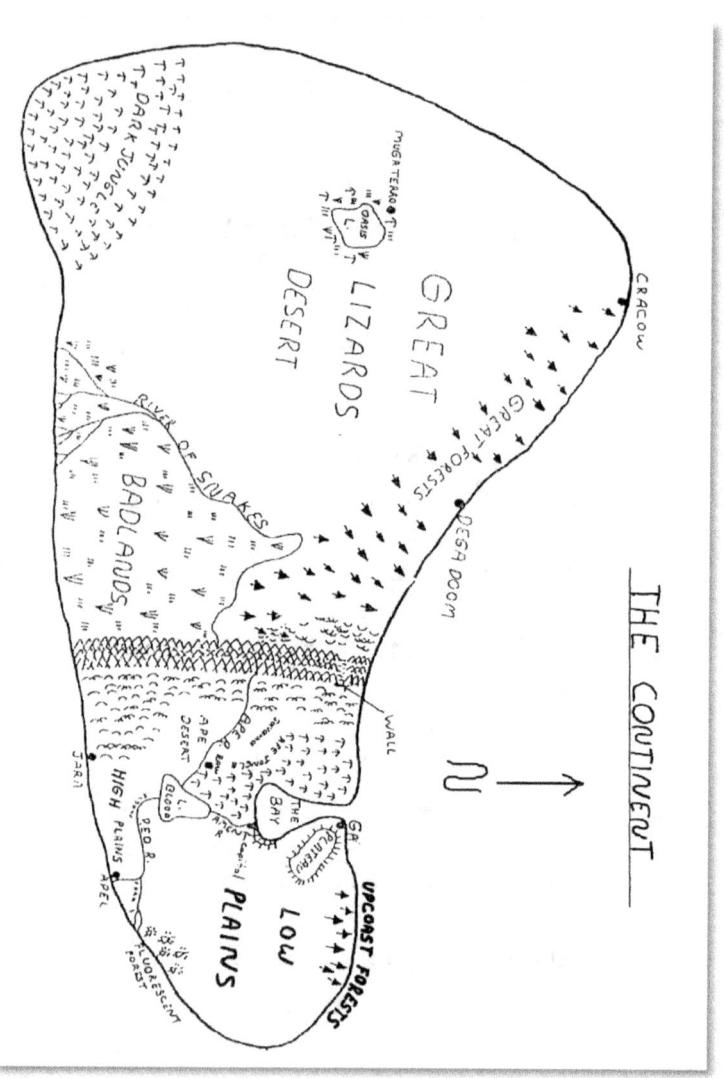

THE CONTINENT

N

Tarawa

The reflection in the mirror was that of a lean and lanky figure with rough, greenish flesh. His crimson eyes were set amongst a mess of facial scars, most notably an ugly scar that spread across his brow; a scar he had received courtesy of a black ape's fang. A serpent skin vest clung tight to his torso, while an intruding beam from the sun revealed the hidden purples, blues and gold's of his fine serpent skin skirt. Gems glistened in the gilded hilt of his scimitar sword, which hung in sheath from his belt.

One of his clawed fingers scratched an itch on his side, while his serpent skin boot tapped upon the marble floor. Yet he was clearly unaware of either, for he bore the sober face of one lost in thought.

All of Tarawa's thinking was locked onto the prods meeting and the part he would play in it. As Prod Commander of Land Forces, he enjoyed considerable influence with Supreme Pid in matters concerning ground operations, yet not nearly enough influence to suggest the supreme reconsider his plans for conquest altogether. It mattered not whether he felt the very idea of invading east was both dangerous and unnecessary. As supreme, Pid's power over his subjects was absolute; and he knew it. None but Prime Prod Dorak could even consider suggesting such, and Dorak mongered for war as much as Pid did.

No, it was not Tarawa's place to ponder politics. Being a prod commander meant his duty was to follow his supreme's orders and ensure all officers and soldiers under his command did likewise. Still, his keen mind could not help but question Pid's wisdom in igniting a foreign war with so many domestic situations in dire need of solutions. Thankfully, a lizarma's thoughts could still be kept secret within the confines of one's own mind. Were it not so, he would have met Morgue long ago.

The hungry ones especially were of great concern to him. Their capable leader, Sickly, was still free to cause chaos despite the efforts of Prod Gila and his silence squads to find and dispatch him. It was suspected that Sickly directed his *spoilers* from somewhere deep within the seemingly endless maze of tunnels and catacombs that crissed and crossed deep down beneath the bustling seaport of Dega Doom. Yet no spoiler had ever stayed of breath long enough to be interrogated. On those very rare occasions when one was captured while still of breath, the defiant captive would simply swallow his or her own tongue to meet Morgue. Such zeal for their cause deeply troubled Tarawa.

Seven cycles past, the hungry ones launched their first ever raids against the nobility. The raids were well-planned and carried out concurrently during a bleak and stormy night in Dega Doom, targeting several shops owned by wealthy merchants plus a small warehouse owned by an enterprising family of noble rank. Fortunately, no nobles or gentry were harmed and all the desperate group stole that fateful night were a few articles of warm clothing and some much-needed food and medicines. Unfortunately, the city's Royal Rep panicked and contacted the local silence squads for help. His overreaction had since proven to be a costly mistake.

Every lizarma knows the realm's silence squads never need just cause for their cruelty. In fact, whenever they find proof lacking, their abuse becomes all the more brutal. As far as Prod Gila's thugs are concerned, poor lizarme are always guilty of something. Thus, they readily obliged the rep by randomly hanging dozens of innocents in Dega Doom's rookery district. Just to set an example.

Tarawa shook his head as he recalled the shocked expression on Supreme Pid's face when, just ten days later, word reached Cracow that a group calling itself the *Hungry Ones*, besides admitting responsibility for the raids, had now retaliated for Gila's actions by snatching and hanging the very rep himself! The insolent group had even pinned a note into their victim's flesh, warning Pid and Gila against any further brutality against the poor.

It was the first time Tarawa ever witnessed the supreme's reason rescinded by rage. Pid's crimson eyes had bulged and blazed not unlike those of a beast taken with the frothing sickness. Gobs of saliva flung from the corners of his mouth while he screamed, "Make them meet Morgue! Put their hovels to the torch! Burn the entire rookery to the ground! Let none escape! You hear me! None! None! None! None! None!"

The silence squads swiftly carried out Pid's orders. Not a single hovel escaped the ensuing sea of flames. A great many innocents were burned or put to the blade; male, female and tot.

For nearly one full cycle, no more was heard of the hungry ones and all in Pid's realm returned to normal. Or so it seemed...

Then it happened. On the fifteenth occasion of Pid's ascension to the throne, the hungry ones struck again. Only, this time it was neither food nor clothing nor medicines they sought. While Pid's troops were proudly parading down Dega Doom's main way, Sickly's spoilers stole through an underground passage to raid the local garrison. Somehow they had evaded notice while tunneling beneath the fortress walls and up through the floor into its weapons cache. Over thirty of the realm's soldiers were slain to meet Morgue, while the hungry ones lost but two. Of far greater concern to the local nobility, however, the spoilers made off with a huge haul of weapons; including tridents, scimitars, metal shields and almost all of the local garrison's entire supply of modern crossbows and bolts.

It was the theft of the latter that concerned Tarawa the most. With barbed tips and a kill range well in excess of 300 strides, the new issue bolts were perfect for assassins.

Pid went raging mad over the matter. He demanded the hungry ones and their leaders meet Morgue at all cost. "Put all to the spit!" he had shrieked. "All! All! All! All! All!" Then he threw himself to the tiles in a tantrum, exerting behaviour which would have earned Tarawa's own tot a stern lecture and the removal of privileges.

An extensive and expensive military operation was immediately undertaken to flush Sickly and his followers from their catacombs deep beneath the ancient city. A number of the realm's toughest combat units poured down into the dark tunnels. Each unit was supported by rexids, the vicious tracking lizards with sabred fangs and retractable claws.

However, it was the hungry ones who ruled inside their subterranean maze; a labyrinth of countless tunnels, impasses, sheer drops and booby-traps. Sickly's spoilers simply cut the soldiers lifelines, thereby preventing entire units from finding their way back out. Torch oil was routinely poured down upon the confused and panicky intruders, then promptly ignited by flaming clay jars dropped from unseen hands.

On one occasion, the clever tunnel-dwellers had unleashed a barrage of boulders down a steep incline, burying more than two hundred of the realm's most battle-hardened troops. On another, the hungry ones managed to seal a large contingent of troops within a cavern and then flood it by diverting the flow from an underground stream; drowning all. Too often the blackness echoed with the screams of soldiers who had unwittingly *stepped* off a ledge. Or had they? No, the catacombs were no place for civilized beings. Whatever civilized means in a *civil* war?

Tarawa thought, *'Even the deities themselves would be loath to venture down into that hot and smelly place, where even the very stones seem to shift and sweat. Where every twist and turn is fraught with danger. Where wandering spirits share freely of their chilly aura when passing.'*

For over six cycles steady, the hungry ones had continued to grow in both numbers and daring. Their revolt had spread throughout the realm like famished flames across parched brush. Wary soldiers now patrolled the roads both day and night. Barely a night passed without at least one organized attack on a military unit or installation. Even the Royal Rep of Cracow had been assassinated. And right in his own bed!

"Dung," Tarawa cursed. "We are embroiled in a civil war that knows no front? A civil war that allows no quarter. These hungry ones strike and vanish like ghosts. They take and surrender no prisoners. Yet Pid keeps blind to it all. Rather than

4

see the much more dangerous enemy lurking beneath our very own cities, he is instead focused on invading foreign lands. The timing is all wrong. We will be fighting multiple enemies on multiple fronts. First, we must defeat the enemy within our own borders before we..."

"Who are you talking to?" a soft voice inquired from an adjacent room.

Turning from the mirror, Tarawa watched his mate enter their bed chamber. How lovely and graceful she appeared in the flowing gown that matched her beautiful blue eyes. Her smooth, greenish flesh shone without blemish. Her playful smile teased him for speaking aloud to himself.

Even though it was common practice for male nobles to take concs, Tarawa had chosen to spend his future with just one mate. And why not? Anole had wed down to share their love and dreams. Just thinking of her always made him feel all nice and warm inside.

"Talking to one's reflection can be cause for concern," Anole quipped. "Especially if you're losing the argument."

He returned her smile as best his mood would allow. "Military matters weigh heavy on my mind, Anole. Soon we will be at war with both the hungry ones and the eastern allies. We could even find ourselves at war with the antemi as well, should Empress Antraha find her own opportunity in our push eastward. As powerful as our army is, I have a gut feeling..."

"I do not understand this needless war of expansion," Anole interrupted. "Have we not already more land than we need?"

Tarawa's reply was blunt. "It is not a soldier's place to question his supreme's motives. Not even a prod's. You know this, Anole."

Noting Anole's hurt reaction to his tetchy tone, Tarawa crossed the room and cupped her cheeks in his hands. He stared deep into her pouting eyes, before gently licking her brow.

"You are right," he conceded. "We do have more land than we need. Much more. Were it within my power, there would be no wars and our poor would be better treated."

Anole smiled and snuggled tight into his long arms so they could feel each other's energy.

Ever so gently, Tarawa slipped his hand up under her gown and began rubbing her growing belly. It brought him great joy to feel his mate in a bearing way and they licked passionately at each other's faces.

"You must speak with your tot," Anole said, suddenly pulling free from his embrace.

Noting the seriousness in her tone, and the fact that their tot had just become *his* tot, Tarawa responded with some concern. "Anole, what has Gekar done to upset you?"

"Your tot brought home this note from his learner. It says he is doing poorly in classes. He even told his learner a noble education is of no use to him – that his own father is low born, and yet he was still granted noble status for his proven courage and loyalty to the realm. He also told her he intends to become a prod just like his father, and since you only learned your letters after becoming a soldier he can't see how reading fits in with his plans. Dearest Destiny, Tarawa, our son's still a tot. He's only in the first grade. Barely six cycles aged and he already glorifies the gory of war! How many other tots think like this?"

Tarawa calmly took the note from his mate's hand. As he read it, his manner sank somber. He huffed heavily before patting her shoulder and departing the chamber.

'The gory of war', he thought to himself as he strided down the corridor to Gekar's room. *'Sometimes Anole says much with few words.'*

He thought of something else his mate had once said to him, spoken upon his return from what proved to be his final hunting trip just for the simple sport of it. *'Perhaps beasts enjoy a superior simplicity of sense from which we who wage war can learn much?'* he mused, growing a grin. Then the unwelcome thought of his tot following in his footsteps shed his smile.

While approaching the door to his tot's room, Tarawa paused briefly to ponder his course of action. He always disliked having these contests with Gekar, even if they were oftentimes necessary. The youngster was exceptionally clever for his age, and Tarawa had learned through experience that a clever tot can and will match wits with any unprepared elder.

Tarawa had never believed in the flawed parental philosophy of, *"Do as I say, not as I do."* Neither had his own father for that matter, or his father's father. Even in his profession, the proud prod would never ask anything of his subordinates he would not do himself. This style of leadership by example endeared him to his troops, and he hoped it would produce fine adults of his tots.

While seven cycles of military service were now mandatory for all male nobles, Tarawa often prayed unto Destiny that young Gekar would not make such his career. Of course, now that his mate was once again in a bearing way, he would soon have to double up on his prayers. Regardless of the new suckler's gender, Tarawa wanted both of his tots to become skilled in matters of medicine or science or law. Secretly, he wished to be the last career soldier in his line, and he often told Destiny so.

After pausing to exhale a parent's sigh, Tarawa turned the latch and swung open the door. He barely suppressed a slight smile as he beheld his son directing a wooden dact in flight.

Upon seeing his father, Gekar lowered the toy to his side and came straight to the point. "Mama told you about the note, huh?"

Tarawa nodded that she had.

"She always tells," Gekar complained, tossing the toy onto his cot.

"Do you remember our little talk from the last time we went netting for finners?" Tarawa asked.

Gekar dropped his eyes to the floor and shrugged his shoulders. "Yes, Papa," he replied meekly.

Tarawa stepped forward and dropped to one knee. He gently nudged his tot's pouting chin upward. "Then tell me why you keep slacking in class?"

It was obvious Gekar had anticipated the question. "Because learning letters got nothing to do with soldiering."

What wasn't obvious to Gekar was his keen father had also anticipated the answer. "Oh, really?" Tarawa bated him, while calmly pushing to his feet.

7

"Well, it don't," Gekar said, parting his hands. "What does learning letters got to do with shooting a bow or wielding a blade? Most soldiers can't read. Even you couldn't until mama learned you, and still not very well until after you became a commander."

"Hmmmm?" Tarawa mumbled as he pretended to ponder. He casually clasped his hands behind his back and locked stares with his defiant tot.

Tarawa continued, "Let us suppose you are made a low commander and a runner brings you sealed orders from your superiors. Orders so secret the runner was not allowed to read them. The message is in code and the orders state you are to send a fixed number of troops to a set place at a set time. Such orders are quite common in battle. How would you know how many troops to send?"

"I can count," Gekar replied rather smugly. "And I know how many soldiers each unit is sposed to got."

Now Tarawa knew he had him. "Ah, but you can't read well enough to understand code. How would you know how many soldiers you were supposed to send to start with?"

Gekar sensed he was being lured into one of his father's traps, yet he didn't know how to elude it. "I would ask somebody who reads code to tell me."

"How would you know where to send the troops?" Tarawa pressed.

"Well – um, I'd ask him that too."

"How would you know when to send them?"

It was obvious Gekar was growing more uncertain with his answers. "Um – I'd have him tell me that too."

Tarawa grinned. "But nobody else can read the message because the orders are so secret and they are meant for your eyes only. Now what are you going to do?"

The confused tot wanted to respond, but his racing mind couldn't catch the right words.

His father persisted. "Even if you were permitted to show another the message, how would you know if he was in fact giving you the correct information? What if he was making a mistake? In battle, mistakes cost lives. Sometimes a great many lives."

Again, Tarawa's questions were met with uncomfortable silence.

Tarawa finally broke the silence. "You have received only one message, yet you have required help three times. And your helper could have misread the message. What he is telling you could be all wrong and you wouldn't even know it. All because you never learned your letters and numbers well enough to understand code. Now think about this very carefully – if you were the supreme, why would you give such responsibility to one who needs so much help just to carry out one order? Why would you not simply promote the soldier who had learned his letters and numbers well enough to understand code?"

Gekar tried to respond, but no words would come. Embarrassed and angry, he merely hung his head and shrugged. "I don't know."

Tarawa bent down and clasped Gekar by the shoulders. It did not always feel good to win an argument, especially over one's own tot. He said, "It is true I could not read when I first became a soldier. It is also true, had your mother not learned me my letters, I would be a common soldier to this very day. If you do choose to make soldiering your career, I will fully support you. Even though I prefer you do something else, I will still support your choice because I love you so very much. Whatever you choose to do, I want you to be your very best at it. Not better than anybody else, just the best you can be. Do you understand what I am saying to you?"

"Uh-huh," Gekar answered, stepping into his father's firm embrace.

"Good," Tarawa said.

"But the learners are always teaching us stupid stuff, Papa."

"Stupid stuff?" Tarawa repeated. He started licking his tot's face. "How so?"

Gekar giggled and wriggled free. "We always learn about numbers and letters and science and stuff. Sometimes, the learner lets us read about beasts, which I don't mind so much. But we hardly ever get to read about stuff I like."

"And what might that be?" Tarawa asked, standing erect.

"About battles and weapons and stuff my papa does," Gekar replied with a sly, manipulative smile. "Like the Great Continental War, or the wars against the bugheads. I especially like stories about the battle for Muga Terro. Or battles in the Dark Jungle. Aunt Agama said her papa's papa fought bugheads in the jungle. Just like you did, Papa. Is it true?"

Tarawa toned cross. "I've told you not to use that term, Gekar. They are called antemi. And yes, your great grandpapa Gekkota was there."

Gekar's face beamed. "I never met him, Papa. Did he ever speak to you of it?"

"No," Tarawa said. "I never got to meet him either. He fought there and he met Morgue there. Now go get ready on the swift. I promised your mother you could come with us to the palace this night."

"Yippee!" Gekar cheered, throwing his arms in the air. "Can I feed the dacts, Papa? Please."

"We'll ask the pen-keeper about it," Tarawa assured him. "Now put on a clean vest and skirt. And scrub those dirty hands. You weren't birthed in a bog."

As Tarawa walked back through the corridor, he could not suppress a slight smile. He was pleased with the manner in which he had just dealt with Gekar. Many of his contemporaries believed young lizarme only heard reason after blows to the backside. He noted how many of those same lizarme also struck their mates. His own family, however, had learned not to fear him. Nor would they ever have to.

Upon re-entry to their bed chamber, he beheld his mate's reflection in her mirror. Anole was seated with legs crossed at her prep-board, seemingly unaware of his return. Unseen skysheep from beyond the castle walls blocked out any beams from the sun, yet her beauty was just as vibrant in the glow from a burning brazier. The furtive flames frolicked and danced to a symphony of silence while she carefully donned her trimmings.

Tarawa watched in muted admiration while Anole threaded her gold wedding band through the pierced flesh between her nostrils. The band bore no gems, as he had been but a common soldier when he begged her to unite with him. Several times since, he had offered to have a talented gem-setter improve upon it. She would hear naught of it, saying the band would always be worth more to her than any sum of coin because it had cost him virtually all of his savings at the time.

Tarawa continued staring in silence as she removed a pair of coral hoops from a clam bowl and began threading them through her piercings, cursing beneath her breath when one snagged her earlobe. Uncrossing her legs, she leaned closer to the mirror for a better look.

Satisfied all was properly affixed, she dipped her hand back into the bowl and took out a short length of gold chain. She carefully clipped one end to a hoop and the other end to her wedding band so that the glinty object festooned against her cheek. The process was then repeated with a second chain against the opposite cheek.

She next removed a fine sapphire broach from inside the bowl and pinned it to her gown. After pausing to ponder its position, she adjusted the glittering object slightly and patted it properly into place.

Glimpsing Tarawa's reflection in the mirror, she flashed him a smile and stuck out her tongue to tease before reaching deep down into the bowl. She produced a gold snake chain with an empty crystal vile for a pendant and motioned for him to clip it about her neck...

The object had cost Tarawa a quarter cycle's pay and he had given it to Anole upon their tenth wedding anniversary. Their tot was already five cycles aged at the time, yet the proud prod lost his battle with teary eyes as he thanked her for suffering the pangs of birthing; for the hundredth time. He explained how the empty vial was to remind them both that he would be nothing without her.

Emotion had swelled up within her and spilled from her eyes as he dropped to his knees and told her how not one single day passed without him thanking Seed and Destiny for gifting him his family. He stated how every time he thought of her and

Gekar it moved him to be a better husband and father; a better being. Adding that he thought of them even when he napped, he promised he would eagerly exhaust his final breath for either one of them.

Both had wept freely when he snatched her up in his long arms and carried her to their cot. There he had confessed how sometimes he was uncertain whether she was real, or was she a warming vision passing by? Adding that if she was such a vision, then he never wanted to awaken. He pressed by noting also that if she was real, then she could only be a gift from Destiny, and one must never show cruelty of any kind towards a gift from a deity. He promised never to raise so much as his voice to her; a promise he'd always made certain to keep.

He had gently slid her wet and burning body atop his own. She had moaned when he entered her, melting her hot body down onto his. Both loved as one, neither knowing Seed had once again blessed her with a fertile womb; that their prayers had finally been answered.

...after Tarawa fastened the clip, Anole reached back down into the bowl and removed a fine silken headband. She carefully slipped the band about her head so that a red gemstone rested flat against her brow. With that, she pushed up to her feet and spun to face her lover.

"Dearest Destiny," Tarawa remarked, staring into her painted eyes. "When Seed created you, she really took her time."

As he reached to embrace her, Anole playfully slapped his eager hands aside. "We mustn't be late," she scolded with a smile.

Tarawa knew she was right. One never kept Supreme Pid waiting. Ever.

"I will have the carriage readied," Tarawa said, returning her smile. He turned from her and, after retrieving his skullcap and skin cape from their pegs, he departed the bed chamber.

Tarawa plopped the skullcap on his head, and then swung the cape about his shoulders. He fumbled briefly through one of its pouches until his clawed fingers found his gemmed prod's broach. He clipped it to a pair of collar rings to secure the cape and turned away from the corridor.

Tarawa descended a stairwell in the manner of a noble but with the mind of a commoner. Although he had been granted noble status eleven cycles past, which was virtually unprecedented at the time, he could never overcome the discomfort he felt upon seeing his many servants scramble at the mere sight of him. It bothered him. He often thought, *'If they knew just how mortal we nobles truly are, then they would not fear us so.'*

Not that he was accepted by the nobility either. Nobody had ever said anything rude directly to him. No noble would dare to openly question any decision made by the supreme. That is, none who value their heads. Be that as it may, he could almost feel their snobbish stance towards him. They looked at him differently. Spoke to him differently. Listened to him differently. Not much differently, yet definitely so. Or could it just be his own mind seeing and hearing them differently? Perhaps he was the social bigot? Could he be putting others off? He wasn't certain?

He had once tried to speak to his mate about it, and received a confused stare for his trouble. Only Prod Commander Sergon seemed to understand, albeit for his own reasons.

Spotting his senior steward, Tarawa signaled for him to fetch the carriage. No words were needed to prompt the swift undertaking of this most routine and anticipated of tasks. However, none of the servants moved to open the door for him. Tarawa would not allow for it in his own home. With two strong arms of one's own, why would any grown lizarma ever permit such foolishness? Let alone need others to help him attire? He did not understand such things, yet those birthed as nobles never seemed to ponder over such matters. Yes, he was clearly moulded from different clay.

Fresh air filled his lungs as he descended the stone stairwell to the lane. Beams from the sun warmed his exposed flesh.

Far off to the east, a small flock of white skysheep floated for the horizon. Circling swoopers seeking tasty prey was all that challenged them for space in the otherwise empty blue above.

Shifting his sights northward, Tarawa took in the splendor and squalor that was Cracow. From his mate's grand estate on the upper slope of Nobility Hill, he could look down over the entire city. Only Pid's palace enjoyed a higher vantage.

Tarawa sighted down upon the clay-shingled roofs of his neighbors' manors, all of whom were resentful that one of common birth dwelled higher up than they. All, that is, save for his friend Sergon.

Like Tarawa, the pudgy marine prod was also scorned by many of the other nobles. Truly a strange stick, Sergon had been birthed with peculiar pinkish eyes. Content to dwell out his days without a mate, Sergon always preferred the company of male lizarme. He spoke softly and Tarawa had never known his friend to carry a grudge or talk ill of anybody. In fact, Sergon was fond of saying, "If you don't like somebody, get to know them better".

Others enjoyed mimicking Sergon's mannerisms, especially his limp and his soft-spoken words. They would often burst bellies with laughter whenever one from their clique would imitate his movements while mocking his speech. Yes, there will always be those who slight others simply for being smarter than themselves; and Sergon was certainly that.

Lesser commanders quietly grumbled on about how Sergon only held his rank because he was the supreme's first cousin. Tarawa knew better. Sergon was both a brilliant inventor and a capable marine tactician. He alone had conceived of and designed the giant combat carrier, plus personally supervised its construction. To win the war, they would need a marine commander such as Prod Sergon. Tarawa knew it. Prime Prod Dorak knew it. And of utmost importance, Supreme Pid knew it.

So let them mock and mimic and snicker and jest. Tarawa had long suspected the nobility's ignorance regarding Sergon was simply a matter of bigotry served up with envy. Despite his private ways, his friend was far more intelligent than any of them – and they at least knew that!

The further down the slope Tarawa sighted, the smaller and blander the manors became. At the base of Nobility Hill were the fine wooden homes of the more affluent commoners. These lizarme were often highly skilled overseers to a vital trade, or they were very prosperous merchants. Some were revered in matters of law, science, or medicine. A select few of the realms most talented scribes, painters and sculptors also dwelled amongst them.

A select few of the most trusted commoners had even secured minor positions in the *Guidance Guild* of the local government. Their charge was to encourage groupthink among the masses and suppress individual thought beginning at the education level; to teach the masses what to think as opposed to how to think, especially the young. They were also expected to report any who spoke ill of the realm, no matter how benign their words may seem. Not by coincidence, vigilant members of Prod Gila's silence squads held all of the Guidance Guild's most senior posts. Always watching. Always listening. Always in control.

Beyond the wooden homes of the affluent commoners sprawled the humble huts of the masses. Usually covering just one small room, these crude hovels were nothing more than large clay shells inverted over a dirt floor. The lone entrance was protected by nothing more than a drape of hide, as no one had anything worth stealing anyway, and the walls had mere slits to peek through. A crude mud or clay stove was usually positioned in the center of each hut's round base, and the smoke was allowed to escape through a hole in the roof; providing, of course, the occupants could afford the wood to feed a warming fire in the first place? And even if they could afford it, all wood sourced from dead trees or gathered off the forest floor was by law property of the rich, leaving only green branches off live trees for the poor. Small wonder their fires produced such an abundance of choking smoke.

The huts were always damp and dingy and smelly. In the hot quarter, they were beyond sweltering. During the cold quarter, shivering inhabitants often awoke to find their dirt floors hardened by frost. At no time were such hovels ever the least bit inviting.

Between the huts and the docks squatted many factories and storehouses. Thick smoke poured upward from stone stacks as weapons of war were forged day and night inside huge, raging hearths. A brownish haze hung over the eastern quadrant of the city, waiting impatiently for the seaside breeze to move it along. The incessant banging and clanging of metal upon metal was routinely shushed by the roar of blast furnaces.

Sporadically spaced out along Cracow's busy shoreline were the even larger storehouses of the dockyards and the bulk of the realm's dry docks. Between them, broad concrete piers, made by mixing volcanic ash with lime and seawater, reached out into the sea; their long fingers trying in vain to grab the distant concrete breakwater that dared to challenge the sea's powerful wetrollers. With each slap from a charging wetroller, frothy foam and spray splashed over the breakwater's seaward face, yet its stubborn caissons refused to budge. Noisy shoresquawkers perched atop the piers, or scoured the seaside in search of finners and crabs.

Great treadmill hoists with wheels two levels high lifted cargo skids laden with crates and sacks and barrels up from the piers and swung them over the gunnels of cogs. The hefty loads were then lowered by block and tackle into the belly of each ship's hull.

Assorted warships were moored all along the shoreside face of the breakwater. Amongst them were the galleys of the invasion force. Dubbed *bashers* and designed by Prod Sergon specifically to disable humanfolk *striker boats,* each basher was fitted with a sturdy battering ram fastened to the craft's prow just below the wetline. Immediately upon impact with a striker, a wide boarding plank atop the basher's prow would be dropped across the striker's gunnel. Two long metal claws beneath the plank's tip would then steady both boats in check while naval infantry stormed across the plank and onto the enemy vessel. Although untried in battle, bashers had performed extremely well in trials against mock-ups of striker boats; plus the bashers wide, flat hulls granted them an exceptionally shallow draft for their size, thus making them suitable for beaching.

Notwithstanding their many merits, bashers were still burdened with some disadvantages. Being much larger and heavier than strikers, the bulky bashers could never match them in speed; not even close. Nor were they anywhere near so maneuverable as strikers, especially in choppy seas and cramped combat. And a basher's many oars combined with its twin masts meant plenty more bodies were needed to crew it. If a basher did ram a striker, it would most certainly disable it; yet 'if' has often been the most pivotal word in warfare.

Even so, it would be extremely difficult for fighters from a striker boat to board a larger basher. Harder still for them to sink one. In fact, even in the highly unlikely event humanfolk did clamber aboard a crippled basher, it would still require many more naval infantry than were aboard a striker to match numbers with those aboard a basher. Plus it is always easier to defend a pitching and listing vessel than it is to capture one. As well, the entire lizarme invasion fleet would enjoy air cover from dacts, further compounding the enemy's woes.

Tarawa steered his sights past the breakwater to where a flotilla of currachs were netting for finners. The tough little boats were fashioned of plaited willow, with tanned hides stretched tight over their frames and stitched together so skillfully they kept even the roughest seas at bay. Being suitable for both deep sea sailing and rowing the shallows of inland rivers, the humble craft dotted the rolling surface, disappearing and reappearing in a timely waltz with the wetrollers.

Further out to sea, a monster ship towered atop the surface. Fully two thousand boatbuilders had laboured for six cycles to build it. Unlike the smaller craft, it squatted motionless in the sea and stretched for over three hundred strides from bow to stern. Even at three tiers tall, its deckhouse was dwarfed by its four masts, each of which threatened to spear any errant skysheep. When unfurled, any one of its four sails could cloak a small village. An entire forest had been depleted to supply wood for its oaken hull, which was six levels in height. Each of the monster ship's two fluked anchors weighed more than some cogs. An ingenious wheel and pulley system steered a pair of enormous rudders – and right from within a covered wheelhouse!

Over sixteen hundred crew could be berthed within its messes; albeit, not all at the same time. They shared the hammocks and slept in shifts. If no hammock was available, a common sailor might simply nap on the hard deck or stretch out upon a lumpy sack packed with beans. The ship's three hundred officers slept in tight racks in separate quarters.

Modern catapults were bolted in place at strategic intervals all around the main deck; powerful new war machines that employ a counterweight to sling their projectiles from the end of a long wooden beam. Dozens of dact pens were secured to the deck about both the bow and stern landing platforms.

Tarawa watched as a lone dact bearing both flighter and lancer flapped wings for the carrier. It glided across the vessel's bow before touching talons to its platform. Within moments the riders had dismounted and hurried their beast off the platform and down into its pen, quickly clearing space for the next dact to land. As ever, troops under Prod Sergon's command were very well trained.

The rattle of an approaching carriage caused Tarawa to redirect his attention back to his immediate vicinity. A team of eight rexids snapped and spat and raked their claws as they hauled their wheeled burden up the steep grade towards the stone stairwell.

Beasts had always intrigued Tarawa. Especially rexids. The ferocious tracking lizards with powerful claws and sabred fangs could sniff out prey from over a kilopace away. Their eyes sighted well during night's rule, and their pricked ears snagged even the slightest of sounds. Powerful tails enabled them to maintain exceptional agility and balance, while their lengthy limbs propelled them to raving speeds. Rexids could even alter their pigment to blend in with their surroundings. This ability made them difficult to detect and most useful for relaying

18

messages between units. Being keen of wit and fiercely loyal to their masters, the noble beasts were well suited for guard duty. And they would force a fight to their final breath.

As the team strained to draw the carriage the remaining few lengths, Tarawa's nostrils sniffed the scent of his mate. Turning his head about, he stretched Anole a smile so broad his scars seemed to shine.

"Your fragrance is deliciously floral," he remarked, noting how stunning she looked in the mulberry silk gown he'd given her for her thirtieth birthday. He marvelled over how her beauty never waned.

Anole grinned slightly and extended him her arm. "I brushed with rose petals."

Tarawa moved to lick her, but was interrupted by a tug on his cape. He looked down into the eager eyes of his tot, who stood with raised arms.

After exchanging an amused glance with Anole, Tarawa reached down and tossed the giggling youngster up into the air before catching him in a warm snuggle. Beaming with fatherly pride, he stepped up to the carriage and extended a supportive hand to his mate.

Once his family was properly seated, Tarawa motioned to the drivers. All aboard instinctively braced for the jolt as a sharp crack from a whip lurched the carriage into motion; before relaxing as best they could for the rough ride up the rutted road to the palace.

Conversation was nearly impossible over the incessant rattle of the carriage, so Tarawa turned his thoughts to the current state of Pid's realm. Many of its services and infrastructure had been neglected out of sacrifice for the war effort. Every lizarma was expected to do his or her part, hence taxes had been raised just as services were cut. Not even the nobility had been spared. At every level of government save for the military, spending had been severely slashed. Roads, bridges, sewers, infirmaries, public baths and local parks were all affected by budget cuts as the royal treasury strained to satisfy the demands of the invasion.

19

To try and compensate for shrinking wages in an already impoverished realm, a strict system of rationing had been introduced. It covered most essential goods including wood, skins, burnable oils, drinkable water and food. What few government services the masses may have once enjoyed were now mostly defunct; including waste disposal and pest control.

Poor sanitation led to an unabated spike in sickness. With infirmaries and apothecaries unable to obtain many of the ingredients needed to brew their healing potions, disease and infection ran rampant in the overcrowded rookeries where the poor dwelt snout to snoot amongst the rodents and filth and flies. Cracow's markets especially had become cauldrons of contagion, forcing many shops to shutter for good. The same social and economic rot had also taken root in other cities and towns all throughout the realm. Not surprisingly, many lizarme were unable to work. Industrial production was at a record low.

To try and correct the situation, some powerful nobles with strong ties to industry had convinced Pid to issue royal decrees denying ration tickets and medicines to those too sick to work; an ill-conceived approach that merely forced the weak to drag themselves back into the factories, where they promptly passed their illnesses on to others.

Not only had industrial production plummeted, costing the realm plenty in lost taxes, but the ensuing lack of goods led to a bustling black market. An enormous underground economy had burst into being seemingly overnight, providing everything from food and clothing to coal and wormwood. Crime now ran rampant all throughout the realm, which drastically increased the cost of combating it. In fact, one enterprising group of peasant farmers from an obscure village near Dega Doom had even constructed a crude press for printing counterfeit ration tickets!

Unfortunately, those with absolute power never admit to their mistakes; hence, Pid's decrees remained in place, punishing the infirm and fueling a growing backlash. Riots had even erupted in one of the largest yards after the dockers learned the coach bringing their overdue ration tickets had been hijacked yet again.

Tarawa himself led the push to restore peace. Acting on his order, the army shackled any rioters who refused to concede. Then, to Tarawa's horror, Prod Gila's silence squads executed them anyway. Of course, the hungry ones quickly used the hangings as yet another rallying cry for their cause. To them it was priceless propaganda.

As for Tarawa, the needless executions made it the single worst day of his command. In fact, he was sickened by it all. It is one thing to quell a riot, quite another to purge unarmed citizens. To him, the hangings were nothing short of murder.

Gila's callous actions had long disturbed Tarawa. He hoped Morgue would duly note the evil lizarma's contempt of all things decent and scourge his spectre accordingly, before banishing it to forever wander through his chilly maze. But what of the suffering Gila should beget before then? Surely Destiny feels some pity towards the innocent?

Tarawa's thoughts drifted into his past. Memories flooded in like he was reliving each moment in the present. Sight. Sound. Smell. Taste. Touch. All senses seemed so real and current to him. Almost like he was there......

****

......Tarawa was just fourteen cycles aged when he departed his tiny mining village in the eastern foothills and trekked west to Dega Doom. His intention was to seek out a master metallurgist to mentor him in the craft. Anything seemed better than toiling below ground in a job fraught with danger, and metallurgy paid thrice that of mining.

Even from a distance, the brownish haze hanging over the city should have warned him this was a place much different than his home. However, the euphoria of youthful adventure overruled his caution; as it so often does.

Being birthed and reared in a tiny village, Tarawa stared about Dega Doom with wided eyes. Everything about the city seemed new and exciting. He watched with wonder how the marketplace merchants would haggle with customers over the cost of their wares. Never had he seen such a selection of garments and pottery and food. Some lizarme offered to reveal one's future by means of dumping bones onto sand, while others offered up advice based on patterns of smoke.

Unlike the humble market back home, Dega Doom's bazaar was busy, chaotic and noisy. Sweet incense wafted from almost every stall and cart. Constant chanting and music mingled in with the incessant chatter and bustle of a crowd.

None of the merchants seemed the least bit friendly, not even to their own patrons. Almost every merchant bore a sharp blade of some design. Coin changers and silk merchants enjoyed the added security of rexids, despite local laws prohibiting the use of such beasts by anyone other than the city's bludgeons, who patrolled the ways and wynds to keep order.

While coinage was quite commonplace all throughout the realm, many lizarme still bartered with goods. Tarawa watched as one angry lizarma berated a stout merchant. The irate patron brandished a serpent in one hand, while wagging a forefinger with the other.

Clearly unmoved by whatever his customer was shouting, the stout merchant simply shook his head and placed a vial of scent back onto a shelf. Tarawa did not blame him. It was not difficult to snare such a common serpent.

There were some amusing sights as well. Performers of every description competed for coinage: musicians and mimes and jugglers and jesters, together with dancers and magicians and poets. And, of course, there were beggars by the bunch. Plus tricksters too. In fact, there were a good many tricksters. Each one of them hot on the scam.

Although Tarawa did not know it, one such trickster was about to drastically alter the course of his future. Also unknown to him, Destiny's will was at direct odds with his own. And Destiny always wins.

Tarawa amused himself by watching a little lizarma with a patched eye perform a seemingly simple trick using three inverted shells on a padded tabletop. Two tall thugs brandishing scimitar swords stood vigil at his sides.

The trickster would place a teeny cloth ball under one of the shells, raise his arms atop his head, and then shout, "Watch whilst me hands be swifter than thine eyes!"

Next, the trickster would swiftly shuffle the shells about the tabletop, before stopping and offering to match coinage with any who dared to wager under which shell the ball was hidden.

Even though all challengers had a one in three chance of choosing the correct shell, virtually none of them ever did. An oddity which at first puzzled Tarawa, until he quickly figured it out.

Tarawa noticed the trickster always tipped the shell away from himself whenever he inserted the ball. Hence, none in the crowd actually observed the ball being placed under the shell. They merely saw the motion to do so, followed by the trickster's empty hand as he raised his arms to begin shouting out his challenge.

Soon the reason for the trickster's unusually loose attire became evident to Tarawa. The little trickster required an oversized robe with long, loose sleeves to dispose of the ball altogether. Whenever he raised his arms the cloth ball would roll down the inside of his sleeve and robe, before stopping where the garment was belted tight at the waist. In fact, many balls could collect above the belt with nobody any the wiser. Tarawa also noted how the trickster would momentarily turn from the crowd and subtly dip his fingers into a pocket before commencing with another challenge. No doubt both pockets kept a ready supply of like-coloured balls, all destined to disappear inside the robe.

Tarawa reasoned any being who cheats others deserves to get taken at his own game. With such thinking foremost in mind, he made his fateful decision to play.

"Watch whilst me hands be swifter than thine eyes!" exclaimed the trickster. As always, he then raised his arms.

Tarawa stepped forward from the mob and emptied his purse on the table.

A murmur flowed from the crowd as the bold youngster counted out thirty-nine coins. Almost a full quarter's wages for a miner.

The trickster swallowed his smirk and exchanged muddled glances with his thugs.

"Thirty-nine coins in total," Tarawa said, adding, "I'll wager the lot, if ye dare?"

The hesitant trickster paused to ponder the young challenger's peculiar rural accent, before slowly stretching a scammer's smirk. After dipping into his own purse, he likewise counted out thirty-nine coins and pushed his pile up against Tarawa's.

The ensuing commotion quickly attracted a crowd of curious onlookers who pushed in tight about the stall. Accordingly, both thugs readied their curved blades over the tabletop. Clearly, any attempt to snatch the coins would cost some foolish thief his hand.

Some in the crowd gasped at the speed with which the trickster's hands shuffled the shells. It was readily apparent he was well practiced at his craft.

"Ye pick," the trickster said, lifting his arms to show empty palms.

"Under the middle shell," Tarawa replied, perfectly aware the ball was not under either of the shells.

"Be ye firm with ye pick?" asked the trickster, hinting at a smirk.

"I be," Tarawa replied, exuding cocky confidence.

Then before the startled trickster could react, Tarawa grabbed both outer shells and promptly turned them over. "See, no ball under these shells," Tarawa said, gloating a grin. "It must be under the middle shell."

A group gasp united the crowd as they realized the youngster had actually won the wager. Most stared in disbelief.

"Patch never loses?" somebody remarked.

"Must have beed a lucky stab?" suggested another. "Patch's hands be much too quick. Nobody ever wins."

Some in the crowd nodded to agree.

A third voice suddenly exclaimed, "Patch's hands may be quick, but lucky stabs count all the same!"

"They do at that!" someone else shouted to concur.

"The lad won fair and just, Patch!"

"Give the lad his coins, Patch! You lost!"

"Yeah! Pay up, Patch!"

A group murmur of consensus preceded an enthusiastic round of applause as Tarawa raked all seventy-eight coins into his bulging purse. He took pride in tricking the trickster and his face made no effort to hide it. Leastways until he looked up to find five angry eyes glowering clean through him.

Tarawa had never experienced such a sinking sensation in his gut. Patch and his two thugs weren't just glaring out of annoyance such as a parent might do when dealing with an unruly tot. No, not at all. These glares were of a kind completely different from any he'd seen before. Their crimson eyes bled hatred.

"Don't spend it too swiftly," Patch growled through clenched teeth.

Tarawa's tongue was too tangled to talk. Bellybees stung inside his knotted-up guts. All he wanted was to get away. Far away. To be anywhere else?

Pouching his purse, he turned away and almost rudely shoved a path through the clapping crowd. He was just vaguely aware of many hands patting his shoulders, yet he was fully aware of Patch's lone eye fixed firmly onto his back. He could feel its spite burning holes through his soul.

All Tarawa could think of doing was to seek out the safety of an inn. The eternal deity, Night, was about to challenge its divine rival, Day, for sway of the above, and the young lizarma had no desire to be out and about beneath the skytwinklers in such a strange and unfamiliar city. Especially not in this city, which had already lost its appeal.

Tarawa was uncertain as to how long he sought out lodging. Nor could he venture a guess as to his route. All of the eastside sectors of Dega Doom began to look the same to him. The merchants were closing up their shops and each section of empty stalls appeared much as the last; and more like the next.

As the sun started its retreat beyond the western horizon, Tarawa finally conceded he was hopelessly lost. And completely alone. He became aware of a scary stillness nipping at his nerves. Something was definitely amiss?

The moon was high atop the eastern horizon and rallying its army of skytwinklers when suddenly a familiar voice sent shudders down Tarawa's spine. He spun about to set sights on three unwelcome figures emerging from the shadows.

"Ye have led us on quite a chase," Patch mused with a gloat to his grin. "Ye really must pay us for our trouble. And our trouble be worth about seventy-eight coins, so I say."

Both thugs patted their scabbards.

Tarawa turned to flee, but the trio had him boxed into a corner where two walls converged. They had picked their place of ambush well. His only route of escape was through them.

"I won these coins just and proper!" Tarawa shouted defiantly. His entire body shook as he reached inside his vest with one shaky hand, while unslinging his back bag to use as a shield with the other. He had never been in a fight before, but he was determined to defend what was rightfully his. Thus, in spite of his gut urge to bow before fear, he brandished a small whittling blade and braced to hold his ground.

Patch paused to ponder this unexpected problem. Not for an instant did he considered the young stranger with the peculiar rural accent might dare to resist. He fully expected the frightened upstart would simply turn over the coins and beg for his pardon. Which, up until now, Patch had fully intended to grant him.

"Dispatch him!" Patch shrieked at last. "Ye will soon learn what value coins hold in Morgue's maze!"

Each thug drew his scimitar and closed in on their trembling prey. Despite their superior size over their young adversary, the pair still approached him with caution. They were visibly unaccustomed to such defiance.

"Stay where you stand!" a commanding voice shouted from somewhere in the blackness. It was joined by clinking and rattling and the stomping of many feet. There was much flickering from torches.

"Silence squad!" Patch shouted, quickly spinning about and retreating back into the shadows. Two tall forms vanished with him.

"Halt! You there, stay where you stand! By order of the realm!"

The approaching soldiers did not need to warn Tarawa again. He froze as several of their number surrounded him with tridents poised to spear, while others ran past and diverged off into the wynds and the shadows.

Several bits later the troops returned empty handed, led by a bespectacled little lizarma with an ugly scar stretching from ear to chin. He bore the amber flesh and purple eyes typical to all desert clans. A black cloak and matching skullcap alluded to his nasty disposition. As did his sadistic scowl. He wore a gold ring on his middle finger. A carved skull was set into the ring, and it glowed a ghastly green in the torchlight.

Tarawa instantly recognized the skull. Carved of bone taken from cadavers and then treated with phosphors to make them glow, the creepy skulls had long been the hated symbol of Pid's dreaded silence squads; squads whose sole purpose is to root out and crush dissent. All lizarme feared the skull symbol, which is precisely why such rings became standard issue to the commander of every silence squad. The symbol by itself usually proved enough to ensure a lizarma's fullest cooperation; especially when one took into account where the bone came from.

For the second time in one day, Tarawa's tongue became tangled and bellybees stung into his guts. He tried to speak. To explain. To tell them about the robbery. Yet no words would form. Again, all he wanted was to get away. To be anywhere else.

A sudden blow to the back punched all breath from his lungs. While rolling and writhing in the dirt, Tarawa became vaguely aware of a raspy voice growling down at him. Then a heavy boot pinned him on his back while foul breath blasted across his face. His bleary eyes could barely focus on the bespectacled lizarma looming over him. Unseen fingers twisted his ear until he winced in agony.

"…doing about beyond curfew?" growled the raspy voice. "Who were your accomplices? Why…"

Tarawa wanted to answer. To explain. But the words still wouldn't come?

"…into the pit with you then – you filthy, unlettered letch!"

Something struck Tarawa up under his nose. All became red and his eyes leaked tears. Then came the darkness. He wondered, '*Will I be cursed to wander Morgue's chilly maze? Or deemed worthy to enter Utopia?*'

Destiny pitied him, however, and he did not enter Morgue's maze. Instead, Tarawa awakened face down on cold stone with a groggy mind and aching limbs. Each gulp of stale air burned his throat.

After painfully pressing up into a sit, Tarawa began shaking his head to sort his mind; before flopping back down to revisit the realm of dreams.

When next he awakened, he became aware of voices chatting nearby.

"He'll do just fine," one of the voices said. "We are always in need of volunteers."

Another voice responded, "A might frail to be sure. Still a youth. I believe it best to start training new recruits when they are a few cycles older. What exactly was his crime, Commander Gila?"

"Plotting," replied a familiar voice.

Tarawa shuddered upon recognizing the raspy voice of the bespectacled lizarma.

"Plotting? Plotting what?"

"A robbery no doubt," Gila replied. "He was caught lurking about past curfew with no good reason to be where he was. Not a coin to his name. All he possessed were the garments on his frame – no doubt stolen. Not a single local could identify him. I only spared him for his youth, and because I know you are always in need of volunteers. Perhaps military service will set his criminal mind right?"

"Oh, it will certainly do that," assured one of the voices.

Another added, "We'll have some soldiers escort him to the local barracks. Have you any other volunteers?"

"Alas, not on this night," Gila replied. "His gang got away – this time."

By such means, Tarawa *volunteered* for military service. Which was probably just as well for he no longer possessed any coinage or belongings anyway. Nor were any friends or family about to vouch for him.

Deciding to make the best of a bad situation, Tarawa eagerly threw himself into the military training. He never fully took a liking to drill, yet he practiced so hard on his own that he eventually became the best marcher in his unit. His healthy attitude towards fitness soon showed results in the development of his body, which became lean and hard and quick. Every night before retiring to his cot he positioned a length of log across his back and shoulders. He then climbed up and down the steep grade behind the barracks until his thighs screamed for mercy and his puffing chest threatened to burst.

What Tarawa enjoyed most of all, however, was the rigorous combat training. Especially training done with a trident. He easily excelled due to his keen wit and constant craving for perfection. Each peek of dawn revealed his silhouette practicing blocks and thrusts and parries long before the other recruits awakened. He further honed his trident skills by thrusting or hurling the weapon into targets fashioned from tightly bound highgrass.

It wasn't long before commanders took note of their exceptional recruit. They nodded each time he outwrestled a much larger lizarma. Heads shook in disbelief at his uncanny skill with a scimitar or his accuracy with a hurling blade. His instructors voiced their approval whenever he routinely disarmed his opponents, then graciously assisted them back up to their feet. All were awed by his speed on the sprint.

One cycle after he entered the military, Tarawa's unit was transferred east to The Wall. It was just the first of his many tours at the forbidding structure, which had been built by apes and humanfolk to secure the eastern continent.

The eastern allies had erected the awesome barrier following the Great Continental War in order to block lizarme troops from taking the north pass through the Divide Mountains. The Divides stretched almost unbroken from the north coast to the south and separated the western and eastern regions of the continent. With the north pass being the only gap wide enough through which one could march an army, it became vital to the eastern allies that it should be blocked. So much so, in fact, that the structure's location and the rugged territory around it became known to both sides simply as The Wall.

Constructed of a stone and mortar base, plus the tallest of bamboo shoots, the defensive structure stretched sixteen kilopaces from north to south, spanning the entire breadth of the pass and creating a choke point through which no army could march; at least in theory. It had been built in the hope lizarme leadership would consider such a risky venture to be counter to any territorial gains they might make. In short, invading the east simply wasn't worth the cost in blood and treasure.

Stone bastions were spaced at strategic intervals to cover any dead angles, while hoarding platforms permitted its defenders to cover the rampart right up to the wall itself. The steep rampart separated the wall's western face from a mucky moat sewn with caltrops and pointed stakes, which was also home to highly aggressive mud vipers; in fact, a great many mud vipers.

While no direct assault had ever been risked against the wall itself, skirmishes were quite common in the surrounding mountains. It was as if the Great Continental War had never really ended, but had merely endured a diluted reprieve until the start of what was now about to become the Second Continental War. Such is the way of things whenever important issues are ignored and left unresolved.

Prior to the Great Continental War, lizarme families had dwelled peacefully for hundreds of generations in the foothills east of the Divides; until famine and war forced them to flee into the western regions of the continent. Now the Black Ape Federation claimed all lands bounded by the mountains, the sea, and the Ape and Amen Rivers. For their part, the lizarme still claimed the eastern foothills as rightfully belonging to them. And therein lay the problem.

During his first tour of duty at The Wall, Tarawa received the ugly scar on his brow, courtesy of a black ape's fang. He brow butted his hairy assailant as they grappled amongst the fallen forms of their comrades. Both were already spent when they rolled as one off a ledge, only parting their embrace as each tumbled heels about hearers down a rocky grade.

They eventually slid across the hard and bumpy floor of a tight ravine, before finally coming to an abrupt and painful halt against an unforgiving slab. There each briefly studied the other's battered and bloodied body before slowly pushing to their feet. Both were stripped of much flesh and the ape had suffered a broken fang. Crimson gushed from Tarawa's brow.

Tarawa's limited knowledge of the ancient continental language was basic at best, yet he still managed a few words. "We can both breath to clash another time," he stated with pleading eyes.

The panting ape briefly raised a palm before nodding and limping away.

Only then did Tarawa take note of the sticky warmth flowing down his own face and taste the blood on his lips. Every fibre of every muscle in his battered body ached as he gasped to suck in air. His pounding heart threatened to burst his chest. Yet somehow he still thought to thank Destiny that the burly ape had understood his words. And that his worthy foe had been of like mind.

During his military career, Tarawa completed seven tours of duty at The Wall and four more battling antemi in the Dark Jungle. The lizarme had seized Muga Terro from the skeletal, bug-like beings three generations past and forced them to migrate south. Even so, the antemi never surrendered their claim to the city, routinely attacking lizarme patrols all along the jungle's northern edge.

Lizarme seldom venture in amongst the thickest jungle foliage because male antemi possess bulging holoptic eyes which allow for wrap-around vision and grant them much superior sight in the shadows. As well, the enemy's agile aeronts can zip in and out of the jungle's musty maze at far greater speeds than the much larger and more cumbersome dacts. Thus, their longstanding conflict against this baffling, bug-like foe had basically evolved into a battle of containment. It was lizarme military policy never to pursue any antemi much beyond the jungle fringe. To do so was to taunt Morgue, for the enemy was most cunning and dangerous, especially during Night's rule, and the sun's rays seldom penetrated through the jungle's thick overhead canopy during Day's. Hence, the Dark Jungle was quite aptly named.

Tarawa's heroics, however, became legendary even amongst the antemi. While other lizarme commanders would have their troops pursue the overgrown pests no further than the fringe, the former miner from the foothills would have his squad pursue them deep into the jungle's sweltering depths. Often for many kilopaces. Often for many days. Always with a favourable kill ratio.

Due to Tarawa's proven courage and battle savvy, several progressive prods appealed directly to Supreme Pid for the young commander to be promoted to prod and placed in charge of his own combat group. Pid, being fully aware of Commander Tarawa's skills and exploits, readily conceded his desire to do so, but pointed out he could not. Lizarme law strictly decreed that none but nobles could rank as prods. Such had been the lizarme way for more than a hundred generations and Pid always considered any deviation from the law to be blasphemous against his ancestors, as well as a threat to his own rule. He believed having none but nobles as prods greatly reduced the risk of rebellion within the ranks. After all, why would those who are always on top ever want or allow change?

It was Marine Prod Sergon who then suggested quite matter-of-factly, "Perhaps, sire, you might bestow noble rank upon such a worthy lizarma? Is it written into law that such cannot be done?"

The older prods gasped at such a shocking suggestion. Bestowing noble status on a lowly commoner? The mere thought was preposterous! Absurd! Insulting!

Cracow's most learned legal scholars were immediately summoned to the palace library, where they painstakingly reviewed each of the twenty tablets of law. Then they reviewed them all again. Constant muttering amongst themselves made it quite apparent they were in disagreement.

Following much heated discussion, they at last appeared to reach some sort of a consensus and the eldest scholar approached Pid. He explained with obvious reluctance that no letters had ever been scribed on the subject and therefore only the supreme himself could resolve such a delicate matter. The scholar then added that, in his humble opinion, tradition failed to support such a happening.

Pid, however, was not interested in some scholar's opinion on tradition, he was only concerned with the rule of law and what best served his military. For that reason, he paced and pondered over what his decision should be, carefully weighing risks against rewards.

After giving the matter ample thought, Pid finally made the choice that would change Tarawa's life. He decided to break from tradition and promote the realm's bravest soldier to the rank of prod, believing it would be good for troop morale and perhaps inspire even more soldiers to seek the army's highest rank through proven loyalty and courage in battle.

Consequently, Tarawa was granted nobility status on the spot and promoted to the rank of prod......

****

......a sneaky rut jarred Tarawa's thoughts free from the past and snapped his mind back into the present. He instinctively braced for balance as the carriage veered up the palace drive.

The palace, with its stone walls and battlements, plus many bartizan turrets for keeping watch, squatted atop Nobility Hill. Having been upgraded from the original castle, it was still fully encircled by a wide, fabricated moat, which was well stalked with nasty little finners whose sharp teeth could strip a beast to bone in mere bits. Venomous serpents skimmed about the surface. Tall barbicans covered each side of the drawbridge, with a walled neck between them leading to a much older and shorter barbican; one which framed a grated iron portcullis, raised to let welcome allies pass. Machicolations were strategically placed outside the portcullis, allowing defenders to pour pitch and boiling oil down upon unwelcome enemies in the unlikely event of a siege. Two taller and newer guard towers flanked the old barbican, both fitted with arrow loops for archers to slaughter exposed attackers long before they reached the portcullis.

Tarawa granted Gekar a loving look as the carriage wheels rolled across the drawbridge's heavy planks, panicking the thrashing finners down below. His tot returned him a smile and clambered over onto his lap.

Soon the carriage rolled into the outer bailey and made straight for the guest stables, where the air always reeked of beasts, feed and dung. No sooner had the driver steered the team of rexids into a vacant stall, when several servants scrambled to assist Anole down to the cobbles. They all knew better than to assist the prod himself, whom they instead met with courteous bows of respect. Some then nodded their heads in greeting and offered him a welcoming smile; something they'd dare not do with any other noble save for Sergon, who likewise treated them with some respect.

"Well pluck out me seers if they don't spy Master Gekar in the skin," a cheery voice suddenly remarked. It belonged to an elderly lizarma with wrinkled amber flesh and purple eyes. His robe of dyed cloth showed him to be the stable master, as only a servant of his stature could afford such.

"Mox!" the tot shrieked as he wriggled free from his father's arms. It was readily apparent he was quite fond of the old lizarma.

Mox nodded a casual greeting to Tarawa as the thrilled tot embraced his legs. "We be blessed as bards to tend to thy team, Prod Tarawa."

"Can we feed them?" Gekar interrupted. "Can we, Mox? Please?"

"Hush," Anole crossly interrupted. "I'm certain Mox has much more pressing tasks to tend to."

"Papa said I could feed them," Gekar argued, offering Tarawa a pleading stare.

"No," Tarawa corrected him. "I said if it was okay with your mama we would ask the stall keeper about it. Don't put your words in my mouth."

Gekar lowered his head in a pout.

"The stall keeper shan't stickle over some help with the feeding," Mox assured them. "Old Slipes is always chattering on about how young Master Gekar has a gifted bond with the dacts."

"That he does," a servant confirmed. "A gifted bond to be sure. Destined to become a flighter, Master Gekar is."

Several other servants nodded their heads in support.

"See, Papa," Gekar pleaded, "I have a gifted bond with the dacts. They really like me. Can I feed them? Pleeeeeze?"

Tarawa glanced at Anole, who begrudgingly offered up a nod.

"Yippee!" the ecstatic tot cheered, taking Mox by the hand and tugging him away.

"I will mind him well," Mox assured both parents.

"We know you will," Tarawa replied with a confident smile.

"You mind their sharp beaks!" Anole shouted after Gekar. "And mind your manners too, you weren't birthed in a bog!"

"Aw, Mama…"

"And do as Mox says – or it's straight to time-out when we get home!"

"I will, Mama! Promise!"

After Gekar and Mox had departed around a corner, Tarawa extended Anole his arm and escorted her across the cobbles to an open doorway. Two guards drew back their halberds and snapped smartly to attention as the couple passed between them and on through the main gate into the inner bailey. They made their way across the grass and up a tiered perron to the main keep, where Pid liked to receive his most important visitors.

Two more guards swung open heavy doors to allow them entry.

A pair of muted toilers averted eye contact as they carefully removed the nobles' capes. Neither toiler dared so much as a glance, so intense was their fear of the nobility. Unlike common servants, toilers were condemned without trial into permanent servitude, it being a crime to set any free. Since it was generally accepted that all toilers were by their very nature inborn liars, their tongues were quite often removed. If their crime was theft, all digits of their dominant hand might be cut off as well. Or both hands if the court was uncharitable. If they had tried to flee from capture, then all their toes could be chopped off as well. Toilers were deemed chattel beneath beasts, and their owners could do with them as they pleased.

"Enjoy spending time with your boons," Tarawa said, before licking his receptive mate's face from chin to brow. "You can tell me the choice gossip later."

Anole responded by licking his cheek before nipping his ear. "I love you," she whispered.

Tarawa licked Anole's face one more time before playfully pointing her in the direction of a spiral staircase and starting her off with a pinch to the backside.

"Ouch!" she yelped, before shooting him a playful stare. "I so owe you for that."

Tarawa stretched a sly smirk. "Promises, promises."

"You had best nap with eyes peeled."

"Hopefully we shan't nap at all this night."

Anole blushed blue and paired her inviting stare with a naughty smile. Then she lowered her sights to negotiate the steps.

Tarawa watched his mate climb the staircase and disappear beyond the lip of an upper level. He resented the thought of battling apes and humanfolk at The Wall while she was in a birthing way. He had been there to greet Gekar. In fact, the slippery tot had passed from Anole's womb straight out into his own trembling hands.

As always, Anole had taken the news of his departure with selfless control. "You must do your duty," she said, adding, "We'll manage until your return."

He had noted her attempt to mask her angst behind a sham smile and a soft tone. But her honest eyes always betrayed the truth.

Pushing her image from his mind, Tarawa turned and started for a guarded archway. Two guards stared straight ahead and presented halberds as he strode between them and on into a long corridor.

His boots clicked cadence upon cold marble as he hastened through the vaulted passageway, completely oblivious to its intricate sconces, cressets and sculpted friezes. Being a prod commander, he had marched the palace corridors more times than he cared to count and their elaborate artistry had long since lost his interest.

Eventually, he approached a sealed archway which was flanked by two tall guards armed with halberds and scimitars. Iron hinges squeaked to bleed ears as the alert pair swung open the heavy hardwood doors.

Immediately upon clearing the second archway, Tarawa mounted a short stairwell and veered down one of two divergent corridors. Here a purple carpet covered the marble floor. Paned windows in the vaulted ceiling allowed dancing sunbeams to waltz about the plastered walls, which were festooned with purple drapes that hung down between frescoes of past ruler's and military heroes of note. A marble sculpture of each noble kept silent vigil beneath their portrait.

Tarawa came upon another sealed archway that was flanked by two more guards. This much larger archway was blocked by a pair of intricately carved hardwood doors with images of various beasts painstakingly carved into their core. A pair of shield-shaped plaques served as door handles. Both plaques were painted with Pid's royal crest; crossed tridents atop a flaming red sun.

Both guards strained to open the heavy doors. Then, because each had served their mandatory military tours under Tarawa's command, they postured proud for their popular prod.

Tarawa nodded his mutual respect as he marched past the guards and on into a large chamber furnished with many wooden stools; plus one metal spittoon. A broad, full-length mirror covered almost an entire wall, permitting prods and other nobles to jointly adjust their attire before each assembly. In one corner a narrow archway opened into a garderobe for relieving oneself.

Tarawa viewed the spittoon with disgust. Personally, the filthy habit of chewing chaw had never appealed to him. He often wondered, *'Why would anyone deliberately choose to chew something that blackens one's teeth and fouls one's breath?'* He hoped Gekar would forgo such foolish habits.

A loud boom echoed across the chamber the instant the heavy doors slammed shut behind him. A red curtain almost entirely obscured a corridor to his right. Directly before him, a raspy voice drifted in from beyond yet another archway. As per always, its familiar tone was ripe with venom.

Tarawa stepped from the anteroom and on into the Royal Library. Along the far wall, a row of padded chairs were lined up facing a lengthy study counter. A candle lantern was placed in front of each chair. All candles had been snuffed until next they were needed.

The remaining walls were fitted ceiling high with cubbyholes for storing scrolls. Wheeled ladders were connected to guide rails, allowing them to slide back and forth as needed. The lowest cubbies were packed full with ancient stone or wood tablets, and a few even contained the newest items for sharing information; bound sheets of calf vellum called books.

Dyed-glass windows, made from melting sand with potash and then adding powdered metals to the molten mixture before cooling, were connected by lead strips to form the library's domed ceiling; thus permitting the sun's warming beams to waltz in colour about the interior. Iron braziers hung from chains to provide ample lighting during Night's rule, or whenever angry black skysheep spurned the sun. Long metal rods jutted high atop the glass dome and were connected by copper cables to thicker metal rods buried deep under ground.

It was the latter rods' unenviable function to absorb the violent wrath of crackling flashbolts.

Located directly beneath the largest brazier, an enormous hardwood table squatted on ten thick legs. The legs were fashioned to resemble those of beasts, complete with sculpted hooves. Tanned hide had been stretched tight across the entire tabletop. There were no chairs set about the table as Pid would not allow it. "Lazy bodies birth lazy minds," he always said.

A lounge of three lizarme stood off to one side of the table. All wore matching vests and skirts and boots. They also donned skullcaps. Each had a scimitar hanging in sheath from his belt. Two of the figures were of greenish skin. The third of amber.

One of the lizarme offered a welcoming nod to Tarawa. He was unusually pudgy for a lizarma and possessed peculiar pinkish eyes. It was readily apparent he was in ill humour. Quite rare for Prod Sergon?

Towering over Sergon, like he did over most lizarme, was Prime Prod Dorak. His cold crimson eyes and nasty disposition left him unrivalled as the meanest looking lizarma Tarawa had ever seen. All save for Pid and Gila feared him.

If Tarawa could suggest anything good about his superior, it would be he was a capable military strategist and one of the few nobles who cared not one iota that his land prod was of low birth. Dorak always valued ability over status. He also had influence with Supreme Pid. Without Dorak's support, it is unlikely Tarawa would have attained his high rank and noble status. Hence, he owed much to Dorak.

All the same, Tarawa had noted on more than one campaign how Dorak's massive ego could sometimes overrule his sense. Plus his lack of tact and compassion regarding discipline kept him most unpopular with the troops. Not that Dorak cared, of course.

The third lizarma was of amber flesh. He wore a black cloak to match his skullcap. Thick spectacles only served to magnify the cruelty lurking inside his purple eyes. An ugly scar stretched from his deformed ear to the tip of his pointy chin. His middle finger bore a ring set with a glowing skull; the feared symbol of the dreaded silence squads. In one hand he clenched a clay mug. Gila, as always, donned a demeanor worthy of his rank: Prod Commander of Silence Squads.

The primary purpose of Gila's silence squads was to deal swiftly and harshly with any dissenters who dared question Pid's rule. For this role, each squad was granted free scope in collecting intel and *disappearing* dissidents; two jobs they did both often and well.

A fourth figure was doubled over at Gila's feet, clasping his throat and gasping for breath. Tarawa instantly recognized the frail little victim with puffy purple eyes and amber flesh. It was the muted toiler, Slerf.

Slerf had been seized for snaring hares on a lord's estate, simply to feed his family. Yet the manorial court showed him no mercy. Age and a clubbed foot made him unfit for military service, so his tongue was severed and his entire family sold into servitude. The court only spared his hands to increase his value at auction. Fortunately, Slerf's family were all purchased in a single lot and not torn apart as other families so often are. Now they ate better as trusted toilers in Pid's palace than they ever did stealing food just to survive. Despite his loss of tongue and freedom, Slerf often thanked Destiny for such blessings. *After all, what good is either to one who is starving?*

Tarawa felt his fists clench as he watched the bespectacled bully berate and beat the timid toiler. Yet he dared not intervene out of fear for his own family's safety. It was no secret that Prod Gila could arrange 'accidents'. None wanted him as an enemy.

"I wanted ale, not mead!" Gila screamed. He kicked the gasping toiler, who dared not block the blow. "Next time guess it right, you servile scrote!"

Suddenly, the irate prod tossed the mead into Slerf's face and then smacked the tankard hard against his victim's brow. Slerf struggled in vain to find his footing as he was unceremoniously dragged across the library; before a boot sent him sprawling face down into the adjoining anteroom.

Gila burst forth with a boisterous belly laugh, removing his spectacles to wipe tears from his eyes. He only swallowed his laughter when a heavy door slowly squeaked open.

All four prods bowed as a familiar form entered the library.

Supreme Pid was of above average height for a lizarma, although not quite so tall as Dorak. His rough, greenish flesh was well wrinkled with age, especially about his glazed crimson eyes and swollen nose. Cracked lips framed his lopsided mouth and crooked teeth.

He was clearly gaunt despite all efforts of his regal robe to conceal it. The loose garment was dyed deep purple and patterned in front with the royal crest depicting crossed tridents atop a flaming red sun. In one shaky hand he clenched a gem-studded sceptre of authority, in the other he carried a bound vellum scroll. A gold crown adorned his head. As always, a crystal vial containing white powder swung from his neck chain.

Pid nodded to acknowledge their gesture of respect, and then motioned for all to gather about one end of the table. Without uttering a sound, he untied the scroll and spread it out across the tabletop.

Etchings in the vellum depicted a crude map of the entire continent, complete with inked markings to enhance rivers and lakes. Symbols scratched into the skin depicted jungle, forest, mountains and other terrain. Every city of any importance had been plotted as near as possible to its proper place. An imprecise key approximated distance. The inscribed date revealed that the map had been etched long before the Great Continental War, when lizarme had dwelled on both sides of the Divide Mountains.

"I trust all is well with my fleet?" Pid asked in his usual deep voice.

"It is, sire," Sergon replied in his usual soft tone. "Your assault craft and your supply ships are crewed and supplied and ready to sail.

"And my carrier?"

Sergon offered his Supreme a satisfied nod. "The very last of the catapults were bolted down yesterday, sire. Your carrier is battle ready."

"Splendid," Pid remarked, shifting his sights. "Tell me, Prod Tarawa, what is the status of my army?"

Tarawa leaned over the map and tapped a claw to an area in the foothills just west of the Divide Mountains. Sire, the bulk of our siege engines are hidden in this valley here. Most of our troops are encamped here, here and here. On your command, they will march east towards the pass. All will take place under cover of darkness to maintain stealth until we opt to be seen. We cannot be too obvious. Morale is high, sire. Your army is eager to fight."

"Splendid," Pid remarked, clasping his hands together. "We must make certain enemy scouts discover Tarawa's troops well prior to the invasion. I want the bulk of the humanfolk army to be camped at The Wall before Prod Sergon sacks Capital. With no home army to defend his kingdom, how long can Myro hold out against my invasion force? Two lunar phases? Three at most?"

"I'll wager less than two," Dorak boasted, leaning over the map and drawing a claw across its surface. "First we'll secure the right bank of the Amen River, then we'll march around Lake Blood and secure the left bank of the Red River as far south as this fork here. It will place us within striking distance of both Raw and Apel."

"The humanfolk will quickly sue for peace," Gila stated quite matter-of-factly. The ignoble prod poked his spectacles in place as he too leaned over the map. "After that our forces will be free to march upon either Raw or Apel. Perhaps even both at once if Prod Tarawa breaches the wall?"

"My troops will breach it," Tarawa stated flatly. "Even if the white ape and humanfolk armies do not hasten home to counter Prod Sergon's invasion force, my soldiers will still defeat them in battle."

"The wall has already proven quite an obstacle for you," Gila taunted, betraying a sly smirk. "Even when it was defended by black apes alone…"

Tarawa was visibly upset by Gila's churlish attitude. "Prod Gila, you know full well we never attempted to breach the wall.

42

Yes, I did dispatch a small squad of scouts to climb atop the structure under cover of darkness, but it was a covert action meant only to gauge the enemy's defenses and gain intel for future use. The mission was never intended…"

"And exactly how many of your scouts returned with said intel, Prod Tarawa? If memory serves me right, I believe not a single…"

"Enough!" Pid cut in, stretching a scowl. "My army will tend to their duties just fine, Prod Gila. Such is not your concern. It is the hungry ones who are your concern. So tell me, what news have you regarding this traitor, Sickly?"

Gila swallowed his smirk and shot a warning glance at Tarawa. As per his arrogant nature, he puffed proud when he spoke. "The hungry ones are all but beaten, sire. It shan't be long before I personally present the scoundrel to you. Either stiff or in shackles, he shall be a thorn in our side no longer."

Sergon and Tarawa exchanged the look of skeptics.

"I don't want him stiff. I want this Sickly brought before me with a beating heart that I may slowly execute him before the masses. He will meet Morgue strip by strip and piece by piece. An example must be set. Do you understand, Prod Gila?"

"Yes, sire. It will be as you wish. My best silence squad is hot for his hide. We shall nab him soon enough. Still of breath as you desire."

Tarawa thought, *'They will never capture Sickly still of breath. Not in a hundred cycles.'*

Pid flushed purple with rage and began pounding his fist on the table. "Yesterday would not be soon enough, Prod Gila! I demand his hide now! Now! Now! Now! Now!"

"Yes, sire. I shall tend to it personally." Gila bowed before Pid, then sighted sinister at both Sergon and Tarawa as he turned and hastened from the library. One could almost smell his humiliation.

"Now then," Pid continued, leaning heavy on his sceptre and pointing a shaky finger at the map. "Let us review my battle strategy one last time in fine detail. As you three are fully aware, our objective in this war is to regain all territory stolen from my line in the last war."

43

Pid paused to pat Tarawa on the shoulder. "With all due respect to your abilities, Prod Tarawa, I am not so confident the wall can be breached. However, with your troops acting as decoy to lure the humanfolk army west to aid their ape allies, I am confident Prod Sergon's invasion force shall encounter little resistance in pacifying all territory east of the Amen and Red Rivers. With very few casualties to our own troops, I might add.

"With his entire realm under occupation, King Myro shall sue for terms. Of course, we will demand his army immediately abandon its camps at The Wall and march home, where each unit will promptly surrender all weapons to our occupation forces and then disband. Some swords and a small home guard should suffice for Myro to keep control over his own subjects. He can always request our help in dealing with any uprisings; which, of course, will be crushed without mercy.

"To the south, our raids and forays across the Red River to sack white ape towns and villages will surely panic King Thorax into marching his army home. Once the Black Ape Federation finds itself without allies and facing the prospect of fighting a two-front war alone, their Council of Elders will duly vote on the side of sense. Subsequently, the northeastern foothills will become lizarme soil once more.

"Our peace pact with King Myro will allow us to maintain several large garrisons on humanfolk soil to keep all sides honest. This will ensure a lasting peace on our terms in the east. That will leave only the antemi for us to wage war against. And them we shall exterminate like the overgrown bugs they are."

Pid paused briefly to sniff a pinch from his vial before turning to face his marine prod. "The keys to success will be timing and stealth, Prod Sergon. You must keep my fleet far from shore until Prod Tarawa has lured Myro's army the full distance west to The Wall. The humanfolk will supply their land troops by boat, using the docks on the north shore. It is much quicker than hauling provisions overland.

"Under no circumstances can you permit my fleet to be detected and reported. While you obviously cannot stray so far out to sea that my ships sail off the edge and plummet into the abyss, you must take every precaution to steer well clear of enemy vessels. Should you encounter a humanfolk cog out netting for finners, you will deploy dacts to capture or sink it. The crew must not make it back to shore.

"I fully understand," Sergon acknowledged, bowing his head.

Tarawa could never understand why Pid always doted on the obvious, especially since the entire invasion strategy had originated with Sergon to begin with. Naturally, neither Pid's nor Dorak's egos could ever allow them to accept the fact a pudgy little prod with peculiar pinkish eyes and a quirky waddle was in fact the true mind behind the plan. Tarawa always felt they'd all be better off listening to Sergon expand upon his own plan rather than hear the supreme blather on endlessly about givens. As always, Tarawa knotted his tongue. After all, he wished to keep it.

"The invasion must be brief, the occupation brutal," Pid asserted. "The humanfolk must be beaten beyond a dissenting breath before their army can return to aid them. With their loved ones held hostage, we will dictate the peace. Such will not be lost on their ape allies. If our eastern enemies can be made to fear us enough, then perhaps less of our soldiers need be deployed east of the Divides. This would free up more troops to rid this continent of Antraha's warriors. The antemi may be overgrown insects, but like all pests they have proven themselves most difficult to exterminate. It's like trying to cage pestilence."

"My Supreme, with the force you have assembled, I will conquer Capital within days," Sergon assured him. "The remainder of Myro's realm should come under our control within a quarter cycle at most. Perhaps within two lunar phases if all goes as it should. We will capture many prisoners to be used as pawns for your peace. Perhaps even King Myro himself will be among them?"

"Remember, all hinges on a quick defeat of their home guard."

"The rout will be quick and total, sire. Victory will be yours."

After nodding his approval, Pid shifted his attention to Tarawa. "Prod Tarawa, it is also vital that the allies believe your resolve to invade east is real and imminent."

"It is both, sire. I will raze their wall to the ground."

Pid actually cracked a rare grin. "Oh, I have little doubt you will pump the fear of Morgue into them, Prod Tarawa. If the wall can be breached, it is you who will do it. But as you yourself often say, *if* is the biggest word in warfare. So 'if' the structure cannot be breached, it is vital that our enemies be engaged without pause in the surrounding mountains. It would also help our cause if a few flocks were tasked to raid and harass enemy supply columns in the eastern foothills. This should force them to divert much needed troops away from The Wall to perform escort duty."

Pid's lack of confidence in the army's ability to punch through the pass irked Tarawa, although not near so much as his constant penchant for injecting himself into military matters. Tarawa thought to himself, *'Does Pid not realize his well-meaning strategy to deploy flocks to draw apes away from The Wall may also deprive our own army of valuable dacts needed to breach it.'*

Tarawa's ire was not unwarranted. It took a full cycle to properly train a flighter, a lancer and a dact to fight together. All three needed to be in complete sync with one another. Replacing downed teams might take longer than the conflict will last. Any flocks squandered for naught could be lost for the duration.

Tarawa often wished Pid would leave combat matters to his prods. He briefly checked his tongue to contain an impulse reply, opting instead to tell his supreme words he would want to hear. "We will harass the enemy both day and night, sire. Their bodies may nap, but their nerves will not."

"Splendid," Pid said, leaning back over the map. "Now let us review some of the finer points of my plan."

Tarawa, Sergon and Dorak stood still and alert as Pid lectured them on the finer points of warfare, pausing only on occasion to sniff powder from his vial. Often he would pause to ask himself questions as if no others were present, or blather on incessantly in gobbledygook. Ergo, by the time Pid finally finished his review, all three prods were well beyond bored. Each made certain, however, that their demeanor betrayed nothing of their thoughts. The last prod to offend the supreme was still paying penance in the labour pits. None wished to join him there.

After the meeting was finally over, Pid invited Dorak to join him in feast. This left Tarawa and Sergon all alone in the library.

The pudgy marine prod forced an exaggerated eye-roll. Hinting at a sarcastic smirk, he took heed to whisper. "Glad I was here today. Otherwise I may have overlooked the cog."

Tarawa matched Sergon's smirk and whisper. "Me too. I would never have thought to concentrate artillery barrages where our troops actually plan to attack."

A brief moment of cynical silence was broken by muffled chortles.

"Come, these walls have ears," Tarawa whispered while placing a hand on his friend's shoulder and guiding him towards the archway. "Why don't you feast with my family this night?"

"A fine idea, old friend. Alas, such is not possible. I must awaken at the peek of dawn and my mind is in need of a long nap. Another time, perhaps?"

"Another time then," Tarawa remarked as they entered the anteroom. "But Gekar will be disappointed he shan't be hearing one of your scary stories."

Both prods ignored the smelly spittoon as they paused briefly to adjust their attire in the mirror.

Noting that Slerf was watching them from a far corner, Tarawa smiled and reached into his vest pocket. "To aid your family," he explained, tossing a silver coin to the battered toiler.

Slerf eagerly snatched the precious object from mid-flight and stuck it into his pocket. He nodded his gratitude before stepping backwards to vanish behind a red curtain.

"You dance with danger," Sergon warned. "It is strictly forbidden to pay toilers."

"Who can he tell?" Tarawa asked. "He has no tongue."

"He has no tongue for a reason, my friend. He is being punished."

Tarawa's tone was sympathetic. "Is it not enough to sever his speech? He merely stole a hare to feed his family. Were it my plight, I would have done the same."

"It is cruel, I agree. Still, I caution you. Should the wrong ears hear of your acts of kindness towards toilers, it could pique the interest of the silence squads. They might question where your true loyalties lie?"

Tarawa started for the sealed archway with the shield plaques. "Spoken like Gila doesn't have our every movement watched as is – like he doesn't know the daily routine of ourselves and our families? Old friend, I know you're not that naive."

"Watched, for certain. Still, that is not cause to give him anything of note to see. You really must be more wary of him, Tarawa. He does hate us so."

"Gila hates, period. We are not so special, Sergon."

Two guards presented halberds as the heavy doors swung open and both prods stepped out into the corridor. The paned windows in the corridor's vaulted ceiling revealed Night's advancing army of skytwinklers pushing Day's orange glow from the western sky. Wall cressets had already been lit in anticipation of the coming darkness.

"You'd think Gila would have little time for such folly given the troubles his silence squads are having with the hungry ones. Did you catch his silly boast that they are all but beaten. Ha!"

"Shhh... Dearest Destiny, Tarawa, remember where we are," Sergon whispered. He glanced back over his shoulder before tactfully finding a safer topic of discussion. "How is young Gekar, anyway?"

"Testing us at each and every turn," Tarawa replied. "He's at that age. Plus he's not applying himself in classes. We received another note from his learner."

"Perhaps he needs a tutor?" Sergon suggested.

"Perhaps?"

The chatting pair descended a short stairwell and shoved open two more heavy doors. The iron hinges squeaked to bleed ears. Two startled guards nearly dropped their halberds as they scrambled to attention.

Boots clicked in cadence upon the hard marble as both prods marched in step down the vaulted passageway. Neither took notice of the sculpted friezes which ran along the upper wall near to the ceiling, or of the watchful eyes peeking down from behind them.

At last they emerged into the antechamber with its spiraled staircase and wall cressets. A pair of muted toilers avoided eye contact as they hastened to hold up the prods' capes. Neither dared so much as a glance, so intense was their fear of nobles.

"For your families," Tarawa explained, slipping each toiler a silver coin.

Sergon nervously glanced about.

"Has my mate passed by?" Tarawa asked.

Both toilers nodded that she had.

Tarawa nodded his courtesy to the pair before he and Sergon followed a smoky corridor out of the palace and on into the inner bailey. They wasted no time passing through the main gate and crossing the outer bailey towards the stables. Two vigilant guards snapped to attention and presented halberds as the prods marched across the cobbles for the stalls. The hot aura reeked of feed, beast and dung. Somewhere, an unseen dact screeched its ire.

Tarawa's carriage had already been turned about and its team of rexids were re-harnessed and hitched for the haul. The ferocious tracking lizards raked dirt with their powerful claws and thumped their thick tails in eagerness to be off. Sharp fangs flashed as the unruly beasts snapped and spat to display their lack of patience.

The drivers tried in vain to calm the beasts with cracks from their whips. To no avail. Only the carriage brake and a firm grip on the reins stayed the spirited team from bolting.

Gekar and his mother stood smiling beside the carriage. They were joined by old Mox and a pair of grubby young servants.

"Uncle Sergon!" Gekar shouted, sprinting headlong into the pudgy lizarma's outstretched arms.

Sergon playfully tossed Gekar up into the air and caught him in a tight hug. He began blowing hot breath across the tot's neck.

Gekar shrieked and giggled as he fought to wriggle free. "Stop – it tickles!"

"What's that in your hand?" Sergon asked, setting Gekar back down.

"A dact talon," Gekar replied, proudly displaying the object. "It's a big one too. I found it out behind the stable. Mox says I can keep it. I'm gonna be a flighter."

"That he is," Mox confirmed in his perpetually cheery voice.

"Not if you don't start mending your mind in classes, you won't," Sergon scolded. "Flighters must be especially swift on the think."

Gekar blushed blue and looked to his father, who promptly returned him an 'I told you so' stare of the kind only a parent can muster.

"Are you coming home with us?" Gekar asked, slyly switching the subject and tugging on Sergon's hand.

Sergon gently patted his little friend on the head. "Not this night, I'm afraid. Perhaps next time."

"Aww…" Gekar responded with a pout.

"Are you certain?" Anole pressed. "We will be feasting on smoked skate wings and boiled sea snails smothered in my very own buttered beetle sauce, with raw locusts in cacao paste pudding for dessert. All washed down with a fine vintage from the vineyards of Muga Terro."

"I am tempted," Sergon replied. "Sadly, I must awaken at the peek of dawn. However, I will make time to stop by your home and share a goblet before casting off."

"I will hold you to it," Anole said, latching onto Gekar's arm. "Come on, you – up into the carriage. And drop that disgusting claw thing on the ground before you cut yourself."

"But it's not just a claw, Mama. It's a talon. See how it hooks."

"Whatever it is, it's not coming home with us."

"Aw, Mama…"

"Now, Gekar. Drop it. Or you can spend some time sitting in the quiet corner when we get home."

"No, Mama. I hate the quiet corner. There's nothing to do there."

"Then do as you're told."

"Thck. I never have any fun."

"I'm counting. One… Two…"

A sharp crack from the head driver's whip lurched the carriage into motion. All aboard instinctively braced for the jolt, then settled into their seats as the carriage rolled away from the stables and across the outer bailey towards the drawbridge. As it swung onto the bridge, nasty little finners began thrashing about the surface of the moat down below. To the east, a partial moon had climbed high to take command of Night's advancing army of skytwinklers. To the west, the sun burned a brilliant orange as it retreated before the onslaught. An unseasonably cool gust of breeze pimpled flesh. Morgue's chilly breath?

The carriage creaked and pitched and rattled as it passed beneath the barbicans and out onto Royal Route; which, thanks to budget cuts, was now jokingly referred to as Ruts Route. All aboard held on tight for balance as they veered onto the rough road that wound down Nobility Hill. Except for when some sneaky rut would jar an intrusion, each occupant was content to wander about their own thoughts.

Tarawa considered his spat with Gila and hoped the vain little crybully would quickly get over it. He certainly didn't relish having the Prod Commander of Silence Squads stewing up a payback. Who would?

Directing his gaze northward, Tarawa took note of a flock of dacts flapping across the wetrollers enroute to a flotilla of bobbing barrels. Each of the beasts was mounted by two riders, a flighter and a lancer, both of whom appeared as dark specks between the beasts' wings. The lead dact clenched bundles of short spears in each of its talons, while the others gripped iron bashing-balls.

As the flock approached the training targets, the capable flighters expertly steered their mounts downward until they were barely atop the wetrollers.

Tarawa watched with interest as the distant barrage churned up a patch of sea, before the wetrollers quickly resumed their synchronized march for the shore. He noted with some satisfaction how most of the bobbing barrels had simply vanished from view. In their place, a haphazard patch of floating debris littered the rolling surface. Even so, the ever practical prod was well aware that barrel targets could neither take evasive action or loose arrows at their winged attackers. *'Target practice is one thing, combat quite another.'*

Settling down into his seat, Tarawa snagged sight of a pair of covered coaches stopped alongside the road. He thought, *'Whyever would they stop here? Do they wish to get robbed?'* It also struck him as odd that a large gap of at least eight coach lengths separated them, yet none of the drivers or passengers were out and about in conversation. *'Strange'*, he thought, as his carriage rolled past the rear coach. *'This coach appears to be intact? So why then is it stopped?'* Curious, he looked about for reasons that might explain such odd behaviour. There were none.

The suspicious prod locked eyes with two grubby drivers in shabby uniforms, both of whom granted him amiable nods of respect. Still, something was off? Tarawa could feel it in his gut. He knew most of Cracow's nobles by name, yet he could not recall ever seeing either driver before. Nor their uniforms or coach for that matter. *'Who are they servant to? What could they be doing there? And why would anybody ride in a covered coach during the hot quarter anyway? At the very least they should raise the roll ups?'*

"Hmmm?" he muttered beneath the rattle. *'Perhaps they hail from elsewhere and have simply gotten lost? Such is not uncommon in Cracow. But if that is so, why not wave us down and ask the way? Very strange?'*

Sensing his apprehension, Anole took hold of his hand and offered up a smile.

Tarawa squeezed her tiny hand in response. He would have licked her face, but the forward coach suddenly lurched ahead and started rolling.

"Dung!" Tarawa's drivers cursed as the forward coach steered into the center of the rutted road, forcing them to rein their team to an abrupt halt. All aboard the carriage were flung forward.

Tarawa quickly reclaimed his balance and shot a panicky glance back over his shoulder. His worst fears were realized as the rear coach was also veering out into the road behind them. *'Ambush!'*

"Pass them now!" Tarawa screamed, shoving his mate and tot to the floor boards. "It's a trap!"

With no hesitation, Tarawa's drivers began shouting and cracking their whips. At once, the rexids dug deep with their claws and the carriage lurched forward.

"Keep down!" Tarawa screamed the instant a bolt clacked off the carriage body. His head driver slumped slack and pitched over the side; a second bolt sticking from his neck.

One of the wheels struck a fleshy bump, causing the carriage to tilt. A third bolt stuck into a body panel just as the forward coach veered to bash the lighter carriage off the road.

A skinny lizarma with hostile eyes and a severed ear snarled as he leapt aboard the tipping carriage. In both hands he clenched a trident, but much stronger hands grabbed the shaft of his weapon and yanked him forward and down. He shrieked and flailed at air after a boot slammed up into his belly and flipped him heels about hearers from the carriage.

Tarawa snapped back up into a sit and spun to swing the trident at a second assassin who, dagger in hand, had also leapt aboard the carriage. This assassin neatly ducked the blow and lunged inside the trident's arc of swing.

Both combatants locked limbs in a grapplers embrace. All became a noisy blur as the carriage hit a bump and they were tossed as one over the side. Each winced in agony as their bodies hit the ground. Ruts and stones battered their tumbling form. Skin was scraped from bone. Teeth gritted dirt. Biting, punching, kneeing, gouging.

Tarawa's ears snagged the sound of busting planks and squealing rexids. Somebody screamed! Then silence…

Suddenly, the assassin gasped with bulging eyes. He parted his lips to speak, but any words were drowned out in a gurgle as he choked forth blood and slumped to meet Morgue.

Tarawa heaved the assassin off of himself and withdrew his blade from its breast. There was shouting all around him. Metal clanged to meet metal. The ground shook to the thump of many feet. Sounds from a fleeing coach were rattling off into the distance…

"Prod Commander…" a voice was saying. "Prod Commander…"

Tarawa found himself staring up into the concerned eyes of a young soldier. Many more soldiers were swarming about the carnage, with some taking control of the second coach and capturing any wounded assassins unfortunate enough to still be of breath. The silence squads would be keen to probe each of them.

"Thanks be to Destiny we were near," the young soldier said. "It is my shame some of them escaped. Charged their coach clean through our ranks they did. We lost soldiers. They were not common bandits, Prod Commander. These were hungry ones, of such I am certain. Nary ye fret, they shan't get far with broken spokes and our rexids swift on the chase. We'll nab them soon enough."

After shaking the spin from his mind and wiping bloodied dirt from his face, Tarawa re-sheathed his blade and painfully pushed to his feet. A tangled mess of busted boards and twisted metal was strewn out all along the road. Several rexids were writhing about the wreckage. One intact wheel squeaked in spin on its broken axle.

Bellybees stung deep into Tarawa's gut as his eyes took in the carnage. Panic seized his thoughts and he limped for the boards and metal.

Frantic with fear, he began clawing through the debris. Boards and panels were flung aside at random as he desperately sought out his family. His heart punched at his chest. Dare he think the worst?

54

Then he cast aside *the panel*. Beneath it, two silent figures stared blank at naught. Their eyes were void of thought. Each was already with Morgue.

"Dearest Destiny…" somebody whispered.

Tarawa stared at Anole and Gekar for some time. Slowly, tears started to seep from his eyes and trickle trails down his dirty cheeks. His lower lip quivered. His body trembled. Overwhelmed with grief, he sank to his knees and screamed his pain at the sky. "NO!!"

Aytik

A river galley rode the swift flowing Amen River without need of sail or oars. The powerful current alone sufficed to sweep it along. Only a sneaky stone or a shrouded shoal could stop the craft from speeding safely out of the river delta and on into Ga Bay.

An able pilot clung to the bowsprit, frantically gesturing instructions back to those crew grappling with the steerboard. The remaining sailors shouted and flailed arms at some smiling faces that peered down at them from atop a stone arch bridge. Not even the spray and foam that soaked their baggy breeches and blouses could dampen their cheer. They were home at last!

One pair of hands gripping the steerboard belonged to a handsome young ladfolk with a tanned face. Golden locks whipped about his cheeks as he struggled to help steer the loaded vessel. His alert blue eyes were properly fixed upon the pilot.

A loud cheer erupted as the galley shot clear of the froth and chop of the river, and glided safely out onto the rippled surface of Ga Bay. It was followed by the dull thuds of oars being dropped into rowlocks.

The craft quickly steered starboard and a drummer began pounding out a cadence. Several inquisitive shoresquawkers swooped low to investigate. To the north, a pod of spouters rolled through the water with complete indifference.

The young ladfolk redirected his sights along the shoreline. Many humanfolk were waving from atop the older wooden docks that for generations had welcomed seafarers to the ancient port of Capital. Others waved from aboard the wide assortment of vessels, both large and small, that were moored all about the harbour. Even a wee woofer yapped out its welcome. The return of any trade boat was always cause for much excitement, and merchants especially would be most anxious as to its cargo?

While helping to steady the steerboard, the young ladfolk scanned his sights over his wet and weary mates. Although he was beyond thrilled to be back home, he still felt a sadness inside. They had all been through so much together. Now their common adventure was almost at its end, and each would go her or his separate way. Perhaps never to meet again?

It had been a long and arduous voyage, fraught with all tempers of sea. Torrents that tossed their galley about like a nut. The stifling stillness of tide over. Sea sickness. A frantic beaching to repair a damaged bow. Yet for all that, Destiny had favoured them. None of their crew had met Morgue.

They had initially set sail from Capital; first putting into port at the small fishing village of Ga, where they had taken on a large load of hardwood planks and many crates of fine calfskin parchment. From Capital they had sailed due east past the Upcoast Forests and around the eastern tip of The Continent. From there they had steered west-southwest past the breathing blue sag which concealed the Fluorescent Forest; a mysterious and foreboding place where no mortal with any sense would ever dare to go. They then straddled the rugged southern coast past the Red River delta until they reached the white ape city of Apel.

While their cargo of wood and parchments was being unloaded, the young ladfolk had seized the opportunity to visit with King Thorax, who was one of his father's oldest friends, and also with the beautiful Princess Toongy. He had remained a guest of the white ape monarch and his younger sister until his galley cast off from Apel for the mining port of Jara.

At Jara they had taken on a heavy load of the quality metal ingots that had become so vital to the humanfolk economy, before setting sail back to Apel. From there they had rowed up the deep and sluggish Red River to Lake Blood, which was so named for the strange reddish sand on its shores and the mystical crimson hue of its surface come dawn and dusk. Favourable winds made for a speedy crossing of the lake. To complete their voyage, they had ridden the swift and treacherous currents of the mighty Amen River all the way home to Capital.

This final stage of the long voyage had proved to be the most demanding. Even with its wide, flat hull and shallow draft, the river galley still weighed too heavy for two of the river's shoals. On both occasions, some of the cargo had been temporarily unloaded to shore while the exhausted crew hauled and winched the stubborn craft over the silty barriers. Many a limb had been bruised whenever boots slipped on slimy stones, which they were often apt to do. Then ankles and feet would be numbed by the frigid water, while sopping wet jerkins failed to yield any warmth.

Yet despite all its delays and difficulties, the river route back home had still saved them precious time over again risking the more dangerous sea route.

The young ladfolk thought, *'We've been away for nearly three quarters. That is how long I have been kept apart from her.'*

He'd known from the start it was not by chance his father had suddenly wanted him to learn something of the sea. Nonetheless, he fully intended to wed Shyamala despite her family's low noble status, no matter his father's feelings on the matter.

Nary a day had passed when his mind wasn't mostly on her. He'd yearned to stare into her brown eyes and run his fingers through her black hair. How he longed to caress her skin. To lick her lips. Many night's had brought him dreams of them lying naked together with tangled limbs.

He muttered, "One would think a king would know time cannot conquer true love. Not that my father would know anything of love."

"You spoke, Prince?" asked one of his mates.

The young ladfolk simply shook his head and re-sighted shoreward to take in the city.

Newer and much larger concrete piers dominated the shoreline, their giant treadmill hoists now loading and unloading more and bigger ships from as far away as Jara on The Continent's southern coast to the docks north of The Wall. Beside the piers stood the huge modern warehouses that were so essential to trade. A new boardwalk, built of sturdy hardwood ties and well designed to let supply wagons steer safely about between the warehouses and dockside hoists, provided for easy and safe public access to the shore. Wisps of smoke spiraled skyward from the stacks of tiny shops that supplied the seafarers with everything from gagweed and jabber juice to clothing and fried finners with bread. Some shoreside inns even offered night mates for a fee; a practice that thoroughly disgusted most humanfolk, yet went on unabated nonetheless.

Squeezed between steep bluffs to the east and the Amen River to the west, Capital had grown from a tiny copper age fishing hamlet into a vibrant, sprawling city; and while wooden hovels still dominated the city's shoreside rookery, the long escarpment leading up to the plains was dotted with the neatly spaced homes of well-to-do guild workers and elite artists, all of whom were highly skilled in trades and crafts. Almost all such homes were square-built of white brick and roofed with clay slabs, and when viewed from the bay they appeared as little white boxes with orange lids, all plotted precisely onto a pinkish cobblestone grid.

Higher up the slope, the cobblestone roads widened and the little brick homes were replaced by the much larger manor homes of the wealthiest commoners, who were known spitefully to all low commoners as *pomps*. Their manors were always complete with properties and low curtain walls. As was the fashion, barbican towers had been erected over each gate, albeit more out of vanity than for actual defense. Sculpted statues and ornate, dyed-glass windows flaunted each occupant's status and wealth. Some even boasted with fountains. Comprised mainly of successful merchants and money lenders, the wealthy pomps provided somewhat of a social link between the lower classes beneath them and the true nobility above. Although, truth be told, the needs of the rookery poor were seldom of much concern to either.

Nearer to the bluffs were the more opulent manors of the local nobility. Made of whitewashed stone and roofed with lead or clay pan tiles, they resembled small castles in their own right;

although, as with the pomps below them, their homes were also built more for vanity and privacy than for actual defense. None of them could long withstand an actual siege. Despite their formidable appearance, their walls were much too thin to withstand an artillery barrage from catapults, especially from the modern siege engines that use counterweights to sling projectiles from the end of long wooden beams. While many had decorative battlements, complete with crenels and merlons, all were without moats or ramparts; such things being banned by Royal Decree. If the king's soldiers wanted to enter a lord's estate, they would enter a lord's estate. And that would be that.

With its keep towering high atop the bluffs, the city's one true castle loomed far greater than all the pretenders. Built upon solid rock and backing onto the plains, it had been strategically placed to allow for an open vantage of the entire city to the west and of Ga Bay to the north. Unbroken battlements ringed the entire structure, allowing defenders to keep cover behind thick merlons whilst shooting their bolts and arrows down through crenels.

The castle's massive plinthed walls and fortified flanking towers would prove quite problematic for ladders and siege towers, assuming the attackers could ever breach the surrounding curtain walls to begin with. Strategically placed bastions also permitted defensive fire in every direction, and the steep angle of nature's rampart rising up to the curtain wall rendered any attack from below all but futile. As a last line of defence, every gate was defended by a heavy portcullis with murder holes for pouring hot oil down onto attacking soldiers. Vast stores of food could be kept in the basement of the tower keep, and three deep cisterns collected countless barrels of rainwater from every storm. Clearly, this was a fortress built to withstand an honest siege.

The young ladfolk stretched a smile as he stared up at his home. This night he would nap in his own bed. Hopefully not alone?

Lowering his sights back to the shoreline, he became captivated by the flow of faces that poured from the shops and streamed down the boardwalk to the piers. A large throng had already gathered atop the pier that serviced the slips. Folks waved and cheered and shouted out in welcome. Some burst into laughter as some drunken rowds shoved several unsuspecting ruffs into the drink.

Whistles sliced wind as more club-wielding ruffs began beating a path through the mob in a desperate attempt to assist their thrashing colleagues. Other ruffs used leashed woofers to gain control over the crowd, while many of the burliest ruffs linked arms to bar further access to the pier. A pair of cage wagons were drawn down the packed boardwalk, forcing the rowds to dive clear for their very being. Several flailing bodies splashed into the dirty drink.

"Ha! Be the same ruckus every time a trade boat returns," an amused seafarer noted before adding, "No matter the size, be it a large cog from the sea or a small scow off the Amen, a mob always packs these piers."

Another added, "Merchants sure be masters of mayhem whenever there be coinage for grab!"

"Perhaps the mob will rise up in riot again?" offered a third. His tone sounded almost hopeful. "Last time…"

"Let us hope nobody meets Morgue from such foolishness," the young ladfolk put in. "Their actions lack sense. All buyers know cargo must be listed on the boards a full day prior to auction. That is the law. Hence, each will have their fair chance to bid. The shrewdest merchants are busy calling on forges to learn of their needs."

The other seafarers exchanged knowing smiles. They mused that if the nobility chose to assume their trade laws were obeyed, then let them keep to their ignorance. Commoners knew better. Most of the craft's cargo would be bought up long before any legal auction. Some even before it was unloaded. Needless to say, the corrupt port masters would take home more coin than their wages allow; as always.

By the time the galley glided into its slip, the dock ruffs had managed to force the mob back off the pier and up onto the boardwalk. Now only burly dockers in boots, breeches and blouses stood atop the pier, along with some robed port masters bearing quill pens and thick ledgers. Merchants jostled and craned their necks to see down into the craft's hull, yet none dared challenge the snarling woofers that kept the growing crowd firmly in check.

All aboard the galley braced themselves as the vessel banged up against the corkwood cushions. Several crew hooked the craft steady while some of their mates tossed hawsers up to the dockers.

Once the lines were fast and a gangplank laid, the weary seafarers pulled on their boots, slung their bulging seabags across their backs and began filing off the boat and up the ramp. A greying paymaster in a floppy bag hat doled out an equal stack of coins to each seafarer as they stepped from ramp to pier.

After making their mark in the ledger, the seafarers started strolling towards the boardwalk. They chatted and waved to each other as they split into groups of four or three or two. All were happy to be back safe at their home port; and they would remain so right up until they once again needed to scratch their strange seafarers' itch for danger and adventure. Yes, seafarers are indeed an odd lot?

The young ladfolk was amongst the last to disembark. He slung his seabag across his back, and then hoisted his seafarer's chest up onto one shoulder. His sturdy legs bucked to shift the heavy load and better distribute its weight before he stepped across the gangplank and climbed the ramp to the pier.

"Pleasant voyage, my Prince?" asked the paymaster, handing the young noble his stack.

The ladfolk pouched his pay. "It was my first voyage, thus I have no other to compare. I can say none of our crew met Morgue."

"Then ye voyage beed a charm," reasoned an old docker in a flat cap. His smile revealed a large gap between his blackened teeth, where he promptly stuck the stem of his puffing pipe. He was hunched by age and labour, and wealthy with whiskers. Even so, his rough hands still boasted a grip.

"Are you the ranking docker?" inquired the ladfolk.

Upon pulling the pipe from his lips, the old docker casually blew his lungs void. "Aye, that I be," he replied. "In the wrinkled flesh. Tindal, I be. Rufus Tindal. Ranking docker on this pier and any pier. Fifty-four cycles I beed a docker. Know this port better than I know me own rump. Ah, be ye Prince Aytik by chance?"

Any other time, the young ladfolk might have felt slighted by such a brash and carefree manner being shown him by a low commoner. However, he reasoned fifty-four cycles made the old docker somewhat of a prince about the piers.

"Well," Rufus pressed. "Be ye or be ye not Prince Aytik? Flap up, lad. I shan't slice off ye tongue. Aye or nye?"

Prince Aytik granted Rufus Tindal a warm smile. "Aye, that I be," he replied, feeling somewhat silly in his feeble attempt to chew salt jargon.

The old docker briefly tilted his pipe in a casual show of respect. "Then I speak a chit from Sir Golab to ye. King's guards come to bring ye a steed and fetch ye swift to the castle. Me self in the flesh will tend to ye chest and ye seabag and see em sure to the castle. Nary ye fret, me Prince, they be safe with ole' Rufus Tindal fixin' a spy on em'."

"I be – uh – I'm certain they will be," Aytik reasoned as he lowered his burdens. "But why not just send a carriage so I can bring them myself?"

"I fancy they wish ye be swift on the snap to the castle, me Prince. Be six days now that soldiers and knights pour in from the plains. Capital be thick as nog with hunches and blabbel. Tongues wag of war."

Aytik became visibly perplexed. "War? With whom?"

Rufus shrugged. "Abroad be the blabble. There be much hugger-muggery, me Prince. No soldiers beed heerd flappin' the gums. All be kept strict to camp. Tis all a poser, it be?"

"Then who told…' Aytik began, but the clop of approaching hooves stayed his speech. He shifted his sights to find soldiers of the king's elite Royal Guard leading a spare steed along by its reins.

Each guard was clad in riding boots and breeches, and padded doublets which served as both jackets and armour. They donned domed helmets and wore hide gauntlet gloves. Hooded cloaks of felted sheep's wool, used both as protective garments and for blankets, were rolled up and strapped down tight behind polished saddles; kept within easy reach should the winds blow cold and nasty.

The guards' weapons proved their high status. Longswords fashioned of the finest steel hung in scabbards from their baldrics. Bucklers were strapped to their forearms, each shield painted with the royal crest depicting a gold crown centered within a sunburst. Several knights couched steel-tipped lances.

The spirited beasts clopped to a whoa directly before the anxious prince, who appeared more as a pauper in his sopping blouse and breeches. A tough old guard wearing the armlet of a knight commander bowed his brow in respect and offered Aytik the spare steed's reins.

Aytik took the reins in hand and asked, "What's all this talk of war?"

"I am not firm of the facts, my Prince. There is much secrecy."

"So tell me what little you do know," Aytik demanded, swinging his leg across the saddle. He expressed annoyance as his boots awkwardly sought out the stirrups. "At least tell me what you have heard."

The cautious knight shrugged. "I know only that our entire army is being mustered and made ready to march."

"March where and against whom?" Aytik pressed, reining his steed about and slapping it into a trot.

"Much secrecy prevails, Prince. We were simply ordered to see you swift to the castle. I can say no more."

"Don't glib with me," Aytik coaxed. "Speak freely."

"Very well," responded the knight, gently pressing his steed from a trot near to a gallop. "But we must make haste. The king has summoned all ambassadors and the witan to court. He knows of your return and demands your presence at once."

The knight slowed briefly to let Aytik catch up. "Supreme Pid's troops are said to be massing in great numbers near the pass. There is evidence the *scaleez* may even be mobilizing to attack The Wall – assuming intel from the black ape scouts is reliable? Ambassador Kryle is already demanding the white apes and ourselves honour the terms of our pact and immediately deploy troops in support. Apparently he's being quite insistent."

Prince Aytik reined his steed back into a trot. "Lag the pace, Sir Knight. The boardwalk here is too crowded. Best we arrive late than with innocent blood on our mounts."

"But your father…"

"… shan't mind waiting a bit longer. Surely, our army is not set to march off this very instant, is it?"

"No, Prince. It's just that Ambassador Kryle is most impatient for…"

"Such is his privilege," Aytik interrupted. "Under the terms of our pact, both the white apes and ourselves must send troops to help repel a lizarme invasion. Our honour aside, surely even the black apes know our army can neither march or fight without supplies. There are logistics to consider.

"I've known Doyen Kryle since long before he was appointed ambassador. Even back before he was promoted to doyen. We first met when I was still a wee tot, back when his father held the post. By pressing us to act, he is simply doing what the Federation Council in Raw demands of him. None of it is personal."

The old knight shook his head. "All the same, my Prince, I still don't like him."

Aytik smiled knowingly as they veered from pier to boardwalk. "Not many do, Sir Knight. Not many do…"

Now the dock ruffs were joined by foot soldiers, who pointed halberds and marched forward in closed ranks to disperse the frenzied mob. More cage wagons were also arriving to accommodate any rowds still spoiling for a spat.

With knights at the lead, the guards weaved their way through and about the chaos with little difficulty as humanfolk ran, jumped and dove out of the way. Nobody, it seemed, wished to be skewered by lance or trampled by hoof.

Eventually, the guards turned from the boardwalk and trotted out onto a rutted road, where they pressed their mounts into a gallop. Some public servants were quite casually replacing broken cobbles. Nearby, a group of irate merchants were busy haggling with some white ape traders over the price of purple cloth. Mighty tuskwoolies, burdened beneath their bulky bundles of the precious product, bellowed defiance at the passing steeds.

Aytik felt pangs of pity as they passed through the rookery, every hovel of which was in dire need of repairs. At one point he even tossed his entire pouchful of coins at a bewildered group of mothers in aprons, all of whom wided eyes and scrambled to snatch up the bouncing and rolling objects.

Soon Aytik and his escorts began the winding climb up towards the castle. As Aytik sighted up from amongst the brick homes of the guild workers and artists, the massive stone walls of his own home seemed to grow more and more imposing with each clop of hooves. As such, by the time they trotted in amongst the elaborate manors of the wealthy pomps, Aytik began taking into account the castle's splendor as well.

In direct contrast to its defiant walls and battlements, the castle's dyed-glass windows revealed a softer side to its soul. And nowhere did grass grow greener than within its well-manicured baileys. The pinks and purples and yellows and blues of its many gardens invited all manner of beast to laugh and leap and sing. Its cobblestone drives converged to meet at the barbican, the stone arches of which were gaily attired by floral vines. This season of the cycle they would be in full bloom.

The road widened as Aytik and his escorts clopped past the faux castles of the nobility. He knew that behind the showy yet useless battlements, unleashed woofers patrolled the courtyards and servants kept a wary watch over tots. In the past, brazen lawbreakers had been known to snatch untended tots and hold them for ransom.

Finally, the group clopped between more royal guards, each of whom stood still as statues outside the barbican protecting the main gate leading to the lower bailey. Looking over the colourful vines, Aytik thought to himself, *'I so hope we never lose those.'* As they passed down the neck and on through the tunnel, Aytik looked up at the murder holes. *'I so hope we never need those...'*

Upon entering the lower bailey, they trotted past the stables and granary. The banging and clanging of blacksmiths plying their craft mixed well with the clopping of hooves; the welcome sounds of home. The prince recognized most of the steeds and carriages parked outside the knights hall.

Aytik dismounted and handed his reins over to the knight commander, then patted his escort upon the shoulder before he started up the winding steps to a second barbican which stood tall before the drawbridge. While waiting for the bridge to lower, he looked up at the guards peering down from the bretèche and thought, *'I feel for those poor souls. I will never miss the smell of standing before this gate. Whyever would my great grandfather have let his builders design the garderobes to drop human waste into our moat? When I become king, I will have my engineers design a new sewage system to redirect all waste into cesspits. Cesspits that will be emptied frequently.'*

The moment the bridge was lowered into place, Aytik wasted no time in crossing over the smelly moat towards the main gate into the upper bailey. His father did not permit beasts in the upper bailey, thus the heavy iron portcullis had been dropped and bolted down for as long as Aytik could remember; yet another thing he planned to change when he became king. Until then, he must enter the upper bailey through the walkers wicket just like everybody else.

After Aytik had passed through the wicket and stepped out into the upper bailey, it was no great distance across the grass and past the castle cisterns to the keep. Located on the first level of the keep was the great hall, where the king often held court. Within a short bit the young prince had scaled the spiralled stairwell and rounded its final turn to the entrance. Hinges squeaked as a guard strained to open the heavy oaken door. Moments later found Aytik striding down a smoky corridor towards two massive hardwood doors with metal forging. Shadows from marble statues danced upon frescoed walls. Guards toting long halberds stood rigid with eyes front as Aytik passed between them. A husky knight stepped smartly forward and swung open one of the doors.

Aytik nodded his gratitude as he strode past the knight and on into the great hall. An enormous oval table squatted in its center. Around it stood an assortment of familiar forms. All bore expressions of a most serious nature.

Only King Myro was seated. He donned his regal red robe and matching slipperboots. A gemmed circlet kept his straggly grey hair in check. He clenched his gold ruler's sceptre with shaky hands. Blue veins glowed about his white knuckles. Purple cushions propped up his frail frame. It was quite apparent age was now his most stubborn foe.

'How feeble he looks,' Aytik thought with some sadness as he locked sights with his father's clever green eyes. It was also apparent age was up against a stubborn foe, as witnessed by the old king's keen and unyielding mind.

King Myro's lips hinted at a slight smile. Then, as if he had suddenly caught himself in a regal gaffe, he quickly soured face and motioned for his only son to join the group.

Aytik could put a name to everyone gathered around the table. To his father's left loomed his ever-vigilant bodyguard, Stork. Exceptionally tall and lanky with unnaturally long limbs, Stork's strange appearance alone was enough to intimidate most would-be assassins. He had a huge, hooked schnozz and blinkless black eyes that seemed to sight through their target. His long throat possessed an oversized larynx which, when he walked, bobbed in cadence with each of his lengthy strides. None had known him to smile – or even hint at a smile. Not one single time.

Even Stork's attire was unsettling. As always, he was fit for a fight. He donned a black robe, a mail coif and metal-tipped boots. A sheathed longsword hung from one side of his belt, whilst a morning star dangled from the other. His long fingers clenched a thick halberd with an oversized axe and spike on the blood end. Many suspected him of packing his gloves with sand, thereby adding force to his punches.

Prince Aytik had known the imposing bodyguard since he himself was but a wee tot, so he offered him an amicable nod of greeting.

Stork ignored him.

To the king's right stood his oldest and dearest friend, Olob the historian. As far back as Aytik could remember, old Olob had been white of hair and beard, but with quick blue eyes that never missed a trick. He wore a hooded blue frock, patterned with orange crescent-moons, and the worn old bag hat he was so fond of donning. Buckled ankle boots completed his attire.

Olob nodded discretely and subtly stretched the prince a slight smile. Aytik eagerly returned both gestures. It was apparent each felt a fondness for the other.

Beside the historian stood the realm's ranking grand knight, Sir Golab, who was clad in the padded doublet, long riding breeches and the hide highboots which were standard issue to all of the realm's knights. Hair red as sunsets drooped past his shoulders. His white skin was overcast with freckles.

Beside Sir Golab stood the white ape ambassador, Princess Tianga. The eldest sister of King Thorax, her tall frame and sinewy limbs were completely covered in coarse white hair; save for her purplish lips, and the blue skin on her face and palms. She had wise orange eyes and a flat nose. Her hide skirt and vest were of the finest quality, and her flanged helmet and spiked wristlet-of-rank further attested to her high status. A hurling dagger was sheathed into one of her highboots.

Ambassador Tianga offered Aytik a courteous smile, to which the prince politely responded in kind.

Aytik next locked sights with the antema ambassador, Viceroy. Antemi were a secretive species who dwelled deep within the Dark Jungle on the southwestern tip of The Continent. They were tall, bug-like beings with hard chitin exoskeletons and long, stilted legs; which made them snapping swift on the sprint. As with all male antemi, Viceroy bore bulging holoptic eyes that enabled him to sight in multiple directions at the same time.

Be they male or female, every antema wore a grass skirt. A hardwood cudgel always dangled from their vine belt. Every antema warrior was skilled with a lance and well trained to pilot an aeront; as many a lizarme flighter would attest.

Antemi were also masters of the small composite bows they fashioned from bamboo, horn and sinew. None but the antemi themselves knew the secrets behind making such light and powerful bows, which could be quickly nocked and loosed by a warrior in flight. Their unique, hollow arrow shafts were another antemi mystery. Fashioned from a secret mineral the antemi call graphene, and tipped with barbed arrowheads, such missiles could easily punch through armour. Having been tested accurate and effective to over three hundred strides, the fearsome weapon had become the bane of every lizarme soldier; a weapon so lethal it encumbers their commanders with many napless nights.

Being a first cousin to Empress Antraha by way of his mother made Ambassador Viceroy an antema of some influence. For that reason, Aytik made a point of offering the bug-like being an especially warm and prolonged nod of respect. He knew ape and humanfolk alike would be aggressively courting Antraha's favour in a war against their common foe and he hoped his father would be pleased by his keen sense of diplomacy.

The ever polite antema calmly returned the gesture. As always, his face disclosed not even the slightest hint of emotion. Nothing.

Aytik thought, *'Viceroy's not revealing a thing until he's received messengers from Antraha. She will not aid us without extracting a high price. Of that, at least, we can be certain.'*

Aytik turned his sights onto a burly black ape in a hide loincloth and spiked helmet. A hefty battle-axe was strapped across his broad back. His shaggy hair was as black as his eyes. His wrinkled skin was worn tough by the winds. He bore spiked wristlets of rank.

Although much shorter than the white ape, Ambassador Kryle's bulk made him of superior weight. He all but lacked a neck. Thick thews threatened to burst through his skin. A braided beard draped down between his powerful pecs. Fists like clubs dangled at the end of his thick arms. He had a flat nose wedged between puffy cheeks; plus a broken upper fang, courtesy of a lizarma's brow butt many cycles past.

Aytik had reserved his best smile for Kryle. He and the ape had pledged themselves as cullies in their youth, sealing their bond with a ceremonial mixing of blood. Accordingly, their bond went much deeper than that of mere friends. They knew each other well. It had come as no surprise to the prince when Kryle was promoted to become the youngest doyen in black ape history and placed in charge of a legion. Only seven cycles later, the talented ape became the youngest ambassador ever. His shaggy friend was by far the toughest being Aytik had ever known, and one of the shrewdest.

Diplomats mostly communicated in the ancient continental language, which was crude yet sufficient. Thus, it had long been the language of diplomacy; even the disparate antemi could speak it. Being son to a senior diplomat, Kryle had been taught the ancient language almost since birth and could speak it as fluently as he spoke his mother tongue.

Yet Kryle had also managed to master both white ape and humanfolk speech while he was still a lad. Next he had become passable in the most difficult of all dialects, that of the antemi; a language with no written words. Five languages in total, and all before he'd turned twenty cycles aged!

Kryle had once confided to Aytik he was intent on being elected to the Federation Council before he had aged forty cycles. Although no black ape had ever obtained such a high and prestigious position before fifty cycles aged, Aytik believed his determined cully would achieve it. He'd even told him such.

Aytik stepped up to the table between Ambassadors Kryle and Viceroy. A hairy hand patted his back in greeting.

Across the table from them stood the kingdom's elders of the court, the witan. All were high ranking nobles. They had

71

long beards and were attired in full arrogance with loud silken robes and long, pointy poulaines.

Aytik had always felt poulaines looked ridiculous, a rare viewpoint on which he and his father fully agreed. He often thought, *'Forget about running, how does one even walk in those clumsy things?'*

"Very well," King Myro stated in his regal voice. He shot Aytik a stern stare. "Now that my son has finally opted to join us, we can at last commence with this moot. I humbly apologize for his cooling our heels this long."

Aytik could feel his teeth clenching. He thought, *'I see naught has changed in my absence.'*

Myro paused and hacked phlegm into a cloth before going on. "As you are all no doubt aware, there has been much wag of war about the realm. I can assure you such gossip is not without some basis in truth."

The king paused briefly for a group murmur to ebb before continuing. "It should come as no surprise to any of you that it is against the lizarme whom we may be forced to wage war. The Black Ape Federation has now confirmed what we recently suspected. Large numbers of Supreme Pid's troops are in fact massing near the pass. Black ape scouts have identified banners from some of his best legions. Even as I speak, the enemy may be attacking The Wall."

Again, Myro paused for the ensuing murmur to ebb. Then he brandished his sceptre and shouted, "We shall never allow a single lizarme to set foot east of the Divides! Never!"

A charged silence briefly filled the court, quickly broken by a boisterous burst of cheering and clapping. Some members of the witan took to shouting their approval, while others slapped palms to tabletop in support of their king. Each grasped all too well the consequences should lizarme legions enter the east. Peace as a word would be best left to folklore.

"Of course, it may not come to war," Myro stated with more than a tinge of hope to his tone. "It is our hope that once Supreme Pid recognizes our black ape allies do not stand alone he will abandon his quest for conquest. Already, King Thorax has pledged full white ape support. The pact between our allies holds firm. A lizarme attack against one will be deemed an attack against all!"

Instantly, the court reacted its approval. Elders cheered and began clapping in earnest.

Amidst the noise and commotion, Aytik stole a quick glance at Viceroy. He noted how the antema's face displayed all the emotion of a stone. Not that such was out of character for the reserved bug-like being. In fact, Aytik had often quipped that Stork would have made a good antema. Antemi nature aside, however, Aytik hoped Viceroy would let slip at least some hint of what he may be thinking? But the ambassador's mien offered up nothing.

Turning to face Kryle, Aytik was somewhat surprised to find his shaggy friend donning a frown of concern. The perplexed prince shrugged palms-up to ask why?

Kryle cupped fingers about his cully's ear. Aytik could feel the ape's moist breath.

"They are much too confident," Kryle explained, adding, "Pid would have planned on King Thorax and your father keeping the pact. He knows both place a high price on honour. War is coming, Aytik. Of that you can be certain."

"I've never seen you so troubled," Aytik noted as the clamour started to calm. "What gnaws at your thoughts?"

"I'm not certain," Kryle replied. "We've suspected for some time that the lizarme have been massing troops near the pass. Logic dictates time can only conspire against them, yet they do not attack? Soon your army and that of the white apes will arrive to reinforce our troops at The Wall. Prod Tarawa is much too clever not to realize our scouts would eventually discover what his troops are about. And it's certainly not in his nature to delay an attack while he holds the advantage – at least not without ample reason. I have a sinky feeling in my gut, Prince. Like we're all missing something? Something vital. A puzzle we'd best solve – and quickly. Olob is of like mind."

Aytik had enormous respect for the opinions of both his cully and the historian. He grinned as he spoke. "Now I share your sinky feeling. Gee, thanks."

Kryle puckered his fat lips, which was the ape way of making amused.

"Perhaps we should ponder Tarawa's reasoning together?" Aytik suggested.

"Oh, there will be plenty of time for that," Kryle assured his cully. "Your father has decided that as heir to the throne you must take responsibility and lead your army. Also, some news recently arrived from Raw. The Federation Council have voted in my favour and I have been promoted to Doyen Commander of our army. Hence, I am to depart forthwith for The Wall. As are you. We will mount up before the first hint of dawn."

"On the morrow! Kryle, I just returned home? I've yet to set eyes on Shyamala or my sister."

"How heedless of me, Prince. Clearly, Supreme Pid and the Winds of War have failed to factor in your personal life. Tyrants and war are funny that way. But thank you for at least heeding my good news."

Aytik sighed heavily. He knew his cully was right. He was being selfish and self-centred. "There's no need to get sarcastic. Of course I am proud of you, Kryle. Doyen Commander of The Army. While the rank brings with it tremendous responsibility, especially in wartime, I know you will meet each challenge with the proper mix of courage and wisdom. You always do. So of course the Federation Council chose you to take command in these uncertain times. There is no one more stalwart or deserving."

Kryle patted his cully's shoulder. "I thank you for that. Prince, it is for our loved ones that we must fight this war. We fight only because we have no choice. Any being who welcomes war has never known one – either that or their mind has spun fully *'round the twist'*. I've heard it said hate and greed can mangle any sound mind, that they are the twin stewards of strife. I believe such to be true, especially when the two merge as one. Logic always loses whenever we allow our thirsts for revenge or power to consume our soul and sink our honour. That said, if what you and Shyamala have is love, then it will stand another test of time. Love and honour always triumph in the end."

"And if it cannot stand another test of time?" Aytik asked.

The shrewd ape was quick to counter. "Then both of you will have lost nothing."

The ruckus only abated when Olob again raised his arms for silence. The old historian's glare prompted the more stubborn nobles of the witan to cease slapping their palms on the tabletop.

"War always accents the folly of the ignorant," Kryle whispered.

Ambassador Viceroy nodded in agreement.

Myro fixed sights on the antema. To avoid any confusion, he spoke in the ancient continental language. "What say you, ambassador? Will your legions aid us in attacking our common foe?"

One could almost hear walls breath as all eyes set upon Viceroy and every ear eagerly awaited his reply. Following a tense pause, Viceroy's monotone voice finally broke the uneasy silence. "It is true we antemi are natural enemies of the lizarme. And why wouldn't we be? After all, it was the lizarme who drove us from our ancestral lands surrounding Oasis Lake. That noted, I cannot commit to war without a Royal Decree from the empress herself, for I am but her humble messenger. I'm sure you will respect my position on this matter.

"I have, however, already dispatched messengers to Antraha, but it will take some time. They must zip around the southern Divides and then zip west along the coast to avoid winged scorps and other perils of the Badlands. Even the most seasoned aeronts have a maximum range before they must land to molt their wings; a process that takes days. Thus, even riding upon the hardiest aeronts and with favourable winds at their back, it will still take my messengers at minimum two lunar phases to reach the Dark Jungle. There is no way around it. You do understand?"

"I understand perfectly well, ambassador. So I ask you again – will Antraha send troops north to attack the lizarme?" Myro pressed, his tone spilling frustration.

Viceroy remained vague. "Again, I cannot speak for the empress, sire. Although, given the right conditions, I suppose anything is possible?"

Tactfully, Olob cut in. "Ambassador, it seems to me that with the brunt of the enemy's army engaged at The Wall, this might bring an opportunity for you to avenge your ancestors and retake Muga Terro."

Heads nodded as the witan muttered their approval.

Viceroy was unimpressed. "The lizarme army is well disciplined and highly mobile. It can quickly redeploy elsewhere. Besides, as yet nobody is actually engaging anybody at The Wall. You yourselves have stated that by standing united against Pid, you hope to deter his aggression. Even should your strategy deter the lizarme, Pid could simply abandon his conflict with you and attack us. We antemi could once again find ourselves fighting a much stronger foe on our own. Were we to engage the enemy beyond the Dark jungle, we would be crushed. So no, King Myro, I see no sound reason for Empress Antraha to send antemi warriors north into the open desert to engage such a powerful enemy – at least not without a firm commitment from both humanfolk and apes that there will be no separate peace. The lizarme threat against our nations must be negated and Pid must be deposed. Otherwise, we cannot ally ourselves with you."

Normally Myro would have been taken aback by any ambassador speaking to him in such blunt terms. That is, any ambassador who wasn't an antemi. Brief and to the point was always the antemi way. Besides, dangerous times merit blunt talk. And these were without doubt very dangerous times.

"Just what exactly do you mean by 'a firm commitment'?" Myro pressed, exchanging intrigued glances with the other ambassadors. A charged hush fell over the court.

Viceroy came straight to the point. "Sire, for more generations than we antemi can count, we have warred against the lizarme. There has been little lull in our suffering. Yet you only offer your support whenever they invade east of the Divide Mountains. Otherwise, neither they nor we are worthy of your concern.

"During the Great Continental War, our repeated attacks against the lizarme diverted many of their troops away from your front, allowing your armies to push the lizarme army back westward through the north pass. You forced them entirely from the eastern foothills, where their kind had dwelt even before Fate forged time. A great many antemi were slaughtered to draw those lizarme troops away from your front. Then, after you had secured the pass, you erected your wall and dug your moat and built up your rampart, leaving my nation to once again fight the lizarme on our own. To this day all you ever give us in exchange for our sacrifice is evasive sympathy and hollow advice – while we, of course, continue to give blood.

"This time we shall seek much more than sympathy and advice. There must be no separate peace made with the lizarme, and Muga Terro must be ceded back to us. As well, all territory south of Muga Terro must be relinquished and henceforth recognized as antemi domain, and the northern desert from Oasis Lake to the Great Forests must be permanently demilitarized. Such terms might prove favourable to the empress.

"If I could dispatch messengers assuring the empress we all agree to accept nothing less than the enemy's unconditional surrender, then perhaps she could be persuaded to fly our warriors north. But barring such a pact, I am certain you can forego any aid from us. And while I cannot speak for the empress, I can offer her my slant on the subject. I am not without influence."

Myro kept mute and looked to his historian for support. Both knew the ambassador's claim of influence was not just a petty boast.

"Ambassador Viceroy speaks historical fact," Olob assured his king. "Our ancestors could never have forced the lizarme hordes from the eastern foothills without help from our antemi allies. Then we did abandon them."

"Surely, we are not to be held accountable for events that took place long before Seed had breathed our own bodies into being?" Myro scoffed, resetting his sights on the dispassionate antema.

Viceroy shook his head and became somewhat more diplomatic in his manner. "Of course not. Nor did I mean to slight your ancestors. I merely want you to fully understand Empress Antraha's precarious position. Our entire nation is well aware of its history. We seek to avoid a repeat of past mistakes. Nothing more."

Tianga cut in. "So what you are really stating, ambassador, is that in exchange for Antraha's commitment to attack the lizarme, you would expect us to invade their homelands west of the Divides? To commit to a long and bloody offensive with no separate peace until the enemy has surrendered and agreed to all of our terms?"

Viceroy continued to evade showing even a hint of emotion. "All I am saying, Princess Tianga, is such a commitment might persuade Empress Antraha to commit troops to aid you in your fight. Nothing more. My only desire is to be helpful."

'Mooer dung,' Aytik thought, 'His only desire is to keep the bulk of Pid's army stuck in the east fighting us.'

"But of course," Tianga responded. "I will dispatch a messenger to Apel this very day to apprise my brother of Empress Antraha's concerns."

"And I will dispatch one to Raw," Kryle put in.

"Not necessary," Viceroy assured them. "Our ambassadors in Raw and Apel have already voiced our concerns to the Federation Council and King Thorax. I'm certain both have since given the matter serious thought. After all, it does appear we will need each other to achieve our joint objectives – complete defeat of the lizarme military and Supreme Pid's early demise. Be it by assassination or execution, it matters not to us how justice is dealt."

"Nor to us," Myro agreed.

"We will need time to call the witan," Olob informed the antema. "We must also confer with our ape allies."

"To be expected," Viceroy agreed. "One mustn't take on such a burden lightly, especially where lizarme are concerned.

The scaleez have always been a cruel and uncultured brood. Quite uncivilized, really. One can best view them as being barely above beasts."

'*Viceroy knows something?*' Aytik thought. '*Antemi spies have gained intelligence assuring them war is coming. Conflict is certain.*'

"Antraha needs our help as well," Aytik whispered to Kryle. "She wants war as much as Pid does."

The ape discretely nodded his agreement.

"Very well," Myro said, leaning on the table to soothe his shakes. He set his sights upon Aytik. "My son will lead our army west to The Wall. They march at dawn. I trust all is in place, Sir Golab?"

"All is, sire. Our knights and soldiers merely await your order."

Myro shifted his sights back onto Viceroy. "I will consult with our ape allies regarding an alliance between all of us – and this matter of no separate peace."

Viceroy merely nodded his approval.

Myro continued, "It may take some time to reach a consensus. You do understand?"

"I do," Viceroy replied. "Serious matters demand sober thought."

'*My father is stalling for time,*' Aytik thought. '*He shan't commit to any invasion of lizarme territory until he is convinced antemi help is vital to our own needs. Neither will King Thorax or the Black Ape Federation. Morgue's maze could be brimmed to burst after such a campaign. Each will try to avert war with Pid first, while keeping the door to invasion closed yet unlocked.*'

"Very well then," Myro said, struggling to straighten his frail frame. His green eyes scanned around the oval table. "Now you all know candor from clack. At the sun's rising, my son will lead our army west to help defend the wall. With the sole exception of my own Royal Guard, nary a knight or foot soldier will stay back. Any deserters will be shackled inside cage wagons and drawn to the front."

The old king paused to choose his words carefully before motioning to Viceroy. "I shall dispatch messengers to Raw and

Apel pledging my full support for such a pact. We shall all shine or matt together?"

Myro gestured to Golab, who bowed his brow in respect before turning and marching for the door.

Viceroy responded in his usual monotone voice. "I will send word to the empress that her concerns were well received. She will be pleased. For far too long the lizarme have been the scourge of this continent. So if we must, we will engage them together – this time on both sides of the Divides."

"Perhaps the same result can be gotten through parley," Tianga calmly suggested.

"Ha!" Viceroy spat out, displaying an extremely rare burst of emotion. "Your kind do not know the scaleez as we antemi do, Princess. The only ways to broker peace with lizarme are with the point of a lance or the head of a cudgel."

Tianga parted her lips to respond, then thought better of it. Instead, she gave the irked antema an understanding nod. His curt reaction to her mere suggestion of peace through parley told her exactly what she wanted to know. Empress Antraha had no desire for peace; she very much wanted war.

Olob and Myro exchanged knowing glances, as did most of the witan. Despite his normally composed demeanor, Viceroy's blunt rejection of a peaceful solution had betrayed two truths: First, the antemi very much wanted to attack their hated enemy. Second, the antemi strategy for victory hinged on waging a two front war, thereby splitting Pid's forces; and any negotiated peace between apes, humanfolk and lizarme would certainly deny them such. The lizarme army was simply too strong for the antemi to ever defeat on their own. Thus, Antraha's demand for an offensive commitment from both apes and humanfolk went well beyond aiding allies against a common foe. She needed such a pact to realize her own ambitions. A pact she seemed confident she was going to get.

It was King Myro who finally broke the awkward silence. "Well then," he stated in his grating voice, "It seems little more can be achieved at this time. We will consider your generous offer to form an alliance, Ambassador Viceroy. Then again, perhaps circumstances of war will decide for us?"

"Perhaps," Viceroy acknowledged. "But my own slant on the matter may also have some influence on the empress. When you finally commit to an offensive…"

"If we commit," Kryle cut in. "Like yourself, Princess Tianga and I are also in positions of influence. However, the decision to commit still rests with King Thorax and the Federation Council. You do understand?"

Viceroy promptly corrected himself. "Yes, of course. I meant to say, if you commit. I would also add the sooner this matter is resolved, the sooner we can all focus on our common purpose – defeating and disarming the lizarme. But we antemi shall go no further. We are not a vengeful species, nor do we condone the massacre of innocents. To do so would invite the combined wrath of Fate and Perish down upon ourselves. Our deities would never condone such savagery."

"Nor would ours," Myro assured him.

Having regained his composure, the antema donned no discernable expression as he nodded his approval.

Myro scanned the witan faces as he spoke. "There is nothing more to be discussed at this time. We all have important matters to ponder. Now you must forgive me for being so abrupt, but I have not set eyes on my son in nearly a cycle. I wish to speak with him and my historian alone. Leave us."

Kryle placed his hand upon Aytik's back. "I will meet you at the main barbican shortly before dawn. We will ride west together."

"I will be there," Aytik assured his cully.

The witan were the first to file from the great hall, followed closely by Viceroy and the ape ambassadors. Lastly, the guards departed, leaving only Stork and Olob alone with King Myro and Prince Aytik.

Stork assisted his king back onto his chair, while Olob positioned the purple cushions to comfort him. Then they each set their sights upon the young prince.

Myro smiled and said, "You look well, my son. It warms my heart that you are finally home."

Aytik did not return his father's smile. "It was you who sent me abroad," he sniped in the ageless tone of resentment reserved for indignant sons addressing overbearing fathers.

"For your own good," Myro sniped back, swallowing his smile.

Instantly, the room became charged with an angry silence. One could almost taste the tension.

Finally, Olob could stand it no longer and had to say something. "Ah – I trust your voyage went well? I mean, it must have been ripe with events of note? Do tell of them."

"Perhaps another time," Aytik stated flatly. "Since I will only be home this one night, I should like to spend some time with my sister and Shyamala. You do understand?"

Myro's tone turned taunting. "Ha! I see he still intends to court well below his status. Whyever should he follow his king's wishes and marry a duchess – or even just a baroness? But a bachelor knight's niece? That's just one rank above squire."

"Father, two should never wed to please others."

Myro toned sarcastic. "Olob, am I not still king of this realm?"

The historian sighed his displeasure at being drawn into yet another of their never-ending quarrels. "Yes, sire, you are."

"Stork, as your king's personal guard, are you to choose which assassins to slay and which to pardon?"

Stork hesitated before responding in his gruff and gravely voice. Like the historian, he too disliked being drawn into such quarrels. "No, sire. I am pledged to slay any who mean you harm."

"Then how is it my only son forgets while my heart beats I am still king? Oh, if his mother had only bore me another son before him," Myro quipped.

"And if only grandmother had done likewise before you!" Aytik spat back. "Perhaps my mother would have married a king deserving of such a benevolent and worthy wife!"

Olob and Stork stared awkwardly at the floor as the prince turned and stomped from the hall.

Struggling and shaking his way up to a wobbly stand, Myro shouted after his son. "Morgue claimed her with the stooling disease! It wasn't my fault! I did love her! You hear me! I did! And she loved me!"

"You only love yourself!" Aytik screamed, throwing open the door. "I hate you!"

Myro's wrinkled face flushed with rage. "You must learn respect for tradition, Aytik! She is not worthy to be your queen! I forbid it! Your king forbids it! Her family is of low status! Aytik, come back here at once! I command you to return! I don't wish to quarrel over this now, Aytik! Aytik! Aytik!"

SLAM!!

Tears trickled down Myro's quivering cheeks as he smacked the butt of his sceptre onto the floor. "Dung!"

While Aytik stomped along the wide corridor towards a mural staircase, he was unaware of the sadness in his father's weary eyes or the ache in his aging heart. He did not witness the frail old man slump sobbing into his historian's arms. All he could feel was rage towards a father he felt did not understand him. Or even want to. Like countless sons throughout countless ages he saw his father as an adversary who didn't measure up. It never occurred to him how he so often misused his father's love for him as a weapon to wound an old man; or that someday he might well regret many of the angry words he now savoured. Take that!

Aytik was nearly atop the stairs before he noted a familiar figure looking down from the landing.

The young galfolk was clad in a belted tunic over trousers, along with hide highboots, and she wore a gold chaplet to check her white hair. She had inherited her father's clever green eyes. Her lips parted her brother a smirky smile.

"Dearest Destiny, somebody sure looks mad as Morgue," she noted, stretching a slight grin. "Were you and father quarreling again?"

"When aren't we?" Aytik responded, stepping onto the landing.

Suddenly, his sibling leapt upon him, wrapping her limbs tightly about his waist and neck. She began wetting his face with her kisses.

83

"Okay, okay," he pleaded to no avail, trying to duck her smacking lips. He burst forth in laughter as they both fell to the floor.

In an instant, she was seated atop his chest, pinning his shoulders down with her hands.

"I give up! I give up!" he shouted.

"Say it," she demanded. "Say it or I will smother you with kisses again."

"Okay, okay, I'll say it."

"Say it."

"Helenia is," he said.

"Say it proper," she said, puckering her lips in warning.

"Okay, okay. Helenia is the best and the brightest."

As his sister relaxed her pin on his shoulders, the sneaky prince suddenly thrust his fingers up under her rib cage. She squealed as he began to tickle her. Then he flipped her beneath him and continued tickling until she begged him to stop.

"Who's really the best and the brightest?" he demanded.

Frantically, she tried to squirm free and could not. His thighs squeezed her firmly in check.

"Who is?" he persisted, wriggling his brows. He smirked and tapped his forefingers to thumbs. "Or would you prefer teeny tiny pinches that take your breath away?"

"No!" she screamed, swallowing her smile. "No, Aytik – ahh! Stop it – ahh! Okay! Okay! Stop, stop, stop…"

"Say it."

"Aytik is really the best and the brightest."

"And the best looking," he pressed.

"No chance – ahh! Okay! Okay! Okay! And the best looking! And the best looking!"

Aytik grinned victorious as he stood and pulled his sister up to her feet. After both had caught their breath, he asked her, "I see you have grown much in my absence. How have you fared this past cycle, sister?"

Helenia replied, "Quite well, really. Although riding is not near such fun without you along. I especially miss our long talks."

Aytik smiled and nodded. "As do I."

"Come on," she said, suddenly grabbing his hand. "I have a surprise for you."

"Where are we going?" he asked.

"To your bed chamber."

"To my bed chamber?"

Helenia grinned devious and nodded. Then she dragged him along the corridor leading to the arched, hardwood door of his bed chamber.

"Eyes shut tight," she instructed, turning the latch. "Both of them, Aytik. And no more peeking."

The curious prince allowed himself to be tugged into the spacious bedchamber. He became aware of his sister stifling a giggle as they passed by the heat of a cresset bearing a wall torch.

"We'll talk more later," she said, releasing his hand and leaving the room. She softly closed the door behind her.

Aytik raised his lids to set eyes on a pretty maiden in a blue chemise and matching slippers. She froze him with her soft brown eyes and full lips. Her black hair shone like polished ebony.

Shyamala smiled and explained, "Helenia and I were pruning in the garden when word came of your arrival. She sneaked me into the castle. Dearest Destiny, Aytik, I should hope the king never finds out I'm here in your bed chamber. You know how he despises me so."

"He's never found out before," Aytik reminded her, gently cupping her face in his hands. He sealed her lips with his own and began probing her mouth with his tongue.

She responded in kind and sank into his embrace. "Mmmmm…"

When they finally finished the kiss, she began nipping at his cheek. She whispered, "I've drawn us a bath."

Aytik heard his heart pound as her chemise slipped from her shoulders and fell to the carpet. He was aware of her kicking off her slippers. Probing fingers lifted his wet blouse over his head and discarded it without tact. She began kissing his chest as she unbelted his breeches.

Aroused by the sensation of her hot flesh rubbing against his, he slid his hands beneath her and lifted her from the floor. And took her without thought of tenderness.

Shyamala squealed in delight with each thrust of his loins. She began grinding her thighs together and digging her fingers into his back. Her teeth gnawed on his hard shoulders. Her flesh became hot with his. She squirmed her hips to draw him in ever deeper, pausing only now and then to savour their sticky wetness. Or to sniff the intoxicating scent of sweat and sex and love..."

****

... when next they awakened, Night ruled the above; its army of skytwinklers hidden by the fog rolling up from Ga Bay to greet the dawn.

"Dearest Destiny!" Aytik exclaimed, kicking free of the quilt and leaping from the bed. He hastened to replace a waning candle.

"What is wrong, Aytik?"

"Dawn knocks at the door," he explained. "I must meet Kryle at the main barbican to depart for The Wall."

Shyamala curled her lip into a playful pout. "I don't wish for you to go."

Aytik bent over and kissed her brow. "Nor do I," he assured her. "But I must. An heir cannot seek respect and shun courage."

"I know," she said, grabbing his arm. "Its just that I've missed you so much for so long. I shall worry."

He kissed her again. "Don't. Destiny will watch over me. Now I must attire in haste while my sister sneaks you out of the castle. Hurry, Shyamala – lest my father should awaken early and come to bid me farewell. Unlikely as that may be."

She swung her legs from the bed and pushed up to her feet. After quickly brushing the locks from her brow, she huffed and searched the floor for her chemise and slippers.

Each felt their heart jump as unseen knuckles rapped upon the door. They exchanged anxious looks.

Shyamala scooped up her chemise and bolted for the garment room. She begged Destiny that the king had not heard them.

Aytik slipped his nightshirt over his head and stepped softly to the door. "Who is it?" he asked.

"It's me. Open up, quickly."

Sighing in relief, Aytik opened the door to set eyes on his sister. "Thank Destiny, I thought it was father."

"Shush," Helenia replied. "Shyamala must swift to my chambers at once. Olob is coming."

"I'm ready," Shyamala asserted in panic while dashing for the open door. She paused only to give Aytik a quick peck on the cheek before stepping out into the cool damp of the corridor.

"Wait," Aytik said, grabbing her arm. "Your slippers."

"Dung," she cussed, sprinting back into his chambers. She snatched up her slippers and dashed for the door, pausing only to give Aytik another peck on the cheek.

"Hurry," Helenia's panicky voice called out from the corridor.

Aytik watched as both galfolk scurried about a corner, only sighing in relief after he heard the familiar slam of the door to his sister's bed chamber.

Easing his own door shut, Aytik leaned against its smooth surface and blew breath in relief. Not that he feared the historian would ever intentionally betray him and Shyamala, but secrets do slip out whenever old friends share a fine wine; which Olob and the king were known to do.

The prince tensed with a start as unseen knuckles again rapped on his door. "Who is it?"

A familiar voice replied, "It is I."

Aytik swung the door open and smiled at the old historian. A knowing smile parted Olob's bushy, white beard.

For as far back as Aytik could remember, Olob had always donned a blue frock patterned with orange crescent-spheres; always completing his attire with buckled ankle boots and his worn old bag hat.

"Fine dawn to you," Aytik said.

Olob returned the smile. "And a fine dawn to you as well. Might I come in?"

"You know you are always welcome," Aytik replied, gesturing his friend inside before shutting the door. "I'm afraid I don't have much time, Olob. We must chat whilst I attire."

"Of course," Olob agreed, snagging a candle from its sconce and following the prince into his wardrobe.

"You've risen early this day," Aytik remarked as he struggled into some tight riding breeches.

Olob handed him a silk blouse. "Always wear this under your arming doublet," he advised. "If an arrow should pierce your doublet, silk threads will make it easier and safer for our healers to remove the arrowhead. It could spare you much anguish and torn flesh."

"I know, Olob," Aytik assured the historian, pulling on the blouse.

"Hmmm – yes, I suppose you should," Olob said, handing the prince a pair of highboots. "Ever since you were fit enough to lift a dagger, you have had extensive combat teaching. You have trained and studied hard. Which is all to the good. An heir must be made ready for his time."

After struggling somewhat to get his boots on, Aytik stomped each foot several times to settle in. Each boot had a special sheath sewn onto it, and Aytik procured two shiny hurling daggers from a shelf and slid them into place. "It has been more than a cycle since I've practiced with these," he remarked.

"Let us hope they shan't be needed," Olob said, taking a steel nasal helmet down from an upper shelf.

Aytik slipped a tunic over the blouse, then snagged his broadsword from a peg and slung it across his back. Unlike the Royal Guard, who were issued shields and short swords, he much preferred the wider and heavier blade for its greater striking power. He also preferred to dismount and fight on foot. At least during mock battles.

Olob handed the helmet to Aytik, who promptly placed it atop his head and began buckling the chinstrap. He quickly checked his attire in a length of mirror.

"I've instructed the stable master to saddle your steed," Olob informed him. "I reminded him he mustn't forget to pack your warmest hooded cloak. You will need it. It does get quite wet and cold in the Divides, especially after dark."

"Thank you," Aytik responded, skillfully tightening the sheath strap to keep the sword from flapping about while he rode.

"Might we take time for a brief chat?" Olob asked.

Noting the historian's tone, Aytik opted to forgo the chat. "I must go, Olob," he said, dodging the question and stepping towards the door.

Olob maneuvered to block his path. "I wish to speak of this ongoing quarrel between you and your father."

"Speak to him. I have to…"

"I'm speaking to you," Olob scolded, growing a scowl. "Sometimes, Aytik, you can be quite selfish. All other eyes see your father is unwell, while your eyes see only what you will them to see."

"I love Shya…"

"I'm still speaking," Olob said, laying his hands on Aytik's shoulders. His words were direct, yet tactful. "You are not the first father and son to have an ongoing wrangle-of-wits. Your father is only trying his best to balance your wishes with what is best for the realm. King's have many responsibilities, Aytik. Someday you will be king and have sons of your own. Maybe then you will learn what it is like to have a son who hates you…"

"I don't hate him, Olob. It's just that…"

Again, Olob cut him short. "I know you don't, Aytik. But sometimes he thinks maybe you do? You tell him so every time you disrespect him. Just think about it – when last did you inquire of his ailing health? When last did you tell him how you truly feel about him? Do you even know how you feel – or care? Sometimes, parents need to hear they matter straight from the lips of their children. Even a king.

"You blame your father because your mother met Morgue, while ignoring his grief over the loss of the one person he truly loved before you and Helenia were even born. Well, he shan't be of this world forever, Aytik. Some day he will meet Morgue. Think about that. Do you want your last words spoken to each other to be words shouted in anger? How will you feel then? As king he could end your courtship of any galfolk. Yet he has not done so. Instead, he has allowed you ample time apart for you to weigh your decision to wed. To make certain it is what you truly want. Perhaps you might put some thought into that as well?"

Aytik kept mute. He knew Olob wanted him to bid farewell to his father before he departed. He also knew his stubborn pride would make him unable to do so. He simply stared down in silence.

The historian patted Aytik's shoulders and, with a huff of frustration, turned to walk away. "Ride with Destiny," he said. Then he paused and turned back. "The king does not despise Shyamala, Aytik. He is merely concerned with tradition. His first loyalty has always been to the crown. As must yours be. In time, I am certain he will give both of you his blessing. He just wants you to think this matter through is all. To be certain she is the right one for you. You are not a normal son, Aytik. You are the son who will be king – perhaps even before this war has ended. Perhaps even before this day has ended. Destiny alone knows when you will take the throne and collect all the burdens that come with it. So stop playing the pampered prince and start behaving like the king to be. Remember, pampered princes make for weak kings – and weak kings become deposed kings all too easily."

"I am certain she is the right one for me, Olob."

Olob offered up a knowing grin. "I do hope so, Aytik. Each time you lay together, you both gamble with Seed. You may find out what it is like to be a father much sooner than you should want."

Aytik's jaw dropped mute, only finding his voice just as the historian opened the door to let himself out. "Will you tell my father of us? Of our laying together, I mean."

"To what purpose?" Olob mused, slowly drawing the door shut behind him. "After all, it was he who told me..."

Olob's parting words left the baffled prince staring at the door. Until he remembered he had to meet Kryle.

While walking the castle corridors, Aytik's thoughts bounced back and forth between Olob's words and Shyamala. With his mind thus distracted, he strode across the upper bailey and on through the walkers wicket without even noting his surroundings; that is, until the foul stench of the moat beneath the drawbridge brought his mind back to the purpose at hand.

He cautiously minded his feet as he descended the winding steps to the lower bailey and the stables. Aytik set eyes upon the stable master, Chaps Bridle, and a frail lad with curly locks and a freckled face.

"Arduk, fetch Warrior for the prince," Chaps instructed. As the youth sprinted off down the stalls, Chaps called out after him, "And see that the prince's cloak be strapped down tight! He will have need of it!"

Chaps turned back to Aytik. "Strange lad, that one. Has an uncanny knack with the beasts. He speaks with them, you know. Sure as I'm standing here, he does. But enough of my blabble, how went the prince's voyage?"

Aytik shrugged. "Wet and windy for the most part. Although Apel was quite pleasant."

Chaps granted the prince a cruddy smile. "I have *heerd* such. I heerd the palace there beed built of magic stones that glow like ghosts in the night. And I heerd the Princess Toongy be the loveliest lass Seed ever sculpted. That be what I heerd."

"The white ape palace is indeed built of the finest stones I have ever laid eyes on," Aytik assured him. "Even so, they are not magic. Nor do they glow at night."

Noting the look of letdown sinking into Chaps' weathered face, Aytik smiled and tried to lift the old servant's spirits. "You have heard correctly regarding Princess Toongy, though. She is indeed the loveliest lass Seed ever sculpted. Just her smile alone can brighten a sunless day."

"That beed what I heerd!" Chaps exclaimed, granting Aytik another cruddy smile. It was quite apparent Chaps Bridle took great pride in his knowledge of such things.

Their conversation was suddenly cut short by two approaching figures. The frail lad led a white steed along by its bridle, while whispering words into its pricked ear. At one point, the beast even seemed to nod its head as if in agreement.

"Ha! Sometimes, I think you two actually believe Arduk can speak with steeds," Aytik mused, noting that both the ladfolk and stable master failed to follow his humour?

After mounting his steed, Aytik stole a stare down at Arduk. He thought, *'How pathetic he appears in his tattered tunic and filthy feet. Yet he refuses boots except during the frigid quarter. And even then he will only wear boots he plaits for himself out of peeling bark, which he then seals with tree tar and lines with warm fur from his howlers' undercoats. Destiny alone knows where he ever learned to do that? Certainly not from any pack of howlers.'*

Abandoned to Morgue at birth, the poor lad had spent his first eight or nine cycles in the care of a howlpack. His howlpack. His family. Had he not been spotted and rescued, he would still be running about the plains in seek of tasty rodents. Even two full cycles after being netted, he'd still been apt to snarl and bare teeth when riled. It was only out of intrigue and pity that the king had agreed to take the peculiar little lad on as a servant.

In the eight cycles since, the young ladfolk had tamed his snarling and learned humanfolk speech. On the outside at least, he now appeared to be just like any other peasant youth. Yet his penchant for sniffing the wind and his odd desire to dwell amongst howlers made him a target for gossip and the butt of many jokes. It was even said he could sight in dark as well as in light, and that he could talk with beasts. Since many supposed he was gripped by a spectre, he was shunned by all but a few. He was feared as those of different ways so often are by those who choose not to understand.

Aytik sometimes thought he detected a yellowish glow to Arduk's piercing grey eyes, but he couldn't be certain. Either way, the lad's penetrating gaze often made Aytik's flesh pimple in warning. Here was a ladfolk lost amongst his own kind. A ladfolk best left to himself and his beasts.

"Hope ye war be swift and final," Chaps said, granting Aytik yet another cruddy smile.

"Perhaps the winds of war will wane?" Aytik replied hopefully. Then he nodded farewell and reined his steed from the stable.

The early morning mist felt cool and refreshing as Aytik trotted through the tunnel and the gate tower, then down the neck to the main barbican. Once he was at the base of the barbican, he gently stroked Warrior's neck and mane as the obedient stallion stood still and alert.

Soon the steed's ears pricked forward. Aytik's ears likewise snagged the subtle sound of unseen hooves clopping slowly towards them. Something snorted from somewhere within the mist.

The clops grew steadily louder and clearer until a vague mass began to take on shape. As it clopped closer, Aytik discerned a familiar black form saddled atop a bulky, horned beast with naturally armored flesh and angry red eyes.

The ape expertly guided his surly snouthorn alongside Aytik and Warrior. "It's a fine morning, but not one for a gallop," Kryle noted.

Gripping the reins tightly to steady his anxious steed, Aytik replied, "Hopefully this mist will lift with the rising sun."

"We must go," Kryle said. "There is precious little time to waste."

"Let's be off," Aytik agreed, squeezing his calves to urge Warrior into a slow walk.

Both friends spoke freely of their mutual desire to avert war as their mounts clopped past the opulent manor homes of the local nobility, before winding their way down about the stone manors of the pomps."

The slope began to level out as they passed by the neatly spaced brick and shingled homes of the guild workers and artists. Somewhere within the mist, an annoyed tuskwooly bellowed its defiance at the unseen source of the clopping, which in turn invited every woofer within earshot to begin yapping up a fuss. An irate voice screamed, "Bite your tongue, Mutt!"

Much of the mist had lifted by the time their mounts commenced cantering along a heavily rutted road, leading them past the decrepit wooden hovels that so dominated the city's shoreside rookery. Drummers beat out a marching cadence for the foot soldiers, while mounted knights trotted alongside the column.

Soon Aytik could clearly distinguish the ranks of foot soldiers who marched in step towards the Amen River. Although they were burdened by heavy packs, the well-trained soldiers managed to march in step at a steady pace. Each donned a nasal helmet and had a buckler shield clipped to their belt. They were mostly armed with long pikes or pilums; along with short swords for close combat.

Soon the air was charged with the clamour of an army on the move. Axles squeaked as beasts of burden hauled carts heaped high with supplies. Catapults and bolt throwers were secured to some of the carts, while other carts were laden with heavy stones and bundles of quarrels. A few carts even supported cages packed tight with cluckers and oinkers, which rolled along to the rattle of boards, buckles and harnesses. One cart even hauled cages of cooers, which would be used to convey messages to and from Capital.

War fever had taken hold over much of the city, whipping many citizens up into a frenzy and provoking a party atmosphere. Banner-waving citizens cheered ecstatically as the troops passed by. Others clapped and shouted approval, many flinging streamers down from rooftops. One exhilarated mob even started fisting the air and chanting, "War! War! War!"

"Their bliss will wane quickly if it all comes to war!" Kryle shouted as they trotted across the boardwalk towards the crowded drawbridge. "If Pid is determined to wage this war, he is equally determined to win the peace! This war will be fought for dominance of the entire continent! And it will be bloody!"

Aytik stared into his cully's solemn black eyes. Unlike most humanfolk and white apes, black ape soldiers knew all too well the screech of a diving dact and the squeal of charging rexids. They had fought many pitched battles for control of the pass.

94

Despite their deep seeded hatred of the lizarme, the black apes still had respect for their foe's fighting skills. And Aytik had naught but respect for the black apes. Donning his own serious expression, he nodded in agreement.

"The prince! The prince!" somebody shouted from atop the wooden drawbridge.

Another voice shouted, "You there – shove aside! Make way for the prince!"

While Warrior clopped across the planks into black ape territory, Aytik looked back at the castle. And wondered, *'Will I ever set eyes on my home again?'*

Chimandara

Chimandara awakened with a start, sitting up and knuckling the sleep from her eyes. She instinctively drew her feet back beneath the warm quilt.

Light from the rising sun was sneaking in through cracks in the shutters, slowly turning shadows into shapes. Dawn's cool breath blew crisp and clean. Off in the distance, the intermittent spray of wetrollers splashing into a breakwater grappled with the squabbling shoresquawkers. Nearby, a cock crowed its wrath at the orange sphere rising to the east. Nearby, an axle creaked as unseen hands began cranking a bucket up from a well.

"Ga," the young galfolk yawned as she sank back into the inviting cot. She curled up tight to trap in warmth.

Soon she could smell the familiar aroma of strips and yokes cooking on a hundred hearths. The soothing sound of a tot giggling assured her all was well.

Meshing her fingers behind her head, Chimandara stared up at the ceiling and thought of the voyage thus far. Her crew had only been back in port for two days when word came that, by order of the king, their cog was to straight away take on military supplies and set sail for the shore north of The Wall. Shortly thereafter the rugged vessel found itself sailing north across Ga Bay. They'd barely had time to visit with their families, such was their haste to set sail. Consequently, Chimandara had only held her sister's new tot but once.

Even with strong crosswinds for much of the voyage, it still took the bulky vessel an entire lunar phase just to reach the tiny seaside village of Ga. They had not intended to set ashore, but the pilot decided the craft was much too heavy to navigate the unseasonably wild swells of the open sea. Thus, they had docked merely to unload low priority cargo before sailing west to supply the army with what they could safely transport.

The village elders, however, had other plans for the weary crew. Falling victim to the age old ailment of war fever, they looked upon the seafarers as heroes deserving of tribute and hospitality. The village reeve simply would not hear of them casting off without a farewell feast, and insisted they stay until the following day. Excited citizens opened up their homes to the visitors, even offering up their own cots along with generous gifts of food and drink. None went hungry, and all had drank and jigged about the fires late into the night. Even the clear night sky with its glowing moon and dancing skytwinklers had seemingly joined in with the festivities.

Chimandara stretched the kinks from her limbs, savouring each crackle of her joints. As she flung aside the warm quilt, a blast of cool air blew across her skin, causing her to shiver. Undaunted, she spun from the cot and dropped her feet onto the cold floor. She snagged the smock her hosts had leant her and hastily pulled it over her head and arms. It felt warm and cozy against her body, and she smiled as she walked across the tiny room to open a shutter.

Outside, wisps of grey smoke spiraled up from the stone stacks of modest wattle and daub huts, before being whisked away by the gentle seaside breeze. To the north, beyond the huts, wetrollers crashed into the rocky shore. They scattered shoresquawkers and gannets alike, before sucking their telltale footprints back out into the foamy depths. Spray splashed high into the sky as crashing wetrollers tried in vain to breach the stoic stone breakwater; while shoreside, many skin currachs bobbed safely at anchor in the tranquil harbour. Soon they would set out to net finners. A lone cog was docked alongside the village's only sizeable pier.

The young galfolk yawned and moved to turn from the window when something unusual snagged her sights. She focused her gaze far out to sea. Her mouth gasped and a shudder ran through her spine. Her stomach sank and panic messed with her mind. She wanted to cry out a warning, but no sound would come. She wanted to run outside, but her legs would not move. Both body and mind seemed frozen in time.

Literally hundreds of warships were bearing down on Ga from the north. Above them, flocks of winged specks flapped south in strict formations.

And yet, as frightening as the approaching armada was, the black hulls and winged specks were not what terrified Chimandara the most. Instead, her eyes were stuck on a monster ship with four masts reaching to scratch the sky. Chimandara knew full well who crewed the monster ship and what its arrival meant. Invasion was imminent. The lizarme had come to them!

Unseen hands began ringing the village bell. Almost instantly, windows were filled with curious faces. Others ran out into the dirt lanes and grassy yards. There was much shouting and pointing out to sea.

Panic quickly swept throughout the village. Frantic mothers scooped up their wailing tots on the sprint. Mature ladfolk of all ages began flailing and shouting for their loved ones to flee into the interior, away from the village.

"Avoid the barren plateau!" screamed one voice.

"All lads to thine boats!" ordered another.

"Dung!" Chimandara cussed, snapping free from her shock and dashing to strap on her sandals. Although panicking and fumbling with the straps, she was well aware of the rising commotion beyond the walls. *The elderly and tots won't have enough time to flee...*'

Somebody was shrieking above the chaos and confusion. "Me tot! I've lost me tot! Shareena! Shareena!"

"We've have her with us, Frithia! Make haste!"

"Trek by night directly to the Upcoast Forests!" a ladfolk commanded. "And keep ye low to the maize and the highgrass!"

Another shouted, "You there, do for thine elders!"

"Forego thy pots, Mother! We must be swift on the sprint!"

"Seafarers, grab ye harpoons and ye bows and sprint swift to thine currachs! We all be hunting lizarme today!"

"Look! Striker boats!"

"Strikers be here to save us!"

"They are too few! We must fight with them!"

"Look out!"

"Ahhh – me foot!"

"You lads, clear that cart from the lane!"

"Now! Make haste! And shoo that nanny and doeling out of the way!"

"Dearest Destiny!" Chimandara shouted in frustration as one of her sandal straps snapped. She quickly kicked them off and dashed barefoot from the cabin and out into the lane; where she was swept along by the flood of faces that poured from the cabins and flowed down the hill to the docks.

It was true. A fleet of strikers was sailing past Ga with full sheets. All oars dug deep with each synchronized sweep. It was confirmed by their tack that the swift warcraft had spotted the enemy armada and were on course to intercept it.

Now Chimandara could make the flying specks out to be dacts. The winged beasts had swooped low to lead the enemy attack and were flapping straight for the village! Most clenched iron bashing-balls in their twisted talons, while some carried what appeared to be bundles of short spears. They came in low with their long tails skipping atop the wetrollers.

Chimandara steered her thoughts back onto the task at hand. She courageously resigned herself to the cruel facts. The strikers and tiny currachs had zero chance of defeating such a large invasion force. Even so, and with Destiny's blessing, perhaps they could delay the invaders just long enough for the young and the aged to escape into the maize and the highgrass? Of course, her own fate was already sealed.

For a brief moment, Chimandara thought of her loved ones back in Capital. She smiled fondly as her memory chose to recall her sister's new tot, before abruptly forcing its cuddly image from her mind lest she should lose the nerve to do her duty and thus meet Morgue without honour.

Soon she felt the rough surface of the pier beneath her feet. She stretched her limbs to the limit as she sprinted awkwardly across the uneven planks. Not even the splinters tearing into her soles could stem her stride, such was her resolve to meet Morgue with honour.

The gallant galfolk never wavered one step as she jumped from the gangplank down onto the deck. She winced and bit deep into her lip as something snapped in her ankle. Almost instantly, she could taste her own blood. Just the same, she did not cry out.

'Must stay focused,' she thought. *'Just bear the pain and row.'*

"Chimandara!" shouted a familiar voice. "Leave that oar be and help steer on tiller!"

"Aye-aye, pilot!"

"C'mon, mates – we must lighten the boat!"

"Aye-aye, pilot!"

Other sailors were now jumping down into the hull. Some began unhitching lines, while others took up oars. Three bulky ladfolk commenced hoisting the sail. Volunteers from the village hopped aboard and began frantically pitching cargo overboard into the drink.

"Cast off!" shouted the pilot. "You there! Take up an oar and lend of thine back to row!"

No time went to waste before the cog and a small flotilla of swift and seaworthy currachs steered around the tip of the breakwater and took up chase behind the much swifter strikers. Together they cut across the chop to engage the fast approaching armada.

Chimandara grunted and licked the blood from her lips as she tugged on the tiller. "Hard to port!" she yelled. "And mind those currachs!"

Steering her thoughts to the approaching bashers with their high prows and twin masts, Chimandara took note of the lanky green figures packed onto the decks. Their crimson eyes gave her the shivers.

A voice shouted, "Sight ye above!"

"Dacts!" screamed another.

All gasped with wided eyes as a flock of screeching dacts broke from the main formation and banked for the striker boats.

The lizarme flighters reined their mounts into a climb, trying to rise beyond range of the bolt throwers. A few delayed and were felled like torn kites down into the drink.

Cheering erupted amongst the humanfolk. Then abruptly ceased when those dacts which had evaded the bolts circled back overhead and swept wings into a dive.

Geysers splashed up from the sea as iron bashing-balls missed their mark. Oak planks were smashed into splinters whenever others hit their targets. Screams silenced the wind as crews cowered beneath shields to avoid the torrent of spears. Strikers listed as the sea gushed in through the gaps in their hulls. Limp forms and debris bobbed about the wetrollers. Survivors flailed for help that would not come, while shivers of sharks swam in for a feed.

Chimandara stared with wet cheeks while enemy vessels with bulging sheets bashed into the smaller strikers. She could only watch in horror as planks were dropped across the crippled vessels' gunnels and the enemy's naval infantry, brandishing both trident and cutlass, stormed across to do battle. Many brave humanfolk were sure to meet Morgue.

Soon the monster ship would be on top of them. Its catapult pouches were already loaded, the counterweights raised and ready. More dacts were taking flight from its decks.

With the combat carrier bearing down upon the humanfolk fleet, Chimandara set her sights upon a pudgy lizarma in a prod commander's cape who leaned out over the gunnel. She noted with some curiosity how his sullen manner seemed somewhat saddened by what his eyes were seeing. Then the carrier's catapults slung their loads, and the pudgy prod turned and solemnly walked away.

An ominous shadow moved over Chimandara, joined by the steady whoop of flapping wings. Telltale gusts blew across her skin. A shrill screech sliced through the screams as Chimandara's mates cried out in warning...

"Chimandara!"

"Atop ye!"

"Dact!"

Chimandara spun about in time to dodge the beast's raking talons, but she could not evade the lancer's point.

Wrenching pain punched through Chimandara's chest as the blow knocked her over the gunnel and into the sea. While the gallant galfolk sank deeper and deeper into the frigid depths, she prayed of Destiny that by sailing their boats directly into the path of the lizarme armada they had delayed the enemy well enough for the villagers to escape east into the maize and the highgrass. She prayed for her unsuspecting family in Capital, begging of Destiny they would be forewarned of the invasion and make good their escape. Lastly, she thanked Seed for the gift of life, and begged Morgue to judge her heart alongside her actions.

Finally, her mind blanked and, with a final discharge of blood and bubbles, she sank to meet Morgue.

With honour...

Kea and Kwok

Prince Aytik lost all track of time as the humanfolk army trekked west beneath the thick canopy of the Ape Jungle. Even at the peak of day, torches were needed to navigate the rutted and winding trail which had linked the black apes and humanfolk for more generations than any could recall. Despite its age, the trail was kept under constant attack from vines and ferns and mosses, all of which were determined to bury it forever. Only heavy use by snouthorns, steeds and wheeled carts denied them their victory.

Many such swathes had been blazed and burned throughout the Ape Jungle to link villages and accommodate mule and ox-drawn tumbrils, with each trail cut wide enough for two tumbrils to pass each other by. This enabled Kryle and Aytik and Golab to ride three abreast at the front of the column.

The bold demeanor of both the ape and his surly snouthorn constantly intrigued the humanfolk. Unlike their own skittish steeds, which would seemingly tense to bolt after each sudden squeal or caw, Kryle's bulky beast would simply clop along with nary a huff. Even when a rare striped slinker had leapt out onto the trail, spooking some steeds to rear, the snouthorn had merely snorted its annoyance and glared the orange beast back into the bush. Kryle likewise hadn't so much as flinched. This was their jungle too, and no beast would be wise to challenge such.

On another occasion, a large boa swung low to study the ape as a potential meal. Until a heavy fist left it dangling in nap from a bough.

"Pesky boas," Kryle spat out. "Seed should do something to evolve their sorry eyes."

Golab grinned and quipped, "Once the poor squeezer awakens, I'm sure it will also *see* things that way. Ha! Ha! Ha!"

Kryle and Aytik both groaned with rolling eyes.

Both day and night, nondescripts blinked forth from the shadows. Buzzing borebugs chomped chunks from flesh. Hairy crawlers scurried across skin. Vipers coiled alongside the trail, hissing their defiance at the noisy intruders. Occasionally, an annoyed slinker would roar its warning from somewhere off in the distance. The ensuing caws, chatter and squeals betrayed the presence of many unseen creatures.

When the humanfolk army finally emerged from the sweltering heat of the jungle and marched out onto the trail that led from the ancient city of Raw to The Wall, they were joined by a long column of black apes mounted on surly snouthorns. Each ape was well-weaponed with axe and shield, and spiky helmets for butting in close combat. Their serious black eyes matched well with the angry eyes of their bad-tempered mounts.

Meshing both armies into one long column, the allies wound their way north and west along the jungle's dark fringe, enroute to the distant foothills. Sporadic gusts blowing in off the open savanna brought with them a choking dust that stung into eyes. On two occasions, the soldiers and their beasts were even forced to take refuge back in the jungle when an attack of whirling sand spirits made sight and breathing too difficult.

For all that, the determined troops persevered until eventually they pushed past the savanna and began climbing up into the scrubby foothills. Here a wide assortment of exposed critters kept the weary soldiers amused.

There were mobs of red roos, a species considered sacred by the black apes and therefore protected by law. Cheeky gophers poked their heads up from their burrows. Horned hooters stood perfectly still in hope of snagging a careless squeaker for a snack, while blue-feathered swoopers dove with talons primed to pluck unfortunate rodents in mid dash. Fanged serpents warmed themselves upon rocks, and rattled their tails in warning. Wary jacks cautiously hopped about, never straying far from their burrows.

After several days, the scrub started giving way to grass and leafy trees. Here Aytik caught a rare glimpse of a distant howlpack roving for chow. The alpha howler paused briefly to stare back at him, before leading her pack off into some brush.

The prince wondered what the proud beast had thought of him? *'She probably thinks I'm just another noisy intruder,'* he mused.

Late one cool evening, while their mounts trotted along side-by-side, Golab drew Aytik's attention to the crest of a barren ridge. Each was awed by the silhouette of a burly black figure without neck who straddled the back of a horned beast. Directly behind them floated the full moon; surrounded, as always, by its eternal army of skytwinklers.

"I'm always grateful that one's on our side," Golab managed at last. "Thank Destiny he's your cully."

Aytik stretched a warm smile while he watched his friend rein his snouthorn out of line with the glowing moon and blend back into the blackness. He thought back to the time in their youth when they had cut themselves and mixed blood to become cullies. And he thought of what that meant; of how it was a special bond of friendship even beyond that of brothers. A bond never to be broken. "I give such thanks often, Sir Golab."

As the troops marched ever higher up into the foothills, the whistling wind added a chilly nip to its bite. Digits numbed and breath rolled out in vapour. Far off in the distance, the Divides thrust their white peaks into the underbellies of floating skysheep. The sun hung brightly atop the jagged summits dividing the western and eastern regions of the continent. One could almost hear the Divide Mountains shouting, "CHALLENGE US NOT!!"

Tall needle trees gradually replaced the leafy trees, and thorny bushes clawed to scratch the flesh of any who ventured too close. Broken boughs littered the mushy ground, all clad in mosses and fungi. Vivid yellow and pink flowers grew from the crowns of decaying stumps. Patches of fescue still glistened with drops from the early morning drizzle. Mist mingled with breath.

The lush basins bore an abundance of beasts. Whenever the winds lulled into a hush, anonymous singwings chirped up a melody. A choir of critters would chatter in tempo, while throaty tree croakers belted out bass. Gobbling gobblers would join in on chorus. Somewhere, a rebel pecker rapped along to its own high-rhythm beat. "Rat-a-tat-tat...rat-a-tat-tat..."

Then, seemingly on cue, the singwings would chirp up a brand new melody, and the entire ensemble would retune its part; until the winds returned and whistled the critters into silence, or the patter of skyshowers would drown out all save the crunching and clopping and clamour of an army on the march.

Masked bandits eyed the intruders from the safety of boughs, while cheeky munks kept vigil from their holes in boles. A scurry of nut seekers leapt about with tails fully bushed, as a prickle of quilled porkeez waddled off into the brush. Only the stinky whitestripes went casually about their business; each displaying complete indifference to the noisy intruders, who wisely granted the arrogant rodents right-of-way passage when crossing their paths.

"What is that?" Aytik asked as a bluish-grey prowler with tufted ears, oversized paws and a stubby tail pounced from the bush onto the trail. It pricked its ears and shot a curious stare at the approaching column, before suddenly springing back from whence it had come.

"That timid prowler is called a screaming slinker," Kryle explained. "A species that is often heard but seldom seen. Their nighttime cries sound much like wailing tots."

"I have heard tell of such felines," Aytik said.

"Now you have seen one as well," Golab noted. "Most rare for any humanfolk."

"And just as rare amongst apes," Kryle assured them. "Including that one, I have now seen a grand total of two. And that's after a great many treks through these very same foothills."

"Let us hope it will prove to be a good omen," Aytik suggested.

Kryle nodded in response. "It well may. According to legend, screaming slinkers can curse any who harm them. In contrast, to spot one and leave it in peace is considered a blessing."

"Did your first sighting bring you good fortune?" Golab asked.

The great ape shrugged. "I alone spotted it. Unlike the one we just sighted, my first screaming slinker did not turn and flee. It simply stared down from its perch atop a crag. With laughing eyes, I might add. Like it knew something I did not?"

"But was it a good omen?" Golab pressed.

A brief silence ensued while Kryle bowed his head with eyes closed. He swallowed before speaking. "I must confess I'm uncertain. It all happened during my first taste of combat. I was to lead a patrol through the north pass and up into the western foothills. Our task was to secretly observe and plot enemy troop movements in an effort to estimate their strength. Nothing more. We were under orders not to engage unless forced to do so. Even so, I was still young and arrogant and determined to make my mark. Three days out, I led my soldiers straight into an ambush."

Kryle paused to tap his broken upper fang. His black eyes misted moist. "This is my memento. Only myself and one lizarma cheated Morgue that day. All others perished in combat. Our decision to part company was mutual, yet I will never forget that lizarma's face. It bore more scars than a drunkard with a big mouth."

Kryle briefly puckered lips to make amused. "So, was the slinker a good omen? You must draw your own conclusion, Sir Golab."

Aytik knew Kryle still blamed himself for the ambush, and that his cully had beaten himself about the mind ever since. The tactful prince also knew that in circumstances of profound guilt, whatever any outside party speaks or thinks can oftentimes mean much less than nothing. Outside advice might be fruitful in healing many pains, but pain of the soul must be healed on the inside; for that is where the worst wounds fester. Soul pain is a pain like none other. It will chew up our insides until we forgive ourselves – a cure often dependent on divine help. Alas, since he knew not what was best for his cully, wisdom dictated the correct course of action was to make mute on the matter.

"Perhaps that lizarma you fought had also sighted a screaming slinker?" Golab suggested as their mounts clopped around a bend.

"Perhaps?" Kryle replied, pointing downward and to the west. "Behold – The Wall!"

Both Aytik and Golab stared without words at the breathtaking barrier spanning the valley below them. Despite being dwarfed on both sides by mountains, the wall still inspired awe. Somehow, it seemed impossible that anyone could have cultivated and built such a structure. Nonetheless, there it was stretched out before them.

The wall stretched north and south, fortifying the entire breadth of the pass. Its stone and mortar base acted as a long planter, supporting thick shoots of the sturdiest bamboo, which were lashed and grown together to form a high curtain wall. Crenels had been cut at precise intervals to allow archers to shoot their arrows down at their attackers while keeping themselves safe behind the merlons. A wooden wall-walk was affixed to the bamboo shoots along the entire length of the wall; except for where the contour of the barrier was broken by rounded stone bastions to prevent dead angles, each complete with battlements and arrow loops that enabled defensive fire in multiple directions. In addition, the allure of each bastion was protected by a wooden roof for overhead cover and the merlons were fitted with swinging embrasures that shielded the crenels and allowed for safe covering fire directly down onto the enemy. The entire wall was, in affect, a living barrier. It was truly a formidable feat of advanced engineering, combining the black apes' mastery of horticulture practices with their proud history of castle building.

Tiny black dots were scurrying all about the entire structure, while vague wisps of smoke spiraled up from amongst the many clusters of tents pitched at its base. Scatterings of crude longhuts were also plotted along the wall's base, plus crashes of snouthorns stood stoic within pens.

108

"Although we cannot view it from up here, a dirt rampart runs the entire length of the wall's westside base and separates it from a mucky moat," Kryle proudly informed them. "Save where our scouts sneak in and out through wickets or sally ports under cover of darkness, there is no berm between the moat and the curtain wall, thereby rendering turtles and rams all but useless. Even if Tarawa did somehow breach the moat, his troops and their portable mantlets would simply slide back down the dirt rampart and splash into the muck.

"Naturally, the moat also prevents enemy sappers from tunneling beneath the curtain wall, and even serves as a latrine for our waste. Its mucky bottom has been seeded with caltrops to pierce feet and paws. Sharp stakes have been angled to stab into legs or torsos, should a clumsy sapper slip and fall. The weeds along the bank are well stalked with the marshland mud viper, duly selected for the toxicity of their venom. In fact, I chose that species myself. One bite and you're done for." Kryle paused to direct their sights past the wall. "Note how the valley beyond is blackened and barren, save for the charred remnants of stumps. All growth in the pass has been purposely scorched to thwart sneak attacks. We allow nothing to grow there."

Aytik asked, "Have the lizarme ever tried to breach the wall?"

"Possibly once," Kryle replied, reining his snouthorn around a muddy puddle.

"What happened?" Golab pressed.

Kryle shrugged his shoulders. "Hard to say, exactly. Following an especially bleak and drizzly night, several lizarme were found floating stiff in the moat. Our guards never heard a sound, not even a splash. Stranger still, the bloats had no siege gear with them? They were just lying there face down in the muck and the turds. I pity the poor sops who had to hook them out. The stench would have been vomit worthy."

Aytik thought of the poor guards back in the bretèche above his own castle's moat.

"Possibly they were just some of many and the others had the ladders with them," Golab proposed. "Maybe the others heard them splash into the water and lost their nerve to follow."

"Or perhaps they were just a wayward unit that became lost in the storm and inadvertently stepped over the bank and splashed down into the moat?" Aytik added.

"Possibly," Kryle concurred. "There was no knowing for certain because skyshowers had muddied all clues. The floating bloats themselves excepted, of course."

Aytik shuddered as he considered the terror of meeting Morgue in a dark and mucky moat filled with excrement and bounded by venom vipers. He quickly forced the chilling thought from his mind.

Soon the trail started winding its way down towards the flatlands of the pass. Kryle kept the lead, marching them ever closer to the wall; with the black dots slowly beginning to grow and take on distinct shapes. Shaggy bodies scurried up and down climbing nets with uncanny grace and zip. All along the structure's battlements, alert ape sentries stood like statues and stared westward up the pass. Along the structure's base, more apes loaded skids with supplies to be hoisted up to the allures. Still more kept tight to ranks as they marched in step and wheeled about inside training paddocks, all under the keen eyes of scowling commanders with folded arms and long, braided beards.

Eventually, the trail leveled off and diverged into many paths. As Aytik's steed clopped out onto the flats and the breezy wind paused to catch its breath, he became aware of the creak, rattle and crunch of an army at his back. His ears snagged the distant sound of a commander barking out orders. Somewhere close by, a restless mule brayed its displeasure.

Then the cooling breeze returned, and the welcome smells of sizzling chow touched curious nostrils. Taste buds awakened, moving many hungry bellies to growl. Hard marching always works up an appetite.

Kryle said, "I will instruct some of my commanders to guide your troops to suitable areas of encampment. Two days hence, after your troops have settled in, they will give your knights a thorough tour of the wall and an orientation of our defenses. Although we don't enjoy all the comforts of home, you will find our camps are kept quite sanitary. If you..."

"I should like that tour at first light on the morrow," Golab cut in. "Perhaps we could straight away form a chain of liaison between your high command and my grand knights. We can sync our strategies to repel the enemy attack. Best we all be reading from the same scroll. The lizarme may not be so patient as we would want and we may not have two days? Besides, we have trekked all this distance to help you fight, not watch from the rear. That said, I am certain my knights shall learn much from your commanders' experience and advice."

Kryle paused before grudgingly nodding his approval. "Very well, Sir Golab. It will be done."

Aytik suppressed a subtle smirk. He had great respect for both of his friends, yet he had fully expected friction to rise between them; for they were too much alike. Neither was afraid to accept complete responsibility for his decisions, and both liked to be in total control of their army. Nobody was going to tell Doyen Kryle how to defend his wall, and nobody was going to dictate troop deployment to a grand knight of Sir Golab's stature. Accordingly, Aytik had chosen to let the stubborn pair sort out their issues themselves. As he knew they would, for both were quite sensible and ever adept in the grim art of warfare. They were masters of their craft.

Golab nodded. "Here come some of your commanders now," he added.

All eyes sighted onto a trio of surly snouthorns, which kicked up large clods of clay as they charged across an open field towards the humanfolk army. Each of the bulky beasts was mounted by a black ape clad in a loincloth and a spiked helmet. Two of the shaggy riders bore axes slung across their broad backs, while the third was unarmed.

Close behind them followed a tuskwooly with humourless eyes and a nasty disposition. Its long proboscis bellowed a boisterous warning to keep clear of its path.

A white ape rode atop the beast's back. His tall frame was clad in a brown skirt-of-battle and a matching hide vest. He donned a flanged helmet of the type worn only by those of the highest ranks. Orange eyes sparkled in his bluish face, and his

111

teeth shone white from between his fat, purple lips. One of his hands gripped tight his beast's thick shag, while the other clenched a long lance. A flanged mace was slung across his back. An oversized buckler shield, shaped and painted to depict a red rose, was clipped to his belt.

Even before the snouthorns had clopped to a halt, Kryle cussed beneath his breath and fixed a serious stare on the unarmed ape. "Where is your weapon?" he demanded of the unarmed commander.

"Doyen?" inquired the unarmed ape.

"Are your ears sewn? I asked you where your weapon is?"

The anxious ape struggled to voice a reply, yet the words kept hold in his throat.

Now Kryle grew impatient. "Is your tongue sewn as well? Speak up!"

"Um – there has been no sign of enemy movement…"

"I didn't ask you about enemy movement!" Kryle shouted. "I asked you where your weapon is!"

The anxious ape shook and stammered in his response. "Uh – my mistake, Doyen. In my haste, I forgot…"

"You forgot?"

"Yes, Doyen…"

"Are you not in command of a combat unit?"

"Yes Doyen, but I…"

Kryle toned sarcastic. "Excuse my ignorance, but I thought we were at war. Are we not at war?"

"Uh – yes, Doyen. But…"

"So I was not misinformed. Good. I should hate to think our allies marched all this way just to observe how sloppy my commanders can be. And given the fact we are at war, do standing orders for our troops not state quite clearly that no soldier shall become parted from their weapon for any reason?"

"They still state such…"

"Well, thank Destiny for that," Kryle sarcastically cut in. "However, I am somewhat puzzled, Commander? If standing orders state our soldiers are not to be parted from their weapons, then why is one of my officers galloping about in front of said soldiers minus his own?"

"No excuse, Doyen."

"So you just feel you are special, that you need not set a proper example for our troops?"

"No, Doyen. I do not. Ah – I mean, I do not feel I am special. I do feel I need to set a proper example. It will not happen again, Doyen."

"Tell me, Commander, what would you do to punish a common foot soldier who was as brazenly sloppy about weapons discipline as yourself?"

The fidgety commander shifted awkwardly in his saddle. "I would make him carry his weapon about with both arms raised high above his head for an entire day so he might be less apt to forget it in the future."

Kryle scowled serious with a gripping glare. "As would I, Commander. Therefore, come the next peek of dawn, you will do likewise."

"Yes, Doyen. Such will be done."

"I'm glad you agree, Commander. Now go fetch your weapon!"

"Yes, Doyen!"

After the relieved commander had spurred his beast away at a charge, Kryle reset his eyes upon the amused white ape. "So how are you getting on, Prince?"

"Still standing and drawing breath, old friend. Too much time has passed since we last shared a cup of mead or hot ale."

"That it has," Kryle agreed. "Your many letters have often times lifted my spirits."

Aytik reined his steed alongside Kryle's snouthorn and tipped his helmet to the white ape. "Prince Torak, I trust?"

The ape nodded and replied, "Prince Aytik, I am sure. Doyen Kryle has spoken much of you."

"Oh? And was any of it favourable?" Aytik looked askance at his cully, who responded merely with a kidding scan of the above.

Prince Torak made amused. "Favourable enough that I have long desired to meet you. My cousin Tianga also speaks well of you. She admires your cheerful nature. Although it may be put to the test soon enough."

Torak turned to the knight. "Sir Golab, time has spun more cycles than I care to count. Have you been well? I heard tell you suffered a jousting wound of sorts. A shard of wood in the thigh, I believe?"

"Merely a scratch, Prince," Golab replied, slapping his thigh. "It has since healed. Has thine army already arrived? I noted few tuskwoolies on our approach down from the hills?"

"Ha!" Torak blurted, flashing a smile. "Always a soldier first and foremost. No, Sir Golab, our army is still on the march. But they have long since crossed the Ape River and should arrive any day now. Perhaps as soon as the morrow?"

Torak paused for Golab to reply. He did not.

"Very well then," Kryle interjected, turning to his two remaining commanders. "Escort Sir Golab and his troops to their camp. Any of his concerns will be promptly addressed."

"Yes, Doyen!" both apes responded at once. Each fisted a salute before they reined their snouthorns about and gestured for the knight to follow.

Golab waved his troops into motion; and the creak, rattle and crunch of an army on the move joined in with the mounting winds.

"Our friends have trekked far to aid us!" Kryle shouted after them. "They are to be accorded a hot scoff! Without bugs!"

Both apes turned in their saddles and nodded acknowledgement. While many humanfolk soldiers soured face in disgust.

"Perhaps my place is with my troops?" Aytik said. "At least until our army has pitched camp."

"As you wish," Kryle stated. His tone was tinged with disappointment. "I had hoped to take you atop the wall. You can still join your army before dusk."

Prince Torak's eyes were hopeful. "Sir Golab is quite capable. And it would afford us an opportunity to become better acquainted."

Aytik briefly pondered Kryle's offer. "Very well then. I am curious to see the view from the wall-walk. Plus it is well past time Prince Torak and myself met and shared in a gab. Besides, Sir Golab can be most unpleasant whenever anybody dares poke their sniffer into his spice. Until *his* camp is pitched to *his* liking, he is well rid of me."

Torak and Kryle each puckered their fat lips to make amused. Both nodded knowingly.

"Come then," Kryle beckoned, reining his snouthorn about. "I am keen to show you our defenses."

"I am keen to view them," Aytik said, patting his steed into a canter.

Torak coaxed his tuskwooly to follow, gripping tight the beast's coarse hair for balance.

Soon the ground became a soggy morass of muck and puddles, which in turn made for some slippery slogging, especially for the snouthorn and tuskwooly. More than once, Aytik stayed his steed to let the slower beasts catch up. He now realized why the pens and paddocks were kept well back from the wall. In the event of an attack, the defenders scrambling to get to their posts needn't be slipping about in the muck. Thus, not a single snouthorn lumbered in amongst the clusters of hide tents, and only a limited few were tethered to hitching posts outside of the crude longhuts.

Ranks of shaggy foot soldiers wheeled about in the mucky paddocks just east of their camps, while drill commanders barked at them to, "Get those knees up!" More soldiers grunted and grappled as combat commanders instructed them in the art of close combat.

Upon noting Kryle, several youths ceased training to fist-up in salute. Their careless actions proved costly.

"What ye sloths be gawkin' at!" screamed an irate old commander with a greying beard and many scars. He rudely kicked an exceptionally large recruit's trunk-like legs out from under him and pinned the terrified youth down with a blade to the throat. He next set his cold black eyes upon the other recruits.

"The enemy just slit Thew's throat!" he berated, glaring about with a scowl. "He shan't ever see his mate or tot again! War is not some game to amuse thee! Be I look amused?"

"NO, COMMANDER!!" shouted the group."

"Thou can wager thine very being I be not! Never let thine eyes be averted from thine enemy! Be I make myself clear?"

"YES, COMMANDER!!"

"Be ye all certain?"

"YES, COMMANDER!!"

"I don't swallow ye scat! Drop and give me three hundred thigh burns! Full extension followed by full stand! Recruit Thew's here will keep count! Now!"

"YES, COMMANDER!!"

While the muddy bunch hastened to keep up with the large recruit's nervous cadence, the old ape re-sheathed his blade and sneaked in a quick nod at Kryle.

Kryle nodded back his approval before steering his beast up onto solid soil. Aytik and Torak followed close behind.

"Why do they train in slippery muck?" Aytik asked.

"To develop a better sense of footing," Kryle replied. "If they can stand firm in soft muck they will be tough to knock down on solid ground. This training method was my own idea."

Aytik granted his cully a smile. He was not at all surprised.

A network of well maintained trails enabled the beasts to gait at a canter and soon they were within the wall's shadow. All apes hastened aside to grant them free passage, with every one of them saluting their doyen commander as he led the two princes between their ranks. Kryle occasionally nodded to some of the senior soldiers. It was quite apparent he knew and respected them. And they him.

Activity buzzed all about the wall. Agile apes swung up and down hemp climbing nets with unmatched agility and swiftness. A throaty commander belted out orders as a team of combat engineers hoisted a heavy skid laden with barrels and fire pots up to the allure of a bastion. Others hoisted smaller skids laden with bundles of arrows and bolts up to the wall-walks. Covered hoardings supported by sturdy wooden braggers were spaced at strategic intervals all along the outer parapet of the shoots. They would provide overhead protection while enabling the defenders to drop rocks and pour boiling pitch down onto any attackers should they somehow reach the wall itself.

At the base of one of the bastions, a ragged column of returning soldiers plodded wearily into camp through a tight wicket. Blanketed forms lay upon stretchers, each stiff in their silence. Alongside the wicket, a grated portcullis remained lowered. Clearly, the defenders were taking no chances.

They have been high up into the mountains," Torak explained. "It is the same scene after every patrol. Badly mauled units return during Day's rule, whilst fresh units depart under cover of Night's. Drawbridges are dropped to span the moat, then raised again after our troops are safely back behind the wall. Powerful bolt throwers have been mounted atop our bastions, which will deny the enemy an easy crossing. Even if they bring floating turtles, we can hurl down fire-pots filled with naphtha and pitch.

"And our alchemists and metalsmiths in Jara have recently developed a lethal new weapon – cast iron fire-pots. Wagonloads of such fire-pots will arrive with our army. When shot from ballistas, they will explode on impact and spray metal shards and flaming sulphur out in every direction. The enemy will meet Morgue in charred pieces. Nasty to be sure, but necessary."

"I thought we controlled all of the pass?" Aytik put in.

"We did," Torak replied. "By sheer force of numbers, the green hordes pushed us back eastward in the pass and in the surrounding mountains as well. Thank Destiny the fools have been slow to capitalize on their success and launch a full-on assault. At times, this Prod Tarawa seems slow of sense?"

Aytik glanced at Kryle. The ape merely huffed his annoyance and bade his beast into a trot. It was apparent Prince Torak's words had him troubled.

Aytik, too, was troubled. Kryle had always spoken highly of Prod Tarawa's skill and daring. He clearly had great respect for the intellect and combat savvy of this particular lizarma. Yet Tarawa had deliberately chosen to occupy only a portion of the pass. Why did he halt his advance? Surely, such an experienced prod realized his vast superiority in numbers would soon be drastically reduced. He would fully expect the white apes and humanfolk to rush troops to The Wall in aid of their black ape allies. So why the delay? Something was clearly amiss. But what?"

Kryle led them to one of the larger longhuts, where he promptly dismounted and tethered his snouthorn to a hitching post. Cords of firewood were stacked neatly in rows off to the side. After waiting impatiently for the others to dismount, he gestured for them to follow him inside. He barely acknowledged two guards who presented halberds as he stomped past.

While swifting to catch up, Aytik snagged sight of three pennants flapping in the breeze atop the longhut's pitched roof. One bore the crest of the Black Ape Federation; crossed battle-axes silhouetted against a full moon. Another was emblazoned with King Myro's crest; a gold crown centered inside a sunburst. The third displayed the crest of King Thorax; a red rose in full bloom.

On entering the longhut, Aytik was struck by the crude simplicity of its interior. A large, oval table squatted in the center of the structure's solitary room. Several partially melted candles were set in braziers on the tabletop, while torches were stuck in sconces and evenly spaced about the walls. Day's warming beams still penetrated in through two open windows, making it unnecessary to kindle the structure's simple stone hearth.

A crude cubby was fitted into a corner and packed with hide scrolls. Beside it, assorted swords and capes hung from wall pegs. Axes, pilums and targe shields were rowed neatly along the wall for quick access. A small table supported a clay urn and some wooden cups. The room bore no stools or chairs, but only a single bench along one of the walls.

About a dozen shaggy forms were gathered around the table, apparently pouring over a large map that was inked onto stretched vellum. Noting Doyen Commander Kryle, they instantly snapped to attention and fisted up in salute.

An aging and portly ape with a grey beard and thinning hair limped forward and extended his pudgy hands. "We were thrilled when we received news of your promotion to take command. We all think of you often. It has been far too long, Doyen Commander."

Kryle gripped the old ape's hands. "Thank you, old friend. That it has. Tell me, Doyen Grob, are you well? Has your wound mended?"

"Mended well enough to fight." Grob made amused and pointed to an ugly scar just above his knee. "Only pains me when the air is damp. Blessed be Seed for granting me two legs. My only regret is the lizarma who cut me met Morgue much too swiftly."

Kryle made amused. "I would offer up an apology, but the scoundrel was poised to sink his trident into your mangy hide."

Grob sighed. "Yes, he had me pinned and set for the prongs when your blade found his neck. That much is certain."

After both apes had embraced, Kryle hung his battle-axe from a wall peg and began introducing Aytik and Torak to every doyen in his high command.

Both princes also hung up their weapons before joining the others about the table. All listened intently until Doyen Grob had informed them of the current situation.

"We cannot find a jot of logic in this game Tarawa is playing," another aged ape added. "It makes no sense for him to delay his attack. He is a fool."

"Prod Tarawa is no fool," asserted a very tough-looking ape-gal. "He does nothing by chance."

"I must agree with…" another began.

"But Tarawa is a fool," interrupted another. "Any prod worthy of his rank would have already…"

"Tarawa is well worthy. His prior actions have shown…"

"You would praise our enemy!"

"Stay your temper, Doyen Goorth. Doyen Barx has merely stated a fact. If the truth so riles you, then perhaps…"

"Whose truth is that, Doyen Zarak? I merely…"

"There is only the truth…"

"Enough!" Kryle shouted, slapping his palm down hard onto the table. "Dearest Destiny. Small wonder the enemy hasn't already breached the wall and captured all of the foothills to boot. Toss in Raw as well. My own doyens would much rather battle each other!"

Although several doyens openly seethed from their squabble, none dared interrupt their Doyen Commander. Only Grob risked some hint of making amused.

"Much better," Kryle stated at last. "Doyen Zira is correct. Prod Tarawa is no fool. She should know. Her legion has seen more combat against him than any other. So the dilemma we face is this – why has a brilliant military strategist like Tarawa not attacked while he holds the advantage? Any theories? Come now, I'm all ears."

"Perhaps he waits with a purpose?" Goorth offered after some hesitation.

"Of course he waits with a purpose," Kryle snapped. "But to what purpose? That is our riddle to solve. And until it is solved, we must remain vigilant to any and all possibilities. Tarawa has something brewing – and it's not tea or ale. Both he and Sergon are cunning and patient, and quite skilled in the wiles of deception. Nothing about those two can ever be taken for certain. Now listen up…"

All eyes became fixed on Kryle. Not one doyen dared appear distracted.

"…Zarak, what say your scouts of the enemy's strength?"

"Doyen Commander, our intel counts the enemy's strength at somewhere between one hundred and twenty to one hundred and forty legions. Granted, these estimates are quite rough. It is rather difficult to be precise under the circumstances. To confuse the matter even more, Prod Tarawa is constantly reshuffling his troops under cover of blackness."

"I understand," Kryle acknowledged. "Were our roles reversed, we would do likewise."

All others nodded to concur.

Kryle paused briefly to scan their faces. "I need lend of your honesty. It is most important you share only your true thoughts, for I am somewhat suspect of my own. My suspicions are Tarawa has no intention of attacking us here at The Wall."

A group murmur passed through the room.

Following some nervous hesitation, one doyen asked, "But Doyen Commander, why then would Tarawa mass so many troops near the pass?

"Because he wants us to believe he intends to attack us here," Kryle replied, tapping his finger to a point on the map. "And he may still do so. But I suspect the enemy also plans to invade from elsewhere. I see no reason why Prod Sergon couldn't land marine troops on the north shore here – where docks are already in place and humanfolk galleys routinely unload supplies. More enemy troops could also put ashore on beaches here and here and here, spread out along the coast east of the mountains. The tides are treacherous and the coastline rugged, but the lizarme certainly have the ships and the prowess to do so. Such landings would then expose us to attack from both the west and the north, and deprive the humanfolk galleys of docks to unload our supplies. Given enough troops, and should the winds of war blow with them, it is possible Tarawa and Sergon could even encircle us.

"The lizarme have laid claim to these very foothills ever since losing them in the Great Continental War. They have chosen to wage this Second Continental War to take them back. Tarawa is much too clever to have delayed his attack without good reason. Thus, I believe he fully intends to attack us from the north here and cut our armies off from Raw in a bid to force a peace. A peace favourable only to Supreme Pid, of course.

"Therefore, I have devised a plan of our own to combat any attack from the north. Listen carefully. I propose dispatching three legions north to the coast, near where the mountains meet the wetrollers, and sending two more mounted legions halfway so they can reach the sea or return here within several days hard riding. Now what say all of you? Speak with full honesty, or hold your tongues so others may."

"We have only twenty-eight legions to the enemy's one hundred and forty, Doyen Commander," noted one of the younger doyens. "Is it wise to send five of them away?"

"Doyen Vinea speaks with wisdom," concurred one of the older apes. "If Tarawa does attack us here at The Wall, we will have need of those five legions."

Torak cut in. "King Thorax is providing me with twenty-one of our finest legions. I will spare two for the north shore and send a third halfway."

"And I will confer with Sir Golab about doing likewise with three of our twenty legions," Aytik assured them, adding, "If I have counted correctly, that allots for seven legions deployed to the north shore to repel an invasion by sea, with a further four bivouacked halfway – leaving fifty-eight camped here to defend The Wall."

"Fifty-eight legions is still slight against one hundred and forty," Goorth pointed out. "While our inferior numbers should still be sufficient to defend a heavily fortified structure like the wall, we have no reliable numbers for Tarawa's troops. What if he actually commands two hundred legions? Or more?"

"And what if they do land troops on the north shore east of the Divides?" Zira countered. "I will concede the rocky coast makes it treacherous to navigate and anchor a vessel – difficult, but not impossible. Humanfolk supply ships do it all the time while awaiting their turn at the docks. Hence, we must have a plan in place to stop the enemy from securing a beachhead as it would mean splitting our forces and fighting a two front war."

"Prince Aytik, could your navy dispatch additional striker boats to help patrol the north shores?" Grob asked.

"I'm certain more can be sent," Aytik replied. "But it will take time. Time we may not have."

"Hopefully wind and tide will prove favourable to your sailors," Goorth said. "It will be much better to sink Sergon's shoddy vessels before his troops can set foot on our shores. Thank Destiny lizarme have always been unskilled at boat building. Which is exactly what one should expect from such a poorly evolved species."

Several doyens nodded their agreement.

Kryle raised a hand for silence. "We will go around the table on this matter. Each will have your say. None will be interrupted, but please speak swift to your point. Doyen Zira, you will begin."

With each ape in turn offering up their opinion, Aytik became intrigued by how intently Kryle listened to every single one of his doyens. He noted how his cully paid especially close attention to those with dissenting views to his own. Aytik thought, *'It is a worthy doyen commander indeed who grants his subordinate doyens their fair chance to sway his thinking. It demonstrates both humility and wisdom – favourable assets for sure.'*

Only after each ape had spoken their mind did Aytik and Torak offer up their own thoughts on the matter. All others stared in silent respect while each prince stated his support for Kryle's plan.

Torak especially stressed how troops can be recalled as well as deployed, and that it was never an advantage in warfare to be taken by surprise. "Never let your foe catch you unawares," he stressed. "In war, one cannot be too well prepared."

Most apes nodded in agreement. Three remained skeptical.

Noting their dissention, Kryle asked each of the trio to restate their positions on the matter. Again, he attentively absorbed every word they spoke.

After the third dissenter had made her case against sending troops north, Kryle motioned for all to keep mute while he plunged himself into deep thought. Clasping both hands behind his back, he began pacing about the room. Occasionally, he would pause to murmur and stroke his braided beard, or to huff and prop his fists against his hips. Then the pacing would resume.

Finally, Kryle stopped his pacing and turned to face the others. "You have all shared honestly, for which you have my gratitude. Those amongst you who do not support my thinking have raised some very valid points. We do not know Tarawa's troop strength, and the wall must hold at any cost. Such is true.

That noted, I must follow my gut instincts on this matter. Eleven legions will be deployed north. The remaining fifty-eight will stay here. As always, I and I alone am accountable to the Federation Council for my decisions. I will accept full responsibility should events prove me wrong."

Aytik could not help but notice how virtually every single doyen nodded in support of Kryle's decision, including the three who had been critical of the plan. Clearly, all knew from past experience that once their doyen commander has given an order the time for dissention is past. His charge must now be obeyed without question, except in only the rarest and most serious of circumstances; for war is indeed fluid and events can change quickly. Even so, any subordinate who rescinds such an order had best be able to convince Doyen Commander Kryle of the sound reasoning behind their decision. Or else...

Having issued his orders, Kryle retrieved his weaponry and gestured for Torak and Aytik to do likewise. All apes saluted as their doyen commander led both princes from the longhut to their waiting mounts.

Kryle quickly mounted his snouthorn and set eyes upon his cully. "I wish to take you atop the wall before dark," he said.

Aytik gripped his steed's reins. "I am anxious to do so."

Activity still buzzed all about the wall as apes swung up and down the climbing nets, or hoisted supplies up from the structure's base to its bastions and wall-walks. Alert sentries stood still as statues while they peered west over the parapet.

"Our wall averages ten stands in height and stretches for sixteen kilopaces," Kryle explained as they approached the structure. He added, "Bamboo from our jungle normally doesn't grow so tall, but the shoots used here have been carefully cultivated by our best botanists ever since the seeds were first germinated for planting. These shoots have increased strength and flexibility despite their unnatural girth and height, and they each retain copious amounts of water to keep them from burning. When the winds blow in angry from the west, the entire structure can sway significantly at its cusp. For those nervous of heights, it can really needle one's nerves. That shan't be a problem this day, however, as the wind blows gentle from the north. The degree of sway should be slight at best."

Several ape commanders scrambled to greet Kryle as the trio trotted along within the wall's shadow. A small flock of skysheep grazed upon the otherwise blue sky. A slight breeze nipped at flesh.

Kryle dismounted and handed his snouthorn's reins over to one of the commanders. He then gestured for Aytik and Torak to do likewise and follow him.

Every ape fisted a salute as Kryle led the pair through a maze of tents enroute to the wall. Once there he motioned for a squad of sappers to clear some supplies from a pallet.

"Sit and rest your legs," Kryle said, pointing to a bundle of bolts. "It is unwise for humanfolk to stand atop a rising skid as it is not uncommon for them to spin and sway and bang against the shoots."

Aytik quickly saw the sense in his shaggy friend's words, for the lift up the wall face was anything but smooth. The skid did in fact spin and sway with each tug of its cable, twice banging hard against the shoots.

"We apes usually ascend by the hemp nets," Kryle explained while making amused. "Unless we wish to take humanfolk atop. Climbing certainly isn't one of your stronger suits."

Aytik forced a grin. "We prefer to keep our feet planted firmly on the ground."

After the skid had safely ascended above the wall-walk, a husky ape used a grapnel to hook the cable and haul in the platform.

"Look," Torak said, pointing to the east. "Night is beginning its assault. Skytwinklers are advancing above the horizon."

Kryle merely nodded as he stepped from the skid onto the allure, gesturing for the pair to follow. Despite the light winds, their legs were still aware of the structure's gentle sway as they advanced along the wall-walk and stepped inside a covered hoarding.

A crisp breeze cooled their cheeks as they stared west up the pass. Far off in the distance lay the rolling contour of the western foothills, with faint puffs of smoke floating up from their crests.

"The enemy sends messages to their scouts in the mountains," Kryle explained.

"Can you not decode them?" Aytik asked.

The black ape shrugged. "Rarely. We never know their true signals from false. Those puffs you see could be meant for us to decipher. Besides, Tarawa's signalers are constantly changing their codes. Oftentimes daily. He is nobody's fool."

Jagged white peaks bounded the charred surface of the pass, their conical crowns stretching high enough to spear skysheep. Green needle trees skirted down their rugged slopes.

Aytik leaned forward and peered straight down the wall's western face. True to Kryle's words, a steep dirt rampart separated the wall from the moat. He was certain he saw something slithering about in the muck. It caused his spine to shiver.

Turning about, Aytik looked down at the activity east of the wall. Black forms scurried about the clusters of tents that were spaced at strategic intervals all along the length of the structure's stone and mortar base. Combat units still wheeled about in drill, always under the watchful eyes of scowling commanders. Crashes of bored snouthorns lumbered about inside numerous pens and paddocks, while others hauled wagons laden with crates and barrels and sacks. Further east, swoopers circled in search of lax rodents.

Finally, Aytik located his own army busily pitching their tents in a clearing to the north. Several campfires were already burning within stone fire rings. The knights steeds were corralled around a glistening pond, kept separate from the palfreys which grazed alongside the sparkling brook that fed it. Nearby, a blacksmith's forge was hastily being erected under the keen supervision of the master farrier. Supply wagons were being systematically aligned into neat rows.

"Ha!" Kryle blurted. "Sir Golab must be the most over-organized being to ever draw a breath. I'll wager the distance between each wagon is accurate to within a pinch!"

Aytik could only smile. He knew his cully would win that bet.

They remained atop the wall until the sun began its retreat behind the western foothills and Night's vast army of skytwinklers once again filled the eastern sky. An alert crescent moon kept constant vigil in the east, knowing full well where Day's next advance would begin.

"Let us go," Kryle said, leading the princes back to the pallet. "Soon there will be naught but shadows to see. Best to reach your camp before then."

Torak seated himself down on the crude platform and said to Aytik, "I must pass by your camp on the way back to my own. Might I accompany you?"

"I would very much enjoy that," Aytik assured the ape.

Once the spinning and swaying and banging had ceased, and the skid had been safely lowered back down to the ground, several apes approached with each of the princes' mounts in tow.

"Where is your snouthorn?" Aytik inquired of his cully.

"I had it taken to its pen for a wash and a feed," Kryle replied. "I wish to inspect some of my army's camps. After dark, all beasts are restricted to specific trails to avoid accidental tramplings. It is critical that a commander always obey his own edicts. My own two feet, however, are free to trek wherever I so choose. Besides, if I snoop about on foot, my unit commanders shan't know I'm coming. Sneaky tactics, I will admit, yet most effective for maintaining discipline. All my commanders are quite aware I might pop up at any place – and at any time. Then they will be held accountable for any lax in discipline."

Torak commanded his tuskwooly to kneel and curl its long trunk for him to step onto. He then signaled the beast to raise him partway up its girth. Lastly, he pulled himself up onto the beast's head, sliding backwards down its neck and onto its back.

From his perch atop the tuskwooly, Torak commanded the beast to employ its trunk to retrieve his lance and shield from an attendant. "Fine night to you, Commander," he said, offering his ally a respectful nod.

Kryle returned the gesture. "And a fine night to you," he responded. Then he turned to Aytik, who had likewise mounted his steed. "Nap well, my cully."

Aytik smiled as only cullies bound by bloodletting can. "Try not to startle too many unwary guards," he quipped.

Kryle's black eyes dimmed most serious. "Any sentry I catch unawares will wish I were the enemy. Of such you can be certain."

"Oh, of such I am. You and Sir Golab have much more in common than you know.

Torak and Aytik steered their mounts along at a slow walk. They stopped often to inquire of the other's personal history and hear one another's opinion of the momentous events now at hand. They shared freely of their concerns and their confidence, of their likes and dislikes. Both expressed their gratitude at having the tough black apes for allies, yet shared some good-natured banter over some of their shaggy comrades more peculiar habits; such as always napping with their mouths fully agape, or their queer quirk of chewing their chow with one eye closed.

But most of all, they spoke of home. They shared of their youth and spoke of their families. Each felt the other's loneliness when they talked of that special lover they had left behind. Both shared of their desire to seed tots and of how they hoped their heirs would never be sent off to war; and of how their other scions might someday aspire to higher education in the arts and sciences, perhaps becoming painters or poets or physicians? Or even alchemists and astronomers? They briefly wondered aloud whether some lizarme might not feel the same about their own offspring?

By the time Torak pointed Aytik down the trail leading to the humanfolk camps, the seeds of a new friendship had been sown. They parted company feeling a mite more removed from the dumps of alone; which was all to the good as loneliness can make otherwise rational beings think and act strangely, often leading them into poor choices that they would not otherwise make.

Day's light had retreated by the time Aytik finally found his own tent. After tending to his steed, he walked down the crude boardwalk for the entrance, whereupon he parted the flaps and stepped inside to find Sir Golab stomping into his highboots.

"Going somewhere?" Aytik asked.

After Golab had sheathed his longsword and strapped his nasal helmet onto his head, he snatched his cloak from a peg and set eyes on Aytik. The glow from the brazier made his hair seem all the more redder.

"I still have much to do this night, Prince. There is pork potage in the cauldron and fresh pandemain in a basket on the table. Plus some honey still sweet in the comb. There are jugs of fine claret or mead to quench your thirst. Or clean water should you so desire. Do fill your belly before you nap. An enemy attack will make napping and eating luxuries for all of us."

Aytik considered suggesting the grand knight follow his own advice, but decided against it. He knew his words would be wasted.

"A warm bowl of potage should stick well to my ribs," Aytik said, blowing on his fingers and stepping towards the cauldron. "The chill certainly dips swift come dark in these foothills."

"That it does," Golab concurred. He parted the flaps and stepped outside. "Nap well, Prince."

"Thank you," Aytik called after him.

Only the sound of fading footsteps replied.

A strange stillness filled the tent, muting even the outside winds. It was the screaming silence of alone.

After removing his tunic and highboots, the weary prince ladled himself a bowl of potage and seated himself at the table. He again let his mind drift to home.

His thoughts found Shyamala waiting for him in his bed chamber. He could almost see her standing before him in her favourite blue gown and matching slippers. How he yearned to caress her skin and run his fingers through her hair; to gaze deeply into her eyes and press his lips to hers. To disrobe her. To touch her breasts. To kiss her pearl. To taste her wetness. To enter her in an act of passionate love.

The beauty of the fantasy only served to arouse him, hence he heeded to stop himself lest release come close in hand. "Morgue is your master," he cussed, slamming his fist to the tabletop and spilling some pottage. "You're heart is carved from stone. How else could a father deny his son such love?"

Only the screaming silence replied.

Pushing the bowl away, Aytik slumped brow to tabletop and began to weep. Drops seeped from his eyes until his lids grew heavy and his mind entered the relaxing realm of deepest dreams...

****

...when next he raised his head, shadows of passing steeds were floating along the tent's walls. He could hear the relaxed clop of their hooves and the voices of their riders. Somewhere off in the distance, metal clanged upon metal. An unseen woofer yapped out its displeasure.

Next, his ears snagged the sound of something scraping within the tent. Twisting about, he found Golab sitting atop a mat, skillfully honing his blade.

Pushing to his feet, Aytik sleeved the cold pottage from his face and started stretching tightness from his neck. His mouth gaped to yawn in a big breath.

"I trust you napped well?" Golab asked, without looking up.

"Too well, I think," Aytik replied, pushing his pelvis forward to crack a kink from his back.

Golab cautiously shaved a fingernail across the blade's edges. Satisfied as to their sharpness, he slid the sword back into its sheath and clipped it to his belt.

"Did you not nap?" Aytik asked, noting Golab's bare cot.

"Some," Golab replied, donning his doublet. "It is difficult to nap with so much yet to be done."

"It will get done," Aytik said. "Why have you not unraveled your bedroll?"

"I might ask you the same," Golab stated with a slight smile as he pulled on his gauntlet gloves. "I might also ask why you prefer to nap slumped over a tabletop facedown in a puddle of pottage, all within five strides of your cot?"

Aytik returned the smile. "My dreams caught me unawares. But why have you not unraveled your bedroll? It is unlike you to set aside such things."

"It is. However, for several nights I will have need of it elsewhere."

"Elsewhere?" Aytik was visibly confused. "You speak in riddle, Sir Golab?"

The old knight donned his padded coif and strapped on his nasal helmet, and then he slung his bedroll across his back. "I wish to view our defences from up high, Prince. I have therefore arranged for a unit of apes to lead a patrol of our foot soldiers high up into the mountains to where I can bird-see the pass. Our troops should share in defending the mountains as well as the wall. I shan't be gone beyond half a fortnight. Commanders Shrike, Leez and Zleta will tend to matters here. All three are capable organizers. They should be, seeing as I trained them myself. Ask for either if you need anything."

"The mountain passes are crawling with lizarme," Aytik said with noted concern, as if he only now felt the closeness and danger of war.

"We came to fight alongside our allies, Prince. Not to hide behind the wall and have them take all the risk. It is a matter of humanfolk honour that…"

"Then I'm coming with you," Aytik interrupted, reaching for his own highboots.

An uneasy expression etched into Golab's stony face. It was readily apparent he did not approve of his young protégé tagging along. He toned stern, as if he was addressing a page. "Your presence is unneeded, Prince. You will remain here. The king…"

"…would expect his heir to do his duty," Aytik cut in, adding, "I too came here to fight. Not to moulder in comfort while others take all the risks."

"Prince, I strongly advise against…"

"I am not asking, Sir Golab. Bring more troops if it will wither your worries, but do not try and alter my choice. How will it look if a future king is unwilling to take the same risks he demands of his knights and soldiers? Will that not make me a coward in their eyes – and in my own? The pampered prince who is too timid for combat. A leader of none."

Realizing the young prince had him trapped, Golab frowned and nodded his head. "I have mentored you too well. Although I doubt your Father and Olob would thank me for it. Very well then, Prince. Bring your bedroll and gloves. Plus your warmest hooded cloak. Also, you are to keep no more than a sword's reach away from me, a rule which is closed to debate. Understood?"

"Understood," Aytik replied with a smirk. "Somebody must watch over you."

Golab neglected to acknowledge the quip. Instead, he huffed and scowled and stomped from the tent, grumbling his displeasure through taut lips. He was clearly upset.

Aytik swore his ears snagged the phrase, "…should have just left him a dung note…"

After splashing cold water onto his face and relieving himself in the chamber pot, Aytik donned his silken blouse and belted trousers. Over his blouse he donned his padded doublet. Next, he pulled on his highboots. Removing his warmest cloak from a chest, he quickly rolled it up inside his bedroll. His mind could hear Golab's favourite refrain, '*A soldier cannot be too ready. Never part with your weapons, your boots or your cloak!*'

After donning his coif and strapping on his helmet, and then pulling on his warmest gauntlet gloves, Aytik next slung the bedroll over his back. Lastly, he clipped his sword to his belt and hastened from the tent.

The puffing prince managed to catch Golab just as the knight veered from the path into a clearing, where several units of foot soldiers and archers stood strict in ranks. An exceptionally tough-looking squad of apes was loosely assembled nearby.

As per their prince, each foot soldier and archer also wore warm trousers and hide boots. Over their silken blouses they too wore arming doublets for added warmth and protection in battle. Each donned warm sheepskin gloves and a nasal helmet, and had a bedroll slung across his back. The longbow archers toted quivers packed with arrows and wore hide bracers to protect their forearms against whiplash from the bow strings, while arbalests toted crossbows and quivers packed with bolts. Many carried pavises to form a shield wall. Foot soldiers bore pikes and bucklers and shortswords. All exuded an aura of angst; each fully aware this was no training exercise. The war was coming to them.

The apes were also dressed for the cold. They were likewise clad in thick trousers and hide highboots. Each wore a plated vest for added protection in battle, plus nasty gauntlet gloves with spiked knuckles for ripping. As with the humanfolk, every ape also toted a hooded cloak wrapped inside a bedroll.

All were armed with axe and shield, with some clenching bendable pilums to pierce enemy shields and render them useless. Most bore an opened-face kettle helmet over a padded mail coif that served to protect the cheeks and neck. Each bore a battle map of scars across their bodies. Male or female, not a single ape appeared the least bit affectionate; or even remotely amicable. Clearly, these experienced warriors were all in for combat.

Aytik toned sarcastic. "Quite a pleasant looking lot, don't you think?"

"Pleasant doesn't mesh with their purpose," Golab replied in his most serious tone. "They are well aware of what might await us. Let us hope the lizarme find their nasty dispositions as uninviting as you do."

Suddenly, Aytik snagged sight of a peculiar looking ape with unusual grey hair and rough blue skin. The ape's unique amber eyes were staring back at him.

Beside the grey ape stood a powerful ape-gal, whose shaggy hair was as black as her eyes. Thick legs bowed beneath the bulk of her torso. Her marred face was a map to past battles.

Something moved Aytik to nod at the strange pair. He was surprised when they actually nodded back. Feeling somewhat confident, he risked a smile. This time they simply ignored him and looked away.

"They seem ill at ease?" Aytik noted.

"You should be too."

Aytik muted his reply. He knew from Sir Golab's tone it was best, for sometimes the knight cared not for rank or title.

No time was wasted on introductions before the troops set march from the clearing. The experienced apes took up the lead, their bulky bodies swaying as one. They were closely followed by the steady crunch of humanfolk marching along in step.

All other apes made way for them, often waving to wish them luck. Even the most impassive commanders bade them gestures of respect.

The column wound its way about numerous tents and fire rings until it eventually reached the southern extent of the wall. There it was joined by a unit of ape archers, armed with powerful longbows capable of shooting an arrow well over four hundred strides. In fact, few humanfolk could even nock and draw an ape longbow.

Together, the troops began their climb up the base of a mountain. The rugged trail quickly narrowed into a path, which was littered with chunks of loose rock and sneaky roots that surfaced to trip careless feet. By midday, the path had tightened to force the troops into single file. Shortly thereafter, the first patches of snow appeared in hollows and fissures, which were well hidden from the sun's seeking beams. The needle trees began thinning out and stones became slippery from frost. Bluish icicles hung from overhanging cliffs, dripping down onto the troops and threatening to drop their frozen spikes.

Chests puffed and hearts pounded. Thighs ached with each carefully placed step. Backs were strained as soldiers struggled to push and pull each other up steep slopes. Breath rolled out in a vapour, stiffing beards white. Even within their gloves, digits took numb from the chill. Teeth were tickled by it.

Bellybees buzzed inside each humanfolk. Planks creaked beneath them as the column crossed hungry crevices, or bridged gaps in broken ledges. Apes, encamped for the purpose, lowered coarse vines to help them climb sheer cliffs. Biting gusts often whipped their cloaks about in warning as to who really ruled on high. At such moments the mountain's jagged peak seemed to be laughing down at the puny intruders that crawled about its frozen slope.

Towards the onslaught of night they arrived at the base of a series of scarps that were stacked one atop the other and, when added together, climbed to well over two hundred stands. Spirits sank as the humanfolk soldiers ogled these latest obstacles.

"No need to fret," an ape commander assured the humanfolk. "Come the peek of dawn, our scouts will lower climbing vines down to aid us – winds permitting, of course. Tonight we will bivouac here on this plateau as there are hollows in the scarp. Most are connected and well stalked with firewood. A few even trickle with potable spring water. Or, if you prefer, you can always melt wetspikes for drink. Do not concern yourself with the sour stench as these caves are home to blackwings. Mostly of the docile type."

"Uh – mostly?"

The ape puckered his lips to make amused. "Nap well, Prince."

Prince Aytik did not nap well. At the first hint of dusk, the nippy air sharpened its bite and the waking winds began whistling their wrath all about the frosted lips of the caves. Fluttering shadows moved mysteriously across the stony walls. Eyes blinked from the shadows. Sour breath seeped up from deep within the mountain's gurgling belly. Distant drips echoed in a splash. Things unseen rattled and hissed, while disgruntled spirits moaned.

Those humanfolk who did nap well awakened to find the plateau covered knee deep in snow; clean and pure. Above them, the mountain's jagged peak seemed somewhat subdued in its fresh attire. Far below, the white skirt of its slope hemmed abruptly at the charred flats of the pass.

North of the pass sloped the white skirts of distant mountains. Day's advancing rays danced about their freshly clad peaks. It was readily apparent the Divides enjoyed showing off their splendor.

From up on high, the wall seemed slight and fragile; merely a thin ribbon of brownish and green growth spanning the breadth of the pass. The barrier's northern and southern tips touched mountains at both ends. Behind it, countless columns of smoke wisped upward to greet the rising sun. Further east stretched the golden crests of the rolling foothills. Somewhere far beyond them, past droughted savanna and stifling jungle, lay home.

Many of the humanfolk swallowed hard as they turned their thoughts back to the task at hand. Then they commenced shimmying up the coarse climbing vines which had been lowered down to greet them.

Each level brought with it a sheer scarp that stretched upward higher than the last. Still, the soldiers persevered until midday found them all safe and sore atop the crown.

"It gets somewhat easier now," an ape said to Aytik. He paused to make amused before adding, "I mean, there are no more vertical scarps. Unless, of course, one is foolish enough to hike for the summit. From here on our biggest challenges will be the nip and the blow."

"Along with trudging deep snow," another ape noted.

"And possibly battling lizarme," the grey ape reminded everyone. His unique amber eyes wided most serious. "Be most vigilant for the unnatural. The enemy is brave and cunning and has been known to wrap themselves in warm skins and hide in wait beneath the drifts."

"Always don your helmets and keep a wary watch to up," advised the powerful ape-gal with the marred face. "The lizarme be apt to drop heavy ice spears down on our noggins. Seldom fatal, but quite apt to bruise flesh or draw blood."

Many of the surrounding apes nodded to agree. One even tapped at a dent in her own helmet.

Humanfolk soldiers drew their cloaks tight about themselves while they trudged across the rugged mountainside. Wisps of powder waltzed atop the drifts in time with the whistling wind. Many feet, crunching in step, kept a steady beat.

Towards the end of the day, they at last began to descend their host's western slope. A shimmering river nourished a lush valley far below.

An ape commander approached Aytik and Golab. Her manner was calm yet serious. "That valley drops down to connect with the pass!" she shouted over the wind. Pointing downward and north to where the slope met with charred flats, she added, "It is crawling with enemy scouts! As are most of the valleys in this sector of the Divides! Many battles have already been fought in them! Many more will be! Territory in these valleys changes sides more often than the pitch of Destiny's breath! As much as is practical, it is vital your soldiers try and keep in constant contact with our scouts – lest they should wander behind enemy lines! We prefer forays there be planned in advance and with a set purpose!"

"Indeed!" Golab concurred, panting for breath. "Soldiers should never be sacrificed for naught!"

Aytik granted the commander a nod of assurance. "Our troops have been instructed to cooperate fully with your own! To be a plus not a problem!"

The dour ape simply stared at Aytik and Golab for several tense bits. Her detached demeanor made it quite clear she was none too thrilled about having a humanfolk prince tagging along.

Finally, the commander returned Aytik's nod and said, "Prince, it often takes two soldiers to evacuate one wounded back behind the wall! From this point forward, only those cases deemed most serious will be taken! Any who meet Morgue will be left behind to smell where they fell! That applies to both ape and humanfolk! This is not a merciful war!"

"What war is!?" Golab shouted, wrestling with his cloak.

Ignoring the knight's rhetorical question, the ape-gal shouted, "If we chop the chat and make haste we can drop back down below the shrub line before dusk! The *nip* and the *blow* will be much tamer for us to bivouac there!"

"Will there be ample firewood!?" Aytik asked."

"Can't do it, Prince!" Golab shouted, shaking his head. "The flickers and smell of a fire would betray our position! From this point onward, its raw chow on the shiver! At least for the soldiers who will be staying behind! I've seen enough to satisfy my curiosity! This terrain is much too treacherous for even a daring commander like Prod Tarawa to march his army through! Advantage greatly favours the defenders! Come the morrow, you and I shall return to our camp!"

"I will arrange for two escorts to guide you!" the ape-gal hollered. "For now we must hurry! The Divides promise to blow bitter this night! A clear sky up here means Night will bite with frozen fangs."

After nodding his gratitude to the ape-gal, Golab bluntly gestured for his soldiers to make haste. The ape commander did likewise.

Thus, they dropped down below the shrub line and made camp. It was well they had warm cloaks and bedrolls for, true to the ape's warning words, the night chill did bite like a beast.

Once again, Aytik did not nap well. The nasty nip kept him in shivers inside his bedroll. He constantly wiggled his toes, less they should freeze. He tucked his fingers within his armpits. Outside his bivouac, needle trees cracked from the cold. He thought, *'This must be what Morgue's chilly maze is like?'*

It was the apes themselves, however, who disturbed Aytik the most. He noted how they had become quite jittery, all of them napping with one eye open and weapons clenched tightly in hand. Also, the ape commanders had put out what Aytik felt was an excessive picket to guard the camp perimeter. Like they were waiting for ghosts?

'Given their long history of battling lizarme in these mountains, I suppose one cannot blame them for being overly anxious,' Aytik reasoned to himself.

Dawn broke crisp and clean. It brought with it some sense of relief, although all of the apes kept scanning their surroundings with much more than cautious concern. Each kept a sturdy grip on their weapons.

"What is wrong?" Aytik finally asked of some apes during a brief lull in the wind.

"No mountain chirpers," an ape-gal whispered in reply.

Another ape whispered, "No matter the *nip* or the *blow*, they always sing praise to the rising sun. This dawn they did not."

"Why are the chirpers silent this dawn?" Golab asked.

"Shhh..."

"Could the enemy be close... ugh!"

The bolt struck Golab in his left chest, piercing his doublet. His face twisted in shock and pain as he sank to his knees. He clenched the metal shaft with both hands. Blood choked from his mouth. His eyes stared briefly at Aytik before he gurgled his last and pitched face down into the snow.

"OOOAAHH!!"

A firm hand clasped onto Aytik's hood and yanked him aside just as a second bolt stuck where he'd stood. A third struck a nearby ape in the thigh.

"Shield wall!" shouted an ape commander, pointing up the slope. "There they are! Up there!"

Disciplined ape archers immediately formed a shield wall and began loading bolts and nocking arrows. Humanfolk archers quickly followed suit.

"Archers, loose at will!" shouted the commander.

Arrows and bolts began soaring up the slope in projectile motion as the archers carefully picked out their targets. Neither apes nor humanfolk wished to shoot in a volley and empty their quivers for naught.

Somewhere above an unseen lizarma wailed in pain. Another slid down the slope, already lost to Morgue's maze.

"OOOAAHH!!"

"Fight, Prince!" a sprinting ape screamed. "Fight or meet Morgue!"

Aytik stood and stared with legs rooted to soil. All around him, scores of lizarme were emerging from behind rocks and crags. They were joined by snarling rexids; the vicious tracking lizards with sabred fangs and powerful claws.

Equally fierce apes charged to engage their foe. Spirited foot soldiers sprinted to aid them. Bowstrings twanged at random as the humanfolk archers closed tight their ranks. Metal clanged upon metal amid screams of fear and pain. The chaos and clamour of battle was everywhere...

139

A hundred times, Aytik had thought of this very moment. Fantasized about it. Yearned for it. A hundred times he had planned his response. For all that, now when his first taste of battle was finally at hand, his limbs were frozen in place. His eyes locked in a stare.

"Fight!" the ape repeated. "Prince, draw thy blade!"

My blade, Aytik thought. Yes, I must draw my blade.

"OOOAAHH!!"

"Prince, mind ye back!"

Something in the ape's panicky tone snapped Aytik from his torpor. He spun about and awkwardly unsheathed his sword.

"Oooaahh!" cried the young lizarma as it whacked the weapon from Aytik's hands. Its momentum carried it crashing into Aytik's body.

They landed in a heap upon the cold ground, with the lizarma on top. In one deliberate motion, it shoved its trident shaft up under Aytik's chin and pinned him firm by the throat.

Aytik too grabbed the shaft, and strained to press the weapon away from his throat. He choked and gasped and gulped. He twisted his torso to wriggle free. He slammed a knee up into his attacker's groin.

Although the determined lizarma winced with each blow, he failed to yield the choke. Aytik gazed up into his enemy's frightened eyes, aware of the strength draining from his own limbs. Every fibre of every muscle ached. His lungs yearned for just one gulp of precious air. His eyes struggled to keep focus. He could sense his thoughts fading. Would he welcome the end? No matter. Soon it would all be over..."

"Whack!"

Aytik did not see his attacker's face torn from its skull, or the strong hands that rudely yanked him up off the cold ground and slung him across a broad and hairy back. He was just vaguely aware of his sword sliding back into its sheath, and of the ground rushing past just below his dangling arms. A thick arm pinned his legs together against a burly chest. He could hear battle sounds fading off into the distance. He could also

140

hear the breath of somebody puffing to keep pace. With great difficulty, he lifted his head and focused his eyes on the powerful ape-gal with the marred face. Then his head flopped back against the hairy back and all became a blur...

****

...when next he regained his senses, Aytik found himself lying alone on a bed of cold moss in the crux of two tree roots. He could hear a river rushing nearby.

His throat felt tight and tender, and he became aware of grit between his teeth. It seemed as though every fibre of his form still ached and throbbed. There was an incessant pounding between his ears and his entire skull suffered from cramps.

Aytik winced as he raised his head. Ever so carefully, he untangled his locks from a knot in a root and struggled to pull himself up into a sit. He tried to shake the mush from his mind.

When his eyes finally found their focus, Aytik started scanning his strange new surroundings. The trees were red of bark and far taller than any he'd ever seen, seemingly touching the sky. Furlike moss dangled down from thick boughs, and moisture glistened like skytwinklers within those strands that were struck by sunbeams. A chilly mist crept across the forest floor, slowly winding its way about the thick growth. A nondescript blinked from a hollow.

Aytik's nostrils caught the musk of an unseen beast; its foul stench and the clop of its hooves giving it away. Somewhere nearby, a tree rapper dug for bugs. Off in the distance, a lone howler was barely audible above the river.

"Ouch!" Aytik squeaked as he slapped to squish a pesky skitter. He quickly muted his mouth and honed his ears. Only the rush of water replied.

With all his senses seeking for any sign of trouble, Aytik silently slid his blade from its sheath and slowly pushed up to his feet. The crackling of stiff joints caused him to pause. He could hear his heart pounding to burst out of his chest.

Satisfied he was in no immediate danger, Aytik turned and trod warily towards the sound of the river; his sword still held at the ready.

While he sneaked through the forest, meandering about mossy logs and climbing over giant roots, Aytik wondered whatever had become of the apes who had brought him to this place? Were they still about? Had they met Morgue? What of the foot soldiers on the mountain? Had any of them escaped? What of Sir Golab?

Aytik stopped still in his tracks. Now he remembered. He swallowed hard at the memory of his old mentor looking so helplessly up at him. Pleading for – something? How could he ever forget that gurgle? Was he truly gone? Forever? Shutting tight his eyes, Aytik sought to erase the horrifying image altogether. He could not. A lone tear trickled a muddy trail down his dirty cheek.

'Must keep my wits together...'

Upon reaching the riverbank, Aytik promptly dropped to his knees and plunged his face well below the surface. The frigid water instantly numbed his brow and temples, momentarily pushing the pain from his mind. He washed the filth from his brow and cheeks. It felt good to get clean.

When Aytik finally pulled his face up from the drink, his thinking had calmed. It all came back so clearly to him now. The ambush. Sir Golab's pleading green eyes. His own scrap with the young lizarma. Their harrowing escape down the mountainside. A vague recollection of an ape with unusual grey hair and unique…"

"Uhhh…" Aytik grunted as a strong hand clasped to mute his mouth. He struggled without success to break free.

"Prince," whispered a stern voice. "We must keep mute. This sector swarms with lizarme."

Aytik ceased to struggle and the strong hand was removed. He turned to find himself in the company of the grey ape with amber eyes.

Several strides in back of the grey ape stood the powerful ape-gal with the marred face. However, she was not looking at

142

them. Instead, her black eyes searched back and forth about the forest edge.

Aytik noted she now possessed a lizarme scimitar to go along with the trident. Both weapons were stained with blood.

"Prince, my name is Kwok," the grey ape explained. "And this is my mate, Kea. We've been ordered to protect you. Please, we must seek refuge back in amongst the foliage. It is too open here and dacts can easily spot our tracks."

"What of the others?" Aytik asked.

Kwok nodded solemnly. "They were vastly outnumbered, Prince. I suspect the worst."

Kea suddenly cut in, her tone void of emotion. "Worst part of war be losing thine own."

"Come," Kwok stated, yanking the startled prince to his feet. "It's not safe here."

"Where will we go?" Aytik asked.

"South," Kwok replied. "We'll keep to the forest to avoid dacts. Later, we'll hike back up over the mountain. It will be hard to detect only three of us. Even so, we must keep our wits sharp and off the nod since the enemy has eyes everywhere."

As they stepped back beneath the canopy, Aytik turned to Kea. "How does one forget?" he asked. "Losing one's friends, I mean?"

The ape-gal appeared confused. She paused briefly in thought before asking, "Why would ye want to?"

"Shush," Kwok whispered sternly. "Keep mute or our friends will be grieving us."

They stole south along the base of the mountain until the hint of dusk, eventually taking refuge beneath the girth of a fallen redwood. Distant skybangers rumbled in warning of approaching skyshowers. Crackling flashbolts spread their crooked claws across the ugly sky. The storm's wet breath began bending and whipping boughs about on a rampage. Cones crashed down upon the ground.

Soon the sky spilt its wrath and the tears of every widow who ever wept fell upon the valley. Winds wailed and skybangers raged. No creature dared be out and about.

Come the peek of dawn, the forest floor was a sea of muck. Pests eagerly buzzed their approval whilst greedy roots slurped and gulped down much more than their fill. Unseen chirpers sang songs of praise unto Seed for sending them such a gift as skyshowers.

"I've never seen such a drenching," Aytik remarked, just as one of the sun's warming beams shone through the dripping canopy. "Not even in The Ape Jungle."

"Blessed be Seed seldom throws such tantrums," Kwok said, donning his helmet. "And that when she does, they never last very long. If they lasted…"

A firm grip on his shoulder stilled his tongue. Kea motioned for all to make mute.

She had good reason for doing so as a peek out from beneath the fallen redwood revealed they were not alone. Mere strides away, lanky figures with crimson eyes were stalking about the muck. Tracking lizards crept along beside them, with snouts pressed low to catch every scent. It was readily apparent a single swipe from one of their powerful claws could mean an early meeting with Morgue.

Aytik could feel his heart pounding to escape while he stared out at the seemingly endless column of lizarme and rexids. Fortunately, they were in hiding downwind of their scaly foe. Nevertheless, Aytik's hands started to shake. A bead of sweat seeped out from under his coif and trickled down his cheek to his lips. He could taste the salt on his tongue. He was fully aware that, should the wind change and the enemy discover them now, their time with breath would be done. A swift spiral down into Morgue's maze would be their souls' final fortune.

A firm hand began patting the panicky prince on the back. He turned to find Kea touching a forefinger to her lips. She nodded and retrained her sights back onto the enemy, but continued with rubbing his back.

"Fear takes some getting used to," Kwok whispered ever so softly into Aytik's ear. "I should know. Black ape father, white ape mother. Been scrapping virtually all my life. Was always afraid. Funny thing about fear is you can't go around it, you can't tunnel under it, you can't climb over it. You can only push through it.

"Don't you fret, Prince. Destiny is wishing us well. Those lizarme don't sense we're here. The breeze blows for us, and Seed's skyshowers have washed clean our scent. The musty stench of the foliage hereabouts is always strongest after a good spill. Even rexids have trouble tracking prey in such conditions. Providing we keep calm and quiet, the lanky lugs shan't know we're about. Just bide your time thinking on things pleasant."

'Oh, sure,' Aytik thought on the scoff. He tried to focus on things pleasant anyway. To little avail. The spectacle of so many enemy so very close gripped his eyes and his mind. It both terrified and intrigued him. Fear aside, he knew two facts. If they were discovered, it would mean an early meeting with Morgue; and this time at least one lizarma was going to feel his blade.

Aytik carefully unsheathed his sword, smiling and nodding at his concerned comrades. "Just in case I pass gas and give us up," he quipped.

Both apes exchanged awkward stares before making amused and resighting on their passing foe.

For what seemed like forever past ever, the trapped trio crouched low in hiding while hordes of lizarme stole past. Neither spoke nor risked any movement until long after the threat had passed. Only then did they emerge from beneath the fallen redwood, albeit warily and with weapons in hand.

"Step soft on the swift," Kwok said, taking up the lead. "And keep your senses on the up."

Kea motioned for Aytik to go ahead of her. "Mind ye not squish noisy in the muck, Prince. Rexids hear much too well."

Aytik was amazed by how quickly the enormous redwood roots sucked the forest floor dry. By midday, the ground was once again firm beneath his boots and, save for a few obstinate muckles, all evidence of Seed's drenching tirade had vanished.

Shortly past midday, they veered from the lush valley and commenced the long climb back up the mountain. As they trudged further and further up its base, the slope steepened to a slide and the towering redwood trees gave way to blue needlers. Then the needlers gave way to scrub. Breath began spouting in vapor. Ears and digits were numbed by the nip. Tired muscles ached and empty bellies growled. Nostrils stuck to themselves.

Night returned soon enough, its breath biting and cold. Ice cloaked the stones, sometimes shining beneath the vigilant moon. Armies of skytwinklers blinked with a brilliance, boasting that they alone ruled the boundless above. Unseen spirits whispered on the wind, or snapped sticks as they stole about the scrub.

Unable to risk a fire for warmth, the weary trio huddled together in a cozy cavity at the base of a slanting crag. There they shivered as one, constantly wiggling their toes and blowing hot breath across numb fingers. They scanned the shadows for shapes. Sometimes, they steered their sights skyward in wonder. Was Destiny really watching them? If so, did it care?

They all relaxed in relief when the sun's glow reached over the mountaintop and the waning moon led Night's army of skytwinklers in a westward retreat. Just the same, even as the shadows stretched long down the mountainside, the three comrades stayed concealed within the cavity; for once again, no mountain chirpers had sung praise to the rising sun?

Tension returned with a rush as their ears snagged the sound of loose stones rattling down a slope. Their flesh tingled in readiness as fear yet again tormented their minds. Hearts pounded and hands shook. Each of the three knew this time there was no avoiding a fight. They were trapped!

For the first time in a very long while, Aytik humbly prayed unto Destiny. Like frightened folk so often do, he promised impractical changes if his creator would help him out *just this once*. Promises his ego knew he would never keep.

Next, the anxious prince wiped his sticky palms on his cloak, and then tightened a grip on his sword. He could feel his thighs burning from the crouch. *'No matter,'* he thought, *'If the enemy does find us, we shan't be spiralling down alone!'*

"Shhh," Kea whispered, as the distinct crunch of a heavy foot finding an errant pebble sounded from just outside the cavity. She tried to block Aytik's body with her own, but he nudged her aside.

A vague shadow started ever so slowly creeping into view. It was followed by the barbed prongs of a trident. Followed by the shaft.

Aytik could take the tension no longer. Like a slinker stalking prey, he sprang from the cavity with his weapon raised and – froze?

The startled ape also raised his weapon, then sighed and lowered the trident back down. When Kea and Kwok emerged from the cavity, the ape nodded in greeting.

Kea and Kwok both returned the gesture before Kwok said, "Drox, thank Destiny. We saw the trident and thought you were a lizarma. Did any others…?"

"Kryle!" Aytik exclaimed, momentarily forgetting where they were.

The ape raised his hand for silence, whilst cautiously glancing about.

"Sorry," Aytik said, suddenly taking note of the battered condition of the ape soldiers. Nary a one was without wounds.

Kryle's tone was calm, yet formal. "Come on, Prince," he said. "We must flee this sector at once. It is no place for foolish heroes. Our pyres have consumed too many. Had you met Morgue along with Sir Golab, what would become of your troops' morale? You have been both foolish and selfish."

Aytik felt ashamed, yet prickly. "We are at war, Kryle."

Kryle nodded. "True, we are at war. And should you meet Morgue without me, your sister and Shyamala would have my hide for a hammock. Come, we must hasten back to our camp. If all goes well, we should reach our side of this mountain before dark."

"Kryle?"

"What?"

"I am sorry. Golab was as much your friend as he was mine."

"I know well the pain of loss, Aytik. When we found where they'd fallen, I was afraid I had lost you as well. When you weren't found amongst the frozen, I begged of Morgue that you were safe and of breath. But we can discuss this another time. For now we must mourn on the move. Zira, have some scouts guard our rear."

"It has been done, Doyen Commander."

As they climbed above the scrub and found themselves trudging through deep snow, the apes became wary of the deep drifts and of the above. When at last they filed into a narrow ravine with sheer cliffs rising high on each side, familiar figures with black eyes stared down from the cusps.

"Our scouts will cause slides if lizarme enter this ravine," Kryle explained. "We have buried them here before, so don't fret if your feet should step upon something meaty beneath the snow."

When they finally emerged from the ravine and started back down the east side of the mountain, Aytik drew tight his cloak and paused to ponder the view.

Below them dropped the series of scarps. Many tiny black forms clambered about them. To the north, beyond the charred flat of the pass, freshly clad peaks still smirked at the mortals who had foolishly dared to challenge one of their own. They almost seemed proud of the suffering their kind could cause.

A thin ribbon of chutes spanned the breadth of the pass; the wall kissing mountains both north and south. Behind it, smoke wisped skyward to greet the awakening skytwinklers. Beyond the smoke, far to the east, a long column was winding its way through the distant foothills like a giant white serpent.

Aytik knew at once they were white apes mounted on tuskwoolies. King Thorax's army had arrived to help out...

Capital

"Ow!" Helenia shrieked, grabbing the balcony balustrade.

"Well, you moved," Tianga noted, adjusting the angle of the comb.

"She always does," Shyamala added, gloating a grin. "She can't keep still for a blink. Never could. I swear she has gnats in her shift."

Tianga puckered her lips to make amused.

"Very funny. Ha, ha, ha – ow!"

"Stay still and it won't tug so much," Shyamala scolded, rolling her eyes. "Dearest Destiny, Helenia."

"My foot has taken nap in my slipper," Helenia protested rather defensively.

"I can't believe how fine it is to the touch," Tianga said, rolling a lock of Helenia's hair between her fingers. "As smooth as a silkspinner's web."

"In fact, I think a silkspinner has moved in," Shyamala said, winking at the white ape.

"I think Shyamala may be right," Tianga concurred, playing along. "Oh, look – there it is."

"Ha. Ha. Very funny," Helenia mocked, refusing to bite.

"All kidding aside, your hair is soft like goose down," Tianga emphasized.

"Don't tell her that, Tianga. She might start honking and laying eggs. Ha! Ha! Ha!"

"My, aren't we the witty little jesters this day. Ha. Ha. Ha."

"Shiny too. Yours as well, Shyamala. Whatever are you galfolk doing to bring out such a beautiful sheen?"

"Aloe plants are cultivated all along the banks of the Amen River," Shyamala explained. "We slop our hair with gel drawn from the leaves and then we rinse it clean by bathing in the artesian wells bubbling up from deep beneath the ground."

"We can't stay in the frigid water for very long before numbing," Helenia added. "Especially our ankles and knees. But the purity of the water makes our skin and hair feel tingly clean for quite some time afterwards."

Shyamala nodded to concur. "Tianga, you really must come with us sometime. You must."

"Promise us you will," Helenia pleaded, taking the ape's hand. "Please. It'll be so much fun. You'll see. We always bring wine."

"We apes aren't much for cold water," Tianga said, acting out a shiver. Noting their disappointment, she added, "Oh, all right. I suppose it wouldn't hurt to try it once. And I do like a good wine."

"Yay! We're going to have so much fun!" Helenia exclaimed.

"Perhaps we can go on the morrow?" Shyamala proposed.

"Perhaps," Tianga said. "We'll see how things are then."

All three gals made mute and stared out across Ga Bay as the ape-gal continued teasing knots from Helenia's hair.

"Ouch!"

"Whoops – sorry."

Some time passed without words as Tianga kept combing the princess' hair. She clearly enjoyed pampering her younger friend.

Finally, Helenia broke the silence. "Tianga – um – have you ever like, done it? Made love, I mean?"

"Helenia!!" Tianga and Shyamala shouted in unison.

The princess stretched a naughty smile. "Well – have you?"

"Helenia!"

"What? It's just a simple question. I mean, we all know Shyamala has. But have…"

"Helenia!"

"Well, you have. Many times, in fact. But have you, Tianga?"

"Helenia, stop it!" Shyamala shouted, flushing face.

"You have, haven't you?"

This time Shyamala and Tianga merely exchanged awkward looks.

150

"With Commander Kryle, I'll wager."

"Helenia!" Shyamala scolded. "Stop it. You're dipping too deep into Tianga's private well."

"Come on, Tianga, just admit it. I can tell by the way you and Kryle look at each other that either you are or will be lovers. Your eyes sparkle whenever he is near. And your face flushes purple. It's quite apparent you lust after him."

Helenia awaited a confession that did not come. So she pressed on into a touchy topic. "Is it not frowned upon for white apes to mate with black? I mean…"

"Yes it is," Tianga acknowledged. "Not by all, but by many. Too many, in fact. Helenia, bigotry never flips quickly. It always drags on time. Which is why you must never speak of this to anyone. Neither of you. Ever. Promise me. Both of you, promise me right now."

"How old were you when you first…"

"Helenia!"

"Much older than you!" Tianga scolded.

"Did it hurt much? I mean…"

"Promise me," Tianga demanded. "Promise me and pinky swear. And hug on our friendship. Both of you."

"We promise," both galfolk stated together.

All three joined in a pinky swear, followed by a group hug to seal their oath.

Tianga moved to speak further, but sudden movement within the bed chamber snagged her sights.

"Hssssssssss…"

"What's wrong with Clive?" Shyamala asked, pointing to the ape's pet spiketail, which had suddenly started hissing and spinning about.

All three friends watched with glee as the spirited creature with warty flesh and eight clawed legs spun around and around. Mucous flung from its fangs as the agitated pet snapped at its own tail. Its angry red eyes glared at its adversary.

"Imagine if our males did that," Tianga quipped.

"Imagine if their tails were near so long," Shyamala added, widening her eyes.

"And had spikes on them," Helenia joked.

"Helenia!" Shyamala scolded. "That's sick. Who says that?"

Tianga made amused. "From what I've seen, most males think with their tails."

Helenia and Shyamala paused in shock, before all three began laughing themselves to tears.

Once the hysterics had subsided, Tianga regained her composure enough to ask Helenia a question. "So, have you?"

"Have I what?" Helenia asked.

Tianga wided her eyes.

"Oh," Helenia said. "No, not yet. Although I think I might like to."

"Helenia, you're not near old enough!" Shyamala exclaimed. "And you don't even have a ladfolk."

"I kind of have a ladfolk," Helenia said. "Uh, I mean, I like him allot. He makes my belly flutter and my heart twist in my chest."

"And who might this unfortunate soul be?" Tianga teased, winking at Shyamala.

"Do tell," Shyamala put in. She was visibly intrigued. "Is it a handsome knight from your father's own Royal Guard?"

"Uh-uh," Helenia replied.

"Who then?"

"First you both must promise never to tell," Helenia said, waggling her baby finger. "You must pinky swear and hug to seal it."

The others rightly agreed, pinky swearing and hugging Helenia to seal their oath.

Helenia lowered her voice to a near whisper. "I love Arduk," she mumbled.

"What?" Shyamala asked.

"Speak up, Helenia. We can barely hear you."

Helenia raised her voice just enough for them to hear her. "I love Arduk."

"The stable lad!"

"Dearest Destiny!" Shyamala shouted. "You cannot be serious!"

The young princess simply bit her upper lip and nodded that she was.

"You mustn't entertain such thoughts," Tianga scolded. "There is something loopy about that one. Even Clive is wary of Arduk. When riled, the lad snarls and froths and bares his teeth like a mad howler. Some say he speaks with wild beasts. And there's been clack his eyes glow yellow at night and he can sight through the darkness. Clack which may very well be true. It's no secret he was reared by howlers. How far have you two…"

"Not that far."

"Well, thank Seed for that," Shyamala sighed. "Imagine if you had acted on your urges and he put you in a breeding way. Your father would have his spitter for bait!"

"Helenia, you mustn't…" Tianga began.

"What I feel for Arduk is not some passing pash," Helenia interrupted. "And you two can't object. Tianga, you are in love with a black ape. Will you end your love for him because of what some bigots may think? Should he end his love for you? And you, Shyamala, have been my brother's lover since before you were my age. My father only objects to Aytik matching with you because your family is of low status. Yet Aytik loves you more than life itself. So who are you two to judge my affections for Arduk? I only told you of my desires because I love and trust both of you. I thought you would at least try to understand. Apparently I was wrong."

An awkward silence roared as the two older gals exchanged looks. Both were shamed by their haste to judge their friend, who had never once judged them for who they loved.

Helenia's face flushed with emotion. Tears began trickling down her cheeks and in between her quivering lips. She would have scolded them even more, except that something across Ga Bay suddenly snagged her sights. With her jaw slacked open, she could only stare northward in shock.

The others turned to see what held their younger friend's gaze. They too stared with slacked jaws.

It was Tianga who finally found her speech. "Dearest Destiny, we must tell the king at once!"

Instantly, the three friends turned and sprinted across the bed chamber. Tianga flung open the door and they all raced out into the corridor. They bounded down and around and down and around a spiraled stairwell until they reached the ground floor of the keep, upon which they sped full sprint down a wide corridor to the king's court. Both massive doors were open, thus they charged past two bewildered guards and on into the great hall.

They were closely followed by an agitated creature with eight clawed legs and angry red eyes, which hissed its ire at all the commotion. At least until Tianga's gentle hand patted it mute.

Three figures stood at the far side of the table, seemingly pouring over a ledger of sorts. King Myro was hunched over in the center, clad in his robe and slipperboots. His grey hair was held in check by a gemmed circlet, and he clenched tight his ruler's sceptre.

To the king's left loomed Stork; clad, as always, in his black robe, mail coif and metal-tipped boots. He held his halberd in his gloved hands. True to form, Stork's face betrayed no emotion. His black eyes stared blinkless on each side of his hooked schnozz, while his large larynx threatened to burst through his throat.

On the king's right stood Olob the Historian. Olob was wearing his hooded blue frock, patterned with orange crescent-moons, and his worn old bag hat that kept his white hair in check. Long pointy shoes completed his attire.

King Myro was visibly annoyed by the intrusion. He glared briefly at Shyamala and Tianga, before anchoring his stare firmly onto his daughter.

Myro toned cross. "Child, have you no need of manners this day?"

"F-Father, climb to the pinnacle and sight north across the bay!" Helenia shrieked, puffing to catch wind.

"Many ships approach," Tianga added

Noting the panic in their tone, all three ascended the stairwell as swiftly as Myro's feeble limbs would allow until they had reached the pinnacle and could sight past the curtain wall. There, even Stork let slip with a rare gasp as they all froze and watched the armada bearing down on Capital. One massive ship dwarfed all others, its sheeted masts reaching to spear the skysheep themselves!

"Olob," Myro managed at last, turning to face his historian. His voice quivered as he continued. "Old friend, never have I needed your wisdom and counsel more than now. What say you?"

The Historian cupped a hand about his mouth and, for a brief moment, he stared down in deepest thought before again peering north past the battlements.

Only an unseen chirper broke the silence as Olob kept to his private thoughts; until, at last, he turned to face his king.

Helenia could not recall ever seeing the old historian appear so alarmed despite his words flowing calm and certain.

At this point, Olob turned to face the bodyguard. "Stork, order the Royal Guard to confiscate all the burnable oil they can find and rush it to the shore. Instruct them to empty our warehouses and shops of every cask, barrel and bottle. Have them spill it all about the harbour, dousing every plank and beam with it. Warehouses. Shops. The rookery. Put it all to the torch. We must create a wall of fire. And make certain they douse the cargo hoists and piers and set them ablaze. Burn all that can aid the enemy. Now go."

"Burn it all, sire?" Stork asked of Myro.

Myro never swung his eyes from Olob as he raised his hand for Stork to wait. "I have always trusted your judgment, old friend, yet now you muddle my mind? Many buildings along the shore are quite aged and constructed mostly of wood. Wood that has dried out over time. And the wind blows inland. Should we do as you ask, all of Capital could go up in flames? Our beloved city might be consumed. All of it."

A lone tear trickled down Olob's cheek. "We must pray to Destiny that it will be so. Pid has duped us, sire. With our army away at The Wall, Capital is already lost. Still and all, perhaps we can spare our folk to fight another day? Even the toughest lizarme troops cannot pass through a wall of fire, and the smoke will do much to hinder their dacts. Prod Sergon will be left with two options. He can wait until the flames have finished their feed, or he can turn his armada around and land his troops north of the bluffs. Regardless of his choice, the flames will grant us time to evacuate the city. But we must act quickly. There is no time for debate."

"Abandon the city!" Helenia blurted. She would have spoke more were it not for a gentle hand patting her shoulder.

"We will assist with the evacuation, sire," Tianga assured Myro. "I will personally see to it that our tuskwoolies use their size and strength to clear the main roads of any obstacles."

Myro merely nodded in response to the ambassador's words. He next turned to Stork and instructed, "Go and do as Olob counsels. Torch it all."

Stork turned and hastened down the stairs, his throaty lump bobbing in cadence with each lengthy stride.

"Why are you still here?" Myro demanded of his only daughter. "Go."

"But Father…"

"Now!" Myro exclaimed. "Fetch your steed and go!"

Helenia wanted to remain with her father, but a hairy hand grabbed her by the tunic and began dragging her forcefully towards the stairs.

"Sire, we will evacuate with the others," Tianga assured the king. "Come, Shyamala. First I must retrieve my battle gear, then we will meet up at the stables. Clive, heel."

"Hsssssssssss…"

"Do watch over my daughter for me, ambassador. And keep keen of wit – both of you."

Soon all three friends were ascending the stairwell in its clockwise spiral, keeping left to the outer wall to take advantage of the wider steps. The nimbler humanfolk took up the lead, with the ape and her pet giving chase.

"Go…" Tianga puffed as they reached the upper landing. "Make haste and I will meet you at the stables…"

"Don't fret if we should tarry," Helenia said. "There are some important items…"

"Forget them!" Tianga shouted, shoving both of her friends towards a corridor. "No object is worth your life! Shyamala, see she does not tarry! Nor yourself! Hurry along now, both of you."

Before either galfolk could find words in reply, the ape and her spirited pet turned and raced across the landing towards another corridor.

"Hsssssssss..."

"We must hurry," Shyamala insisted, tugging on Helenia's tunic.

"Uh – yes, of course," Helenia replied. "Come. Let us be swift on the sprint."

Both girls turned and dashed headlong down the corridor until they came to an abrupt turn. From there they raced into a second corridor and charged across the tiled floor to Helenia's bed chamber, barging through the door together.

"Remove your gown and slippers," Helenia said as she kicked off her slippers and commenced pulling on her highboots. "I have tunics and boots that will fit you, and hooded cloaks to repel the chill and the wet."

"No thank you," Shyamala replied from the garderobe. "I prefer my gown and my slippers."

Helenia considered pressing the issue, but thought better of it. There was no time for squabbling. "Suit yourself, Shyamala, but at least bring one of my warmest woolen cloaks. Make it a long cut and hooded so it can double as a naproll. We may have to bivouac."

"I'm good," Shyamala replied as she stepped back into the bed chamber.

After pulling on her highboots, Helenia procured a pair of hurling daggers from a shelf and slid them securely into their sheaths. "These may serve us well," she explained, noting that Shyamala was eyeing her with some concern.

"You know I don't care much for weapons," Shyamala stated.

"Apparently you don't care much for reality either," Helenia snapped. "I need to use the privy, then we must swift on the sprint. Tianga will be wondering what has happened to us. Will you not at least consider packing a tunic and boots? They may prove quite practical given the pressing situation that confronts us."

"No, I am comfortable as I am. My slippers have fine padded souls and they are much lighter than boots. They will keep me fleet of foot."

"Fine then," Helenia huffed as she rushed to use the garderobe. "I'm still bringing a long cloak for you! Along with a tunic and boots! You can thank me later!"

"Do as you wish!" Shyamala replied. "But I am particularly fond of these slippers and this gown!"

In quick time, the princess re-emerged into her bed chamber. Her tone was clearly vexed. "I'm quite certain my brother would understand you leaving them behind given our present plight . He can always have the royal cobblers and clothiers replace them. You are aware he is heir to the throne, are you not? That he will be king?"

Shyamala would not be swayed. "Ha. Ha. Funny. You know they are my favourite gifts from him, Helenia. While I wear them I feel as if a part of Aytik is always embracing me. Like the sleeves are his strong arms about me, and the slippers are his feet gently caressing mine."

Helenia rolled her eyes. "Dearest Destiny, Shyamala. Dare I ask which part your chemise might play?"

Shyamala blushed. "You may ask, but I shan't tell you."

"I don't think I care to know. Come, before Tianga grows frantic. You know how she frets."

Moments later found the pair bounding down some winding steps, before sprinting into a smoky corridor where shadows from marble statues danced together upon frescoed walls.

Hinges squeaked as a guard strained to open a heavy iron door. Beyond the door a narrow stairwell wound its way down into the upper bailey. It was no great distance across the grass and past the castle cisterns to the walkers wicket; however, the heavy iron portcullis had been raised to allow for rapid evacuation of palace servants and their families.

Helenia thought, *'I cannot remember that portcullis ever being raised. Not even once.'*

"Gather your families and flee for the plains!" Shyamala shouted at some bewildered servants. "Lizarme are nearing the harbour!"

The drawbridge had already been lowered and the two galfolk wasted no time sprinting onto it, both pinching their nostrils in a futile attempt to stem the stench of turds bobbing in the moat. After crossing the bridge, they quickly raced through the barbican and beneath the bretèche. Scooting down more winding steps brought them into the lower bailey and near to the stables.

A cross-looking ape stood with both fists propped against her hips. Her skullcap and the flanged mace slung across her back made her appear even taller and more menacing. She wore thick breeches, tucked into her highboots, and a sleeveless jerkin over her padded doublet. Clearly, her mind was bent on battle and her purple lips were not at all puckered to make amused. She was Tianga the warrior now.

"What kept you two?" Tianga demanded to know. "Do you think this is some sort of game we're all on about?"

"W-We came as swiftly as we could," Helenia managed in her own defense.

"Which wasn't near swift enough," Tianga snapped back. "You heard the king, Helenia. I am to look out for you. Not a responsibility I intend to take lightly. Now come, let us make haste."

"Tianga, you are not my keeper..."

"No, Helenia, I am not your keeper. What I am is your friend. I love you both as sisters, but this is no time to tarry. Your father's Royal Guard is already feeding oil to flames all about the docks. Prod Sergon is no sap. The moment he sees what we're about he will dispatch flocks of dacts to batter our carts and wagons – anything to slow the flow of refugees out of the city. He needs as many humanfolk hostages as possible to make your father capitulate.

"Chaps Bridle and Arduk have already gone to fetch our mounts. It shan't take their skilled hands but a few bits to saddle your steed, Helenia. Then we must be off. Shyamala will ride with me. See there, smoke already billows skyward from the piers. We will exit the curtain wall through the eastern gate. The southern gate will be opened as well. There are still many pockets of woodland scattered across the plains. Perhaps the forest spirits will shield us?"

Looking westward, Helenia saw that Tianga's words rang true. Thick black smoke was already billowing skyward from several points along the shore.

Suddenly, a loud bellow trumpeted the arrival of a tuskwooly. A frail lad with curly locks and a freckled face rode atop the enormous beast's back. Clad merely in a tattered tunic and without footwear of any kind, the lad gently patted the anxious pachyderm's head and leaned lower to speak strange words into one of its flappy ears.

In response, the tuskwooly raised its long trunk as if to trumpet again, then simply shook its head and bowed low to let the lad slide off its haunch to the ground.

Arduk locked his eyes upon Tianga.

Tianga and Shyamala exchanged wary glances.

Noting the ape's hesitant demeanor, Arduk motioned for her to mount the tuskwooly. "Bowing pains Masshag's legs," he explained.

Again, Tianga and Shyamala exchanged wary glances.

"Thank you, Arduk," Helenia injected just as an old stable master with a weathered face led her royal steed along by its bridle. "And thank you as well, Chaps. Breakneck seems fresh as dew this day."

Chaps granted her a cruddy smile. "Aye, Princess. Fed and fit for a gallop, she be."

Helenia took the bridle from Chaps wrinkled hand and placed her own hand on his shoulder. "Chaps, you must gather your family and make haste away from the city. A large lizarme invasion force is about to attack."

"That beed what I heerd," Chaps acknowledged, patting her hand. "Nary ye fret, Princess. Right as we chew the blabble, me missus and me tots and me grandtots all be loading thine carts to be off. Arduk and I will stay to help feed the flames and slow the *scaleez* so others can flee. In due course we will follow."

"No!" Helenia shouted in shock. "I-I mean, you two mustn't – I mean, the city is lost and the Royal Guard is tending to such things. You and Arduk must leave at …"

"Shhhh," Chaps whispered. "We will fare fine, Princess. Destiny always be fixin' a good watch over us. Arduk says the forest spirits be liken to side with us as well. Now best ye ride off at a gallop."

Helenia was muted. She turned her eyes onto Arduk, who merely shrugged and gestured for her to mount her steed.

"Hurry, Helenia," Tianga coaxed as she pushed Shyamala up onto her tuskwooly's back. "We must be off before the roads are crammed."

"Princess Tianga speaks sense," Chaps noted, patting Helenia's shaky hand. "Ye must be off on the swift. Nary ye fret over us. Arduk and me will keep keen of wit and his howler pack will warn us of trouble. The scaleez shan't take us by stealth."

Helenia was disturbed by Chaps' racial slur against the lizarme, for she did not favour such speech; war or no war. Still, she pressed her lips against the old stable master's clammy cheek, and then turned to do likewise with Arduk. But the young ladfolk had already turned from her and was rushing back into the stable.

"Arduk must tend to more steeds," Chaps explained. "Aeronts mostly. Aside to the antemi themselves, his be the only voice they heed. An odd lad, that one. Much prefers beasts over humanfolk."

Helenia had long been a skilled rider. She stuck her highboot into a stirrup and effortlessly swung her leg across Breakneck's back. "Keep keen of wit, Chaps. And do look out for Arduk."

Chaps Bridle grinned knowingly. "Nary ye fret, Princess. Young Arduk can fend for himself. Him beed reared by howlers in the wild. Seed blessed him with speed and spit and strength well above his size. Ye can pity any scaleez who seek to scrap

161

with him. A few dockside brawlers can vouch to such. One of their mates be less an ear and some teeth for seeking a scrap with Arduk."

"Yes, I heard all about that," Helenia noted with disgust.

"Gnawed it clean off, Arduk did!" Chaps exclaimed with pride. Then, noting the princess' disapproval, he explained, "Big Butch cornered him and taunted him with a stick to start things up. Kept poking him with it. Figured he'd force a few bellybursts from his mates. Demanded the young lad snap n' growl like a howler, he did. Big Butch shoulda' knowed better. Arduk's yellow eyes gave his warning. Only Butch beed so smashed on stalk sauce and so set on makin' his mates laugh that he never seed what toppled him till he was sprawled flat on the boards being choked to the throat. Thank Destiny I beed there to stop it or Butch apt to be rotting with the worms. So nary ye fret, my Princess, young Arduk will fare just fine."

"Even so, please keep watch over him. Promise me, Chaps."

Chaps offered her a cruddy smile. "Ye know I will, Princess. I will keep him at me side until we've beaten the scaleez back clean across the Divides."

Helenia offered Chaps a smile of her own. "Thank you," she said, before prompting her steed to catch up with Tianga and Shyamala.

Before fleeing east onto the plains, the three friends paused to sight west over the city. Capital was now a buzzers hive of activity. Already, the opulent coaches and carriages of the nobility were turning from their long castle drives out onto the cobbled roads. Below them, the panicky pomps were scurrying about their stone manors and hastily loading their own carriages with every item they could jam inside.

"Fools," Tianga spat out. "As if any of those items should matter right now. It never ceases to baffle me how so many humanfolk place objects above what truly matters in life. They'll lose their own tots before they misplace a brooch."

Shyamala and Helenia could only nod in agreement.

Lower down the slope, tiny dots were scurrying about amongst the brick homes of the guild workers and artists. Many wagons had already drawn out onto the cobblestone roads and were veering up the steep grade towards the mansions.

Helenia thought, *'There is going to be a jam if somebody doesn't bring order to this chaos.'*

Far below the brick and shingled homes sprawled the wooden hovels of the shoreside rookery with its mucky roads. The girls watched in silence as a mob of humanfolk started moving in mass up the slope.

A thick and dirty haze hung heavy over the tiny seaside shops with stone stacks as black smoke billowed up from the roofs of the warehouses and dry-docks; every single one of which was now offering itself as feed for the famished flames that devoured them. Some of the older wooden structures were already collapsing and splashing their orange embers about the boardwalk and onto any craft moored nearby. Several bulky supply vessels already had flames climbing up their masts and devouring their sails.

"Dearest Destiny," Shyamala gasped as one of the larger hoists snapped and crashed down onto some mounted guards. Both they and their steeds seemingly vanished within a pyre of flame and smoke.

"The bravery of your Royal Guard is unmatched," Tianga said with noted esteem.

"Many of their tots will be orphans," Helenia noted, her moist eyes still glued to the bedlam below.

"Helenia, we have done all we can here," Tianga noted, steering her tuskwooly about. "Come, we must get on before the road is blocked. Clive, follow!"

Helenia moved to spin her steed about, when activity out over Ga Bay snagged her sights. Shivers raced up her spine. Flocks of dacts were flapping in V's towards them!

"Helenia, what are you waiting for?" Shyamala asked, beckoning the young princess to follow. "We must make haste."

Reining Breakneck about, Helenia peered east across the fields and forest of the plains. Crude trails cut swaths through the swaying highgrass and husk crop, passing by an occasional barn or hut; perfect terrain for hiding from enemy troops or blending in to ambush. Providing, of course, that any telltale carts and carriages were abandoned.

Helenia again sighted her eyes west to take in the carnage and chaos of the evacuation. Carriages and wagons were moving in orderly file towards the south gate. However, the road leading up to the east gate was jammed due to collisions between carts and carriages. Down below, the mob was advancing, growing in power and scope. Vulnerable humanfolk were being trampled and left in its wake.

"Dearest Destiny," Helenia muttered, resighting her eyes past the shoreline. The dacts were now dropping altitude and closing ranks into single line formations. Clearly, they were preparing to attack. There was no time to waste.

"Those dacts won't matter if somebody doesn't quickly bring some semblance of order to this chaos!" Helenia yelled at no one in particular. "We are doing Sergon's work for him!"

"Helenia, come on!" Tianga shouted, drawing Masshag about. "My knights can help clear the road with their beasts!"

"Hurry, Helenia!" Shyamala added.

Helenia pointed out past the shoreline, directing their sights to the approaching flocks. "We can't just leave! We must bring some order to this chaos or few of our folk will even make it to the highgrass! Come on!"

"Helenia, what can we do!?" Shyamala shouted.

Helenia dismounted and drew one of her daggers. "We must clear the main road leading east! All coaches and carriages are to be commandeered and used to convey the tots and the feeble! Able-bodied adults will trek on foot in an orderly fashion! By my order, all else with wheels will be abandoned alongside the road and set ablaze! Tumbrils and barrows and wagons – put them all to the torch! Smoke may hinder the dacts!

"You knights over there! See to it that all evacuees bring with them only what they can carry and that they keep to the road! Have our foot soldiers deal swiftly and harshly with any troublemakers regardless of rank or status!"

The knights responded at once. "You there, surrender your carriage at once! You as well, duke and duchess! Surrender it now, by order of Princess Helenia – daughter of the king!"

"Foot soldiers, start filling the carriages with the young and the feeble!"

"You there! Move that beast and tumbril off the road! Now, or you'll feel my sabaton up your backside!"

Tianga and Shyamala exchanged bewildered looks before sighting back on Helenia, who was busy stomping about and shouting out orders. They watched with jaws dropped as the young princess did in fact put her boot to the backside of one brightly plumed duke who dared protest the loss of his carriage.

"I have never seen her behave like this. What shall we do?" Shyamala asked.

Tianga made amused. "What else can we do? She is her father's daughter. Hey, you there, did you not hear Princess Helenia! Move that wagon off the road at once lest my tuskwooly will move it for you! Hey, you! Yes, you! What do you think you're doing!? Get that tumbril..."

Helenia and Shyamala began running up and down the roadside, shouting orders at bewildered nobles and commandeering coaches and carriages. Tianga and Masshag opted to bash aside any wagons or carts blocking the road. Even Clive joined in, hissing and snapping to *encourage* slower beasts to pick up their hooves and vacate the road.

"All on foot keep to the right side of the road in orderly file!" Shyamala shouted. "By order of Princess Helenia!"

"Carriages keep to the left!" Helenia added. "You soldiers over there, see to it all abandoned wares are put to the torch! Make plenty of smoke and leave nothing of use to the enemy!"

"Yes, Princess! At once!"

"Conscript any bodies you need!"

"Yes, Princess! Hey, you lot over there! You're in his majesties army now! Pile up debris to be torched!"

"You two, commandeer that coach for the tots and the feeble! Quickly!"

"Do pray Morgue is merciful to us this day!" Shyamala shouted, pointing to the north and west.

Helenia sighted up to see the first flocks of dacts swooping in low for an attack. Lizarme flighters and lancers sat saddled between tilting wings. "Get under the carts!" she screamed; all to no avail, for the intended victims were too far away to hear her.

"Destiny, no!" Shyamala shrieked as the first barrage of bashing-balls and spears were dropped onto the terrified humanfolk.

Screaming erupted all along the road as carts were smashed and spears found their mark. Debris and bodies littered the center of the roadway, some still and some writhing.

"HOORRAY!!" shouted the humanfolk as an arrow stuck into a dact's eye and the wounded beast fell like a torn kite. "HOORRAY!!"

"Come on!" Helenia shouted at nobody in particular. "We must keep this column moving! Delay means Morgue! You there, take up and carry that tot!"

"It is not mine, Princess?"

"Are you questioning the princess? Perhaps my mace will…"

"N-No, Sir Knight. Come, little one. I will care for you until we find your family."

Plumes of choking smoke began billowing skyward, forcing dacts to climb and making it more difficult for flighters to sight in their targets. Cheers erupted whenever a careless dact dropped too low and came within range of humanfolk bolts; gasps and screams whenever a flock accurately targeted its drop.

"Eeeeeeeeee…"

"Whoop – Whoop – Whoop – Whoop…"

"Helenia! Look out!"

Heeding Shyamala's scream, Helenia spun about and ducked in the nik to avoid the sharp talons of a swooping dact. The momentum tripped her to the ground.

"Dacts to the north!" Tianga shouted, waving frantically with her hands. "Hide those tots under the carriages!"

Shyamala reacted at once. Scooping two tots up into her arms, she whirled about and scrambled beneath a wagon; where she hugged the wailing pair tightly as the dull thuds of spears sticking into wood sounded above them. She breathed deeply and stared out from between wheel spokes, taking in the violence and chaos raging all about her.

166

Iron bashing-balls were smashing carts and wagons into kindling. Some humanfolk wailed in pain from their wounds, while others would never feel pain again. A wounded dact crashed into a coach, sending both of its riders to an early meeting with Morgue; while above them an aeront and its lance-toting antema zipped off to find more prey. Everywhere, there was shouting and screeching and confusion.

Shyamala gasped as a shadow suddenly appeared over Helenia, mere moments before the dact fell to the ground behind her. "Helenia!" she shouted, handing the tots over to a galfolk and then dashing out from beneath the safety of the wagon.

Lancer and dact lay with Morgue, but the flighter slid from his beast's back and hobbled towards the young princess. He fumbled to unclip his scimitar.

Helenia likewise fumbled to unsheathe one of her hurling daggers, but her fingers would not do as she wished. It seemed as though they had become tangled together. "Dung!" she cussed.

"Oooaahh!" chanted the lizarma as he bore down on his much smaller adversary. His eyes looked at her with both mettle and dread.

Helenia lunged inside the lizarma's arc of swing, his blade slicing naught but the wind. She rudely slammed the palm of her hand up under her attacker's chin, grabbing hold of his arm with the other. Together, they fell to the ground.

Helenia wailed in pain as the lizarma bit into one of her fingers. Then a blow from her knee caused him to grunt the digit from his mouth.

"Help!" Helenia screamed, desperately trying to hold onto her attacker's arm lest he be able to thrust his weapon. "Somebody…"

Suddenly, a slender shape in a blue gown pounced upon the lizarma's back and long fingernails raked across his eyes. The wounded attacker was forced to neglect Helenia as he stood and spun to toss his tormentor from his back; all to no avail as the gallant galfolk's long legs were locked fast about his torso.

167

"Ahhhh!" screamed the lizarma as Shyamala again raked her fingernails to scratch out his eyes. He wailed in agony as her teeth chomped into one of his ears.

Around and around he spun, desperately trying to dislodge one antagonist, whilst the other held firm to his arm. With his free fist, he started striking out in blows. Again to no avail as neither galfolk had any intention of relaxing her grip.

Helenia dared not let go, for the blade slashed but a pinch from her face. "Help!" she screamed. "Help us!"

Neither galfolk was aware help was close at hand. A tall and lanky figure with blinkless black eyes was sprinting to aid them. His large larynx bobbed in cadence with each of his lengthy strides.

A black sleeve wrapped itself about the lizarma's throat and slammed all three bodies to the ground in one thrashing heap. The tall and lanky figure landed atop the scaly being and stabbed the tip of his sword deep into its chest; albeit not before he himself winced with a gasp and his face twisted in agony.

Both girls watched in muted horror as their rescuer gawked at them. In obvious pain, he pressed both palms to his ribcage. Blood squirted out from between his fingers, soaking his gloves and his lap. He nodded briefly, then gurgled his last and pitched forward atop the motionless lizarma.

"Stork!" Shyamala screamed, dropping to her knees and rolling the bodyguard over. Stork's head felt heavy in her lap. A crimson stain spread across her torn and dirty gown as she held him tight. "Stork! Please move, Stork! Please. Dearest Destiny, why is this happening? Why did you do that, Stork?"

Helenia dropped to her knees beside her friend and they both wept as one. Both galfolk were aware of a welcome swarm descending all about them. Their ears snagged the comforting hiss of a nearby spiketail.

"Princess, you must mourn on the move," a monotone voice asserted. "We must go now."

Both galfolk looked up through wet eyes and sighted upon a tall, bug-like being with bulging holoptic eyes. Blood dripped from the cudgel in his hand.

Glancing about, Helenia could see Tianga trying desperately to pry Clive's fangs from about the head of a downed dact. A limp lizarma was choked late in the spiketail's powerful tail.

"Ambassador Viceroy," Helenia managed at last. "Have you seen my father?"

The antema merely pointed behind her.

"Father!" Helenia shouted as she took in the sight of her father and Olob approaching just as fast as the old king's limbs would allow.

King Myro threw his frail arms about his only daughter and held her more tightly than her racing mind could ever recall. Tears of joy fell from his eyes.

"Sire, Ambassador Viceroy speaks with sense. The dacts will attack again. We must mourn on the move so as to hide in amongst the highgrass before they return."

Myro continued to hold his only daughter as he nodded to his historian. Then he shifted his eyes onto Shyamala and deliberately blinked his lids in gratitude.

Shyamala was surprised, yet nodded back at her king.

"We must bring Stork's body with us for a proper burning," Myro ordered. "His many cycles of loyal service have earned him more than a few drops of tears before we leave him as feed for the vultures. See how the gluttons circle above in wait of their feast."

"It will be done, sire" Olob assured his king.

Myro released his hold on his daughter and gently patted his historian on the shoulder before walking away.

Before moving to follow her father down the road to the plains, Helenia turned to steal one final stare back at Capital. Night was already preparing to attack, and the retreating sun now painted the western sky a bright orange. The enemy armada was sailing east and north along the coast. Sergon's plan had been thwarted by Olob's quick thinking. Most of the city's inhabitants would escape the invaders, and breathe to fight more battles.

While they trudged the rutted road towards the safety of the highgrass, the young princess could still smell the entire city engulfed in flames. Even so, she would not grieve. Her busy mind was already raging for revenge!

Sickly

Light from his oil lamp flickered off warm stone walls and calcite pillars as the gaunt old lizarma limped his way through the labyrinth of damp and slippery tunnels that crissed and crossed far beneath the bustling seaport of Dega Doom. Dug before the dawn of time by the eldest deity, Creation, the deepest tunnels were ever hot and ever wet and ever stale.

The constant drip from overhead stalactites thoroughly soaked the old lizarma's sleeveless tabard. Except for that of drops plopping into puddles, the only sounds were those of his own panting mixed with the shuffle of his mangled limb whenever he dragged it along behind him.

His movements were slow and laboured, and a sturdy walking stick was needed to help propel his hunched body forward. Cracked and swollen lips were parted to show his black teeth, and a slight wheeze bore witness to the effort his one able leg must make when bearing the burden of two.

Despite it all, his solitary eye was filled with the spit and spirit of youth. If he was nothing else, Sickly was a lizarma driven by the passion of his beliefs.

As he continued winding his way down ever deeper into the labyrinth, the determined leader of the hungry ones took little note of his surroundings. His thoughts were far removed. He barely even noticed the reek and the rustling of camps of blackwings, having passed them by countless times before.

The purpose of Sickly's descent weighed heavy on his mind. He must now order into battle the legion of spoilers whose prods were already gathered about the three turquoise pools that lay still and clear and glowing deep down inside the bowels of the weeping cavern; the very same sanctuary where rebels had met in secret since before his own birth. It was a secure and hostile place where even Prod Gilas silence squads dared never venture, having long ago learned the subterranean maze below Dega Doom was the rightful domain of the hungry ones. Any who pursued them down into the maze were much more apt to meet Morgue than they were to return safely to the surface.

According to legend, the turquois pools have been in place since Creation first forged time; that they are filled by the tears of every widow whose mate had been slain in battle. However, Sickly did not believe such tall tales, for he was always practical and secular in his reasoning. He had long ago concluded the pools were fed by subterranean streams flowing beneath the surface of The Continent; frigid streams that had never once felt the warmth of the sun. Eyeless finners had been seen swimming about in the crystal clear water, plus Sickly himself had drank from such pools and not once had he detected even the slightest trace of brine; which, of course, one should surely taste if the pools had been filled by tears.

Yet Sickly's thoughts were not about how or when the pools were filled. Not at all. Instead, his thoughts were focused on one task and one task only; how to properly address the legion and make its spoilers eager for battle – and for freedom. He himself had long wanted a new structure for his nation. Not just for his fellow hungry ones, but for all lizarme. A structure whereby those in power must be elected to their posts, hence power would no longer be the sole privilege of the ruling elites. One lizarma, one vote. Both genders. Such was his vision.

Albeit, Sickly had also spent many restless nights worrying about such a structure: *'What of lizarme nature? Would it place lizarme in positions of power who would misuse the public purse to maintain power and thereby bankrupt the nation? Could the typical lizarma be trusted to place the collective good before their own selfish demands? Or would they flock to those who would buy their votes with their very own tax coins? And what of justice? Suppose the masses should become dependent on lizarme leaders for their own protection. Would that not render them once again mere vassals of the state? And what of education? Would lizarme tots be taught how to think – or would young minds be schooled in what to think? If it becomes the latter, then are they not simply trading one despotic tyranny for another?'*

172

One question more than any other troubled Sickly most: *'What if the masses should fail to grasp that the only true protection they will ever have against tyranny is political and social freedom of speech – that those with power must never be permitted to decide for all what each lizarma can or cannot say – or read – or write – or think – or feel – or believe? History has long shown that those who seek power often crave it absolute. They want it all, even though all will never be enough.*

'Given the chance, they will enact laws to still dissent; always for feigned righteous reasons, of course. Youth will become their weapon of choice, with the aged branded an enemy. The young, so infused with a hatred of free thought, will rashly condemn themselves into servitude without even knowing it. Could such events come to pass? Why not? Time alone will tell...'

Sickly was not a leader drunk with power. To rule over others had never been his ambition. He often told his fighters, "Revenge has no place in our struggle." To him, there was nothing just in swapping an old tyranny for a new tyranny. Where is the merit in that? *'After all, opposing extremists often have more in common with one another than they do with those trapped in the middle. Both crave power. Both are bullies.'*

Sickly's thoughts turned to the battle yet to come and the consequences should the hungry ones suffer defeat. Defeat that was more probable than possible.

"Destiny," he muttered in a rare prayer, "If I am mistaken in my beliefs and you do exist, please bring about an early end to this war so both sides will be spared the senseless spillage of blood. The youth of our new nation deserve a chance to find their own way to Morgue without the aid of a blade or a bolt. So I beg of you, Destiny, will you please keep with us in our struggle. It is my only wish that by defeating Pid and ending this civil war we may all strive to build a better continent. A continent where all lizarme dwell alongside one another without quarrel. A continent where lizarme and apes and humanfolk will prefer trade over conquest. A continent at peace."

As he continued his trek through the maze of corridors and caverns, Sickly took note of the many hovels his hungry ones had cut into the rock. Entire families were often crowded into tiny caves no bigger than a small carriage. Caves that were empty now, as every dweller had gathered about the pools to see their small army march off to engage the enemy above.

He took note of the near empty ration shelves where his selfless followers would divvy up their meager resources, doling out equal shares of food based on a family's size and needs. He recalled how long before he began to organize his rebels they would quarrel over the tiniest morsel of food, or even over a strip of ragged cloth from the body of one departed. Thankfully, things were much different now. His followers had one thing they had lacked in the past; they now possessed the one quality that can topple empires: HOPE.

Such a small word, hope. Small, yet powerful. For without hope one cannot tap the well of courage hiding deep within the soul of every being. However, with hope, even the smallest and most timid of beings can muster a strength of mind that can conquer fear. And to conquer fear is to conquer all.

Sickly became aware of the growing rumble of many voices off in the distance. He was getting close now and could feel the energy of his hungry ones waiting for him to speak.

A faint glow appeared before him as two guards parted tattered curtains to expose the interior of the Grotto of Elders. It was in the grotto where he and his prod commanders had often met to discuss the future of their nation. Learn valuable lessons from the past, yes – but never dwell there. Starve the past, feed the future. For without dreams of a better future, one has already met Morgue – they just haven't stopped breathing yet.

Sickly dragged his mangled limb into the grotto, then paused briefly to take in those aged hungry ones who were gathered around the oblong slab. The very same slab where countless raids had been planned. The very same slab where the concept of a free society had been birthed so many cycles ago.

He exchanged nods and smiles with all of the rough and familiar faces that offered him stares of love and respect. His eye returned their fondness in kind.

Finally, Sickly set his sights upon a aged and frail lizarma with wrinkled amber flesh and sightless purple eyes. "Ah, welcome Squamata," he said, limping closer to his old friend. "You have trekked far and at great personal risk to join us. We intend to attack in mass this very night. Not just here in Dega Doom, but also in the streets of Cracow itself. With smaller raids in hamlets all throughout the Great Forests."

Sickly paused to pass his lamp to one of the elders, then placed a hand upon Squamata's shoulder. "Tell me, how are things in the desert?"

Squamata frowned and shook his head. "Not well, I'm sad to say. Recruitment to our cause is stagnant. We have enlisted barely one thousand new spoilers this entire cycle. The silence squads have been most brutal of late, even for them. It seems dissention in his home territory has brought much chagrin to Gila. And we both know how Gila feels about being made to look the fool. It matters not that he is one.

"Despite our small numbers, those who are with us will rise up against Pid's troops this night. Their passion and pluck are second to none. It is the silence squads who will feel their wrath first. Call it revenge woven in strategy. From this dusk forward, Gila's thugs will greet every dusk with needled nerves. That I can promise you."

Sickly fondly patted Squamata's shoulder. "Old friend, it matters not their numbers just so long as they strike first and strike hard. From this dusk forward we will attack the enemy every single night until Pid himself bows before Morgue. Our cause is just and we shall prevail. That I can promise you."

Mumblings of support flowed about the grotto as every elder nodded his or her approval.

"Large or small, any raid against Pid is a good raid, Squamata" one elder put in. "Each soldier Dorak must deploy into the desert is one less we must contend with elsewhere. It is all to the good."

"Such is so," Sickly agreed. "We have finally assembled and equipped an army we can all be proud of. Now let us send our spoilers forth into battle."

"To victory!" shouted one of the elders.

"TO VICTORY!!" echoed the others.

All elders moved aside to permit Sickly and Squamata to take up the lead. Thereupon they followed the pair across the grotto.

At the furthest end of the grotto, two young lizarma hastened to part a pair of hide curtains which sealed the cave's mouth. Sickly and the entire group then filed out onto a rocky ledge that provided a clear vantage over all of the weeping cavern.

Sickly drew his biggest breath as he scanned over the awesome spectacle before him. The rocky ledge was located about halfway up the massive cavern's towering walls, thus permitting him an unobstructed view down upon the three turquoise pools that lay still and clear and glowing in its center. Like the panes of a blue mirror.

Numerous rafts drifted gently about the surface, each supporting its own small group of torch bearers. The glow from the torches reflected off the pools' smooth surfaces and bounced about the cavern's glittering walls. Tapered red stalactites speared down from the concave ceiling above.

Ranks of armed spoilers stood still and proud all around the pools. Many more hungry ones were packed amongst the army of stalagmites that reached up like bloody claws from the cavern floor, while still more dangled their limbs freely from the lips of ledges or were packed tight into the mouths of caves.

Suddenly, a lone lizarma started to bang her club hard against her shield. Another quickly joined her. Followed by yet another....

Tears seeped from Sickly's eye as virtually all of his fighters hastened to join in. Some began banging the butts of their tridents on the stone floor. Others slapped their blades against their crude armor. Even those hungry ones without weapons started stomping and clapping to the beat of the shields; whilst tots of suckling age wailed their displeasure at the crescendo that pained their young ears.

The noise within the cavern soon climbed to pain all ears, yet Sickly would not cover his. To him the booming echo was a song of love, and he permitted it to continue unabated.

Eventually, the crescendo began to ebb and the cavern became filled with the restless rattle of an army anxious to be off. All eyes locked upon their aged leader, who had taken the servants and villeins of their society and forged them into the well-disciplined and proud fighting force standing before him. Not a single eye was without tears as they eagerly awaited his order. They would follow him into Morgue's maze itself.

Sickly could not call out. Emotion had dammed his throat. No matter how hard he tried, he could not swallow the ball of feelings lodged there. So he merely raised his stepping stick high atop his head and waited for silence to rule the moment. His moment. No, their moment. It was a moment for every lizarma who had ever wanted opportunity and who had always been denied such based solely on the level of their birth. It was a moment for the masses.

Soon one could hear naught but the rhythm of breath and the pounding of hearts as the crowd stood tense and ready for Sickly to act. Not a single hungry one offered up so much as a whisper. It was as though each knew this was a turning point of history.

Sickly stared down into their eager eyes. *'Yes,'* he thought, *'Their time is now. They are no longer ruled by fear. The hopeless have become the hopeful. From this night forward, let fear forge itself a new prison in the minds of the master class!'*

With that thought fixed firmly in mind, Sickly brought the shaft of his stepping stick down hard upon a rocky crag. The impact from the blow sent a sharp clack across the cavern. It bounced about the ceiling and walls.

"HOORRAY!!!!"

At once, unit leaders wheeled about and started barking orders to their spoilers. Almost as though they were all lashed together, the entire army started to move in orderly sync towards their assigned corridors. Rank upon rank marched in lockstep behind their commanders, as if filing off to war was the most natural thing for them to do; perhaps because, at this critical point in their long and tormented history, it was.

Sickly and the other elders watched with pride as their brave followers started vanishing into the darkness of the corridors leading up to the surface. Not a tongue wagged until the last troops, as well as their families and supporters, had all passed from view.

For some time thereafter, Sickly simply stood and looked out over the empty cavern, staring in silence until all of the torches were snuffed. Then he smiled briefly at Squamata before turning and stepping back into the stillness of the vacant grotto. There he humbly bowed before the oblong slab and offered prayers unto a deity he did not even believe in. Such was his fear of failure.

High above the grotto, only the rumbling skysheep witnessed the multitude of dark forms silently emerging from the bowels of the ground and spilling into the narrow streets of Dega Doom. In Cracow, and in many hamlets and villages all across Pid's realm, similar scenes were unfolding. Each vague form seeking to butcher others of their own kind; such being the cost of civil war – and, be it Destiny's will, of victory...?

The Wall

A chilly blast of wind whipped Prince Aytik's cloak about his shoulders and head. Peeling the cloth from his face, he wrestled it tight about his torso and held it firmly in check until the gust had waned. Intense winds had always blown eastward through the pass, but they felt especially powerful when one was standing high atop the wall. In fact, were soldiers not alert to quickly brace their stance, an errant gust catching them unawares might blow them clean over the edge. Such had happened before.

Aytik kept both feet planted at the ready. Peering west over the wall, his straining eyes sighted naught but blackness. Even the moon and its army of skytwinklers were hidden behind black skysheep. Only at brief intervals did the moon find a break in the flock; then its beams would fill the charred pass with shadows.

To the east, Day's fingers reached atop the distant horizon, pushing up beneath the skysheep. Soon warmth and colour would return, negating the need for torches and lanterns.

Aytik turned to the tall figure at his side. "I sense we're in for a wetting."

"I agree. But not this side of midday," Torak's replied.

"Be quiet," Kryle's husky voice berated from the shadows. "Engage your ears west."

For a time, only breath disturbed the silence. Until Torak noted, "Chanting?"

"It is," Kryle concurred, stepping into the glow of a lantern.

"I don't hear anything?" Aytik offered.

Prince Torak cocked his head to better snag any sound drifting up the pass. "Ah, yes. I hear it much clearer now. The lizarme are certainly on about something. Are they trying to unnerve us?"

"No, Prince," Kryle replied. "They mean to do battle."

"How can you be so certain?" Aytik asked.

"I can feel it in my bones," Kryle explained, keeping his gaze to the west. "Prod Tarawa will attack shortly past the peek of dawn. We must make ready and move our troops into position now. Once he attacks, there will be no time to dither. There is nothing hesitant in his nature, hence there must be nothing hesitant in ours. This battle will be a slugfest. Tarawa's strategy has always been the same; plan your offensive carefully, then strike fast and hard. He is a brilliant strategist who will swiftly change tactics as the battle unfolds. Doyen Zira!"

"Yes, Doyen Commander!"

"Have our troops mustered for battle!"

"At once, Doyen Commander!"

"Also, inform our allies the enemy is mounting their attack!"

"At once, Doyen Commander!"

"Kryle, shall I order our archers to spread out along the wall-walk?" Aytik asked. "They are of no use on the ground behind the wall."

"Doyen Grob and Commander Shrike have already sorted the matter, Aytik. Your archers will gather atop any bastions that have wickets or sally ports – especially any with portcullis gates. They are the weakest links in the wall and it is there where Prod Tarawa will concentrate the brunt of his barrage. He will try to exploit any breaches before our engineers can plug them. It is then and there where your archers will be needed the most. Return to your army, I can manage things up here."

Aytik placed a hand upon his cully's shoulder. "I fight alongside you. From up here I can best view the field of battle and better direct my own troops."

Kryle turned to set his serious black eyes upon his much smaller cully. His breath spouted in vapor. "After the battle begins, there may be little chance of you directing anything from up here. My commanders have signal flags to relay my orders as best they can, but there will be chaos on both sides. I think it best you rejoin your army on the ground."

Aytik offered up a defiant frown. "And I think we must trust in Destiny – and in the ability of our commanders and troops to think and act on their own this day. Either way, I'm staying up here with you. If Destiny does not smile on us this day, then you and I will meet Morgue together."

Kryle sighed and made amused. He fondly rapped his knuckles on Aytik's helmet. "When last did I tell you I love you?"

"Long ago," Aytik replied, pushing his helmet back in place. "But none ever had a better cully than I have in you."

"None save for myself," Kryle responded. Then he blew breath to warm his numbed fingers.

Both turned to peer west past the parapet. Already, some shadows in the pass were beginning to take on shapes.

Aytik thought briefly about meeting Morgue. About how either nothing would matter post life – or everything would? Perhaps the answer was due him this very day? He thought of Shyamala.

"She will fare fine," Kryle said. "I have no intention of meeting Morgue before you two are wed. Especially given that there will be much feasting and merrymaking. And plenty of wine and ale I'm sure."

Aytik offered up a smile. "There will be all of that. How did you know I was thinking of her?"

"Ha!" Kryle blurted. "When are you not thinking of her?"

Aytik blushed before speaking. "What of you and Tianga? When will you two wed? Simply choose a date and do it."

Kryle's face sank with a sigh. "I wish it were that simple."

"It is that simple," Aytik scolded. "You love her. She loves you. You are properly betrothed. Her family approves. To Morgue with the judgement of bigots. I thought you were past all that, Kryle?"

"I was always past it, Aytik. It's just that with so much going on…" Kryle began, before something snagged his sights and stayed his tongue.

"What is it?" Aytik asked, straining his sights to the west.

"Look, there. Movement in the forest beyond the clearing. The enemy advances."

Training his gaze upon the distant treeline, Aytik noted a slight rustling of the foliage. His ears snagged the faint sound of chanting floating in on the wind.

"OOAAHH!!"

"Strange," Kryle suddenly said, "This thing we mortals call power, I mean. It makes us mad as frothing howlers."

Uncertain of how best to respond to his cully's words, Aytik at first bit his lip in silence. Then he offered up his own thoughts on the matter. "Perhaps it is our inherent inability to be content with what we do have that makes us crave power all the more. Or perhaps it is our lack of faith in Destiny that fuels our ambitions?"

"Perhaps both," Kryle replied. "Still, it is hard to believe these bamboo shoots are all that stand between freedom and tyranny. This very day so many youths on both sides of this barrier will meet Morgue. And all for what? Our passion for power over others? Our desire to possess that which we do not need? Our inability to share freely with those around us? Foolish pride that bars us from hearing one another? Why do we mortals behave like this? Why are we so lost? What is the matter with us?"

"I suppose it all depends on what one is fighting for," Aytik offered.

"I don't know what's wrong with we mortals," Torak put in. "I often ask myself how it is so many can be so foolish so often? So lacking in common sense? I believe every war ever fought was driven by greed. Somebody wanted to take something away from somebody else – or was afraid somebody else would take something away from them."

"OOAAHH!!"

Kryle huffed his displeasure. "Let's just hope when this Second Continental War is over we will have finally learned our lesson. It is certainly a sad account of our mortal stupidity that we must assign our wars numbers."

Both princes nodded in agreement.

"OOAAHH!!"

"Doyen Commander!" an ape shouted, pointing frantically to the west. "The enemy emerges from the forest!"

It was true. All along the treeline, bushes were rustling and shaking as a dark mass began emerging out into the open.

"OOAAHH!! OOAAHH!! OOAAHH!!"

"This could be the deciding battle of the war," Torak suggested.

"It will be," Kryle replied.

The apes and humanfolk could only stare in nervous anticipation and wait as rank upon rank of enemy troops kept emerging from the forest and began marching up the pass. Amongst them, teams of snapping rexids hauled catapults and wagons heaped high with shot. Many of the lizarme bore long siege ladders, or sturdy planks to bridge the moat.

Others carried flaming torches, or bows and quivers packed with arrows. A great many bore long pikes with their unit colours flapping in the breeze, or waved banners depicting crossed tridents atop a flaming red sun. All marched forward with purpose, stepping in time to their own chants and the blatant beating of shields.

"OOAAHH!! OOAAHH!! OOAAHH!!"

The green hordes were led by a tall and lanky lizarma brandishing a scimitar high atop his head.

"Tarawa," Torak muttered.

"You've seen him before?" Aytik asked.

"No, but see how he waves his scimitar to encourage the others. It is he. I'd wager my breath on it."

"It is he," Kryle said knowingly.

"Look!" Torak suddenly blurted, pointing far to the west.

Aytik felt a swarm of bellybees buzzing about his guts as he took in the source of Torak's alarm. Enemy flocks were flapping skyward from the forest. Each dact bore a flighter and a lancer, and clenched bashing-balls or spears in their sharp talons.

"There are too many to count," a familiar voice observed.

Aytik turned to encounter a grey ape-lad with unique amber eyes. Behind him hunched a serious ape-gal with a marred face.

"Kwok? Kea?" Aytik said with some surprise.

"We're not letting you hoard all the fun?" Kwok stated in jest. Then he made amused.

Kea, of course, did not.

Aytik faked a smile before turning about to sight down the eastern face of the wall. Activity and organized chaos were in full swing amongst the troops. Both black and white apes were scrambling up the nets to the wall-walk, while crude block and tackle hoists lifted skids packed with humanfolk archers atop the bastions to help cover the wickets. Further back, units of ape and humanfolk soldiers were being quick-marched to their positions, while snouthorns, steeds and tuskwoolies all trotted about nervously in their pens.

Aytik could not help but admire the discipline of some white apes as they raised and lowered their long pikes in perfect sync. Each blue face was overwrought with thought.

Black apes stood still at their posts, clenching their axes and shields. All donned spiked helmets for butting. None seemed assured.

Further north, mounted humanfolk knights in full battle armour were lining up to defend portcullis gates. All along the base of the wall, ape riders were doing likewise.

One irate tuskwooly bellowed its displeasure at the ruckus, which encouraged many others to do likewise. It prompted the steeds and the snouthorns to snort in accord.

"They know a battle is coming," Torak said. "I sometimes wonder if beasts can sight into the future."

"Perhaps they can," Kryle suggested.

Aytik shifted his sights onto the nearest bastion, where the apes had already cocked their bolt thrower and aimed it at the empty sky. All knew it would soon feast on targets as the first flocks of dacts had already passed over their ground troops and were dropping in low for an attack.

"Shields up!" Kryle screamed. "Keep tight to the shoots!"

"You there!" shouted an angry voice. "Come out from beneath those planks! Both of you!"

"You heard the commander! Move it! And keep a firm grip on your shields!"

Aytik deliberately drew his sword and crouched close to the shoots. While peeking out from beneath his shield, his ears caught the distinct twang of the bolt thrower.

"HOORRAY!!"

Cheering erupted all along the wall-walk as an errant dact fell like a torn kite. Aytik watched with gritted teeth as both riders splashed down into the moat. He thought of the mud vipers.

"That water should cool their cockles," Torak jested.

A torrent of arrows filled the sky as humanfolk archers loosed their bows. Once again, Aytik's ears caught the distinct twang of the bolt thrower.

"HOORRAY!!"

And once again, cheering erupted all along the wall-walk as two more lizarme fell from their dact, which flapped aimlessly about with an arrow sticking from its neck. A flighter and lancer clung tight to another dact's back, until it rolled and pitched them to the wind; each flailing at air as they fell.

"Brace for attack!" a voice shouted.

"Here it comes!" added another. "Hug tight to the shoots and overlap thine shields!"

Aytik found himself wedged between Torak and Kwok. Initially he could only feel the shake of projectiles slamming into the shoots, until his ears caught the loud crack of a bashing-ball breaking off a piece of the parapet. Next came the steady *thud, thud, thud* of spears sticking into wood, and the *clack, clack, clack* of many more deflecting off shields. Several wounded apes could be heard wailing close by.

"Healer! We need a healer over here!"

"To the south!" somebody shouted. "Dacts to the south!"

Setting his sights south caused Aytik to gasp with wided eyes. It was true. A long column of dacts was bearing down on them from behind the wall. This time the shoots would afford them no protection!

"We've been tricked!" a frightened voice shouted.

"Get beneath the wall-walk and the hoardings!" Kryle shouted over the chaos. "Now!"

"Beneath the wall-walk and hoardings!" another voice echoed. "Dacts approach from the south!"

Suddenly, Aytik was yanked rudely from behind. The force of the grab stole his breath and stripped his shield from his grip.

He could only watch it fall while he dangled helplessly beneath the planks. With his guts sinking like stones, he looked up into Kwok's concerned amber eyes. Kea also kept a firm grip.

All along the parapet, apes and humanfolk were scrambling to swing beneath the wall-walk. Or to take shelter inside the hoardings.

Next came the crack of another ball bashing off a piece of the parapet, followed by the steady *thud, thud, thud* of many more spears sticking into planks.

Somehow, Aytik managed to grab hold of the climbing net and stop his body from swinging. That's when he became aware of a dark shadow above.

"Whoop – Whoop – Whoop…"

Aytik gasped as his eyes beheld the dact flapping in place near to where he clung for his very being. He could feel gusts from the wings blowing cool across his face, and see the crimson eyes of the frightened flighter as he fought to steady his mount. Bellybees swarmed into his gut as he watched the lancer spit an ape from the net.

Quickly gathering his wits and tapping his courage, Aytik struggled to re-sheath his sword. He fumbled for one of his hurling daggers. After what seemed like forever, his fingers felt a familiar hilt and he pulled the blade from its sheath. Without hesitation, he threw the weapon with all his force.

At first the flighter was stunned by shock. He reached down and pulled the dagger from his thigh. Blood dripped from the blade. Then he winced in pain and pitched forward; a bolt sticking into his back.

"EEEEEEEEE!!" screamed the dact as an arrow pierced its gizzard.

Two powerful hands grabbed onto the lancer's weapon and yanked him rudely from the wounded beast's back. The unfortunate lizarma flailed at breeze as he fell to meet Morgue.

Aytik could only stare in shock as Kryle spun the lance about and thrust it into the dact. The beast gurgled and spat blood before falling from flight.

Aytik retrieved his sword just as another dact streaked past without riders. Then he turned to see Torak climbing back atop the wall-walk. "Torak! What are you about!"

"I can't do battle whilst clinging to a net!" Torak shouted back. "I need to plant my feet!"

"Stay here with Kea!" Kwok instructed. "I will ascend and guard his back!"

"I'm coming with you!" Aytik shouted, struggling to break free of the ape-gal's grip. "We're no safer here!"

Kea looked to Kryle for direction.

Kryle hesitated before nodding at her. Only then did the powerful ape-gal lax her hold on the prince.

As Aytik pulled himself back atop the wall-walk, he sighted many still forms strewn about the broken planks. Their eyes stared at naught.

Pushing to his feet, he peered west over the parapet. The spectacle below punched him in the gut.

Lizarme engineers had built floating footbridges and enemy soldiers were now filing across the moat and clambering up the ramparts. Some had already braced their siege ladders and were climbing for the parapet. The dacts had clearly succeeded in their tasks of clearing the parapet and buying their ground troops much needed time.

Aytik's ears snagged the distinct *clack* of enemy catapults hurling their stone or iron projectiles. He could only watch as a barrage of the latter slammed into a nearby bastion. Chunks of stone crumbled and fell to the plinth, before rolling down the rampart and on into the moat.

"Screeeeech!! Screeeeech!!"

Aytik ducked just in the nik as a lance clipped his helmet.

"Screeeeech!! Screee…"

The dact fell silent as an arrow found its mark.

The lancer dropped his weapon and dove from the beast's back, barely clinging onto the merlon. With much effort, he began pulling himself over the parapet.

Aytik was momentarily frozen by the spectacle. He quickly gathered his thoughts and swung his sword downward with full force, chopping off fingers. With his enemy dangling helplessly by the other hand, Aytik hesitated and looked deep into pleading eyes. He noted no hatred or anger in them. Just fear. Pity forced him to close his own eyes while delivering the fatal thrust; only by doing so was he able to slight his own conscience.

Aytik had expected his blade to sink effortlessly into soft tissue just as if he was skewering meat at a feast, but its tip struck bone and jammed his elbow. Dropping to his knees, he opened his eyes to see the lizarma's severed digits. The sickening sight moved him to retch.

Once he had reclaimed his senses, the shaken prince pushed up to his feet. Solemn winds bore the stench of Morgue. Pressing one hand against a shoot to steady himself, he brandished his sword with the other. His eyes shifted to survey the carnage and chaos all about the wall.

Lizarme archers were loosing flaming arrows, while catapults hurled fire-pots filled with burning pitch. Nonetheless, the stubborn bamboo was proving quite slow to catch. Many dacts still swooped low over the parapet as their lancers tried to spit the defenders, thereby buying their ground troops more time to climb the ladders.

Many of the hoardings had been smashed and long sections of the wall-walk were broken away. Lifeless forms were strewn all about the debris, some with eyes frozen wide with fright. Other bodies dangled from planks or climbing nets. A downed dact was impaled on sharp shoots. Beside it lay a lizarma's headless torso.

Shouting, screaming, wailing, whistles, horns; these were the sounds that filled Aytik's ears. Stealing another glance along the west face of the wall, he saw that in some sections the lizarme had climbed almost up to the parapet. In most other sections, motionless lizarme were piling up or floating face down in the moat. Everywhere, patches of dirt were stained dark by blood.

True to Kryle's words, Tarawa's troops just kept coming and coming. Lizarme soldiers were still filing across the footbridges, while their engineers were hastily floating more into place. Enemy catapults kept pounding away at every bastion, trying to breach its portcullis. Already, some lizarme commanders were pointing excitedly at a demolished portcullis and flailing their arms for assault troops to storm through the gap before ape engineers could plug it.

Turning about, Aytik took in the spectacle along the eastern base of the wall. Many corpses lay still amongst piles of broken planks and shoots. Wounded soldiers were writhing in agony, while stretcher bearers scrambled to evacuate both humanfolk and apes to the infirmary. Lizarme wounded were being put to the spit.

Black apes on snouthorns were primed and ready behind the crumbling bastions. White apes on tuskwoolies were poised to plug any breaches. Further north, Aytik could see his own knights couching their lances to charge. In every case, ranks of foot soldiers were being wheeled about into position behind the beasts.

"Dacts!" a panicky voice screamed.

"Shields up!" shouted another.

Aytik felt his stomach sink as he turned about to find a flock of dacts flapping directly for his section of the wall. Each beast clenched bundles of spears. Behind them a second flock clenched bashing-balls. A third flock took up the rear, with each rider holding a hide sack.

Aytik thought, *'I am without shield... Destiny, side with me!'*

"Aytik, take cover with us!" a familiar voice shouted.

Moments later Aytik found himself wedged between Kea and Kwok, each taking cover beneath their shields. There they anxiously awaited the barrage.

But the barrage never came. Instead, as they swooped near to the wall, all of the dacts with bashing-balls suddenly broke formation and veered towards the damaged bastions. The balls slammed into their targets, crumbling stone and rolling up clouds of choking dust.

Dacts clutching spears overshot the parapet and dropped their missiles down upon the mounted warriors and their beasts. Some even swooped in low enough for lancers to skewer their foe.

The dacts bearing sacks also overshot the parapet and dumped caltrops down amongst the beasts; the simple yet ingenious weapons certain to pierce many hooves.

"Dung!" Aytik cussed.

Panic ruled the ranks as apes and humanfolk fell from their mounts. Some beasts reared and bolted with wooden shafts flapping from their haunches, while others limped about with caltrops stuck into their hooves.

"Tarawa knows we will charge our beasts to plug any gaps!" Torak shouted, joining Aytik beneath the shields. "Thus, he seeks to render them lame!"

"Whoop – Whoop – Whoop…Screeeeech!!"

"Prince – behind you!"

Aytik whirled about with sword in hand and parried to avoid being run through by a lance. Having cheated Morgue, he ducked and dodged to evade the dact's beak. He could feel gusts from its wings as its talons raked the wind.

"Screeeeech!! Screeeeech!! Scree…"

Suddenly, the flighter fell from the beast's back. An arrow stuck into the retreating dact as it veered and flapped away from the wall, while the lancer dropped his weapon and took hold of the reins.

"NO!"

Aytik wheeled about to find a grey ape cradling the head of a fallen ape-gal and weeping openly as he rocked her back and forth in his lap.

"Kea!" Aytik shouted, stepping towards his slain comrade. But a firm hand gripped his arm and he found himself staring up into familiar orange eyes.

"Leave them!" Torak shouted. "Look!"

Aytik gasped as he noted the source of Torak's alarm. A short sprint away, the rungs of a siege ladder were propped against the parapet.

Aytik spun about to find Kryle yelling something to a runner. Kryle kept on yelling even after the runner started swinging down the climbing net.

"Come on!" Torak shouted, dragging Aytik along with him. "We must defend the parapet!"

"I'm with you, Torak!"

The two allies bounded clumsily across the boards, arriving at the rungs just as a greenish face poked atop the parapet.

Torak deflected the prongs of the lizarma's trident with his shield, and then grabbed his foe by the throat. Somehow the determined lizarma still managed to swing a leg over the parapet and then pull himself entirely over the top. Both combatants fell to the planks.

Suddenly, a second head poked atop the parapet. A young lizarma was visibly frightened as he climbed over the top and dropped down onto the wall-walk. His eyes locked with Aytik's.

Without breaking stride, Aytik charged beneath the lizarma's trident and butted his helmet full force up into his face. He thrust deep with his blade.

Having dispatched his young foe, Aytik wheeled about with blade in swing. It sliced into a leg that dangled over the parapet. Next, the frightened prince stabbed his blade into an exposed belly. The doomed lizarma grunted before Aytik grabbed the wounded leg and flung his victim back over the wall.

"Aaaaa!"

Aytik barely stepped out of the way as Kryle charged towards the ladder. He watched as his cully grabbed the rails, wasting no time in shoving the ladder aside and sending several lizarme plummeting down to the rampart.

Next, Kryle grabbed the lower jaw of a lanky lizarma who was climbing over the parapet. The hapless being could only watch in pain and horror as the powerful ape popped his jaw from its socket while rudely shoving him back over the top.

Yet another green form was sent flailing over the parapet, his hands grasping naught but wind during his fall down to the rampart.

Torak pushed up to his feet, clenching a trident in hand. He bore a nasty gash about one of his eyes. Claw marks were raked across his face. A deep cut bled from his thigh. Seemingly undaunted, he nodded to tell the others he was still fit for a fight.

"There!" a voice screamed. "The enemy breaches the wall!"

It was true. The constant barrage of heavy stones and iron balls had knocked down one of the bastions. Some lizarme were already clambering over the heap of rubble and broken timber, locked in mortal combat with equally determined apes. Elated lizarme commanders were frantically pointing and flailing their arms for more foot soldiers and rexids to advance and storm the gap.

"What can we do to help them?" Aytik inquired of Kryle and Torak.

Kryle placed his hand upon Aytik's shoulder. "We can do nothing more from up here. Success now lies with our troops on the ground. My cavalry will charge their snouthorns together in a crash to plug any gaps. As will yours and Torak's. Then the foot soldiers will follow. We shall know soon enough if we are victor or vanquished. Until then, all we can do is protect the parapet and accept Destiny's will."

"Watch and pray," Torak added, wrapping a strip of cloth around his wounded thigh.

"If you feel you must," Kryle muttered.

"There!" a voice screamed.

"The white apes charge!" added another.

All eyes shifted to take in the spectacle unfolding below them. White ape commanders were charging their tuskwoolies directly into the breach.

"They'll trample their own soldiers as well," Aytik noted.

Kryle's tone was somber. "It must be done."

Aytik felt a stone sink in his belly, despite knowing his cully was right. The enemy must be stopped at any cost.

"We must keep vigilant for dacts," Kryle stated.

"We must," Aytik concurred, yet his eyes could not divert from events down below. Nor could his ears, for horns were sounding the attack.

One could almost feel the ground shake beneath their hooves as the shaggy herd charged into the gap. Their defiant eyes spit rage as they lowered their long ivory tusks to skewer. White ape riders did likewise with their long pikes. Foot soldiers followed close behind the beasts.

A chill shot up Aytik's spine as the lead tuskwooly scrambled atop the heap of rubble and timber. Several tridents flapped from its shaggy haunch as the furious beast skewered an unfortunate rexid and tossed it aside like a tot's doll. Terror and anguish splashed across the faces of both apes and lizarme as they desperately scrambled to get clear of the beast. Those who did not were trampled to meet Morgue.

Without warning, the tuskwooly lost its balance and tumbled back down the heap, leaving many crushed and breathless bodies in its path. With its leg now broken by the fall, the beast took to lashing out with its tusks.

More tuskwoolies were scrambling up the heap now. Again, both apes and lizarme scrambled to get clear; and again, those who did not were trampled to meet Morgue.

Aytik watched as the shaggy beasts continued their charge through the gap, emerging on the west side of the wall. The first beast through slipped on the steep slope of the rampart and slid down into the moat. Mangled green forms littered its wake.

A second beast also lost its balance and rolled down into the moat, crushing its own riders.

Panicky figures scurried about the mound as lizarme tried to flee the tuskwoolies, only to find there was no place to run. The beasts were steered both north and south along the rampart, struggling to maintain their balance. Some continued to slip and roll down the steep grade. Others managed to lumber onward.

Screams sliced the wind as a tuskwooly charged out onto a floating footbridge. Almost instantly, the wooden planks snapped beneath the beast's bulk and it splashed down into the moat.

One of the beast's riders somehow landed clear of any stakes. Pushing to her feet, the ape suddenly tensed and grabbed her leg. She flung aside a serpent, before cautiously slogging through the muck and the caltrops.

Aytik thought, *'Mud vipers never choose sides.'*

Soon so many tuskwoolies lay still in the moat that attacking lizarme took to using the carcasses as makeshift bridges. White ape foot soldiers began pouring through the gap to engage them.

Brave soldiers on both sides held their ground and fought well. The ramparts were littered with bodies, while many more floated about the moat.

Similar scenes were now unfolding all along the mound as the black apes and the humanfolk were likewise charging their beasts through breaches in the wall and engaging the enemy. Snouthorns snapped planks beneath their massive bulk, splashing down into the moat. Many a fleeing lizarma was trampled or spitted upon ivory horns as they sought escape. Even the normally fearless rexids were quick to cower and flee before the enraged pachyderms.

The smaller but more agile steeds were also having some success at pushing the enemy back from the gaps. Plus the steeds were also forcing the enemy back across the floating footbridges, which bowed but did not break beneath their weight. Lizarme legs and weapons became tangled as they turned to escape the galloping onslaught.

Pride seeped from Aytik's eyes as he watched a courageous unit of his foot soldiers battling their way across the planks. Then he gasped as he watched a stone barrage from an enemy catapult wipe them instantly from view.

The battle raged on and on as combatants fought to control the breaches. Catapults clacked with every shot, followed by bursts of flame or the crumbling of stone. There was the hiss of incoming projectiles and the twang of bolt throwers. Commanders blew incessantly upon their whistles. Signalers waved their flags and banners to relay messages.

Shortly past midday, with the battle showing no sign of waning, a series of crackling flashbolts and ground shaking skybangers announced the arrival of skyshowers. The ensuing spate swept up the pass like a river. In quick time the ramparts were churned into a slide of mud that poured into the rapidly rising moat.

"We can win!" Kryle shouted to top the wailing winds. "Such a deluge favours the defenders! Lizarme artillery will be hard-pressed to sight in their targets! Dact flighters will be hindered as well! Now our troops need only battle the ground forces before them! In such a quagmire as this, we can win! We will win!"

"Should we descend and join our troops beyond the wall!?" Aytik asked, scanning above for dacts.

"No!" Kryle replied. "We can be of more use by hurling debris down upon the enemy! See how Torak's troops are pushing them back along the muddy rampart towards our section!"

It was true. The white apes were beginning to push the green mob back along the slippery rampart. Some enemy troops now found themselves directly beneath the hoardings. Apes and humanfolk had already began dropping stones and pouring boiling oil down upon them.

"Look!" Torak shouted, pointing beyond the moat. "The enemy retreats! We have prevailed!"

Cheering erupted all along the parapet as lizarme began wading and swimming to get back across the moat. Others were sliding down the muddy ramparts, or slipping their way across the wet carcasses of beasts.

The sight of their comrades scrambling in retreat sapped lizarme morale and started siphoning soldiers away from their units. In short time, a great many more began breaking ranks and fleeing their posts. Even the most disciplined lizarme units, being assailed from both their flanks and above, were disobeying their commanders and retreating back across the moat. What began as a tiny trickle of angst had become a flood of panic. A flood that was feeding a rout.

The allies too could sense a turning of the tide. Apes and humanfolk seized the momentum as a new current flowed throughout their ranks; a current which swept away doubt and brought faith in themselves. And in victory!

Across the entire breadth of the pass, a greenish tide slogged its way west as it fled for the safety of the foothills. Lizarme who did not retreat were quickly overwhelmed by allied calvary. Or put to the spit and the blade by vengeful foot soldiers.

Aytik watched with cheering eyes as the tide flowed about the catapults, simply leaving them in its wake.

Allied commanders were hard pressed to call off the attack when their troops captured the catapults. Even so, Doyen Commander Kryle thought it unwise to press the attack and pursue the lizarme into their home territory where the deluge would now favour them. Not that he didn't want to. He very much did. But why put Destiny to the test? When next he attacked Tarawa it would be in his own time and on his own terms. And he would strike without warning. When Tarawa would least expect it.

Until then, Kryle would simply accept those spoils of war which Destiny had gifted him and have his victorious troops haul the enemy's war machines back behind the wall for its own defence. Unlike the fallen, at least the survivors could regroup and attack again. For now they would tend to their wounded. But their doyen commander vowed not to wait long. *'I will attack before you can recover, Prod Tarawa. And sooner than you suspect. Much, much sooner. Although you are unaware, you have already lost this war.'*

Taking in the carnage all about him, Aytik felt the euphoria of victory drain from his limbs. Suddenly his sword arm felt heavy and the stench of Morgue offended his nostrils. His eyes took in the corpses. Some knights he knew. A few he had even shared a cup with.

Foot soldiers were wading about the silent forms, sticking any lizarme still of breath. Somewhere, a pike silenced a squealing dact.

Turning about, Aytik set his sights upon a grey ape with sad amber eyes. He cradled a limp ape-gal tight against his chest. Her matted hair was sticky with crimson and her eyes stared at naught.

"He wishes to hold her awhile," Torak explained. "He very much loved her."

"He always will," Aytik noted. "I owe them both a great debt. They twice spared me an early meeting with Morgue."

Torak nodded knowingly. "Such is true. Sadly, there is little time to mourn. Prod Tarawa will regroup his forces and attack

196

again before we can plug the breaches. He is not one to…"

"No, Prince Torak," Kryle injected. "Tarawa will not be attacking us again."

"How can you be so certain?" Torak asked with a shrug. "Tarawa is not the kind to quit so…"

Kryle spat blood over the parapet. "I am so certain because this very night we are going to advance our armies up the pass under cover of darkness and attack him at first light. From this moment onward, the battlefront only moves west. It is we who attack, and Tarawa who retreats. Give the order for a forced feed and sleep. Inform your commanders that once we attack there is not to be one step backward. Do you both understand?"

Torak and Aytik dropped jaws and stared with wided eyes. They glanced briefly to each other before staring back at Kryle.

"Doyen Kryle, our troops have just fought a brutal battle," Torak protested. "They are exhausted. The bodies of the fallen must be buried or burned to prevent pestilence. We cannot simply leave them…"

"Tarawa's troops are equally exhausted," Kryle interrupted, taking hold of a climbing net. "I will assign troops to gather up bodies only after we have secured our flanks. Until then, those on the ground will decay where they lay, and those in the moat will bloat where they float. Callous, to be sure. But it must be so if we are to catch our enemy unawares. Which is exactly what I intend to do.

"Since secrecy and surprise are crucial, have only your grand knights join with my senior doyens in the command hut. Also, order the forced feed and sleep for your troops as soon as the wounded have been brought to the healers. No matter the weather, every able foot soldier will take part in the initial assault, both ape and humanfolk. Our cavalry will advance only after the battle has begun. We cannot risk some high-strung beast giving us away."

Again, both princes exchanged startled stares. Then the white ape quickly grabbed hold of the net and swung down after Kryle.

Aytik turned his attention back to Kwok, yet chose to respect the ape's grief. There would be a better time to offer up sympathy. For now, his friend must pour his eyes dry.

Retraining his sights far to the west, Aytik caught sight of a lean and lanky figure standing alone atop a distant outcrop. He wondered about the solitary figure who stared towards the wall. "What are you thinking, Prod Tarawa?" he muttered out loud. Then he turned to climb down the net.

Aytik was unaware that all along both edges of the pass salivating vultures were perched like judges in the hollows of cliffs. They tilted their bald heads and ruffled their filthy feathers in gleeful anticipation as they gawked over the entire field of battle. The verdict was in. It was going to be a splendid feast!

Arduk

Daybreak found four crouching forms straining their eyes to detect even the slightest hint of movement amongst the tall husk crop, which was now ripe for harvest.

"Hsssssssssss…"

"Shhh," the tallest of the forms whispered, "Clive senses there is something moving amongst the husk crop. Keep still."

The spiketail slowly raised its tail, with the sharp tip of spiked bone poised to bash. "Hssssssssss…"

"Clive, shush," the ape scolded in whisper, patting her pet's warty hide. "You too, Shyamala. Quit rustling about."

"Sorry, Tianga."

"Don't be sorry. Just be quiet and keep your trident at the ready," instructed another muffled voice.

"I'm trying, Helenia. It's just that bellybees are buzzing and my heart is pounding…"

"All of our hearts are…"

"Cork thine gobs, both of you." Tianga commanded crossly. "Dearest Destiny…"

"Hssssssssss…"

"Shush."

"For what seemed like forever, the four forms crouched low in silence. Each continued to scan about the husk crop for any hint of movement.

As Day's light chased Night's skytwinklers from the sky, what were mere shadows started taking on shape and colour. Unseen chirpers started singing to greet the giver of life and warmth. The chill morning air felt crisp to the flesh, and the four forms could now discern their own breath spouting in vapors.

Helenia readied her sword and offered a comforting smile to Shyamala. The blue gown her friend had placed so much value on was now torn and stained with dirt and blood. Her black hair was matted and long overdue for a brushing. In her dirty hands she awkwardly held a trident like it was a growers' hoe.

Helenia thought, *'Shyamala looks so out of place in a combat unit.'*

Next, Helenia set her sights upon Tianga. In contrast to Shyamala, the ape seemed so in sync with herself. Clad as always in a battle skirt and vest, she clenched her mace with purpose. She had purposefully soiled the shine from her skullcap, lest its glint should alert enemy dacts. Her eyes had grown puffy and lacked their usual sparkle due to fatigue, yet her resolve held firm.

They were all so very tired, and Helenia wondered what she must look like to the others? Not that it really mattered given their plight.

Tianga's pet spiketail was ripe for a scrap, its warty body swelling and shrinking with each anxious breath. A spiked ball of bone dangled menacingly at the tip of its powerful tail. Unmistakably, Clive was not a beast to challenge lightly.

After wiping a moist and filthy palm on her tunic, Helenia reached to check the hilt of the hurling dagger sheathed inside her highboot. She had but one dagger left, having stuck the other into a passing dact's neck, and she did not wish to squander it for no good purpose.

The three friends and Clive had become separated from their unit when it was ambushed by a much larger enemy force in the mucky marshes along the northeastern shore of Lake Blood. Having fled north by northeast for several tense and uncertain days, they had eventually emerged from the thick reeds of the marsh and ventured forth beneath cover of darkness into the golden highgrass and tall husk crop of the low plains.

Now they found themselves hopelessly lost and hiding in a grower's field, uncertain as to what or who was stalking them? Nor were they inclined to even guess as to the whereabouts of King Myro and his Royal Guard, whom they were especially determined to find; assuming, of course, the king and his court were still breathing?

As Day's beams began to reveal more of their surroundings, the group saw they were at the edge of a small clearing. Within it, the husk crop was broken and trampled flat, except for where shards of stalk stuck up like fibre spikes. Amongst it all, many still forms stared at naught.

One pair in particular moved Shyamala to tears. A young lizarma lay twisted and bloated, his claws still tangled in the locks of the breathless galfolk who'd stabbed him. The brave little galfolk lay partially beneath him, her stiff fingers still clenching the blade. A shard stuck up through her heart.

Without meaning for them to do so, Helenia suddenly found her eyes nervously scanning the above for dacts. Then a shiver rattled her spine as her ears snagged the distinct call of an alpha pair howling to summon their pack. "Tianga, we must go. The howlers make ready to hunt. They will smell Morgue's scent."

"Shhh…" Tianga whispered, placing a forefinger to her lips. "We must keep still and keen of wit. Something lurks nearby. Note how Clive spoils for a scrap – and how the chirpers cease to sing."

It was true. The angry spiketail was warily whirling about with its tail cocked to swing and baring its fangs for the bite.

"Then shouldn't we be off?" Shyamala asked, her eyes wide with alarm. "I mean, if there is…"

"Hush," Tianga replied. Reaching out, she yanked Shyamala closer to her and Helenia. She cupped her fingers about the trembling galfolk's ear. "I know you are scared, but you must not move or speak."

Shyamala was too fear frozen to reply. Her heart beat over her breath. After closing her eyes and counting to stay her nerves, she somehow managed to firm up her awkward grip on the trident. Above all, she had sworn to fight alongside her friends come what may. And she intended to do just that.

Helenia fondly reached over to rub her friend's back. She thought, *I must remember to tell Shyamala how proud I am of her. Although she is by her gentle nature ill-suited for warfare, she still tries to do her part. She is truly worthy to be my brother's queen. I must mention such to Father. He has already shown her some kindness since she leapt upon that lizarma's back during the evacuation. It shan't hurt him to hear more of her courage and efforts to defend the realm. That is, if we ever find him?'*

Suddenly, the alphas again called out to their pack.

"The howlers, they come closer," Shyamala whispered.

"Shhh…"

With bated breath and blade held ready, Helenia shifted her eyes back and forth to scan between the tall stalks directly across the clearing. She could feel the pounding inside her chest. Despite the cooling breeze, a bead of sweat trickled down her brow. A nasty cramp began gnawing into her thigh.

While adjusting her crouch to ease the pain, the nervous princess suddenly became aware of yellow eyes staring at her. Instinctively bracing to do battle with howlers, she instead found herself shocked into muted disbelief. Her jaw slacked and she gasped in astonishment. Then she sighed in relief and lowered her sword.

Alerted by their friend's gasp, the others also braced for battle…

But there was no need of combat. Tianga and Shyamala both wided eyes before likewise sighing in relief.

"Hsssssssssss… Hssssssssss… Hssssssssss…"

Ignoring Clive's hiss, all three kept their eyes glued to the figure crouching before them.

A familiar and frail ladfolk with curly locks and a freckled face was watching them from across the clearing. His eyes bore a yellowish glow. He was clad only in a tattered tunic. No sandals or boots covered his filthy feet. In one hand he gripped a sturdy longbow. A packed quiver was strapped across his back.

Two larger than average howlers with glowing yellow eyes flanked the young ladfolk. One of the howlers bore the scars of many scraps all about its matted grey fur, while the other bore a black coat. Each bared its fangs as they growled back at the spiketail.

The ladfolk spoke something to his companions, both of whom softened their growl while keeping their wary glare.

Next, the ladfolk hissed something to the spiketail, which in turn softened its own hissing while keeping its wary glare.

"Arduk?" Helenia managed at last. "What – er – I mean – uh – where is…"

A sudden flapping from above startled all three friends, panicking them into raising their weapons. But each exhaled and slowly lowered their weapon as a bald swooper touched talons to perch upon the ladfolk's shoulder.

Arduk nodded as the swooper beaked something into his ear. Then he pursed his lips and piped his reply.

The swooper nodded before taking flight. Circling about the clearing, it squawked something down to Arduk before soaring and vanishing off into the bright of the sun.

The ladfolk then growled a command, prompting both howlers to turn and leap back in amongst the husk crop. In the bat of a blink, they too were gone.

"Arduk…" Helenia began.

Stepping forward into the clearing, the frail ladfolk set his serious stare directly upon Helenia. His tone was beyond scolding. "Howlers say ye three been rousing enough ruckus to rile up rocks."

"You are right, Arduk. We have been much too noisy," Tianga acknowledged.

"Arduk, where is Chaps Bridle?" Helenia asked. "You two are always together…"

"Chaps' spirit floats with the winds."

All three gals exchanged bewildered glances as Arduk then placed both thumb and forefinger between his lips and blew through clenched teeth. Although Shyamala and Helenia heard no sound, Tianga cupped her hands over her ears while wincing in pain.

Almost instantly, countless howlers called back in reply. Then all went silent save for the rustling of leaves and the shushed blow of gusts passing through husk crop.

Arduk started sniffing for scents on the breeze. "Scaleez be close," he explained.

All three friends stood still as statues while the young ladfolk closed his eyes and placed a forefinger to his brow. Only leaves and breeze saw fit to respond.

After what seemed like forever, Helenia moved to speak. However, even with his eyes shut, Arduk somehow sensed such and motioned her mute. The others could only gape in awe.

"What is he doing?" Tianga finally whispered.

Helenia merely shrugged.

At last, Arduk opened his eyes. "Them be here now," he explained.

"Who?" Tianga asked, glancing about. "Who is here now?"

"I don't see anybody?" Shyamala added.

All three galfolk were growing concerned. Had the war and the loss of Chaps Bridle made the ladfolk numb-of-sense? Had Arduk spun *round-the-twist*?

"There," Arduk stated, pointing to the edge of the clearing.

When nothing appeared for them to view, Tianga sneakily thumbed at the young ladfolk and rolled her eyes to scoff. Shyamala nodded to agree.

Suddenly, without any warning, an odour most foul wafted into the clearing. It burned nostrils and eyes, moving all three gals to retch.

"Whitestripes?" Tianga spat out in disgust. "Seriously, Arduk? You've summoned whitestripes?"

"Hzzzzzzzzzz…" Clive railed angrily, glaring daggers at Arduk before attempting to burrow his own warty face deep into the dirt.

"He sure did," Shyamala affirmed, struggling to stifle a gag.

"Whatever for?" Helenia asked, joining the others in pinching her nostrils. "Arduk, whitestripes are gross."

"Them be that," Arduk agreed, stretching a broad smile just as a family of whitestripes began emerging from the husk crop. Each fearless critter completely ignored the gals and Clive as they waddled directly for Arduk.

Suddenly, all ears snagged the sound of rustling foliage. Unmistakeably, a dry stalk crunched underfoot.

Crouching down low to gently pet some of his striped friends, Arduk purred out something for them to ponder. All of the whitestripes nodded and waddled off in the direction of the rustling. None even gave a glance to the gagging gals or wheezing spiketail. They knew they were in charge – for whitestripes are always in charge!

A seeking silence seemed to pass over the land as the group waited with lips locked for something to happen. Not even the wind stirred. It was as if the very gusts themselves were forbidden to interfere in the drama about to unfold.

Somebody shouted their lungs clean. Another voice screamed out in a panic. More shouting and snarling and commotion followed as unseen bodies crashed recklessly through the husk crop. One could clearly discern the distinct squeals of fleeing rexids.

All three gals could no longer contain their giggles as the crashing and shouting and commotion waned off into the distance. They cupped their hands over their mouths, trying their best to muffle any sound; all to no avail.

"Ar-Arduk," Tianga finally managed at last. "I salute you."

"And your stinky friends as well," Shyamala added.

"You've certainly earned a big hug," Helenia said, stepping across the clearing and wrapping her arms tight about the startled ladfolk.

"That he has," Shyamala concurred, moving to hug the now blushing ladfolk.

Even Tianga put her arm about Arduk's shoulders and squeezed him tight to her bosom. "That was smart thinking, Arduk. Now we must go. They could still come back."

"I doubt it," Shyamala giggled.

"At least we'd know exactly where they are," Helenia added in jest, scrunching face and plugging her nose.

Tianga puckered her lips to make amused. "We still need to go. Arduk, do you know where we can find more humanfolk?"

The ladfolk merely shrugged his shoulders.

"What are you doing way out here?" Helenia asked. "I mean, why aren't you with anybody else? How did Chaps meet Morgue?"

"I beed kept safe with me howlers," Arduk replied. "They love me. Now ye be safe with them too."

Before anyone could question him further, the frail ladfolk started out across the clearing and led them in amongst the husks. He veered northeast, swiftly winding his way amongst the tall stalks; pausing only on occasion to prick his ears or sniff at the wind.

Helenia was becoming even more intrigued by the strange lad who had been reared by howlers. In fact, she was almost unable to strip her eyes from his back as he guided them out of the husk crop and in amongst some tall highgrass; although she sometimes found herself distracted by glimpses of agile shapes prowling the fields beside them, or by the sight of blinkless, yellow eyes watching from amongst the golden stalks.

By midday the temp had climbed well enough to warm flesh, which was not uncommon in the late quarter. The group even took a brief respite to quench their thirst and wash in a clear-flowing rill. All knew dusk would return soon enough and they would once again find their breath spouting in vapors.

On occasion, one or more members of Arduk's pack would appear and they would confer with him in howler speak. Sometimes, swoopers would land on his shoulder and beak into his ear. Once, he even hissed in speak with a venom spitter, before patting its flattened head in gratitude.

"Spitter says many scaleez stomped by here three days past," Arduk explained.

The amazing spectacles continued as their young guide also paused to exchange dialogue with furry cheekers, wild gobblers, horned hooters, masked bandits, and even one of the very rare roos that humanfolk growers had hunted near to extinction. Even tiny squeakers offered up advice, often pointing about excitedly as they spoke with him.

Yet the most astounding spectacle happened when Arduk approached a very nasty rattler. The coiled serpent was clearly not up for a chat. However, when it sprang to strike at the ladfolk, it instantly found itself choked tight in his grip. All three galfolk gasped as one when Arduk's hand grabbed quicker than the rattler could strike. Who would think such even possible?

Arduk's tongue flicked in and out as he hissed in dialogue with his scaly captive, who struggled for wind and for words. Yet the determined ladfolk kept on until he was satisfied with what the rattler had to say. Then he gently placed the rattler down on the ground and motioned for it to slither away.

"Rattler says no scaleez be lurking about," Arduk explained.

A sudden cry from a howler drew an immediate response from several others. Arduk also joined in, cupping his hands about his mouth and howling his reply to the pack.

"What did the howlers say?" Tianga inquired, not fully believing she was actually asking such. *'Have we all spun round-the-twist?'*

"Howlers say many scaleez be to the north. So we will go east."

Veering due east, the group continued their trek through the swaying highgrass. The galfolk tried to ignore the pesky borebugs that needled their flesh, as well as the annoying itch from highgrass seed that stuck to their sweaty skin.

Arduk continued to converse with critters both big and small as the group kept on at a steady pace. Sometimes, he would guide them to a clear rill where they would gulp greedily and the young ladfolk could fill the water skin he kept in his quiver. There howlers would join them on the bank, where they would quietly confer with Arduk before prowling off back amongst the highgrass.

Come the first hint of dusk, the group opted to bivouac in a small clearing alongside a pond. Arduk assured them his howlers and many other critters would keep an alert vigil, while Tianga sent Clive to patrol the perimeter. Then they all curled up for a much needed nap. That is, all but one.

Helenia could not nap. Fatigued as she was, she simply could not get the young ladfolk out of her thoughts. She tossed and turned to no avail. She knew he was curled up mere strides from where she lay thinking about him. Fantasizing about him. Wanting his flesh pressed tight against hers. Wanting him inside her. It moved her to touch herself. *Wet.*

Finally, she could deny her desires no longer and, after pausing to assure herself that her friends were both deep into their dreams, she slipped out of her tunic and slowly began crawling across the moist ground towards him. Soon she could discern his form. She could even hear his breath. Then she was beside him. Reaching out to touch him.

Before Arduk could speak, her tongue was in his mouth. Two shaky hands cupped his head and guided it between two soft breasts, before latching onto his tunic and pulling it off over his head…

****

…she turned to face him and kissed him on the lips. Then she gently pushed away and started the short crawl back to her own bivouac, silently praying unto Destiny that none had noticed her absence. Or worse, heard her and Arduk and knew what they'd done. Stretching the smile of one in love, she curled up to take nap. But could not.

Arduk also could not drift back into dreams. His heart pounded, pumping his loins with desire. He could still feel her. Smell her. Taste her. And she was delicious. Never before had his tongue savoured such a taste. He only knew he wanted more. Much more.

While each lay awake thinking only of the other, neither could possibly know Seed had blessed Helenia with a fertile womb. Or of the trouble such would soon bring.

Come the peek of dawn, Helenia and Arduk kept tight of lip. They offered one another secret glances, yet neither uttered a sound. When others spoke to them, each simply nodded in reply. And even then, only when necessary.

Noting such, Tianga sighed and frowned knowingly. She turned to Shyamala and muttered beneath her breath, "It seems so natural for us to always desire that which we cannot have."

Shyamala's lips were drawn taut with deep concern. "Helenia really must be more careful," she whispered. "Her desires could cost young Arduk his head."

The ape moved to speak, but instead nodded her agreement.

Soon after, a black crow descended and took perch on Arduk's shoulder. It cawed something into his ear before soaring off into the blue above.

"Us be safe," Arduk explained, failing to look the others in their eyes.

Thus, they departed the bank of the pond and plunged back in amongst the highgrass. Arduk took the lead, along with the pair of alphas that had since rejoined them. Helenia kept tight to his heels, with Tianga and Shyamala following close behind. Clive took up the rear, crawling along with eyes peeled; all the while hissing his displeasure at the pack of howlers guarding their flanks.

After dark, unseen blackwings would flap down and touch feet to Arduk's shoulder. They would quickly chirp words only Arduk's ears could hear, before flapping away and vanishing off into the night. Clearly, the ladfolk had many spies.

The group ventured due east, winding their way through husk crop and highgrass. From Day's advance until its retreat, they trekked across firm ground and slogged through marsh. Always, they were careful to avoid stepping into one of the many deep sinkholes that were quite common in the weeded areas of The Low Plains; for some of them could swallow a beast whole.

During the day, Helenia and Arduk were inseparable. Come each night, they would bivouac slightly apart from the others, while Clive and Arduk's many critters kept vigil about the perimeter. When they felt it safe to do so, the young lovers would eagerly seek each other out, before sneaking back to their own bivouacs with the mistaken belief they were fooling the others.

Neither youth could know that while they were tangled in passion, Shyamala and Tianga were also awake; each brooding over the young lovers while coveting the same for themselves. For both were lonely. And although neither would admit it, they were each torn with envy...

****

Early one damp and chilly dawn, even before Night's army of skytwinklers had fully completed its westward retreat, an old hooter with molting horns and feathers touched talons upon Arduk's shoulder. The hooter *whooed* something to the ladfolk, before taking flight towards a distant grove of hardwoods.

Arduk turned towards the others. "Hooter says white apes be camped to the north by slight east."

"White apes?" Tianga asked, clearly perplexed. It was plain by her tone that she was skeptical. "Arduk, are you sure of this?"

"Way out here?" Helenia added. "Whatever for?"

Before Arduk could respond, a pack of howlers emerged from the highgrass. As they approached the ladfolk, his eyes began to glow in kind.

After trading thoughts with the alpha, Arduk turned to Tianga. "Howlers will lead us to your apes."

Arduk began to walk alongside the howlers, often joining in sniffing for clues on the wind.

Finally finding themselves alone with Helenia, Shyamala and Tianga tried to warn their younger friend of the risk she was taking. In response, Helenia grew angry and stomped off to join Arduk.

"Perhaps Helenia is right?" Tianga proposed. "Perhaps her love life is none of our concern? Perhaps we are tilling where friends should not sow? Perhaps no good will come of it?"

Shyamala huffed to agree. "Helenia is right. Her love life is none of our business. Still and all, I shudder to think what may become of young Arduk should the king learn of their affair."

"Then we must agree he will not learn of such from her friends."

"Absolutely not," Shyamala concurred. "Gossip of their affair shan't leave my lips."

"Mine are sealed as well," Tianga said. "Let us speak no more of it lest such tattle should slip by blunder. Are we agreed?"

"Agreed."

"Pinky swear?"

"Pinky swear."

In time the gals noticed many more howlers were joining up with them, and swoopers began to arrive and depart by design. Upon advice from the swoopers, Arduk and the howlers would alter their course.

They trekked through husk crop and highgrass, and slogged across marsh. Twice they even wound their way through mazes of sneaky sinkholes. Despite their fatigue, they ignored the ache in their feet and kept on. And on...

When at last they emerged from the fields and found themselves standing on the shore of a large pond, each was stopped mute in their tracks. All along the shore, resting ape-gals stared back with wided eyes. Several startled spiketails sprang to their claws with tails raised and hissed at the strange group that had just emerged from the highgrass.

"On your feet!" somebody suddenly shouted. "It be the Princess Tianga! Me seen her in the flesh in Jara!"

"Tis her. Me seen her on Royal Parade in Apel!" vouched another.

"Form up in ranks for inspection!"

All along the shore, startled ape-gals snatched up their weaponry and sprang afoot. They quickly formed up into ranks and stared straight to the front with nary a murmur or flinch.

Four of the eldest ape-gals, all donning skullcaps and wearing homespun wristlets-of-rank, marched smartly up to Tianga and bowed low in respect. Neither offered up speech.

Tianga blushed purple as she took in the four commanders, each of whom was greying with age. "At ease, my sisters – and order our troops to do likewise."

When the uncertain apes proved unable to respond, Tianga moved to take charge. "At ease, all of you. We are safe here." She paused and motioned to Arduk. "My friend's spies assure us there are no lizarme in this sector. Trust me, they would know."

All of the apes paused before relaxing their stance and lowering their weapons. Still, they kept staring in silence at Tianga and her companions.

Tianga retrained her eyes on the four commanders before her. Her voice toned strict. "So tell me, just what in Morgue's maze are four squads of armed ape-gals doing roaming about these plains?"

All four apes exchanged glances, yet neither uttered a sound.

"Any one of you," Tianga pressed. "Speak freely."

All four apes began talking at once, then promptly made mute and exchanged confused glances.

Finally, the eldest of the foursome stepped forward. "I-I am Deena," she stammered. "We – uh – we…"

Noting that the ape-gal was quite intimidated by her presence, Tianga placed a gentle hand upon her shoulder. "From where do you hail, Deena?"

"From Apel, Princess," came a nervous reply. "That is, we mostly hail from Apel. A few hail from Jara, Princess."

Tianga made amused and released the shoulder. "Well, Deena, I have a request of you. Might I make one?"

"Y-Yes, Princess. Whatever your wishes, we will carry them out at once."

"What I really wish is for you to stop addressing me as Princess. There is no need for such folly and formalities way out here. An enemy trident would see no difference between you or I – would you not agree?"

The uncertain ape-gal hesitated before nodding.

"Good," Tianga continued. "Also, I think you might want to scrape the shine from your skullcaps and smear them dull with dirt and muck. Any alert dacts will catch the sun's glint off your heads from a great distance. Understand?"

All four commanders nodded to show Tianga they understood.

"Excellent!" Tianga exclaimed, again making amused. "I should dislike seeing either of you dangling from the spit end of a lance."

The ape-gals flushed purple and made amused. It was apparent they were quite quickly becoming comfortable in the presence of their princess.

"My friend's spies and his howlers have been tracking after you since the peek of dawn," Tianga explained. She paused to draw a deep breath before going on. "You've really given us quite a challenge catching up to you. I must admit, I am impressed. I do, however, have some questions. Actually, just one question. Could somebody please tell me what four squads of ape-gals are doing roaming about the low plains? Deena?"

"My Princess, we…"

"Tianga, please. Call me Tianga. And do not bow before me in the field or the enemy may reason I am somebody worth slaying or taking hostage. Understand? Also, look up at me when you speak. My eyes do not bite."

Deena giggled nervously before going on. "Princess – uh – I mean, Tianga. We four commanders felt we were serving little purpose keeping safe in Apel whilst our soldiers and our allies were battling the enemy on two fronts. So we recruited some volunteers and marched east to help the humanfolk fight. Did we do wrong, Princess? Uh – I mean, Tianga?"

Tianga moved to speak, but emotion muted her tongue. Tears leaked from her eyes. At a loss for words, she turned to Helenia for help.

Helenia smiled. "No, Deena, you did nothing wrong. We welcome your help. Destiny knows it is needed. I am Princess Helenia and these are my… Deena, you need not bow before me. If anything, it is I who should be honoured by your presence."

"Absolutely," Shyamala agreed. "My name is Shyamala and I am betrothed to Prince Aytik, heir to the humanfolk throne. I am honoured to meet such brave and selfless warriors. You are all welcome in our land."

Tianga finally found her words. "Did you four organize this combat unit all by yourselves?"

"No," Deena replied. "All the others played their part. It is only because four of us are older and have schooling that we were chosen to lead. But now we have a real leader."

Tianga wiped the wet from her eyes. "My friends, you are real leaders. True dames if ever I met any. All four of you. When this war is over I intend to have my brother, the king, formally dub you as such. Come, I should like to meet more of your soldiers before we move out – and I long to hear tidings from back home. You say you hail from Apel?"

"Yes, Princess."

"Tianga."

"Uh – sorry. Yes, Tianga. I hail from the east end – near to the river."

"Close to the wharf?"

"Yes. Very close. My folk mostly net finners and dig clams."

"And what of you? Where do you hail from?"

"North by west of Jara. Me folk be mostly miners."

While Tianga and Helenia went to meet with the other apes, Arduk motioned for his howlers to follow him. He then hissed something to Clive, which moved the spiketail to eagerly scurry over to the shore and mingle with its own kind.

Arduk walked down to the shore and waded in up to his knees. While his howlers drank, he retrieved the water skin from his quiver and started filling it with fresh drink. He was quite indifferent to the slender figure in a tattered blue gown wading in beside him.

"Arduk, might I speak with you?" Shyamala asked.

The ladfolk trained his suspicious grey eyes on her.

Shyamala was a bit taken back by the unlettered stable lad's eerie stare. It had always disturbed her, although not near so much as when his eyes burned a warning yellow. "Arduk, I do wish to speak to you about a matter of grave importance. I want to talk about what is going on between you and the princess."

Shyamala paused to permit Arduk a verbal response. She paused for naught.

"I know you think you're in love," she continued. "Which you may very well be. It's just that – well, there could be trouble if the wrong folk should find out about you and Helenia. I mean…"

"Ye be a snitch?" Arduk asked rather defensively.

"No, Arduk. I am not a snitch. Nor is Princess Tianga. We are concerned others may find out and tell the king. It would mean big trouble for you. It could even mean your head. Do you understand what I am telling you?"

Arduk kept mute and expressionless, making an already awkward situation even more cumbrous.

Shyamala drew a deep breath to better organize her words. "Arduk, I like you. I really do. So does Princess Tianga. It's just that in our structured society only nobles can mate with nobles – unless a noble is willing to forfeit their title and stature to wed down. Do you know what I am saying?"

Arduk hesitated before shaking his head.

"What I am saying, Arduk, is this thing you have going on with Helenia could cost the princess her noble status. Worse, you could be punished very badly just for touching her."

Arduk was clearly confused. "Helenia likes me to touch her?"

Shyamala wanted to discuss the matter further, but the clatter of apes moving out averted her attention. She could see Helenia and Tianga waving for her and Arduk to join them.

Turning back to the confused ladfolk, she offered him a sympathetic smile. "I know she does, Arduk. Come, we must go."

Arduk waded ashore and motioned to his pack.

The howlers instantly sprang from the pond and shook the wet from their fur. They then split up and passed from sight into the highgrass.

No sooner had the apes formed up into their squads, when they received the order to move out. As they marched off into the highgrass, each soldier nervously scanned their flanks with weapon held ready. Hissing spiketails crawled along beside them.

Arduk hissed his ire at two spiketails for alarming a pouched roo that had hopped over to speak with him. At once, the spiketails turned and crawled off to join the column.

The roo relayed her intel to the ladfolk, then glanced warily at the spiketails before hopping away in the opposite direction. She clearly wanted no part of them.

On and on the apes marched, pausing only for brief rests during the day. Come dark they would bivouac for the night, while enjoying the protection of Arduk's strange ensemble of critters; although the call of distant howlers often disturbed their dreams.

While the landscape did seem flat to the eyes, the further north they trekked, the higher they gradually climbed; until finally they found themselves atop a golden escarpment, the rolling contour of which was often broken in places by thin, shimmering aquaveins or patches of leafless woodland. On occasion they would come upon cart trails leading to abandoned farms; always taking care to send howlers on ahead, lest lizarme soldiers should be making use of the barns.

Whenever they encountered oinkers or cluckers or mooers, Arduk would always pet them and ask questions. Always, the beasts were quite eager to answer.

Often the howlers led them to frightened families that were hiding amongst highgrass or in patches of woodland. Thereupon they would collect the displaced humanfolk and bring them along. Shyamala always explained to the terrified tots that they were trying to get to the Upcoast Forests in the hope of finding King Myro and his Royal Guard, assuring them that once there they would be safe from the screeching dacts.

Time and again they passed by barns that had been put to the torch, where they often encountered bloats covered in buzzers. Wakes of greedy vultures fought over the spoils, always eager to savour the bounty of war.

At such times the apes would scoop orphaned tots up into their strong arms and shield their eyes from such sights. Although even they knew their trembling bundles had already seen much to mess up young minds.

Early one misty morning, a very excited swooper descended and told Arduk that they were marching almost on course to connect with a large unit of humanfolk. The swooper added that if the column veered slightly to the east and made haste they could overtake the others before Night's army of skytwinklers reclaimed the above.

The ape-gals immediately altered course, and quickened their pace under orders from Tianga herself. No further rests were granted as they thrashed their way through swaying highgrass and swifted across small glens. Yet each seemed content as the quick pace warmed their bodies against the gusts sweeping down from the north, which nipped at their cheeks and ears and fingers and toes. Already, the new quarter's first dusting of snow was beginning to fall.

"The frigid quarter is now upon us," Shyamala observed, scooping up snow to quench her thirst. "It will prove much harder for troops to move about. We will have to garrison. The only question is where?"

"The cold and the blow will prove worse for the lizarme," Tianga noted. "The many dessert dwellers amongst them are not used to your harsh climate and time is no ally to their cause."

"Nor is Destiny," Helenia added. The princess would have said more, except suddenly she felt nauseous and reached to her friends for support. Then she threw up.

"Helenia!" Shyamala shouted, dropping down to aid her retching friend. "Did you eat spoiled potage?"

Tianga calmly reached down and pulled Helenia's hair from the mess. "No, she did not. I ate the same potage. Perhaps we have pressed on too fast. I will order a rest."

"No," Helenia said, grabbing hold of the ape's arm and pulling herself back up to her feet. "I am fine. Shyamala is correct. It is probably something else I ate. I feel much better now that my belly is clean. Come, we must keep pace with the others."

Thus, they continued their trek without rest, hurrying along behind the apes in an effort to intercept the humanfolk unit before the onslaught of dark would make such an encounter much more difficult.

"Me and the howlers will swift ahead to scout for scaleez," Arduk explained, suddenly bolting into a sprint.

"Please be careful," Helenia called out as the young ladfolk and his howlers swifted away. "I love you…"

Both Tianga and Shyamala exchanged glances.

"Are you certain you are well?" Shyamala asked. "You seem to have taken ill."

"I am well," Helenia assured her friend. "Come, we are falling behind."

217

They kept on at a pressing pace, pausing neither for feed or for rest. Fatigue wearied legs and blisters burned feet. Frigid gusts coloured their cheeks and numbed their digits. Yet in spite of it all, not a single humanfolk or ape complained. Not even one. Not even once.

They kept mostly to highgrass or forest, seldom venturing out onto barren or scrubby patches of terrain; constantly scanning above for any sign of dacts, or of lizarme assassins hiding in the treetops.

After some time, Arduk and his howlers returned. Only now he was wearing a pair of boots he'd plaited himself from waterproof peeling bark, along with a hooded cloak that hung well below his knees.

"That lad is one strange stick," someone noted.

"He is that," another concurred.

Helenia thought, *'Okay, I know he makes his own boots. But wherever did he get that fine sheepskin cloak? It's of the kind only lizarme commanders wear? – No, he couldn't have... He didn't...? Oh my... – Well, at least there's one less enemy commander for us to fret about.'*

"Humanfolk wait for ye in the scrub," Arduk explained to Helenia, pointing due north. "There beed a few scaleez napping about a pond, but now they nap with finners."

"How far north are the humanfolk?" Tianga asked.

Arduk shrugged. "If ye swift on the stride, ye can meet up by dark."

As the apes and humanfolk hastened their pace to the north, Arduk and Helenia started to avoid one another. By now both were becoming uncomfortably aware of Tianga and Shyamala's constant looks. It seemed as if the pair were always staring at them.

Eventually, the tension grew so tight the uneasy ladfolk beckoned his howlers to follow and vanished into the growth. He didn't even turn to look back at Helenia.

She was both saddened and relieved to see him depart, for she was battling back shame. Not because they had done anything to be ashamed of, she reasoned. But the obvious disapproval of her friends had moved her to question her own thoughts and desires. She needed time apart from her lover to sort through her own feelings.

Neither Helenia nor her friends spoke a single word as they pressed on across some fields. That is, until they at last emerged from the highgrass and found themselves standing in a small clearing of stunted, brown scrub. Nervously, they scanned their exposed above. Thankfully, their eyes sighted naught but Night's advancing skytwinklers straining to peek through some gaps in the skysheep.

"There they are," Shyamala said, folding her arms tight with a shiver. Her breath spouted in vapors. "Dearest Destiny, they look like cadavers."

It was true. Spread out across the clearing was a combat unit of battle-hardened galfolk, all of which were in dire need of a feed. Already, many of the apes and the humanfolk were gripping one another's hands in greeting. Some even embraced. A few of the apes were offering out chunks of brined meat, which the starving humanfolk gulped down in large chunks.

Arduk led a gaunt galfolk across the clearing towards them. Her dull black eyes were puffy from fatigue. A loose mantle hung from her frail frame and a sword hilt stuck from the sheath on her belt. Both boots had holes. Her bony hands clenched a trident. Blue veins glowed about her white knuckles. It was readily apparent she was in dire need of a feed.

"Princess," the galfolk said as she bowed before Helenia. "At last you are found. The king has been frantic since wounded soldiers from your unit arrived to tell of the battle. Thanks be to Destiny you are well."

Helenia reached up and placed her palm against the galfolk's brow. "I am quite well, but you appear ill? Your flesh burns like embers."

"Merely a nip of a fever bug," the galfolk replied with a forced smile. "I should fare fine now that we've found you. The king and his historian are in hiding deep within the Upcoast Forests. All units have been ordered to find you and escort you safely to them without delay. I will order my soldiers to make ready to march at once."

Before the frail galfolk could fully turn about, Helenia locked a firm grip on her shoulder. She gently guided the galfolk about so she could look into her eyes.

"What is your name?" Helenia asked, offering up a warm smile.

"Myrna," the galfolk replied. "I hail from Ga, Princess."

"Well, Myrna from Ga, I think it best you let the apes share with you of their food, then bundle up warm and take nap all this night. We will depart on the morrow."

"But the king…"

"Will manage just fine without me for one more night," Helenia cut in. "For now, we must try and make you and your soldiers well. Is there no food in the Upcoast Forests?"

Myrna nodded that there was.

"Then why are you all so famished?" Shyamala asked.

"We have not been to the Upcoast Forests for quite some time. Enemy patrols are all about the perimeter. They hunt us day and night. We seldom have time to forage for feed. Often we risk dact attacks simply to fill our water skins. Fully half of my unit have met Morgue. Many from starvation."

"And the other half will soon follow if we don't get some hardtack biscuits and cured meat into you," Tianga said. "And plenty of tree needle tea to warm you. Go rest your weary limbs while my soldiers tend to your ill. Deena, see to matters."

"At once, Tianga."

Myrna looked to her own princess, clearly uncertain of what to do.

Helenia nodded. "Go with Deena, Myrna. Your soldiers have well earned your feed and a rest."

Myrna stretched an eager smile, which seemed to put twinkle back into her eyes. "Yes, Princess," she said, already turning about to follow after the ape.

Helenia looked to Shyamala. "We should likewise take nap and nourishment. I am familiar with this area of the plains. My brother and I have hunted for wild gobblers here on several

220

occasions. The Upcoast Forests are two or three days hard march to the north. Perhaps we can sneak through the lizarme lines unseen? There must be many gaps along such a broad front. Arduk, can you have some of your spies probe the forest fringe for us?"

"Me already sent hooters and slinkers to spy," Arduk replied. "Each sees clean in the dark."

"Good choices, Arduk. None sight better at night than hooters and slinkers."

"To slip through unseen would be best," Tianga put in.

"Swoopers warn there be much war to the north. Vultures bellies bloat from the feasts," Arduk explained.

"In that case we may have to punch through enemy lines," Helenia responded.

"With Myrna's three squads, that brings our total to seven," Tianga noted. "Quite a formidable fighting force if we must do battle. Plus our spiketails are ample match for rexids. All the same, I should prefer we avoid the enemy. At least until we have been relieved of the tots we've collected. They shiver at night, and come daylight their sights are fixed on the above. They have seen and endured far too much for such a tender age."

"Many more of Myrna's soldiers may have been bitten by the fever bug," Shyamala pointed out. "Plus the temp will dip colder with each coming night."

Helenia sighed. "Such is true. Come, let us feed then take nap. There is nothing more for us to do this day."

True to Shyamala's words, the temp dipped quickly as Night's army of skytwinklers pushed the retreating sun back beyond the western horizon. By midnight, the above had cleared of skysheep. While the full moon kept its glowing vigil over the plains, hissing spiketails and alert howlers patrolled the perimeter.

Come the peek of dawn, a rolling blanket of clean snow covered the ground. The howling gusts had softened into a purr, yet the temp still nipped sharp at cheeks and digits. Breath spouted in vapors. Numbed digits were kept on the wiggle for warmth.

Apes and humanfolk alike wrapped the smaller tots snug into bedrolls and carried them tight against their breasts. Many of the tiniest tots were even packed into back packs, with their faces beaming smiles at those around them. Others were toted on shoulders, or pulled along on makeshift sleds.

Night's skytwinklers had yet to retreat when the apes and humanfolk broke camp and moved out. The constant crunch of snow beneath boots kept cadence as they marched north, while many eyes scanned above for dacts.

"Dung," Tianga cursed, looking behind them. "We cannot avoid leaving a trail."

By midday, the snow had melted into mush and slogging became slippery and slow. Especially for those in the rear, who had to slosh about the mucky footprints of their comrades. All the same, they marched on without complaint.

Later on, the lie of the land began to descend. Although suspect to the eyes, feet and limbs were quite aware of the gradual slide of the slope. Many a cuss and guffaw were heard as soles slipped from beneath bodies and butts splashed down into the muck. At such times, the wee ones giggled in delight, which moved several of the apes to start routinely falling down on purpose. Some even engaged in snowball fights; their cold and sopping forms being warmed by the joyous laughter of tots.

For three days and nights, they kept to their course. During the day, they marched as fast as their slowest could travel. Come night, they made camp and cuddled up in blankets and bedrolls.

With each passing night, the temp dipped lower than the sleep before. Come the next peek of dawn, the ponds were covered with slush and thin ice. Soldiers had to break through to refill their water skins.

Early on the fourth day, the contour of the Upcoast Forests rolled atop the north horizon. Despite the dump of fresh snow, the more stubborn hardwoods were still clothed in leaves; even so, most raked the wind with naked branches. Green needlers were clothed in clean snow, their boughs bent for the ground.

A yellow swooper descended and touched talons to Arduk's shoulder. It quickly beaked something into the alarmed ladfolk's ear before taking flight up into the above.

Arduk looked at Helenia but stayed his speech.

"What did your spy say?" Helenia asked with noted impatience. "Are there enemy troops about?"

Arduk nodded. "Many scaleez be to the east."

"How close?" Tianga pressed.

"Too close. If the wind shifts the rexids might smell ye spiketails."

"Then we will keep marching north," Helenia said. "Hopefully they shan't know we're about."

Tianga and Shyamala nodded in agreement and turned to trek onward.

"Lizarme catched galfolks," Arduk added.

The others stopped still in their tracks.

Arduk addressed Helenia directly as he spoke. "Swooper says galfolks be beaten. Says scaleez do cruel things to galfolks."

Myrna and Deena exchanged horrified looks, while Shyamala buried her face in her hands. All were at a loss for words.

"How many lizarme?" Tianga calmly asked.

"Swooper counts over one hundred," Arduk replied.

"Do they have rexids?" Helenia pressed.

The ladfolk nodded. "Twenty."

"We have near that many spiketails," Deena said to Tianga. "Princess, should we alter our course and mount a rescue?"

"No," Tianga said, shaking her head. "We will escort Princess Helenia to her father."

"And what of our sisters?" Helenia asked. "Would we just abandon them to their fate?"

"I feel saddened," Tianga maintained. "But we must see these tots safe into the forest and then find your father. Helenia, we cannot lose sight of our purpose."

"Tianga, it is our purpose to win this war," Helenia insisted. "You cannot be serious about leaving our own to the lizarme?"

A tense silence intervened before Shyamala finally spoke up. "Tianga speaks sense, Helenia. We have many tots with us."

Myrna also offered her thoughts on the matter. "My Princess, our orders came from the king himself. If we should find you, we are to bring you to him at once. We must avoid the enemy."

"Myrna is correct," Shyamala concurred. "We must obey your father's orders."

"Princess, my apes will return and attack them after we have seen you safely into the forest," Deena assured Helenia.

"You all heard Arduk's words," Helenia scolded. Those galfolk have been beaten and forced upon. They are soon to meet Morgue. I will not abandon our sisters to such a fate. I will not."

"Helenia…" Tianga began.

"Tianga, I have closed my mind on this matter. We hold the numerical advantage over our enemy. Destiny only knows when we will again. Your apes…"

"But…" Shyamala began.

Helenia's look cut her friend short. "Tianga, you and your ape-gals can do as you please. None here will judge you. But this is humanfolk soil the green hordes occupy and we galfolk are going to engage them. Myrna, make ready to quick march east."

"Yes, Princess – but what of the tots and the aged?"

Tianga sighed heavily. "We can help with them. Deena, assign one squad and three spiketails to see the humanfolk tots and the noncombatants safely to the forest. Have the other three squads readied for battle. Anything that can make sound is to be fastened or forgotten. We move out in fifteen bits."

"Yes, Princess," Deena replied, already stepping away to carry out Tianga's orders.

Myrna turned and hastened to obey Helenia.

Three howlers suddenly lunged free from the highgrass and, whilst keeping a wary stare on Clive, walked straight up to Arduk. After a brief exchange, the ladfolk turned to Helenia. "Me pack will also attack the enemy."

"Thank you, Arduk," Helenia said. "I will tell my father of their part in defending the realm. Howlers will be hunted no more."

Shyamala nodded to agreed.

"Ye must step soft on the swift," Arduk stressed. "We will sneak attack from downwind like howlers on the hunt."

Fifteen bits later found six squads of warriors quick-marching across powdered snow. Not a one of them spoke, for all knew surprise mattered most. An unready foe is a panicked foe, and a panicked foe is a careless foe.

Arduk and his beasts sprinted on ahead of the others. Although enemies by nature, both slinkers and howlers held to their truce. Several circling swoopers kept watch from above.

Eventually the much nimbler ladfolk stopped to let the others catch up. He motioned for all to keep wary while pressing a forefinger to his lips and pointing east through the highgrass. Quietly dropping to his belly, he signaled for the others to do likewise. He then motioned for them to keep still while he led the princesses and their commanders crawling through snow and scrub until they found themselves at the crest of a slight slope. There they carefully kept low to the snow and peered down at the mucky bank of a shallow pond.

Helenia gasped in horror as her eyes beheld the spectacle of three greenish forms slobbering over several tethered and gagged galfolk. Other lizarme jeered and mocked the battered and crying victims, while slugging in gulps from potted jugs. It was quite apparent they were well soused on jabber juice.

One tiny galfolk squirmed and screamed through her gag as a lanky lizarme climbed onto her. Her screams were wasted, however, as hard fists made her submit; all to cheers from the drunkards who watched.

Many more lizarme stood some distance away with their backs turned in disgust. Some covered their ears and shook their heads in shame. It was quite clear they were sickened by the spectacle.

"Watch!" screamed a drunken commander. "I order you all to watch!"

His order was disobeyed.

"Dearest Destiny," Helenia said, drawing back and looking away.

"Helenia, shush," Tianga scolded in whisper, pulling her shaken friend down from the crest. "They mustn't know we are here."

Arduk tried to embrace Helenia to comfort her, but she pushed him away.

After Helenia had somewhat regained her composure, Tianga took her young friend's cheeks in hand and gently kissed her brow. "Save your anger for the attack, my friend. The guilty will pay for their war crimes, including those who share blame by their silence. These lizarme are not soldiers. They are thugs and cowards. All are without honour."

Once they were back with the others, Tianga spoke directly to Deena. Her hushed tone did nothing to mask her rage. "Deena, lead two squads around to the left, keeping downwind of the enemy. Take half of our spiketails with you. Keep strict silence as rexids can snag even the softest of sounds.

"I will keep the others here. When we charge, you attack the enemy from the flank. We will have them trapped with their backs to the pond. Make all of them meet Morgue. Spare not one of them. By my direct order."

Helenia too was emboldened and starved for vengeance. "Myrna, take half our troops and prepare to cut off any path of escape along the bank. I will command the other half from here. Do not betray your position until we attack. Then hit the enemy fast and hard. War has naught to do with what is going on down there. Remember, these are not true soldiers we fight. These sadists are unworthy of quarter."

Myrna scowled and brandished her trident for effect. She clearly wanted this battle.

Shyamala added, "We do have them outnumbered."

"Not by much," Tianga cautioned. "Leave nothing to chance. Fight as if we are outnumbered. Heavily outnumbered. Come, let us take up our positions quickly lest any change in the wind should betray us."

While Deena and Myrna led their units into position, Helenia and Tianga dropped back down to their bellies and crawled up to the edge of the crest. As all of their soldiers crawled forward behind them, a dark energy passed over the troops. Without speaking to one another, each was fully aware of what the others were feeling and thinking. *'No quarter given. No quarter gained. This fight is personal!'*

226

Galfolk cautiously slid swords from their sheaths, or made ready with tridents claimed from cadavers. Some withdrew hurling daggers, which they clenched between teeth. Archers made ready to nock their arrows. White apes with sweaty palms squeezed tight their pikes, maces and shields. Anxious eyes. Needled nerves. Buzzing bellybees. Heaving chests. Muscles tensed to stand and charge. Every soldier alone with her thoughts.

Sensing the tension boiling about them, the spiketails started to hiss below their breath. Apes started patting their beasts to quiet them.

"Patience, my pet," Tianga whispered to Clive. "Soon."

Helenia could hear her heart pounding inside her chest as she watched the cruel events still unfolding before her; until she could watch no longer and simply stared down at the muck. Even so, her ears could not shut out the cries of the victims.

A firm hand began to rub her back. Looking up, she found herself staring into compassionate orange eyes.

"Do you have any idea how much I love you?" Tianga asked, lending a warm smile.

Helenia felt emotion lodge in her throat. She wanted to tell Tianga how much their bond meant to her, to apologize for berating both her and Shyamala earlier on. However, the words would not come. She merely smiled through wetted cheeks and nodded.

Tianga continued rubbing her friend's back until a blue face poked out from some parted reeds alongside the pond. After granting Deena an affirmative nod, the ape princess steered her sights downwind of the enemy.

Myrna granted her and Helenia a thumbs-up before carefully closing the reeds back into place.

"Ready?" Tianga asked.

Both Helenia and Shyamala nodded nervously, while Clive hissed his eagerness to get on with it. Several nearby soldiers murmured their impatience.

Helenia signalled for the archers to move up and nock. Once they were slightly short of the crest she gave the signal to draw.

"Let us attack," Tianga said, pushing to her feet. All about her, other anxious forms also stood and readied their weapons.

227

Tianga turned and nodded to an ape with a Bovidae horn.

The ape returned the nod and pressed the instrument to her lips. She squinted as she puffed her cheeks to blow.

Flappers of every size and colour took flight from about the pond as the blast stampeded the very skysheep above. The ensuing roar of an armed and angry mob drowned out all else as the apes and humanfolk charged down the slope to attack.

Others emerged from growth all about the pond, shouting and sprinting for the startled lizarme. Each brandished their weapon with purpose. None intent on giving quarter.

"Loose!" Helenia shouted.

Lizarme fell to the ground as arrows found their mark. Some met Morgue quickly while others screamed and writhed in pain with shafts sticking from limbs.

Helenia watched with horrified pride as the first of Deena's soldiers swept upon the stunned lizarme. Many of the enemy met Morgue even before they could take hold of their weapons. Others fled into the pond, or tried to retreat into the reeds and highgrass. However, accurate arrows felled many while Myrna's soldiers cut off any route of escape.

"To Morgue with them all!" Helenia shouted out as she sped down the slope. "Spare not a one!"

Shouting, wailing, the clash of metal against metal; these were the sounds that filled Helenia's ears as she swung her sword to slice flesh. All about her, other galfolk and apes were charging headlong into their panicked foe.

Suddenly, a trident smacked Helenia's blade from her grip and she found herself staring into the frightened eyes of a scaly youth with a pimpled face. Instinctively, she grabbed hold of his weapon and they both splashed down into the pond.

As they thrashed about in the muck, Helenia slammed her brow repeatedly into the youth's face. In retaliation, he clawed a deep gash across her brow. Both became slopped in muck and tangled in weeds, where they were further weighted down by their sopping garments. They rolled over and over, both gulping for each breath.

Somehow, the youth wound up on top. With both hands fixed firm to his trident, he made ready to press the prongs. Then he groaned with bulging eyes as Helenia's dagger cut the bowels from his belly.

Helenia grunted as she drove the blade in to the hilt. Flipping her enemy beneath her, she began stabbing his chest. Some blows shot shivers up her arm whenever the tip struck bone; until finally the blade found his heart. The defeated youth gasped his last as Helenia twisted the blade in deeper. Then he went limp and his eyes stared at naught.

Helenia kept her grip on the dagger until her mind made sense of the sounds waning about her. Releasing the youth, she struggled to a stand and pulled her blade from his chest. She still choked and sucked for air as she started wading through the thick muck. All of her limbs felt heavy. Very heavy. Something warm and thick flowed from her brow and trickled down her face into her mouth.

She wiped blood from her eyes and took in the carnage about her. Not ten strides away, a crazed spiketail refused to release a slain rexid. Several apes were trying to calm it with speech, yet none dared venture too near. Nobody wanted to be first to pry the beast's jaws from its prize.

Shifting her eyes along the bank, Helenia was momentarily relieved by what they saw. Very few of the enemy were still of breath, and angry allied soldiers were quickly putting them to the spit. One mace-wielding ape in particular seemed almost indifferent as she bashed in a pleading lizarma's skull.

Other humanfolk and apes were untying each captive and wrapping them tight in embraces and blankets. Still others were gathering up weaponry, which now lay strewn all about the cluttered bank.

Suddenly, Helenia gasped. A panicky shiver shot through her spine. Something unseen punched into her gut.

Floating face down amongst some broken reeds was a familiar white form in a hide vest and battle skirt. Crimson stained the water as it flowed from a gash in the motionless ape's back.

Now Helenia's weary limbs found a new strength. She kicked her legs high as she splashed through the muck and the wet.

Upon reaching the still form, Helenia dropped to her knees and wrapped her arms tight about the form's torso. She grunted as she rolled her friend over, before cradling the ape's head in her lap. Two familiar orange eyes blinked up at her.

"Tianga?" Helenia muttered in near panic. "Morgue, please no…"

The white ape reached up to grab her friend's sopping tunic. She tried to speak, but merely gurgled and spat.

Instinctively, Helenia lowered her ear to hear.

Tianga grunted as crimson gobs spat from her quivering lips. She vibrated violently and pulled Helenia's face nearer to her own. Trying without success to speak, she slowly began to lax her grip. A prolonged gasp of escaping breath was all she could manage as her trembling body suddenly slumped slack. Her void eyes sighted on naught as her head rolled heavy into Helenia's lap.

Helenia could merely stare in shock. She was now oblivious to the gash in her brow, and to the many apes who were watching her. With a weeping heart she used her fingers to close her friend's lids. With wetted cheeks, she pressed her lips to Tianga's cheek.

Rocking Tianga's still form back and forth in her lap, she muttered, "Forgive me, dear friend. My ego has cost you your being. W-We could have passed the enemy by as you wanted. I am sorry. P-Please know how much I love you – and I will tell Kryle how often and sweetly you spoke of him…"

Helenia cradled Tianga's head tightly against her chest. "Don't dwell long in Morgue's maze, my friend. You are worthy of Utopia."

Next Helenia noted a solemn hissing beside her. She turned to find Clive nudging Tianga's arm. Then the whimpering spiketail tried licking her face and neck, all the while emitting a pitiful whine.

Feeling pity for Tianga's grieving pet, Helenia reached out and began stroking its flesh. It felt oddly cold and clammy.

Two gentle hands gripped Helenia's shoulders and she found herself staring up into sympathetic brown eyes. Shyamala comforted her friend while Deena applied a cloth to the gash in her brow.

"Keep still, Princess," Deena instructed, while holding a hide pouch. "This healing sap contains a remedy of vinegar and myrrh to stem the flow of blood and help cleanse the wound. But it must sting to fulfill its purpose. I must also apply it to the wounds on your cheeks and chin."

"Ahhhh…" Helenia groaned as the sap did indeed sting. "Stop…"

"Princess, keep still," Deena repeated.

Cupping Helenia's cheeks in her palms, Shyamala spoke to her straight. "Helenia, Tianga wanders Morgue's maze because it is her time to do so. Not for any other reason. In time she will find peace in Utopia. You know such to be true. For now we must make haste. The sounds of battle carry far on these plains. More lizarme will come."

Helenia eyes flooded over with tears as she clenched Shyamala's arms. Sorrow strained her voice. "W-We must grant her a proper burning," she stammered. "W-We must…"

"Tianga's spectre knows we cannot," Shyamala reasoned, tugging on Helenia's tunic and pulling her to her feet. "She would want us to go."

"Come quickly, Princess," Deena urged. "We mustn't…"

"Dacts!" a galfolk suddenly shouted, pointing to the west.

All eyes shifted to sight in the source of the galfolk's panic. She had not shouted in error. Far to the west, tiny dark dots were barely visible against the distant grey backdrop.

A weeping white ape stepped up to Helenia and pointed down to the still form floating at her feet. "This is not your doing, Princess," she said with noted sincerity. "Princess Tianga was always destined to meet Morgue in battle."

"Such a noble death befits such a noble warrior," added another.

All the surrounding apes nodded their agreement.

Helenia thought to herself, *'What is noble in any of this? I sometimes wonder if Seed's carefree creatures might not enjoy a*

231

superior simplicity of sense from which we so-called 'higher'
beings could learn much?'

As Shyamala gently peeled Helenia's stubborn fingers from
Tianga's vest, several apes moved to assist with Clive. The
distraught spiketail whimpered in grief as they led it away.

"Come on, Helenia," Shyamala urged, pulling her towards
the highgrass. "We must…"

The galfolk were muted by the sudden appearance of a
pack of howlers, which ignored the carnage and trotted straight
up to Arduk. The ladfolk briefly joined them in sniffing the
wind, before motioning them back into the foliage.

Concern conquered his face as he relayed the latest intel to
the others. "Ye must flee on the swift. More scaleez close in
from the north."

Despite her mounting concern over the emotional
condition of the princess, Shyamala could not help but be
impressed by how Deena and Myrna now took control of the
situation. With no further hesitation, each began assigning
soldiers to carry the wounded and appointing others to keep
guard on their flanks. They strictly ordered all to make mute
and keep low to the growth to hinder the dacts. Lastly, they
directed their troops to line up into orderly ranks and motioned
for them to keep formation as they all filed back into the
highgrass.

Whenever roos hopped by to help out, Arduk nodded his
gratitude and sent them to scout ahead for enemy units; also to
act as decoys to distract any rexids. Swoopers and flutter bugs
also played their part, departing and returning at regular
intervals.

Evidence of war was everywhere. Patches of highgrass and
husk crop were often flattened and stained with death. These
clearings were oftentimes filled with buzzers and bloats, along
with greedy vultures who squatted like judges and kept a gawky
watch on the column as it wound its way through the carnage.
Their popping white eyes seemed to taunt those still of breath.
Even challenge them. They seemingly enjoyed the disgusting
role Seed had gifted them.

232

All soldiers pinched tight their nostrils whenever they passed by the rotting carcasses of downed dacts and the bloated bodies beside them. Stench rode the breeze unabated.

"Gross," Shyamala said, looking to Helenia.

Helenia merely nodded her agreement.

When Night advanced its army atop the eastern horizon, the apes and humanfolk all huddled together and shivered in silence. They were drained well beyond weary, yet much too nervous to nap. The temp dipped to a right nasty nip, yet none dared move lest they should draw the attention of any lizarme patrols and their rexids. All knew it was going to be a very long night...

****

Even before Day had reclaimed the sky, the entire column was back on the march. They were encouraged by the welcome promise of the Upcoast Forests, which were now but a few kilopaces to the north.

Eventually, near to the forest fringe, they came upon an island of hardwood amidst the sea of golden husk crop. Here they were stopped in their steps. Every stomach sank and nary an eye kept dry as they stared in shock and horror at the sad scene before them. Each felt the nagging knots of guilt.

"What is it?" Helenia asked, pushing her way past some motionless apes before she too was stayed in mid step. Instantly, tears brimmed past her lids, and she sank slowly to her knees. She felt as if the very desire to exist was being sucked from her body.

Before her lay the bodies of both apes and lizarme. Amongst the combatants lay the corpses of the innocents.

Helenia could no longer cope with events. Sinking to her knees on the soggy soil, she gripped her guts and started sobbing uncontrollably. "It's all my fault," she wailed, as Shyamala and one of the apes dropped to comfort her. "I could have simply passed the enemy by. I should have passed them by. My ego has cost so many so much. Dearest Destiny, why didn't I pass them by? Why did I have to stop and fight?"

Shyamala embraced her friend and pulled her in tight against her chest. Both she and the ape began rocking the sobbing princess back and forth to sooth her inner pain.

Arduk also rushed to his lover's side. Uncertain as to exactly what he should do next, he began nuzzling her back and shoulders.

"It's all my fault," Helenia continued. "Dearest Destiny, why did I have to fight? Why didn't I listen to others and just pass on by?"

"Ye spared many galfolk from torture as well, Princess," the ape noted. "Ye choice beed a noble one."

For reasons unexplained, the ape's comforting words only served to make Helenia feel worse.

Arduk gently cupped his hand beneath Helenia's chin and guided her head about to face him. He gently pressed his lips to her brow. Then he scooped her up into his skinny arms and started carrying her past the sickening scene.

She buried her face in his cloak, pulling him tight against her. "Destiny, forgive me," she pined. "Forgive me."

Arduk's eyes teared over as he embraced the only galfolk he had ever desired. Helenia's trembling frame unleashed a storm of whirling emotions upon him. Unfamiliar emotions? He would have given himself to Morgue right there and then if it would drain her suffering; however, he knew it would only bring her more. Somehow, he sensed that all he could do was hold her and share in her pain. He pondered, *'How can one feel so needed and yet so helpless at the same time?'*

When Helenia at last ceased her sobbing, Arduk set her down upon her feet. Wrapping her arms about his neck, she squeezed his head against her own. "I so love you, Arduk," she whispered into his ear. "Please don't ever leave me."

Her words moved him to tighten his embrace. He meant to reply, but instead started sniffing her skin. Pulling away from her, he placed his hand on her belly and hinted at a smile.

"What is it?" she asked.

Arduk did not reply. He simply took her by the hand and led her along behind the others.

"What?" she pressed.

"We must swift on the snap," he replied.

"Can we beat the enemy into the forest?" she asked.

Arduk nodded, if only to comfort her.

Now that they sensed overhead cover was near, the column began marching for the treeline at a very swift pace. None wished to come so far only to lose the race now.

At last, the immense hardwoods which dominated the fringe of the Upcoast Forests were barely a hundred strides away. Unfortunately, the highgrass was quickly giving sway to scrub and weed, thereby exposing them even more to overhead attack. Plus howlers had arrived to tell Arduk there was now a third lizarme patrol skirting the forest edge near to the east. Might they be trapped?

"Dacts to the west!" somebody shouted.

"Them spies us!" added another.

Terror gripped the entire column as all eyes sighted west. It was true. A large flock of dacts was flapping straight for them!

"Into the forest!" Myrna shouted. "Now!"

"Be swift on the sprint!" Deena added.

"Swift! Swift! Swift!" shouted several soldiers as they frantically motioned for the others to make haste.

"OOOAAHH!! OOOAAHH!! OOOAAHH!!"

"Dung!" Helenia cussed as her eyes snagged the spectacle of lizarme foot soldiers charging towards them from the east. "There's too many of them!"

"We'll be cut off!" Shyamala shouted. "We must hurry!"

"Look!" an ape shouted to top the others. "To the treeline!"

Helenia was amongst many who stopped still in their tracks to watch the incredible events unfolding all along the forest fringe. Packs of howlers were charging from the forest and running directly into the path of the bewildered lizarme, causing them to panic and trip over one another to avoid being bitten; while rexids spun about in vain attempts to sink their fangs into the more agile howlers who bit at their tails.

Even swarms of buzzing stingers descended into the fray, and swoopers swept down to rake at scalps and eyes. The

235

lizarme started swatting frantically about their heads, or slapping stingers from exposed flesh. One could almost see the ugly welts puffing up on their skin.

"Quickly!" Arduk shouted. "Into the forest!"

Every ape and humanfolk started sprinting across the scrub for the forest. Each was fully aware of the dacts descending from west. They could also hear the chants of more lizarme marching to overtake them from the south, along with the squeals of more rexids.

"OOOAAHH!! OOOAAHH!! OOOAAHH!!"

Apes and humanfolk leapt from the scrub and plunged into the shadows of the hardwoods. Helenia and Arduk were amongst them.

"Hurry, Shyamala!" Helenia shouted, suddenly realizing her friend was lagging behind. "Sprint!"

"I – I am," Shyamala puffed. She lowered her head for the final dash to the fringe.

"Screeeeech!! Screeeeech!"

"No!" Helenia screamed as an eerie shadow passed over her friend. "Shyamala – faster! Hurry!"

"Screeeeech! Screeeeech! Screeeeech! Screeeeech!!"

"OOOAAHH!! OOOAAHH!! OOOAAHH!!"

Then it happened. Abruptly, and without any warning, a flood of arrows streamed upward from the forest, seemingly shot from the bows of ghosts. Some arrows tore deep into the dact, while others found their mark in the flesh of the beast's rider and lancer. All three slammed into the ground.

"Under thine shields!" an ape shouted, pointing to two more dacts swooping in low for an attack. Each beast clenched bundles of short spears in its twisted talons.

"Screeeeech!"

A loud cheer erupted as a second stream of arrows felled both beasts like torn kites. They crashed onto the hard ground, barely missing several diving apes.

"HOORRAY!!"

"OOOAAHH!!! OOOAAHH!!! OOOAA..?"

Charging lizarme chopped their chanting and scattered for safety as a third stream of arrows arced down amongst them.

Many screamed out in pain or wailed for help as barbed arrowheads stuck deep into their flesh. Rexids wailed and snapped and tried to bite the flapping shafts from their haunches.

A fourth stream of arrows filled the sky, before arcing down amongst the lizarme.

"HOORRAY!!"

Panic gripped their minds as terrified lizarme tried to flee the tapered onslaught. Caught out in the open, many of them tripped over their own stumbling brethren in their haste to escape the fifth stream of arrows, which was already on its way. To their horror, there was no place to take cover. Still and writhing forms quickly littered the scrub.

"HOORRAY!!" cheered the allies as all around the forest fringe frantic lizarme were running away.

"Screeeeech!"

Helenia shivered as a dark shadow glided atop the forest canopy directly above her. She wanted to flee, but her limbs defied her thoughts. Then somebody tackled her hard to the ground, shielding her body with his own. Nearby, a spiked bashing ball pounded a small crater in the soil before bouncing off into a group of diving galfolk.

Helenia sighed in relief as the heavy object finally rolled to a stop. Destiny had smiled on them, for not one galfolk had been harmed.

Twisting about, Helenia found herself staring up into the freckled face of her lover. His eyes glowed yellow like she had never seen before.

Noting her unease, Arduk offered up an explanation. "Aura be dim in the forest, Helenia. Me eyes glow to catch shapes moving through shadows. Just like howlers do."

At first, Helenia simply stared at him. Then she kissed him on the cheek.

Arduk moved to hold Helenia, but their embrace was interrupted by a stumbling galfolk in a tattered gown.

Shyamala dropped to her knees and pointed past them. "Look there," she puffed.

Both twisted their heads about to find many humanfolk archers were now emerging from their hiding holes, which they had dug into the forest floor and covered over with sticks and fallen foliage. Others were stepping out from behind hardwoods and bushes. A few were even lowering themselves down from the forest canopy by use of vine climbing cords. One tiny archer even crawled out from her hiding spot within a hollow log!

"Dearest Destiny," Helenia muttered. "We wouldn't have ever suspected they were even there."

A hunched and aged archer in a flat cap stepped directly up to Helenia. He stretched a prideful grin, his blackened teeth parting his white whiskers. In one of his puffy hands he gripped a sturdy longbow. The other cupped a puffing pipe.

"Aye, Princess, ye be blessed by Destiny we beed about. Me name be Tindal. Rufus Tindal. At thine service, I am."

Helenia grinned fondly as the old archer offered up an awkward bow, before struggling to straighten his spine.

"This be no time to chew the fat, Princess. Scaleez be apt to return. Me scouts shall see ye safe to the king. Nary ye fret, Princess, we will keep the scaleez well jittered on the skits. They not so keen to be scrappin' it up with ole' Rufus Tindal and me mates."

Several more archers nodded to concur.

Helenia was quite unaccustomed to salt jargon, yet something in the old archer's words and mannerisms made her feel safe for the first time in a very long while. Somehow, she just knew Rufus Tindal was one tough elder any lizarma would be hapless to meet.

"Thank you," Helenia said. "For saving us from the enemy, I mean. I assure you that my father will hear of your noble deed. You will be well rewarded, Rufus Tindal."

The old archer stretched another prideful grin. "No need of that, Princess. Spitting scaleez be its own reward. Ye best be off now."

Rufus Tindal nodded to a pair of young scouts, each of whom motioned for the princess and her soldiers to follow them deeper into the forest.

"Mind ye above," one of the scouts explained while thrusting his bow towards the canopy. "Lizarme assassins beed apt to hide in trees."

"My swoopers will warn us," Arduk responded with casual confidence.

Several apes exchanged puzzled looks.

"Uh, do you know how far it is to my father?" Helenia asked, taking hold of one scout's shoulder to slow his step.

"Three days trek," the scout replied. "King Myro keeps deep in the forest."

"The king and Olob make ready their troops to attack Prod Sergon come the next thaw," explained the second scout. "By then we apt to have a fit and proper army to scrap with. We will avenge Capital."

'Dearest Destiny,' Helenia thought with a grin. 'As if it is not enough for my father to fight a defensive war, now he plans to attack.' Naturally, she was not at all surprised.

They trekked onward for the entire day, pausing only once to replenish their grumbling bellies. Come dusk, they made camp and huddled together beneath blankets. There they listened to the incessant nattering and squeaking of the *unseens*. That is, all except Arduk, who, with bow in hand, had joined up with some prowlers and hooters. Together they set off to dispatch enemy assassins while Night's rule gave them an advantage, for lizarme could not see so well in the dark.

Just past the next peek of dawn, the soldiers broke camp and continued their march deeper into the forest. All senses were alert to the growth that surrounded them, yet only wee chirpers and curious critters peeked out from the foliage. Gentle gusts passing through the treetops rustled a soft song.

"Beed no battles this deep in the forest," one of the scouts explained to Helenia. "Scaleez be spooked on account of our archers. Natheless, we must keep keen of wit for assassins. They be our match with stealth and bow."

"They be sly of wit and bold of spirit too," added the other. "We must grant them such."

The scouts' words kept all eyes darting back and forth between their flanks and the canopy. All had learned from experience that lizarme were every bit as brave as apes or humanfolk. Neither side held a monopoly on daring.

Helenia would have stayed at the front of the column, except she once again took ill. Dropping to her knees, she spewed clean her belly. This time, however, Seed made it clear to the heaving princess the true cause of her sickness.

Thus, while being helped along by Shyamala and one of the apes, Helenia grew increasingly worried. She now understood the reason for Arduk's hinted smile after he'd touched her belly. With his peculiar howlers' senses, he had known even before she did. How was she going to tell her father a new life grows inside her womb? Or that it had been seeded by an unlettered stable lad? What would become of her tot's father?

Allied Armies Strike West

Aytik leaned against the stone and mortar base of the wall, thinking about his decision not to race home. The messenger from his father had arrived shortly after the battle, and the panicked prince had at once given orders for his troops to break camp. That was before Kryle and Torak had intervened and convinced him the king was quite right in ordering him to stay put; that the best way to save his homeland was to destroy the main bulk of Pid's army at The Wall and prevent it from marching east of the Divides.

"Pid wagers on you marching your army home," Kryle had noted with strong certitude. "It is part of his strategy that you should do so, thereby sapping our strength here at The Wall. He does not expect you to stay put and fight, let alone join forces with us and attack westward."

"Nary you fret, Prince," one of the eldest doyens had added. "I'd wager a full cycle's coinage your father and ole' Olob will make Prod Sergon's stay in your lands taste bitter on his best days. You can wager your crown Sergon will soon be keen to float his ships back home to Cracow."

"You know such is true," Torak had put in. "This very day, Prod Sergon surely finds himself mired in a form of warfare he had discounted, a form of warfare that cuts away at his troops morale bit by bit and day after day. Now we must do our part and crush Tarawa's army before it can recover. But we need your army to do so."

The apes' words had made sense. Thus, by pushing reason atop feelings, Aytik had buried his instincts and made the decision to press westward with his allies even though the thought of his homeland under lizarme occupation weighed constant on his mind. *'What of Shyamala? Helenia? Olob? Stork? My friends? The king?'*

Hanging his head in guilt, Aytik wiped wet from his eyes and thought of his final words to his father: *'I hate you!'* He

241

quickly pushed his mind to focus on Kryle's plan instead. Such a simple plan, really. Shortly past the close of dusk, all foot soldiers were to step softly up the pass and sneak in amongst the distant foliage.

Destiny had seemingly taken sides as well, for a thick flock of angry skysheep and the constant patter of skyshowers would veil sight and sound. A third gift from Destiny, a constant wind blowing due east, would help mask their scent; providing, of course, such perfect conditions were to prevail without change, for even the slightest shift in wind could betray their scent to enemy rexids.

"We must act this night or we may not see such an opportunity given to us again," Kryle had noted. "Destiny does not take well to having its gifts spurned."

The second phase of Kryle's plan called for the foot soldiers to keep hidden and merely observe the enemy camps in prep for a dawn attack. Accordingly, none were to engage the enemy until they heard the whistles, lest they should betray the allied strategy in its entirety and foil any chance of catching the lizarme army unawares. However, once the attack signal was given, they were to set upon the enemy swiftly and severely.

Once the battle had begun, all knights were to trot their beasts west through the muck in orderly formations before charging into the fray in support of their foot soldiers. All mounted attackers were to grant the enemy no quarter, their objective being to break the lizarme forces up into smaller units for allied foot soldiers to encircle and cut down piecemeal.

Kryle had mandated the attack would continue unabated by day and by night. At no time was the enemy to be free of a fight. At no time would allied units retreat. "Not one step backwards!"

Nap and nourishment would be slight until the enemy was pushed westward beyond the foothills and on into the Great Forests. Only then would the allies pause to rest and plan their campaign to surround and sack Dega Doom; providing, of course, Destiny and the winds of war should allow them to get that far?

Aytik thought of how Kryle often stated, "If is the biggest word in warfare." Yet never had the word *'if'* loomed so large as at this moment. *'What 'if' the enemy proves to be much stronger than we imagined? What 'if' Prod Tarawa suspects our attack? What 'if' Empress Antraha and her antemi warriors should turn their backs on us? What 'if' Shyamala…? No, I mustn't dwell on the 'ifs'… In Destiny's universe there are no ifs. What must be will be. My role is to show courage with honour – and leave the outcome to the deities.'*

Snapping his thoughts back onto the task at hand, Aytik looked about for any sign of Torak. The prince had promised to meet him here so that they could fight side-by-side. Torak's pledge had made Aytik feel somewhat better about Kryle's risky plan, for he much admired his new friend and knew the prince would have his back in battle. Even so, a swarm of bellybees buzzed about his guts.

Briefly, he allowed his mind to think of Golab. *'Are you enjoying Destiny's reward, my friend? Or are you still wandering about Morgue's maze in search of Utopia? Either way, be strong. In time I will join you. Then we will chew the blabble just as before. Once again we shall share in laughter. Until then, just know I think of you often.'*

Tears welled up in Aytik's eyes as he felt the warmth and energy of his friend's spirit flowing about him. He reluctantly pushed his thoughts away from Golab and redirected them onto his surroundings.

All about him, white ape commanders were belting out orders to scurrying soldiers. Wagons packed with brined meat and hardtack and other staples of warfare were being unloaded a short distance from the wall and stuffed into back packs. Some soldiers were gathered about fires, skewering chunks of raw tuskwooly meat for cooking, while others gnawed hardtack and slurped down bowls of hot potage. Battle-scarred tuskwoolies, many with their shag stained crimson, bellowed their woes to the dreary sky above. A column of spiketails hissed and snapped and glared about as they were led past on tethers.

Further south, the black apes were acting out similar scenes of preparation; while to the north, humanfolk commanders were busy forming their depleted forces up into long ranks to be divided up into brand new units.

Slightly to the east, many wounded soldiers were rowed out along the mucky ground, each waiting his or her turn in the infirmary. Already, piles of amputated limbs were filling the burn pits, which had been dug to prevent pestilence. Aytik pondered briefly as to the purpose of separating upper limbs from lower? What difference does it make, he wondered? All must be burned or buried?

Beyond the infirmary tents, weary looking knights tended to their skittish mounts. Some of the knights themselves bore bandages, yet they carried on with their tasks as though nothing out-of-sorts had occurred. Aytik's heart warmed with pride.

"You will pay dearly for what you have wrought, Supreme Pid," he muttered beneath his breath. "Even if I must sneak into Cracow and sever your head myself."

"My Prince?"

Aytik shifted his eyes to find a young knight commander bearing a puzzled expression and looking up at him. Behind the knight, a unit of humanfolk archers stood erect with fixed stares and muted tongues. Each archer bore a full pack and a quiver packed tight with arrows. Some were caked with dried blood from their helmets down to their highboots. More archers than not were bound with bandages, although not a one appeared in any way hesitant or distraught. In fact, Aytik detected a new eagerness in their rigid demeanor and fixed stares; one that demanded another go at the enemy!

"And soon you shall have it," Aytik muttered.

"My Prince?"

"Nothing, Sir Knight," Aytik said, offering up a disarming smile. "I was simply thinking out of mind."

The knight nodded that he understood. "These are the archers you summoned to serve with the white apes. They are battered, Prince – but they are far from broken. Wag of troubles back home has blown fire into their souls. They are spoiling for a spat and eager to march upon our enemy. As per the doyen commander's order, we vow not one step backwards until Cracow itself is sacked and Pid's head is spit on a pike."

Aytik reached out and patted the eager knight's shoulder. "One battle before the next, Sir Knight. In Morgue's time such may come to pass, but for now I want you to respect our white ape allies and deploy our archers wherever they see fit. They are to have our full accord. Is that understood?"

"Yes, my Prince."

"Very well then. Also, the black apes should be made an offer of archers as well. Commanders Leez and Shrike will provide all we can spare. I have already spoken with Doyen Commander Kryle."

"Yes, my Prince. Ah – my Prince?"

"What gnaws at your mind, Sir Knight?"

"We – that is, myself and the archers – well, we wish you comfort on account of Sir Golab. All know you two were close as kin, so I've been chosen to offer up sorrows."

Emotion welled up inside Aytik's chest and sank down into his gut. A lone tear seeped from his eye.

"My Prince, am I too loose with my tongue? If so…"

"No," Aytik assured the nervous knight. "Your words are welcome. Please offer my comfort to all archers who have lost mates and loved ones during this war. I too have taken on much rage over the rape of our homeland. That said, we must not let our feelings rule our sense. We must and will win this war, regardless of whatever sacrifices must be made."

The knight stretched a broad smile. "Nary you fret, Prince. Your father is not a king liken to welcome Prod Sergon with smiles and hugs. Ha! I'll wager a cycle's coinage the scaleez have long soured on slogging about the plains. No doubt much husk crop and highgrass has been stained crimson with lizarme blood."

Aytik likewise stretched a smile. "A wager you are sure to win, Sir Knight. I know my father well and, by the time we are triumphant and free to march home, Prod Sergon may well find his own head spit on a pike. Supreme Pid and his prods will all suffer the sorrows of their choices. You have my pledge."

A group murmur floated free from some archers as they nodded their heads in approval.

"Surely such will come to pass, my Prince. Leastways, if I have any sway in it. May I now tend to some tasks? There is much to be done."

"There is and you may."

As the knight turned away to tend to his duties, Aytik snagged sight of a much taller figure with sparkling orange eyes striding towards him. A flanged mace was clipped to his belt, and his hands were protected by armoured gauntlet gloves. A concave targe shield of iron-plated wood was slung across his back.

Noting the startled expression on his friend's face, Torak punched one fist into his palm before holding up his hands. "Like my gauntlets?" he asked, re-clenching his fist to show off his gloves. "Our best armourer fashioned them special for me. The spikes on the knuckle plates were her doing. Quite a nice touch if you ask me. She did make me pledge I would put them to good use, which is exactly what I intend to do. This night some unsuspecting lizarma will taste the quality of Jara steel."

"Uh, I'm sure more than one," Aytik responded.

"Oh, on that you can wager," Torak gloated. "Many lizarme tongues are going to taste the steel of these spiked gems. So how go the preparations?"

"Quite well," Aytik assured him. "In fact, it seems our knights and commanders are all so well suited to their tasks that I've begun to feel like more of an ass than an asset."

"Ha! That's because you are," Torak jested, turning away. "As am I. Come, we are of no further use here."

"Where are we going?" Aytik asked, swifting to catch up with the much taller ape.

Torak merely waved him to follow.

Torak led him about the muck, winding their way through the maze of toiling soldiers. On several occasions, Aytik was forced to halt or dodge to avoid colliding with some of them.

As they trekked further away from the wall, Aytik took note of some white apes sitting and scribing letters to their loved ones back home. Many more sat in circles about fire pits, some honing weapons while others cooked with skewers. The strong smell of tuskwooly meat goaded Aytik's belly to growl.

Other apes tended to their brethren's bandages, or flipped coins to relieve one another of their pay. Some chatted and laughed loudly, while others kept silent to themselves. A few swung axes to split logs for the flames. Many more were curled up in nap atop tough coir mats.

"I have instructed my knights to have our commanders work the foot soldiers in shifts," Torak explained. "Once the fighting resumes, it may be quite some time before any of them can take proper nap or nourishment."

"I have done likewise," Aytik said. "Kryle is quite adamant about there being no cease in hostilities until we've pushed the enemy back beyond the west foothills all the way to Cracow if need be. Hopefully Tarawa's soldiers are just as battered and weary as our own."

"They are," Torak assured him, pointing to the longhut with the three pennants flapping atop its pitched roof. "Come, let us take nap and nourishment. Keep keen of wit, stay spry and fit, I always say."

"But there is much to be done before dark?" Aytik noted.

Torak snagged hold of Aytik's sleeve. "Do you not have faith in your knights and commanders?" he asked.

"Yes, of course I do. Golab trained them well. It's just…"

"Then let them tend to their tasks," Torak cut in, making amused. "You have already admitted you are more of an ass than an asset. Besides, if we fail to keep ourselves sound of sense, then of what possible use will we be to others?"

"Uh – yes, I guess such is true. It's just I feel some degree of guilt at…"

"Guilt at what? At not being able to control everything? Ha! It certainly is humbling when we who wield power are forced to swallow our pride and admit just how little control we actually have over events. Powerlessness leaves a bitter taste on a royal tongue, won't you agree?"

"I – well, I've never really thought of it like that. I mean…"

247

Torak stopped still in his tracks. "Then perhaps you should, before you make yourself mad. You didn't start this war, Aytik. Nor will you end it. Only the deities can decide such things. The sooner you stop trying to figure everything out, the better off you are going to be. Are you to be held culpable for every humanfolk who meets Morgue in a war you did not start and cannot stop? Of course not.

"Many more will perish before this horrible war ends – both innocents and soldiers. War is unbiased and leaves no tears in its wake. War holds no favour with Morgue. War is evil in one syllable. I do not know where the solution lies, but we mortals had best find it before War devours us all. Otherwise, we are doomed."

"Torak, you speak of war as though it is a deity. Yet it is we mortals who give it breath. Without us war would not exist. It could not exist. So then, does the burden of war not fall squarely on ourselves? Is it not ours to own – and to overcome?"

"I think you give us mortals too much credit, Aytik."

"And I think you give us too little."

Torak sighed and placed his hand upon Aytik's shoulder. "I must apologize. You did not seek my opinion or my advice. It was vain of me to offer either without invite. Certainly not behaviour worthy of a friend. I am sorry."

"Torak, your apology is as unwanted as it is unnecessary," Aytik said as he followed the ape up the slippery steps and on into the longhut. "Friends must speak from the heart. True vanity is demanding others think with our mind – see with our eyes – hear with our ears – speak with our mouth. Forever holding others to feel and act as we do. Now that's arrogance!"

"You are right when you say friends must speak from the heart. The trick is knowing when to speak and when to hold one's tongue. Not always an easy choice to make."

"Even enemies must speak openly if they wish to make peace, Torak. After all, shouting and blaming is still discourse. I deem silence to be the true enemy of peace. For it is silence which first seeds resentment. Resentment next seeds revenge. Revenge then seeds conflict. Be it a lover's spat or a war, revenge too often plays its part. Hence, the mess in which we now find ourselves. Had we met the Lizarme offer to parley after the last war, perhaps we would not be fighting this one?"

"Perhaps? We will never know," Torak noted. "But we do know we must win this war. We can debate the peace afterwards."

After stomping the muck from his boots and hanging up his sword and cloak, Aytik paused to scan the room. All shutters were open to allow light and fresh air to enter, while the crackling stone hearth added much warmth.

Ape commanders were lying about on the wooden floor, either scribing letters or snoring in the realm of dreams. Several more sat and napped on the bench along one of the walls. A few sat in a circle on the floor, staring at an aging and portly black ape with a grey beard and thinning hair who was rapidly rattling something about in a tin cup.

"They're playing bone craps," Torak explained. "I don't know the rules, but many of our soldiers seem stuck on it. And as you can see, so do some of our commanders – including our doyens. Doyen Commander Kryle does not approve of wager games as such, but he does turn a blind eye to it. I myself see no harm in it if it gives their minds a brief reprieve from the horrors of war and from pining for home. It is also a game both white and black apes enjoy playing together. Camaraderie can form over such things."

"I've never understood why white and black apes would fight each other to begin with? Are you not both apes?"

Torak sighed. "I have often wondered how so many could be so foolish for so long? What matters most is we are coming together now, albeit perhaps not as quickly as I would wish. The key to goodwill is to learn from the past, but always with a focus on the future. It is important to avoid blame. We must take heed never to rip scabs off old wounds and make our former enemy bleed all over again. Bigotry can be most patient, Aytik. Too often it takes but one careless comment to raise the wrath of Morgue."

Aytik watched as Doyen Grob suddenly tipped the cup downside-up, thus spilling its contents across the tabletop. Different coloured bones rattled to a stop beside a pile of coins.

"Yes!" Grob exclaimed, pumping his fist before raking in all of the coins.

Several of the losing apes buried their faces in their hands.

"It's turning out to be a fine game for Grob," Aytik noted. "Although I'm not so certain it's all that fine for the losers."

Torak made amused. "Don't worry. Grob will probably lose it all in the next few spills. Then it will be another's turn to gloat."

"So why keep playing once you've already won?" Aytik asked.

Torak shrugged. "Mostly to help ease the dumps of alone, I imagine? And to give your comrades in arms a chance to win back their coin. After all, the same soldiers you are playing bone craps against one day may be fighting alongside you the next. Your very being may depend on them guarding your back in combat. For that reason alone, there can still be camaraderie even in rivalry. No one soldier wins every time and they all share pretty much everything anyway. It all works out in the end. Come, let us fill our bellies."

After leading Aytik over to the small table with the clay urn and a smaller jug on top, Torak retrieved a metal skewer from one bucket and speared a large chunk of cooked meat from another. "Feast freely," he said as he raised the dripping gobbet to his mouth. "It is still warm and it may be our last cooked meal for some time."

Aytik quickly unsheathed his hurling dagger and stabbed a chunk for himself. Tearing a piece off with his teeth, he was surprised at how tender and tasty tuskwooly meat was. He savoured every bite as the juice trickled down his chin.

"Here," Torak said, offering forth a basket of hardtack. "These biscuits may be bland of taste, but they still stuff a hole."

No sooner had Aytik taken one of the biscuits, than an aged ape with missing teeth handed he and Torak empty goblets. With some effort, the old ape then raised the jug to pour.

"Ah, warm mead," Torak said, savouring a sniff. He purposefully raised the goblet to his lips and slugged down a hearty gulp. Then he motioned for Aytik to partake. "Enjoy it my friend, for this may be the last pleasure we know for some time."

"Just don't know it too well," Aytik said with a smirk, raising his goblet to sip. "Kryle would blow a bulge if he knew we were downing jabber juice just prior to battle. You know how he feels about such things having their proper place and time and all."

"One drink won't slay us, Aytik. After we've feasted, we'll simply nap it off. I must allow myself one simple pleasure amidst the gory of war. The strange thing is, before all this fighting began I never much cared for mead. Always found it too strong, both in flavour and in fallout. Or should I say fall down. Ha! Now mead has become like a warm friend to me. It softens the sads. Hence, I will keep drinking it until after the war. Then I shall return to drinking wine and ale."

Aytik felt the claws of concern scratching his mind. "We must all deal with sorrow in our own way, Torak. I hope when this war is over you will find mead less a friend to you."

After gorging their bellies near to burst, both exhausted princes stretched out to nap near the hearth. Aytik lay awake for some time, just listening to the crackle of burning embers and savouring the warmth before drifting off into dreams...

****

...when next he awakened, Aytik found himself seemingly alone in the longhut. Beyond the walls, an unseen commander was shouting out orders that all foot soldiers were to be at their posts by the first hint of dusk.

"Torak?" Aytik said, drawing himself up to a sit and looking about. He sighed in relief as his eyes found the white ape making amused and offering him his garbs and sword.

"I was just about to waken you," Torak explained. "There is barely enough daylight for you to stretch and wash. But you mustn't dally."

Aytik quickly donned his trousers, and then washed his face from a basin that had been placed atop the table. The cool water awakened his senses.

After stretching stiffness from his joints, Aytik struggled to pull on his boots. His toes eagerly welcomed the snug, warm fit. With such in mind, he slid his hurling dagger into its sheath.

His cloak had dried from its hanging and he noted the difference in weight. It hung proper about his shoulders.

"The lighter your attire, the swifter in battle you will be," Golab had often stated with a wagging forefinger; always adding, *"And the swifter in battle you be, the further from Morgue you will be."*

Aytik smiled as he clipped his sword to his belt and snatched up his gloves. So far, the battles fought had proved Golab correct. Speed was indeed crucial in battle. After all, what good was strength if you missed with your blows? Then again, what good was speed if your blows did not count?

"Balance!" Golab had often scolded. *"You must keep an equal balance between strength and speed!"*

Pushing his friend from his thoughts, Aytik sighed and stepped from the longhut. More skyshowers had fallen during late day, so he took caution as he descended the slippery steps towards Torak.

"The temp dips near to the freeze," Torak noted, making amused.

"Tis that quarter of the cycle," Aytik reasoned, relieving himself on the ground. "Warm by day, cold by night."

"Tis," Torak agreed.

Thousands of foot soldiers were quietly forming up into ranks directly in line with the wider breaches, while shivering sentinels kept an alert vigil from atop the wall's bastions. Ape and humanfolk knights were either tending to their beasts at the pens, or taking nap and nourishment well back from the wall.

Just beyond the breaches, sappers floated about the moat on rafts laden with planks. A faint glow from small, shaded lanterns assisted them with quietly laying the planks onto piles. The lanterns would also help guide the combat troops safely across the moat while masking their movements from any spying eyes to the west.

252

"Perhaps Destiny will bless us with skybangers and skyshowers to mask sound? Such would be welcome."

"Do not wager on such, Torak," Aytik replied. "You yourself noted how the temp dips close to the freeze. If it stays its course, we are more apt to get snow. That would place our dark shapes at risk against a white blanket. But it would be best if the temperature held and offered up naught save for steady skyshowers – minus any crackling flashbolts that could light up the pass. The darker it stays the better our chances."

"I will implore Destiny for such," Torak assured him.

Aytik merely nodded as his mind was now busy going over the battle plan one last time. Placed at the fore of the army were the elite spiketail squads, who would cross the moat and advance up the pass first. It would be their unenviable task to sneak in amongst the enemy camps and silently dispatch any sentinels. None but the most capable handlers and their best trained spiketails had been chosen, as one errant cough or hiss could cost their entire army its all-important advantage of surprise.

Next to advance would be the humanfolk archers, whose first task was to flood the enemy camps with a torrent of flaming arrows precisely upon hearing the attack whistles. All tents and huts were to be put to the torch. The objective was to wreak such terror and chaos that enemy commanders would be hard pressed to offer up an organized defense.

The remaining bulk of the allied foot soldiers would then charge into the enemy camps and dispatch without quarter any lizarme who dared stand their ground, while many more spiketails would be hastily brought forward to engage the rexids.

At the onset of battle, all mounted knights, both ape and humanfolk, were to advance from behind the wall and trot cautiously up the pass. Upon reaching the foliage at the western end, scouts and the clamour of battle would lead the knights to the heaviest fighting, where they would lower their lances and spearhead a charge. By using such tactics, larger enemy units would be broken up, allowing allied foot soldiers to surround and destroy the smaller units piecemeal. Whenever possible, lizarme commanders were to be captured alive and taken at once for *'probing'* by *'specialists'*.

Aytik cringed as he recalled Kryle's tone: "We have developed methods of making even the most loyal lizarme find their tongues. We are not losing this war."

With dusk descending over the pass, nervous soldiers kept mute and tended to their own thoughts. Some broke ranks to relieve themselves. Others took sips from their skins or clay costrels, not all of which carried water. All knew this night could change the course of the war. All knew this night could be their last.

Night finished routing Day and twilight settled over the pass. Soon all would be blanketed in blackness. Neither shapes nor shadows stirred in the chilly drizzle.

Aytik's eyes sighted the faint glow from shaded lanterns. His ears caught the rustle of an army breaking ranks and marching softly towards the breach.

"Stay close to me," a familiar voice spoke from the dark.

"I cannot see you, Torak" Aytik replied.

"Just hear my breath and keep near to it."

Aytik became very aware of the many forms moving forward all about him, yet he had no inkling as to who was whom? He could only pray unto Destiny that somehow he and Torak would find their way into battle together.

A dull *splush* announced the careless drop of one of the spanning planks. It was promptly followed by an irate voice quietly cursing out some sappers. The glowing lanterns formed two rows leading to the planks, and the troops began soft marching up the middle. An occasional creak or clunk revealed that somewhere in the blackness soldiers were already crossing the moat.

Aytik's ears snagged the whisper of a spiketail being scolded for expelling a nervous hiss. Then he felt a plank underfoot. The slippery surface seemed to bend and bounce beneath his feet, forcing him to extend both arms to maintain his balance. Directly before him, vague shapes were passing by the lanterns. Hot breath blew across his neck.

"Mind your footing, Aytik."

"I'm fine, Torak,"

"You up there, button thy lips."

It seemed like forever had come and gone by the time Aytik's feet again felt the slop of muck under his boots. He gasped beneath his breath when one of his feet stepped upon something solid, yet fleshy.

"Mind you don't trip over any bloats," Torak whispered. His tone was tinged with amusement.

"Not funny, Torak."

"Shush."

Aytik was fully aware of the many forms moving west all about him as he slogged through the chilly muck. On occasion, a muffled cuss would reveal that yet another soldier had wandered directly into one of the unseen stumps, or bumped into another soldier. Or tripped over something fleshy?

Soon the temp dipped below the freeze and the mucky ground began to harden. Shortly thereafter, Destiny either cursed or blessed the attackers by blanketing the pass with the type of soft, powdered snow that favours sneaky steps. Whether or not the troops were blessed or cursed would depend on if the moon found a gap in the skysheep, for it would not take many moonbeams to expose such a large bulk of dark shapes creeping slowly in mass across a white surface.

Even so, the frozen ground and the snow were a welcome change from the drizzling skyshowers that had fallen all throughout the day. All knew that if the moon remained hidden, the chance of them catching the enemy completely unawares would keep more to the better. The enemy should be remiss to any attack under such conditions. If they were apt to consider any attack at all?

The allied army crept on without rest for most of the night, stepping softly across kilopaces of frozen ground before finally sneaking in amongst the foliage at the western end of the pass. Here the snow became much deeper and they often found themselves trudging through drifts up to their knees. Still and all, no incidents took place to suggest their attack had been compromised as they regrouped at their jump off points along the fringes of the enemy camps.

Peeking out from between the boughs of a thick needle tree, Aytik was astonished to find many lizarme huddled about a huge fire pit. It had been strategically dug in the center of a large clearing so the intense heat from the flames would send warm air into the hemp tents pitched in a circle around it.

One tent in particular troubled Aytik's mind. Whenever a nurse or an orderly parted the flaps, he could see inside its walls. He noted with some guilt it was an infirmary tent, for its floor was strewn with straw and packed tight with writhing forms on canvas stretchers. The moans of the amputees were broken only by their screams.

Somewhere in the distance, a lone dact screeched its ire at the frigid temp.

"Pin him still whilst I saw it off!" a gruff voice commanded in the ancient continental language.

"Dearest Destiny," Aytik muttered to nobody in particular as he allowed the bough to gently swing back into place. "They're no better off than we."

"Which is precisely the purpose of this attack," Torak reminded him, also guiding a bough back into place. "Their thoughts are with the past battle, hence none foresee this new battle. The fools even neglected to post sentries. Our scouts found very few necks to snap and zero rexids to cull."

"So why do I feel qualms of conscience?" Aytik whispered.

Aytik felt a heavy hand upon his shoulder. "You feel such because you are a decent being. Despite all that has happened you still see the enemy as something more than fodder for flame and blade – which may be an admirable quality in times of peace, my friend, but we are trapped in a time of war. A war we must win at any cost."

Steering his eyes to the east, Aytik took note of the first fingers of daylight poking atop the horizon. He also noticed the flock of skysheep was quickly blowing over.

'*Even the winds grow angry,*' Aytik thought, removing his gloves and rubbing his hands together to warm his fingers.

'Before long the sky will be blue and all warmth will escape us. It promises to be a bitterly cold day for a fight.'

"The frigid temp will hinder the enemy as much as ourselves," Torak noted, as if he could read Aytik's thoughts. "Breath easy and keep alert for the whistles."

Aytik kept still and awaited the whistles, while dawn gradually exposed the allied soldiers to each other.

"What are they waiting for," somebody whispered. "Let's get on with it."

"Shush..."

Glancing about, Aytik took note of a great many allied soldiers crouching behind drifts and boughs. White forms with blue faces and orange eyes gripped maces and pikes. Eager humanfolk archers who had wrapped oily rags about the shafts of their arrows and bolts were now poised to ignite them; after which a torrent of flame would shower down upon the clearing, burning hemp and straw and flesh. Such is how the coming slaughter would begin.

Day was quickly forcing Night into a westward retreat. All knew the attack whistles must be but moments away. Bellybees swarmed within knotted-up guts.

Finally, they heard the signal blow from somewhere far to the north. Although stifled by wind and distance, it was undeniably the blast from a whistle.

A second, clearer whistle sounded a bit closer on down the line. Almost instantly, it was followed by an even louder third. Next, a fourth...

Aytik's ears were pained by the blast from Torak's whistle. He jumped up with a start and glared daggers at his friend, who totally ignored him and kept blowing hard and fast.

The stillness was shattered by the cry of many thousands of apes and humanfolk shouting as one. Even so, Aytik's ears snagged the distinct whoosh of a stream of flaming arrows passing over his head. The battle was on!

Aytik watched with mixed emotions as arrows tore into hemp and straw and flesh. All about the fire pit, panicked lizarme tripped over one another in a mad scramble to avoid the flaming missiles. Some grabbed hold of their targe shields and tridents, frantically looking about for the source of the onslaught.

A composed middle commander took control and pointed to where a group of apes were abandoning their hiding places and trudging through deep drifts. At least until a well placed bolt pierced his breastplate and he sank to his knees, before pitching face down into the snow.

Another stream of flaming arrows whizzed over Aytik's head, finding their mark in hemp and straw and flesh. More tents were set ablaze. Badly wounded soldiers screamed in pain as the burning canopy of the infirmary tent melted down upon them. Merely a few managed to stagger out through the flaps, where they were cut down by bolts from the crossbows.

Chaos claimed the clearing now as more allied soldiers raged forth from the drifts and trees and set upon their disorganized enemy. Humanfolk archers advanced with the apes, taking aim and shooting on the swift. Several spiketails began tearing a squealing rexid to pieces.

Aytik felt his stomach spin as he watched a burning lizarma roll about in the snow. Until a thrust from an ape's pike mercifully silenced his screams.

"Come on, Aytik!" Torak shouted, pushing to his feet and brandishing his weapon. "My mace craves crimson!"

The flames had fully engulfed every tent, and those lizarme still able were fleeing deeper into the forest; ignoring a high commander's wasted orders to stand their ground and fight. The stubborn officer kept screaming for his soldiers to engage the advancing apes. That is, until an arrow stuck into the frozen ground between his feet. With his enthusiasm for battle suddenly run dry, the shaken commander desperately hurled his trident at a charging ape, before turning and fleeing after his troops.

Aytik pushed up to his feet. Torak was already charging into the fray, followed closely by even more apes and archers. Across the clearing, some well-disciplined lizarme had somehow managed to regroup and were now hurling spears at their attackers. The apes countered by advancing from behind a shield wall.

"Madness," Aytik muttered, unsheathing his sword. Then he too charged forward to join in the attack. "Not one step backwards!"

Antraha

A bug-like being with bulging dichoptic eyes and a red chitin exoskeleton stood stoic as she peered out over a bamboo balustrade. A crown of pink ivory sat atop her head. She was clad merely in a grass skirt which hung past the patellae of her long, stilted legs. A hardwood cudgel dangled from her vine belt. Her fingers were wrapped tight about a blackwood sceptre of authority. Her other hand clenched a vellum scroll; tightly rolled and bound with a length of vine.

Shifting her sights, she briefly took in the aged aeront that stood saddled and ready by her side. Six skinny legs still steadied its body like it was newly hatched, but greying bristles on its legs, head and abdomen betrayed it to be many cycles past its prime; as did the age blotches staining its chitin. Its four wings were visibly brittle and frayed about the fringe.

'No matter, old friend. You are still able to zip in and out of this jungle's maze at ample speed. The cycles have slowed our bodies, but they have also tutored our minds. Age is Fate's will for all beings of breath and none should feel shamed by such. Even if the chitin about my face has started to dry and crack, am I to be less an empress for it? I should think not.'

Antraha proudly inspected her attack force. Orderly ranks of antemi knights and their aeronts lined the clearing before her, each armed with a cudgel and a long wooden lance. Carved whistles dangled about their necks.

Many more antemi warriors and aeronts were crouched high up in the trees all about the clearing. As with the knights, every antemi warrior bore a cudgel. They were also armed with composite bows fashioned from bamboo, horn and sinew. Hide quivers, packed full with their unique graphene arrows, were slung across their backs.

260

Silence stirred in the jungle as thousands of bulging eyes and anxious ears awaited her command. Nary a knight or a warrior moved save for breath.

Five legions in all would take part in the attack. Thirty thousand warriors in total, led by an additional three thousand knights. Every one of them eager to avenge their ancestors and willing to meet Perish to do so. Thoughts of valor in victory filled every young mind, while the eldest warriors and knights prayed unto both Fate and Perish that their victory would be simple and swift; that the conflict raging far away at The Wall would draw elite lizarme troops east and further away from Muga Terro.

Antraha mulled over the past events which had made her risk war against such a powerful foe. Oasis Lake had been home to the antemi for over a thousand generations. Legend states Fate had gifted them with an abundance of sweet water so they could dwell and prosper in peace, which was exactly what they were doing right up until the lizarme attacked and conquered the great city of Muga Terro, slaying every antema they could find with neither grace nor pity. Those antemi who somehow escaped the slaughter were forced to flee on foot to the south, trekking across burning desert sands to seek refuge deep within the sweltering depths of the Dark Jungle, where they had hidden and adapted ever since the *'Great Slaughter'*.

In time, Supreme Pid ascended to the throne. Being an especially cruel and ambitious tyrant, he quickly ordered his armies to march south and conquer the Dark Jungle. To ensure against any future rebellions, Prod Gila's silence squads were to exterminate the oversized bugs once and for all. It was to be a genocide, with not a single antema left of breath. Every egg was to be found and crushed. The antemi were to be completely erased from history.

However, the antemi's bulging eyes granted them far superior vision in the dark. A second advantage was the jungle aeronts they had tamed for flight. The agile beasts could easily zip about the jungle's tricky maze at far greater speeds than the lizarme's larger and more awkward dacts. Thirdly, the aeronts and antemi both bore extremely hard chitin exoskeletons. Being much tougher than skin or bone, chitin was less prone to lacerations; a vital advantage when zipping about the tall thistles and thorny vines that grow in abundance all throughout the Dark Jungle. The fleshy dacts simply could not compete. As a result, the antemi species had not only been spared extinction, but they were able to claim mastery of the jungle. This enabled them to breed and grow in safety, thereby increasing in numbers and power.

To further fuel Pid's frustration, his soldiers had been entangled in a costly battle of containment ever since. Antemi swarms had even taken to attacking lizarme units at night in the desert, keeping them napless with needled nerves. Skittish lizarme foot soldiers seldom forayed in past the jungle's fringe, for the skilled antemi warriors would almost always win such skirmishes with small cost to themselves. Lizarme soldiers were constantly forced to scurry for cover, lest they should be spit by a lance or pierced by an arrow. Every lizarma knew they were at a disadvantage when fighting outside of their element, that they were simply no match for antemi in the jungle. Morale had long since sunk to the bottom of their minds.

For generations the antemi had patiently longed for revenge. Antraha's own mother had promised her that in time Muga Terro and Oasis Lake would again come under antemi rule. Never one to reap reckless, the former empress had also stressed to her daughter and heir that she must never attack unless they could match might with their foe. *"Only attack when you know you can win."*

Empress Antraha was not fully certain if such was presently the case, for *if* can be a very big word. Even a dangerous word. Still, she was forced to admit to her innermost self that events now unfolding across The Continent certainly seemed like a gift from Fate? And almost since Hatch had first breathed her into being, Antraha's mother had often warned her, *"Anta, never dismiss a gift from Fate – for to reject such a powerful deity never bodes well. It may even mean a quick meeting with Perish."*

Messengers from Raw, Capital and Apel had arrived barely a half cycle past with news of the war raging between the lizarme and the allies. Not that she was totally without her suspicions. For over a cycle, lizarme activity about the jungle fringe had steadily waned. In fact, large scale engagements had ceased altogether.

'A ploy to lure us out from the safety of the canopy?'

However, her own spies had recently informed her that the hungry ones had grown in strength and numbers. Unlike their limited raids of the past, they were now attacking in force and causing chaos all throughout the realm. In fact, they were causing so much chaos that Pid had burned red with rage and ordered the immediate execution of any lizarme even suspected of aiding the rebels. There were to be no more interrogations or forced confessions. Mere suspicion alone was the new standard. Retribution to be swift; whatever was more convenient, the chop or the noose. As well, any lizarme considered *impure* by the Ministry of Visual Acceptance would be put down. Only those skilled *deforms* considered essential workers would be spared to toil in war production; albeit in shackles, of course.

Antraha felt her gut wrench with disgust. *'So now you slaughter your own innocents as well. Clearly, you have lost all sense of sanity. You have become a blight on all that is good – a disease feasting on virtue. Who can say how much suffering we must all endure before your reign of terror is ended? But I can promise you this, Supreme Pid – end it shall.'*

Antraha always found it strange how she could pity young lizarme, and for a moment her heart warmed with compassion. She grasped all too well the cruelty rulers with great power and no pity can exact upon their own kind. She understood how the young could be molded by *'education'* to despise those they had never met. Molded to hate those who think differently than themselves. Yes, the trick to tyranny is always to poison the minds of the youth. Teach them what to think instead of how to think. Teach them what to believe and say and feel. Teach them that any who question the mob must be canceled. Since Pid's ascension to the throne, lizarme youth had been taught to believe they were the moral ones. The enlightened ones. Taught to believe older lizarme are wicked.

Especially those elders who resist the regime, and most especially those who would seek to topple it.

Antraha sighed and thought, *'Indoctrinated youth – they know not that they know not. Sickly, I beg of Fate you will win. And that you will keep your promise to me.'*

Antraha had long believed it was her calling to drive the lizarme out of Muga Terro and reclaim it as her own. She would not pass such a burden on to future generations. With the bulk of Pid's troops mired in a much broader conflict of his own making, and with much of his army either fighting defensive battles in the east or preoccupied fighting domestic enemies at home, it seemed now was Fate's chosen moment for her to strike north and re-capture what is rightfully hers. The future could not grant her more favourable conditions than those in the present. *'I must act.'*

She would venture no further north, however, for conquest was not her intent. If the allies wish to dominate the lizarme, then let them raze Dega Doom and Cracow by themselves. There would be no repeat of past mistakes. This time around, antemi legions would not be sacrificed to spare apes and humanfolk, only to be abandoned to battle the lizarme all on their own. Her ancestors had been duped by the allies during the Great Continental War. She had no desire to become history's latest fool after this Second Continental War was over. Especially since the allies had neglected to assure her they would refuse any separate truce with Pid. No, her kind would take back only what was rightfully theirs, but no more.

However, if Pid were deposed, then perhaps she could come to terms with a battered and bloodied lizarme nation? Perhaps there could be peace and trade agreements? Maybe her nation would opt to share the sweet water of Oasis Lake with lizarme nomads and traders. To view their former enemy as partners and guests. It would take time as much prejudice exists. Still, such might become possible if Sickly and the hungry ones should win?

Antraha again panned her sights over her warriors, comforted by the fact that those within view were just a small token of her entire force. They would zip north beneath the jungle canopy, gathering others along the way until they reached the jungle's northern fringe. From there they would fly only at night, making camp beneath the desert sands during the day. All warriors would be ordered to burrow deep and allow the dry desert winds to mask their tracks. None of her scouts were to engage or even reveal themselves to the enemy until after the assault on Muga Terro had begun. Victory would depend on stealth and surprise; plus, of course, on courage. This time the enemy would be fighting in their own element, thus there would be no tall thistles or thorny vines to hinder the dacts.

Satisfied with her thoughts, Antraha turned her attentions back to her knights and warriors. There was no need for further delay. It was time to act. She could almost feel Fate's fingers prodding her.

Without speaking a word, she raised the scroll high atop her head and began wielding it like a cudgel. Almost instantly, commotion erupted all about the clearing.

"AN-TRA-HA!! AN-TRA-HA!! AN-TRA-HA!!" chanted her warriors.

Quickly, the orgy of hysteria began to increase in both cadence and intensity.

"AN-TRA-HA!! ANTRAHA!! ANTRAHA!!"

Antraha was moved to cover her ears, for the roar of shouting combined with the clack of cudgels banging on boughs shook the very jungle itself.

"ANTRAHA!! ANTRAHA!! ANTRA…"

Empress Antraha respectfully held her tongue until the crescendo had waned, for she was much moved by her warriors passion for battle. She had briefed her knights over and over again, continually emphasizing the pivotal nature of the arduous task before them. For the direction of history is not so easily altered.

When at last Antraha moved to speak, she removed the cord and unraveled the scroll. She loosened her tongue into the monotone voice that was just as much a part of any antema's being as were their bulging eyes or chitin.

"Hear me! Hear me all! It is written on this, our most sacred scroll, that Oasis Lake was gifted to our ancestors by none other than Fate itself!"

"AN-TRA-HA!! AN-TRA-HA!! ANTRAHA!!"

Antraha paused to let the chanting wane.

"And as Fate's gift to us, Oasis Lake will always belong to us – and to us alone!"

"AN-TRA-HA!! AN-TRA-HA!! ANTRA…"

"I hereby swear to it that before the hot quarter returns Muga Terro will be ours!"

"HOORRAY!! ANTRAHA!! ANTRAHA!! ANT…"

Antraha's dichoptic eyes sparkled the colours of pride as she looked out over her zealous and devoted knights, each of whom was fisting support and pounding the butt of their lance upon the ground. Even the feisty aeronts were shrilling their desire to take part in whatever it was their riders were on about. The entire spectacle made her insides warm with love for her subjects.

With nothing more to say, she simply passed the scroll and sceptre to a courtier and swung her leg over her aeront's thorax. Then she skillfully coaxed her aged pet to hover.

A deafening drone filled the jungle as thousands more antemi followed her lead. Gusts from transparent wings rustled leaves and felt cool against chitin. Keeping true to their antemi ways, not one face exposed any emotion.

Soon every aeront was hovering in place. Knights perked up spry in the saddle, their lances clenched firmly in hand. Warriors bridged their reins in one hand, while brandishing their bows with the other.

Satisfied all was as it should be, Antraha fondly patted her aging aeront's head before gripping tight the reins and pressing the eager beast to take flight. Thousands more antemi pressed their beasts to follow.

As the swarming mass flew north beneath the jungle canopy, many more colonies arrived and began swelling the ranks on its flanks. All riders clenched their weapons with purpose as the feisty beasts zipped in and out of the thick

266

foliage. The deafening drone of mass migration testified that literally legions of antemi warriors were now on the move. Even the jungle itself seemed to part in respect.

Antraha looked about and nodded at some of the familiar faces she recognized. One elderly drone, mounted upon a rare white beast with pink eyes, tipped his lance in salute. She nodded to acknowledge him, before steering her eyes ahead. Although the drone was her oldest and dearest donor, she had never thought it wise to act too informal around him. Such behaviour, she reasoned, might create the impression she chose favorites, which was something every egg-layer would be wise to avoid. Still, she felt comfortable knowing her most virile and loyal drone was close by, and that he would gladly battle beyond his final breath to defend her.

Antraha thought, *'It is sometimes difficult being both empress and egg-layer to the warrior class. Why did Fate choose me for this role?'* Satisfied that none but Fate would ever know the answer, she let slip with an extremely rare smile of satisfaction; for Hatch had again blessed her with a fertile sac, and it was always good for an antemi ruler to provide her nation with some two hundred future knights.

Night attacked and retreated and attacked and retreated, but it could not hinder the massive swarm from making quick progress. Antemi had long been accustomed to taking nourishment in the saddle, touching down only to tend to their mounts. Their moments of rest were always brief, before the droning legions would once again rise up from the desert sands and swarm north to Muga Terro; guided only by Night's watchful skytwinklers and Fate's pointing hand.

Antraha did not count the passing days as her warriors zipped beneath the canopy. To her, what did it matter? Her army would do their part to reach Muga Terro, but the moment of attack had always belonged to Fate. Faith in the ancient deities had long been her strength. It relieved her of fear and doubt.

Long before she became empress, she had wisely trusted her future to Fate. In return, the deity had blessed her with the strength of character needed to lead so many young antemi into battle, knowing many would soon rest with Perish.

Eventually, the thick canopy began to thin out and more beams from the sun warmed the jungle floor. Antraha amused herself by watching the lesser creatures scurry or swing for safety below her. From time to time, some of the terrified creatures would stare up at the droning swarm and natter or growl or squawk forth their ire. One frightened and furious family of bough swingers even tried hurling banana fingers at the noisy intruders; a futile act that placed rare grins upon the faces of their amused tormentors.

'They look like tiny apes,' Antraha thought. 'Or perhaps even very hairy humanfolk. I wonder if there might be a link?'

Shortly thereafter, the sweltering dampness of the jungle began to cool. Leafage thinned and the sky took to peeking in through gaps in the canopy. A cooling breeze could be felt alongside gusts from aeront wings. An army of skytwinklers blinked its vigil across the above. High above, the full moon glowed to assert its command.

'Not much further now,' Antraha thought. 'We should reach the desert slightly past the peek of dawn. We'll make camp along the forest fringe until darkness returns.'

Sure to her estimate, they reached the jungle fringe just slightly past the peek of dawn. However, save for dispatching a few trusted and well-seasoned scouts, she would not allow any others to venture off into the desert. Instead, she ordered a forced nap beneath the safety of the canopy, instructing her knight commanders to post a triple guard around the perimeter, with a strict dictate to slay any lizarme they encountered.

"None can escape to warn their army in Muga Terro," Antraha stated. "We cannot risk granting Pid ample time to send reinforcements. We must keep keen of wit at all times. Also, my sac throbs swollen and fertile. Send me some mating drones at once."

Her knight commanders simply nodded before leaving their empress to her thoughts. All knew her well. Antraha would no longer wish to discuss strategy. In her mind, the pieces were set in place. She could do no more. Fate alone held sway over events yet to pass. What should be, would be. Besides, the thirsty desires of her mating instincts were parched. And until such desires were quenched, her mind and body would be of one focus: Mating Drones.

After allowing the drones to spray her sac, Antraha shooed them away to expire. She would not feast on them. For now she would gorge herself on bugs and bumblesweet, before curling up tight to take nap...

****

Enticing dreams kept Antraha at peace for most of Day's rule. By the time she aroused, Night's army of skytwinklers was fast advancing from the east.

Antraha looked up at the moon and thought to herself, *'You command your army, eternal one – now let me command mine.'*

Upon pushing to her feet, she at once became dizzy and spewed clean her belly. Once recovered, she raised her eyes to the above and offered a humble prayer unto Hatch. "Thank you for these joyous gifts which grow inside of me. As Perish is my witness, I promise you this batch will break shell in Muga Terro. And the first pupa hatched shall be named after you."

Satisfied her prayers had been heard with approval, Antraha quickly ordered her mount be re-saddled, while she herself devoured a small feast of nuts, fruit and bumblesweet. Yet more than anything else, she craved meat. Most any meat. Saliva mixed with acids dripped from her chin. Past experience had proven such would be her curse until the next laying.

Developing larva required an abundance of protein. Without it, an egg-layer risked spoiling the entire batch. Antraha still carried the guilt of one such tragedy, and she had no desire to weep through another. Tissue of decaying aeront wings would add vital nutrients into her diet.

Several of the best hunters were informed of the empress's condition and dispatched to find flesh. Until they returned, she would have to gnaw her next meal from the severed thorax of an unfortunate aeront. A necessary act that much disgusted her, yet was still preferable to the tart taste of her own brothers and sons.

Shortly thereafter, some hunters returned with the breathless bodies of three bough swingers. Instantly, Antraha began to gorge the raw flesh, her sharp teeth tearing off chunks by the glut. Crimson stained her cheeks and dripped down her chin as her jaws ground up the fresh gobbet. More crimson dripped from her greasy fingers. Still, her greedy belly growled aloud for more.

More hunters arrived with fresh flesh for her feed, and then quickly re-took to their task. Each knew well they would take little nap or nourishment until after the laying, for the sac of an egg-layer knows no fill. Yet, they were content in their role. They would tend to their Empress day and night without gripe.

Night had once again conquered the above and spread its dark blanket across the drifting desert sands when the droning mass took flight. It zipped northward while keeping low to the dunes, for a clear above and a full moon greatly increased the risk of a sighting.

Antraha had planned her moves well. When she attacked, the moon would be waned to a sliver. She had timed it so the moon would only wax back to full shine after they had laid siege to Muga Terro. Hence, her nocturnal warriors would enjoy a huge tactical advantage throughout the first crucial night of the battle. A quick campaign was what she desired. Nevertheless, she was firm to see the conflict through to its divine conclusion; no matter the cost.

While steering her aeront above the rolling blanket of sand, Antraha savoured the cooling sensation of chilly desert air flowing across her chitin. She could also feel the eggs forming inside of her, painfully stretching the protective membrane of her sac. The thought of her next batch breaking shell in Muga Terro pumped pleasure into her heart, while cravings for raw meat forced foam from her mouth.

Carrier

Arduk was rudely awakened by a boot to the bone cage, before being yanked to his feet by the scruff of his tunic. Next, a shove sent him face first into the snow. His mind raced to catch up with the events swirling about him.

"Move along, ye unlettered letch!" growled a burly guard with a gruff voice. "Thy king fancies a chat of ye!"

Once more, the young ladfolk was yanked to his feet by the scruff of his tunic. He growled and bared his teeth at the guards who poked and shoved and prodded him along one of the slushy paths that wound its way about the tall needle trees of the Upcoast Forests. Yet he chose neither fight or flight, for he had fully expected to face the king's wrath at some point. There could be no avoiding it.

In a way he was relieved the time was now at hand. The waiting and worrying had been his torment ever since Helenia had first conceived. Arduk ventured the king would not banish or behead the father of his very own grandtots. Or so he hoped?

"Keep thine legs on the swift!" growled the burly guard with a gruff voice. "Steer ye eyes straight to the fore!"

"Mind this one close!" warned a nervous guard. "It is he who put the bite to big Butch. Chomped his ear clean off, he did."

"Me heerd Butch beed beggin' a bashin'," noted another guard.

"Big Butch always be beggin' a bashin'," offered a smaller guard, whose oversized helmet slid past his eyes.

"Silence! Just tend to thine tasks!" ordered the burly guard.

Arduk took note of the curious crowd lining the path. Smug grandfolk especially smirked with satisfaction at his plight. Other humanfolk poked their faces out from the flaps of hide tents, squinting to sight in the source of all the commotion.

"That young ladfolk surely did something amiss," a voice noted.

"That's for sure," concurred another.

Arduk had wanted to tell the king himself, but Helenia strictly forbade it. She insisted she be allowed to tell her father in her own way and in her own time; stating, *"Tact and timing must rule over this matter, Arduk. I know my father best and you need to trust me. I shall tell him."*

Helenia's logic was simple. By telling her father while Arduk was elsewhere, then his cooker might cool before he passed judgment on the only soul he was sure to blame for his daughter's expanding state. Kings have never taken kindly to servants lying with their daughters, therefore the princess wanted some distance between her father and her lover before the dung flung.

Displaying both tact and patience, Helenia had timed her news well. Arduk had just returned from five full days on the scout and knew she had told her father about them immediately following his departure. Still, he wondered if maybe he shouldn't have kept to the forest for a little while longer? Like maybe a full lunar phase? Or perhaps even a quarter cycle? *'Oh well, me must face the king sometime. Just as well be now.'*

Catching sight of his howlpack making ready to rescue him, Arduk's thoughts warned them to hold back their attack. No good would come of it.

"Just keep moving!" growled the burly guard, "And ye best be shrewd with thine tongue. Me never seen such wrath in King Myro save for when he vowed vengeance on the scaleez!"

A crowd began lining the path and nodding their heads with either scorn or pity, depending on one's own nature and their sentiments towards wrongdoers. The story of the feral ladfolk who had been reared by howlers was well known and had been ever since the time of his rescue. And while none were surprised that the ladfolk would display such an appalling lack of sense and judgment, what with his being so prone to beastly instincts and all, many still felt pity for him and thought mercy should be the king's recourse for one so ignorant of civilized ways. Most felt banishment from humanfolk society should suffice. After all, with the ladfolk having spent his first eight or nine cycles running barefoot about the plains in search of tasty rodents, what else could be expected of him?

Needless to say, not a single voice in the crowd dared suggest the princess herself might also warrant some blame. It simply stood to reason that the crude stable lad had obviously tainted her thoughts with his magic mind.

Most had long suspected Arduk was gripped by a spectre anyway. How else could one explain the yellowish glow to his eyes? Those same intense eyes through which he saw just as well during dark? And what of the way his neck hair would rise to a challenge, coupled with his instinct to snap and snarl and bare his teeth when riled? Then there was his penchant for sniffing wind. Not to overlook his odd knack with the beasts? Whispers had it he could even think to them without speaking words!

No, the young stable lad was definitely shaped from different clay. A strange pot to be sure. So perhaps it was best the king simply sent him away? Should such a primitive creature be held to hang or led to the block for his ignorance of civil norms? Destiny itself would never approve of such. Even the most stringent grandfolk themselves would protest such an absence of mercy.

Eventually, the guards prodded Arduk free of the foliage and out into a large clearing with a wooden platform in its center. Atop the platform, Myro scowled livid in his regal red robe and matching slipperboots. A gemmed circlet kept his straggly grey hair in check. Blue veins glowed beside his white knuckles as he clenched his ruler's sceptre. His piercing green eyes sighted clean through the prisoner.

Arduk was quite aware of the knot tightening his gut. A hive of bellybees stung at his nerves.

Old Olob stood beside Myro. As always, the historian donned his blue frock patterned with orange crescent-spheres and his buckled ankle boots. Plus his worn old bag hat. His concerned blue eyes looked only at Arduk.

Uncertain as to what he should do, Arduk braved a subtle nod at Olob. He was surprised when the historian actually nodded in reply.

An eager crowd ringed the forest fringe, with many of the younger humanfolk perched upon boughs to gain a better vantage. None wished to miss even one letter of the king's sentence; after the guilty ladfolk had been duly tried and convicted, of course.

As Arduk was being escorted up the platform steps, his eyes scanned about the court. He pretended not to notice the scowls on the faces of the witan, each noble assuming in their arrogance that their opinion somehow warranted merit in this matter. Arduk knew they did not. Nor did the opinions of the royal guards who stood ready with halberds within quick striking distance of any who would threaten the king. Ultimately, it was only King Myro's judgement that held sway in his royal court; consequently, Arduk was fully aware he was now at the mercy of his unborn tots only grandfather, who sat silent and brooding upon his makeshift throne fashioned from sticks and hide.

Arduk continued to scan the platform for any sign of Helenia, but his shifting eyes sought her out in vain. His lover was nowhere to be seen? A fact which would have brought him further worries, were it not for another calming nod from Olob. The old historian discreetly touched a forefinger to his lips to signal Arduk not to speak. A signal that best be heeded.

Arduk thought, *'If anyone can sway the king, it is Olob. They are close as skin. And me and Chaps always taked proper care of his steeds.'*

A charged hush settled over the crowd as Arduk was led directly before the king and shoved to his knees. However, when one overzealous guard attempted to push Arduk's head down to kiss the planks, the defiant ladfolk turned and bit the guard's fingers.

A murmur rolled around the clearing as the guard grabbed his injured hand and squinted to keep mute. Then he cringed and swallowed hard as piercing yellow eyes glared him a warning.

"Me King," Arduk said, steering his sights away from the wounded guard and bowing his head before Myro. "Me loves Helenia more than breath itself."

Upon looking up, Arduk took note of Olob subtly shaking his head for him to bite his tongue. Alas, the historian's warning came too late.

"Love!" Myro screamed, nearly falling off his throne. "Love! What could an unlettered stable lad reared by howlers ever know of love? Hmpff."

Only the wind and clacking boughs replied.

"Now thanks to you, my daughter fancies herself to be smitten as well. So tell me, Arduk of the howlers, just what could two rash saplings such as yourselves possibly know of love?"

A subtle nod from Olob encouraged Arduk to speak.

"Me King, age does not stop love. Howlers mate..."

"Howlers! You dare liken my daughter to howlers! Olob, are my ears deceived, or did this insolent little wretch just slight the princess in my presence?"

"Sire, I don't think the lad meant any dis..."

"Are you really comparing my daughter to a howler? Speak up, lad."

"Uh – um – M-Me King..." Arduk tried to reply, but his tongue kept tripping over his teeth.

"Enough from you!" Myro shouted. "Honestly, I don't know which of you two I find all the more foolish, you or my misguided daughter?"

"But, Me King…"

"But nothing! There is no need for you to speak. Your guilt in this shameful matter is decided. The only issue left to resolve is your punishment. I have instructed my nobles of the witan to study any law scrolls pertinent to crimes of this magnitude, and they have found no such edicts pertaining to your actions. Never before has any subject been so brash as to commit such an act against their king. You mock me without shame. You humiliate the one who took you in. You are without honour."

Noting the muddle on the anxious ladfolk's face, Myro opted to re-state his position in much simpler terms. "You are bold! You are daft! You are selfish! Bold! Daft! Selfish!"

A strong murmur of approval flowed around the clearing.

Myro flushed face and turned his sights away in thought. It was apparent the usually quick-witted and decisive king was quite puzzled as to his next course of action. He steered his sights back upon the anxious ladfolk, huffing his disgust and propping his chin upon his fist. Rubbing his brow in frustration, he looked to Olob for counsel.

"What say you, old friend? Morgue would surely condemn me were I to sever the head of my grandtot's own father."

Myro glanced back at Arduk and, upon noting the dread draining from the relieved ladfolk's face, he shouted, "Bold and daft and selfish!"

Cautioned by Olob's stare, Arduk bit his tongue and merely nodded to agree.

Suddenly, a bug-like being in a grass skirt stepped forward from amongst the nobles and offered Myro his thoughts on the matter. His monotone voice brought a calming influence. "Sire, the youth merely succumbed to temptation. Given the unequaled beauty of your daughter, can we blame the youngster for his lack of – shall we say, restraint? Given his savage history, I should think not. Anyway, regardless of all that, I have devised a plan to sink the enemy carrier and could benefit greatly from this young lad's daring and passion. Can he not be granted a pardon – one last chance to redeem himself?"

Myro near leapt from his throne. "Redeem himself! Ambassador, surely you jest. Just how does one redeem such a base act done to the king's daughter? Hmmm? And what's with this wag of sinking the enemy carrier? I thought you antemi were keen to keep neutral?"

Ambassador Viceroy stepped forward to stand over Arduk. "Sire, we antemi are neutral no more. Messengers just arrived with news from Empress Antraha. It seems much has changed. I have been ordered to combine my forces with yours in waging total war against our common enemy. Again, as we speak, fully five swarms of mounted aeronts are in flight and soon to join up with us. Also, there will be no separate peace – at least not on our end. We will accept nothing less than the enemy's unconditional surrender. Even as we speak, thirty swarms of our bravest aeronts and warriors are zipping north to attack the lizarme garrisons scattered along the shores of Oasis Lake. First we will take back Muga…"

"HOORRAY!!"

Viceroy paused in mid speech for the cheering to ebb. He even noted a hint of joy peeking out from behind Myro's veil of ire.

"Go on," Myro eagerly encouraged, while the nobles of the witan eagerly motioned for all members of the king's court to make mute.

Ambassador Viceroy kept on with his dull demeanor, albeit his eyes did hint at a cautious confidence. "We will first crush Pid's forces at Muga Terro before routing all of his garrisons about the lake – thereby forcing him to withdraw a great many troops away from his eastern front in order to defend Cracow itself. He will be left with no other option as the desert north to Cracow will be wide open leaving the hub of his nation fully exposed. He must divert the troops."

"HOORRAY!!"

After the commotion had subsided, Olob spoke firmly to the antemi ambassador. "Can we assume then that the empress also intends to attack Cracow?"

Although Viceroy knew full well Antraha's intentions, he opted to feign ignorance and spin the jargon of diplomacy. "As of this moment, I have received no such message. Therefore, for me to answer would be mere conjecture – which is something I much prefer to avoid."

Both Olob and Myro leered skeptical.

"Perhaps she does not intend to attack Cracow at all," Olob suggested. "Perhaps she intends to let ourselves and the lizarme fight it out to the bitter end?"

Viceroy shrugged ignorance. "Again, I prefer to avoid conjecture. However, I do know our warriors and their aeronts are now free to join with you in our common fight. That matters. No longer will the enemy rule the skies above these plains. Empress Antraha has graciously provided us with five of her best, battle-hardened swarms. All veterans of countless battles against dacts. Already, I have given orders for them to divvy up and attach themselves to your units. Together, we will make Sergon's stay in your land much more taxing. Now that I am free to speak on such things, I must say your tenacity in battle will be the source of legends. It is good we should have such a bold ally."

Olob and Myro exchanged knowing glances. Each knew Antraha most likely had no intention of ever attacking Cracow. Not that they could blame her. Why should she risk her warriors for land she did not need or want?

Still, the ambassador was correct in his assertion that an antemi assault on Muga Terro would do much to relieve the pressure on themselves and their ape allies. Besides, they could greatly use help from aeronts in defending against the dacts that continued to attack humanfolk soldiers with ravaging results whenever they ventured out from beneath the safety of the forest canopy. This had kept the humanfolk almost always on the defensive. At least now they could take the fight to the enemy. And so they would!

Myro stood and stretched a smile. His tone was tinged with hope as he reached up and gripped the much taller antema by his arms. "Ambassador, you must send a message of my gratitude to your Empress. Tell her I know Destiny – er – I mean, Fate will side with her and deliver what is rightfully yours back to you. Tell her our thoughts and prayers are with her and assure her there shall be no separate truce. Past mistakes will not be repeated. This time we shall fight alongside our allies until the last drop of blood is spilled. Tell her I so swear it – upon my crown."

"A messenger will depart at once," Viceroy assured the king, while hinting at a rare smile. Clearly, he was quite pleased with Myro's solemn promise. A promise he trusted the humanfolk king would be sure to keep.

Myro almost turned to walk away, but abruptly stopped and pointed down at Arduk. "What possible use could you have for this one?"

Viceroy clasped his long digits deep into Arduk's shoulder, causing the ladfolk to flinch. "As noted, sire, I have devised a plan to sink the enemy carrier."

"As yet you have not told us how you shall sink it? It has the girth of a mountain."

"Such is true, sire. It does have the girth of a mountain. But it is a mountain made of wood – and that makes it vulnerable. I trust it will supply ample feed for the flames. It should also provide quite the morale crushing spectacle for our enemy as they watch it burn and sink beneath the bay, the message being they are never safe in your lands. We can and will strike anywhere and anytime – and at any target, no matter how formidable. Such will surely sour their spirits. Do you not agree?"

After pausing to take in their muted smiles, Viceroy detailed his plan. "It stands to reason the many torches needed to mark the vessel's landing platforms at night, plus the lamps needed to provide light within its hull, must all be fuelled by burnable oils. Lots of oil. Many barrels of which must be stored somewhere? Ergo, if we could sneak a pair of brazen fools with flints aboard the carrier under cover of darkness…"

Almost all in attendance promptly deemed the risk factors as being far too great for such a seek and burn raid to ever succeed. They only heard Viceroy out as he detailed his daring plan because it was so very rare indeed that an antema would express enthusiasm for anything. They were intrigued?

Only after Viceroy had finished divulging all the details of his plan did Myro move to speak. "Just to be sure I understand you, ambassador. You believe one of your warriors and this insolent little rogue here can actually sneak onto the carrier unseen, skulk deep down inside its belly, find ample barrels of burnable oils, ignite them all – uh, and then escape to see another day? Is that correct?"

"My plan does not allow for an escape, sire? Such an outcome would be a most gracious gift from Fate, I will admit – or, as per your humanfolk beliefs, a gift from Destiny. That is assuming young Arduk even believes in your deities? What with his having been reared by howlers and such, he may have faith in his own. Or in none."

Arduk gulped down his anxiety. "We will sink the monster ship, sire."

Viceroy motioned for Arduk to keep mute before he continued. "I hesitate to press our deities too far on this matter. If they should guide these two brazen fools to the barrels and allow them to ignite such an inferno within the carrier's hull, then I would be quite content to sacrifice their escape."

"The lad's daring does warrant some merit," Olob noted. "Despite his insolence and lack of – uh, shall we say, restraint in matters of the flesh, young Arduk certainly does have the pluck to partake in such a risky raid. Plus he can sight through shadows as well as any antema, and he is quite familiar with the terrain of the plains. In those respects at least, he has proven his worth many times over since the invasion. Whatever his other failings may be, the lad is no coward. Of that there can be no doubt."

"It's not his pluck that got him in trouble!" Myro snapped, glaring daggers at Arduk. "But can he be trained to fly an aeront?"

"The beasts do like him," Viceroy added. "His is the only humanfolk hand that can touch them."

"Yes, but can he actually fly one?" Myro pressed.

"Yes, Me King," Arduk offered up with enthusiasm. "Me often sneaked zips on the aeronts when ye were all bedded down for the night."

The others exchanged muted stares of intrigue.

"You did what?" Viceroy managed at last.

Arduk nodded. "Me sneaked zips on aeronts just for fun."

"How often?" Viceroy pressed.

Arduk shrugged. "Most nights."

"But your legs are too short?" Viceroy noted. "If your beast should ever hit into a spin or a loop you would surely fall from the saddle."

"If only Morgue should show me such favour," Myro quipped, although only partly in jest.

Now Arduk swapped muddle for pride. "Me clipped straps from me belt to the saddle rings and wore riding gloves for good grip on the reins. Stirrup straps help too. Now spins be most fun on the dive."

Viceroy was clearly impressed. "You executed spins without any training?"

Arduk blushed forth a guilty grin.

"Ha!" Myro sneered, leering contemptuously at Arduk. "So you're a thief as well as a scoundrel. No surprise there. Get up lad. On your feet. It seems Morgue has shown me such favour after all. If you should somehow escape the inferno, which we both know you shan't, then I shall make you a noble. Before witnesses, I so pledge. Hahaha! Now best be off with you – and stay away from my daughter until after you've met Morgue. Do you hear me, stable lad? Keep your peasant paws off the princess!"

There was no cause for King Myro to repeat his words. The grateful ladfolk had clearly heard his king and was already scooting away on the swift. Despite the king's ire and complete lack of confidence in him, Arduk was fully intent on sinking the carrier and returning home afterwards. Only then would he dare remind the king of his promise to make him a noble. Not that Arduk could give a worms wiggle about such titles. He just knew that without such he could not wed Princess Helenia; and that he did care about.

The crowd parted in a scramble to let the feral ladfolk pass on through. There was no telling what one so different might do to them? Especially one with such hard teeth.

"Ambassador, I am quite pleased to see the last of that one," Myro stated as he watched the ladfolk swift off into the foliage. "All the same, it saddens me to see one of your own sacrificed in such a brazen attempt to sink the carrier. Are you certain sending two raiders is even necessary? Why not just send the little scoundrel?"

"I am quite certain, sire. Two raiders can keep watch for each other. Like having eyes in the back of their heads. We just need two who can sight well in the dark – and who are both bold and daft enough to think they can do it. Imagine it. Plan it. Do it. That's what I always say."

Olob could not resist a chance to needle his king. "Both bold and daft. Sire, that sounds like somebody we know. Then

281

upon his return you can grant him a royal title. Like baron? Or earl? Or duke? Or perhaps even prince..."

"He shan't return!" Myro snapped. "I merely spoke in jest. With all due respect to Ambassador Viceroy, the entire plan is absurd. It cannot be done."

"But if he should return..." Olob began.

"He shan't. The risk is too great. He might make it inside the carrier, but he will not make it out. Impossible."

"Unless, sire, it is Fate's will he should become your son-in-law?"

"See what you've begat, Olob. Now even the antemi ambassador mocks me! We are indeed privileged. Both a hint of confidence and an actual jest from the same antema in the same day! All laws of nature must be in flux. Come, both of you. Your jests rake at my nerves. Perhaps a good feed will busy your mouths and thus spare my ears."

"Uh, sire? Might I tend to preparing Arduk and our warrior for their task? I want them zipping across the wetrollers by the first hint of dusk."

"As you wish, ambassador. Although I must ask, do you truly believe such a brazen plan can succeed?"

"Yes, sire. I truly do. Flames lick wood every time. Granted, it is a risk to be sure. One that will require stealth and spirit and spine. Young Arduk has shown..."

"And luck," Olob put in. "Don't neglect luck. They are going to need it."

Viceroy nodded to agree. "Yes, some luck would be welcome. Now, as I was saying, young Arduk has proved himself adept at all three. This is why I choose him to raid with me. Do not fret, sire. If we should both meet Perish, antemi warriors will still fight on alongside you – and you won't be honour bound to knight the father of your grandtots. Unless I am mistaken, that would make him a noble. A noble of the lowest order, but a noble nonetheless. And worthy to wed your daughter."

Having stunned Myro and Olob silent, Viceroy parted his arms to invite a response. After a prolonged pause, he added,

"Then again, we might escape and return. Sir Arduk. Hmmm...? It does carry a nice roll off the tongue, won't you agree? Sire?"

"Hmpff," Myro scowled as he turned to step from the platform. "An antema jester. Who knew? And it's just grandtot, ambassador. As in singular. Do not bid to double my shame. Very well then. If you two sink the carrier and escape to breath another day, I will examine the possibility of noble status for the little $?#t! But no higher than knight bachelor. Some lessons in basic etiquette will also be in order, and that is not subject to debate. I've never met a ladfolk so lacking in basic social skills. To lay with his king's only daughter. Such behaviour can only be described as..."

"Spirited with spine," Viceroy offered up.

"I know, I know. Youthfully brazen was how my parents worded it when I seeded Aytik out of wedlock. Olob will remember how the shortest engagement and quickest royal wedding in our kingdom's history immediately followed as a result."

"I remember it all quite well, sire," Olob agreed with a smirk and a nod. "Thanks to her birthing sickness, you were forced to confess the truth at dawn and you were wed before dusk."

"Yeah, yeah. Ambassador, have you seeded your own scions?"

"Yes, sire. I have seeded many larvae. That said, antemi donors never really know which larvae were seeded from our loins. Egg-layers can store the seed of many donors in their sac for up to ten cycles; therefore, not even the layers themselves ever know for absolute certain who the father is. For us breeding is quite communal. Everyone participates."

"Ha! Apparently for us too. Come, Olob. Let us gorge our growls."

Viceroy bowed his parting to the king and Olob, then turned and strided through the dispersing crowd. His long, stilted legs allowed him to move swifter on the stride than almost any humanfolk could on the sprint; young Arduk being the sole exception to this fact, which was another reason

Viceroy had chosen the strange stable lad to accompany him on such a dangerous and vital mission. Once the fire was set, they would need to get out fast. Very, very fast. And Arduk was by far the quickest humanfolk he'd ever known; both in speed and mind.

Arduk's detailed knowledge of the kingdom's terrain, his uncanny spare sense, his knack with beasts, and his ability to snag even the slightest of sounds from great distances were also factors. As were his soft-stepping nature and contrasting refusal to flee from fear. He would fight through it. Or meet Perish trying.

Viceroy nodded in satisfaction at his choice. *'You and I will sink that floating monster, Arduk of the howlers. Then you will have your knighthood and your princess, while I will gain stature with my empress – perhaps even securing a position of ample influence in her court?'*

Quickly snapping his mind back to the task at hand, Viceroy strided from the clearing and plunged into the foliage. Unlike humanfolk, burr bushes and thorns did not attach to or slice through his chitin; thus, he seldom took to paths. He always felt closer to home amongst the vegetation of the Upcoast Forests, even if it was still a far cry from the dense growth of the Dark Jungle. He much preferred it to glades or the wide-open spaces of the plains. They always made him feel naked and ripe for attack.

Soon Viceroy found himself back at his camp. Bulging eyes peeked out from between vine curtains or stared down from the boughs of trees. Some familiar faces nodded to him in greeting.

Rows of aeronts stood tethered to vines. Several warriors kept busy with bucket and cloth, washing their aeronts' chitin. The beasts hummed in gratitude.

Viceroy snagged sight of a familiar figure in plaited boots and an oversized cloak. "Does the cold not numb your fingers?" Viceroy inquired as Arduk stepped directly before him.

Arduk shrugged. "Yes. But me keeps riding gloves in me flight sack. Me always be ready." Then he reached inside his cloak and slid a hurling dagger out from its sheath.

"A fine weapon indeed," Viceroy acknowledged.

"Dagger beed a gift from Prince Aytik." After slipping the blade back into its sheath, Arduk reached into his cloak pocket and procured a hide pouch. He opened the pouch to reveal a stone flint and metal striker, along with assorted fibre wicks with frayed ends. "Twisted wicks fire fastest," he explained. "Braided burn slower."

Viceroy nodded his approval and patted the eager ladfolk on the shoulder. "I knew you would be well suited to this task. Keep those wicks dry, Arduk. We may get only one chance to fire the barrels."

"We will burn the big boat," Arduk assured him.

"Have you a favourite aeront?" Viceroy inquired, directing Arduk over to the pens. As they strolled down the row, each beast moved to lick the ladfolk's hands.

"They like licking my hands," Arduk explained.

"They like you, Arduk. As do I. Anyway, you can have your pick of the swarm. Ride any beast you want."

"Me will ride wee Whitezig. She be bad swift on the zip and fearless in a dive."

Viceroy slighted an almost smile. "A fair choice, my friend. I will ride my most trusted mount, Redzag. He has aged grey of bristle and is frayed of wing, but his heart beats strong and his eyes are wise. Together, we have clashed with countless dacts."

Arduk smiled in return as he snagged a small sack from Whitezig's stall. He loosened the draw cord to reveal its contents.

"Gloves. Biscuits. Smoked meat. A bulging skin costrel. Arduk, were you planning to mount Whitezig and flee from your punishment – perhaps taking Princess Helenia with you?"

Arduk merely shrugged.

"Somehow, I don't think the deities are quite finished with you just yet, my young friend. So perhaps it is best you should keep your head fixed to your body. Come, let us saddle up. If we depart at once, we should be at the forest fringe by the first hint of dusk. From there we must zip near to the ground to avoid enemy scouts. As Fate would have it, three nights hence we begin a new phase with a sliver moon. Six nights hence, we will be at our target. Perhaps Fate will send fog or snow to shield us when we approach the carrier. We will welcome either to conceal our shapes."

After slinging his sack over his shoulders, Arduk turned and reached out to pet Whitezig. She eagerly responded by humming softly and rubbing her head against his hand.

Once both had prepped their mounts and Arduk had taken the additional step of clipping his safety straps to the saddle rings, Viceroy pointed his cudgel to the above and bid old Redzag to zip. Straight away, Arduk and Whitezig took flight and followed close behind.

With heads lowered and legs swept back, both aeronts easily maneuvered about the thin forest foliage. The frigid quarter had returned in full flurry, and the season's nippy north wind quickly frosted each beasts' chitin.

In time, both riders and mounts began to shiver in the chill, but they zipped on regardless. Being much smaller and shorter of limb, Arduk had some problems with sliding about the slippery saddle, which forced them to land for a brief bit to tighten his safety straps. After a bite of biscuits and meat, plus a quick gulp of weak ale from the costrel, they zipped back into flight.

True to Viceroy's estimate, they broke free of the forest just slightly past the hint of dusk. Nonetheless, they were quite disappointed to discover an army of vigilant skytwinklers. Being quite fit to sight well through darkness, they would have preferred the cover of skysheep.

After veering west by south-west, Viceroy stole a quick glance back over his shoulder. He could not hear Whitezig over the steady drone of his own aeront's wings, yet he knew the ladfolk was there as two glowing yellow eyes shifted about in constant vigil.

Noting he was being watched, Arduk waved to say all was well. Then his wary eyes took back their task.

"Fate, I thank you for such an ally as Arduk," Viceroy offered up in prayer. "If it be your desire, please see him safely back to his princess. Move Myro's heart to forgive him and bestow upon him the rank of knighthood. Surely, he will have earned such."

All throughout the night, they zipped over the white blanket that covered the dormant growth of the plains. On two occasions they encountered beasts, both times howlers. A brief chat with the first pack revealed a flock of dacts with riders had landed and set up camp southwest from their current position; hence, they immediately altered course to swing around the enemy's flank and avoid any risk of exposure. A similar chat with a second pack revealed there were no longer any enemy units in the area. Given such news, they veered back on course for Capital. Or for whatever was left of it?

By the peek of dawn, they were weary and cold and hungry, therefore they set down in a small wood and put up in a razorback's den.

"Are you certain we should be in here, Arduk? I mean, I have heard tell that wild oinkers are mean of spirit and prone to evil. Do they not have long tusks called cutters?"

"Them do," Arduk acknowledged, barely suppressing a smirk.

"What if it comes home and finds us hiding in here? Are you certain this is wise?"

"I do not know. Why don't ye ask him?" Arduk replied, pointing past Viceroy to a hairy mass with mean eyes and sharp tusks.

"Yikes!"

The startled antema was torn between confusion and relief as the hefty beast grunted its joy and rolled over onto its back. It lapped out with its tongue as the ladfolk dove onto its huge belly and started tickling it.

"Slurp, ye growed too fat to tickle. No! Don't! Ha! Ha! Stop! Slurp..."

Viceroy and the aeronts could merely stare in silence as the enormous oinker suddenly rolled onto its side and started to lick and slobber all about Arduk's face.

Pushing to his feet, Arduk wiped his face on his sleeve. He spoke briefly to Slurp before gloating at Viceroy. "Slurp not speak ye words.

Him be my friend and says we can stay in his den until dark. Him keep watch for lizarme so we can nap. All will be well, Viceroy."

"How do a ladfolk and an oinker become friends?" Viceroy managed at last, casting a skeptical sideways glance at Slurp.

"We meeted when me beed a tot. Slurp beed just a wee oinker then. No tusks, even. Me spared him from a howlpack. So now we be friends. Ye take nap, Viceroy. Howlers and Slurp will keep keen on the watch. We be safe in here."

Despite a cold draft, the den at least sheltered them from the full force of the wind. Arduk set a small fire by burning hardened oinker dung and the warmth quickly made peace with the smell. It allowed the weary pair and their beasts to nap in some comfort, for the frigid quarter could chill one's blood thick. Arduk assured the anxious antema that the mounting storm would force the enemy to likewise seek shelter. There would be no lizarme out and about on this day.

By the time Night launched its expected assault upon Day in their never-ending struggle to rule the above, both riders and mounts were well rested and most eager to be off. The storm had waned by dusk, so Arduk quickly bade Slurp farewell and promised to visit him again after the war. Then he and Viceroy departed on the zip.

Although the storm had passed, a thick flock of grey skysheep still shielded the skytwinklers and moon from view. Perfect for stealth.

The pair flew their aeronts close to the drifts. They were confident they would reach the bay unseen as there were now only two more nights before the moon dimmed to a sliver. The above would then be at its blackest and their flight through occupied territory would be all the more difficult for the enemy to spot. Therefore, they wished to travel as fast and far as possible while their shapes were thus shrouded. Viceroy reasoned if they could make Capital in five nights instead of six it would give them an extra night to study their target before the sliver moon started to wax.

"We can ill afford a lapse in judgement," Viceroy had stated. "Not even once."

The following two days were spent snug in the dens of howlers. Viceroy was intrigued by how Arduk was content to curl up cozy amongst their furry hosts, although he himself declined their gracious offer to help warm his chitin with heat from their bodies. Instead, the weary antema opted to stiff into the dormant ball of hibernation that protected his kind from the desert's nighttime chill. Just the same, even with his metabolism slowed, his holoptic eyes kept keen to the slightest of movements. He could instantly rouse himself to fend off danger.

Not that Viceroy lacked faith in the howlers who had been charged with guarding the dens. He was just fully aware they were now very deep behind enemy lines and lizarme had been known to pull off some extremely daring and successful forays of their own. In fact, Prod Tarawa especially had become somewhat of a legend even amongst the antemi for his ingenious use of stealth and cunning in such matters. Viceroy had little doubt more than a few commanders in Sergon's invasion force had at one time or another served under Tarawa. He also knew any lax in readiness on their own part might quickly find them spitted on trident prongs.

No, Viceroy had no intention of trusting the safety of their being entirely to others, even if the howlers had long proved themselves to be most capable sentries. His lofty political ambitions depended on sinking the carrier and gaining much favored status with the empress. For that reason above any other, once he and Arduk had sighted the vessel he would risk his very being to burn it.

Late on the fourth night of their journey, they sighted a flock of dacts patrolling near to northeast. They promptly averted any chance of being spotted by landing and blending in amongst a thicket of brush, where they waited patiently until the enemy had flapped from view. Only then did they make haste on the zip, quite confident they would be shielded by darkness since the slivered moon struggled with little gain to peek through the gaps in the skysheep. Still, they kept vigilant to their surroundings, knowing full well there would be a steady increase in enemy patrols the closer they came to Capital. And to their floating target.

Twice during the fourth night, they sighted lizarme foot soldiers camped in amongst some brush and warming themselves by open flame. On both occasions, they easily averted the enemy by flying near to the snow.

"Them be fools to feed flames out in the open!" Arduk noted once they were safely out of earshot.

"They are cold and probably very hungry!" Viceroy reasoned.

As Day peeked atop the eastern horizon, two vague shapes zipped down to shelter within an abandoned barn. Viceroy and Arduk were aware they were placing themselves at some risk as there was no other shelter from the biting gusts to be found, yet both reasoned they could easily spot any enemy patrols approaching from land or sky. Plus their agile aeronts could easily out-zip the more cumbersome dacts if events came to a chase.

"This night we will be to Capital," Arduk noted while pointing west.

"We mustn't pass directly over the city," Viceroy noted. "Instead, we must keep to the perimeter."

"Huh?"

"To the edge, Arduk. We must keep to the city's edge. There will be no shortage of prying eyes within the city proper – or along the crest of the slope, where some of the stone manors may well have survived the inferno. It is probable their insides will have been gutted by smoke and flames, but their charred walls could still stand to provide a break against strong seasonal gusts blowing off Ga Bay. Even their hearths and ovens might be intact. Lizarme commanders will make good use of such shelters.

"We will hide amongst the charred ruins of the hovels within the rookery. Why would lizarme make camp where nothing of use is offered them? Would we?"

"No."

"Exactly my point. We wouldn't. Nor would we expect a pair of brazen fools such as ourselves to sneak back into the city and bivouac right under our noses either."

The day passed without incident and the onslaught of darkness found two well-rested aeronts eager to be off. Their shivering riders were all too willing to oblige.

Arduk slung on his flight sack, blew to warm his fingers and then clipped his safety straps to the saddle rings. Next he twisted about and stared directly into Viceroy's eyes.

"What?" Viceroy inquired, already anticipating a question.

"Viceroy, we be friends, huh?"

"Yes, Arduk We are friends."

"Will ye pledge to stand witness when me weds Princess Helenia?" Arduk asked.

"Stand as your witness! Arduk, right now I'm still trying to spare your neck the chop. King Myro is furious with you for bedding his daughter. Let us first sink the carrier before we discuss weddings and witnesses, shall we? Will I stand as your witness? Sheesh..."

Arduk thought he heard Viceroy blurt out a muffled chortle as the antema bade Redzag to zip. Then he bid Whitezig to follow.

The flock of skysheep still grazed across the dreary above, exposing the slivered moon at only the briefest of intervals. Regardless, the pair took no chances. They kept low to the snow, constantly monitoring the above for any sign of dacts.

It proved well they did too, for a patrolling flock of dacts flapped almost directly over them. Only after the enemy had vanished in the distance did the wet and shivering pair emerge from beneath a drift and bid their aeronts to take flight.

Eventually, the terrain started to slope upwards towards a distant crest. Near its top, blackened structures stuck from the snow.

At once, Arduk and Viceroy knew they were seeing the charred remnants of manor homes. They had indeed made Capital in just five nights. No small feat over such a great distance.

Viceroy tightened his grip on the reins and steered Redzag sharply to the south. Soon he zipped into a dive, pulling out only when they were zipping barely atop the slope. In fact, he could feel a slight drag every time his mount's dangling legs clipped the peaks of drifts, kicking up snow behind them.

Whitezig followed close behind, with Arduk cussing beneath his breath whenever a kick of cold snow splashed across his face. *"Dung."*

After they had zipped around the city proper and descended the west slope towards The Amen River, Viceroy reined his mount into a hover and waited for Arduk to draw alongside. There they dismounted and began cautiously searching on foot amongst the charred ruins of hovels for a suitable hiding spot with a good vantage of Ga Bay. Each felt confident the frigid gusts off the bay and the falling snow would cover their tracks long before the first peek of dawn.

They eventually found a small shed that had somehow eluded the brunt of the flames, although its stone base and wooden walls were scorched and part of its roof had caved in onto its floor. A scattering of feathers and straw indicated the shed had been a small coop of sorts.

There were no shutters, only the entrance minus its door; although, as a plus, it did provide a clear line of sight along the shore of Ga Bay. Unfortunately, the lack of shutters would prevent them from spotting lizarme approaching from any direction other than north.

A chirper's nest was tucked between a wooden beam and the crux of the roof. Tiny squeakers' holes had been chewed through the skirting boards. There was no evidence the enemy had ever been inside the shed and there were no prints in the snow outside.

"We'll hide in here until…" Viceroy began, but the spectacle of Arduk squeaking into one of the tiny holes muted his words. He slacked jaw as tiny snouts with long whiskers suddenly peeked out from behind the skirting board and started squeaking in chat to the nodding humanfolk.

"Squeakers say no scaleez ever come inside shed. Say they will keep watch for us. Squeakers not like scaleez. Scaleez eat squeakers. Squeakers say too that hungry prowlers ate the chirpers. That's why the nests be bare."

When many more snouts began poking out from holes in the skirting boards, Arduk simply squeaked for them to tend to their tasks. Every single squeaker nodded before vanishing back behind the walls.

"We got many eyes sighting to spare us from ambush," Arduk explained to the stunned antema. "Sad that nests be bare. Me thinks for more chirpers to come help?"

Once again, Viceroy found himself intrigued as the ladfolk closed his eyes in trance. Day ruled all of the above by the time Arduk finally opened his eyes and steered his sights to the shed entrance, where a mixed flock of squawkers and cooers and chirpers all landed together and began filing into the shed, closely followed by a brood of cluckers.

"Fowl took long to come so scaleez not take heed," Arduk explained, before he himself took to squawking and cooing and chirping and clucking. Clearly, he was engaged in some sort of detailed dialogue with his diverse group of guests. Sometimes, the squawkers would even beak draw images in the fresh snow that had blown into the shed, and the cooers would bob their heads to agree.

At one point, the conversation was interrupted when a proud cock strutted into the shed and angrily denounced Arduk. A brief, heated exchange ensued before the irate cock finally retreated, albeit with several of *his* cluckers in tow.

Arduk looked to the remaining cluckers and shrugged palms-up in frustration. They responded with outstretched wings.

By now, Viceroy was beyond befuddled by all the squawking and cooing and chirping and clucking. "Arduk, whatever are you all going on about?" he demanded to know.

"Me sorry, Viceroy. Cooers tell where scaleez be in city. Squawkers tell of ways to sneak into carrier. Chirpers and cluckers offer to fool any scaleez to help us hide."

"They have been aboard the carrier?" Viceroy asked, muffling his monotone voice into a hush. It was readily apparent he was now quite interested in Arduk's intel.

"Uh-huh," Arduk said. "Squawkers sometimes sneak into boat to scoff scraps."

Viceroy had been so intrigued and frustrated by Arduk's discussions with their feathered guests that he hadn't checked outside for some time. So he cautiously peeked out through the shed entrance.

Along the crest of the slope, blackened stone manors still showed some potential for shelter, yet every home below had been razed into rubble. Not a standing stack could be seen among the charred ruins of brick homes, all of which were blanketed with snow.

Whereas before the invasion, rookery hovels and busy shops and warehouses had dominated the shoreline, now only charred timber and stone gave evidence of a once thriving port. Lizarme dockers were even forced to unload their cogs by hand as not a single dockside hoist had survived the inferno. Teams of rexids were busy hauling carts laden with supplies along scorched piers.

Viceroy would have commented on the destruction were it not for the spectacle of several very excited squeakers suddenly scurrying out from behind the shed's skirting boards and pointing and leaping about with great passion. They were clearly in distress.

"Hide," Arduk whispered, shoving Viceroy clear of the entrance. Their feathered friends instantly followed suit. "Squeakers say many scaleez approach on the march."

Viceroy and Arduk exchanged heedful glances as their ears snagged the distinct crunch of many feet marching past the shed in perfect step. They could also hear the hoarse voice of the troop's commander barking out the cadence.

'Just pass us by,' Viceroy thought, gripping his cudgel. *'That's it – just keep marching...'*

Viceroy and Arduk bated their breath as one lizarma suddenly broke ranks outside the shed entrance and glanced within. Satisfied he had found his place, he stepped inside and raised his skirt to relieve himself. A few lizarme teased him as they marched by, but he ignored them and took to his task.

Viceroy and Arduk stood still as statues while the lizarma straddled the ground with his back turned to them. In his haste to relieve himself, their scaly foe had taken no notice of the fresh prints in the newly blown snow, or realized there were an antema and a ladfolk standing directly behind him. Regardless, as soon as he finished doing his business and turned to exit the shed, they would be discovered. Trapped!

Both realized all they could do for the moment was hope the entire enemy column marched past the entrance before the prints were noted. They knew full well if they were caught inside the shed, they would breath their last there. Their only options to avert such an end were to either slay the lizarma before them without alerting his unit, or to fly free of the shed before the other lizarme could react. At the moment, neither option seemed all too promising.

Arduk slowly reached inside his cloak and drew out his hurling dagger. It felt firm and familiar in his hand. All those times old Chaps had made him practice with blades seemed ripe for this moment. Knowing he would not get a second chance, he signaled his feathered friends for help.

Suddenly, one of the cluckers darted from the shed and began flapping up a ruckus. Feathers fluttered everywhere, while laughter and commotion erupted amongst the lizarme. Those soldiers nearest the shed started shouting and chasing after the tasty treat which Destiny had seen fit to award them. After so long feeding on brined meat and hardtack, fresh meat was simply too tasty a treat to pass up. Every soldier wanted to catch the tasty treat for themselves.

Arduk wasted no more time in thought. The lone lizarma had already tended to his task and was turning about to seek out the cause of so much commotion.

He never found it. A slice to the throat severed his speech. Then a blow from a cudgel slugged his entire frame clear of the entranceway.

While Viceroy hastily dragged the limp form off into a corner, the undaunted ladfolk casually wiped the blade clean on his cloak before slipping it back into its sheath.

A loud cheer erupted outside the shed, signaling to all within that the brave little clucker had been caught. A loud snap silenced the ruckus.

Some time passed before the pair risked peeking out of the shed. Beforehand, Arduk had sent squeakers to patrol the area just to be sure. Neither wished to come that close to the enemy again, least ways not until they were safely aboard the carrier.

"It is too risky to stay here. We must board the carrier this very night," Viceroy reasoned.

"Yes, the skysheep and moon both favour us," Arduk agreed, sneaking another peek out from the shed.

"It is clearly an omen. Thanks be to Fate, all is ripe for stealth. To rebuke Fate's gifts is always unwise. We will go after dusk. What did the shoresquawkers tell you about the carrier?"

"Squawkers say there be big windows at stern. Squawkers say we can squeeze in through windows."

Viceroy once again peeked out from the shed and sighted far out over Ga Bay. He fully realized the enormity of the task before them.

The frothing wetrollers were dotted with the hulls of countless bashers and bulky cogs. Their rowlocks were vacant and their sails furled. Many more ships were moored about the mouth of the Amen River.

Further out from shore, a floating monster towered high atop the rolling, grey surface. Its four horns threatened to spear the very skysheep. Unlike the lesser craft, it squatted almost motionless in the swells.

Viceroy reasoned the carrier stretched well in excess of three hundred strides from bow to stern, and that its hull must exceed at least six levels in height. Maybe more? Even at such a distance, his keen holoptic eyes could discern a three tiered deckhouse, which was itself dwarfed by the vessel's four masts. Modern catapults were spaced at strategic intervals around its main deck and dozens of dact pens were secured both fore and aft of the deckhouse.

"Its enormous. Just the anchors and chains weigh more than loaded cogs," Viceroy surmised.

"Flames do not fear size," Arduk noted, nodding towards the charred ruins of capital."

"It's about much more than just a ship, my friend. Before Night's skytwinklers have next retreated, Sergon's troops and sailors shall have witnessed the fiery sinking of their own pride. All while we zip safely away."

"Back to Helenia," Arduk added.

"Yes, Arduk. Back to your princess. If we succeed, you will have more than earned your noble status – even should it be merely as knight bachelor, King Myro shall be hard pressed to deny you at least that. Still, to wed a princess without her father's blessing is not…"

"King Myro will bless us," Arduk assured him.

Noting the confidence in the young ladfolk's freckled face, Viceroy opted to encourage him. "I'm certain he will, Arduk. Why would he not?"

Each offered to keep vigil so the other could nap. Yet neither could. Both were much too focused on the tricky task ahead of them. So instead of napping, they took nourishment and talked throughout the day about the war and their plans for after it was won.

Later, as darkness descended over Capital, they hastened to saddle the anxious aeronts.

Arduk dipped a hand into his cloak pocket and retrieved the hide pouch. "See, the wicks keep dry for burning."

The antema nodded his approval as he threw one of his legs across Redzag's saddle. He then waited patiently while Arduk clipped on his safety straps.

Arduk smiled and nodded his gratitude to his host of furry and feathered friends, before steering his sights back onto the antema. "The gusts howl with spirits, huh?"

"Out atop the wetrollers, the spirit gusts will howl all the louder," Viceroy assured him. "And the sliver moon is cloaked by skysheep. All is ripe for stealth. Fate is surely with us. I just hope our aeronts will hear my whistle in time to whisk us to safety before the carrier blows."

"Me will just think them to come for us," Arduk replied with a casual shrug.

Viceroy was often intrigued by the things Arduk could do, yet the unique ladfolk's sway to move thoughts back and forth between minds had always left the antema feeling somewhat unsettled. *'Could he be hearing my thoughts as well?'*

Breath spouted in vapors as they clenched tight the reins. They kept still in their saddles, listening to the whine of a spirit gust who had become trapped in some nearby rubble. Somewhere in the dark, an unseen plank snapped from the chill. *'Or did it?'*

"It is time," Viceroy said at last, gently reining Redzag to crawl from the shed and out onto the snow-covered road.

Arduk told Whitezig to follow and gently patted the aeront's head; as much to still his own bellybees as to calm the beast. All knew this night could well be their last. From this point forward their minds must stay sharp on the snap. There could be no foolish mistakes.

Without speaking another word, Viceroy bid Redzag into a slow zip just slightly atop the snow. Aytik and Whitezig followed close by the abdomen.

They wound their way cautiously about the rubble, pausing briefly in a controlled hover whenever they snagged even the slightest of sounds. Usually the sounds came to nothing, except for when they encountered a ragtag unit of slurring lizarme singing in stagger and swinging jugs of jabber juice. Both aeronts quickly zipped in amongst the ruins of a demolished hovel, where they all waited in hiding until the cheery drunkards had passed.

Once some new animal friends had assured Arduk all was safe, he and Viceroy emerged from the ruins and cautiously zipped about more rubble and drifts until, at last, they reached the shore of Ga Bay. There they bid their aeronts to make swift for the carrier, taking heed to steer well clear of other vessels, lest they should be spotted by an alert lizarma on watch. Both were aware modern metal horns could blow warning blasts a great distance across wetrollers, which would without a doubt rob them of the element of surprise; and without surprise as their ally, they would surely fail at their task.

True to Viceroy's words, the spirit gusts did howl much louder out over the wetrollers. In fact, the aeronts were at times hard pressed to challenge them. On more than one occasion, the beasts were forced to hover in place until the spirits paused to draw new breath. No matter, regardless of the adverse conditions which hindered their progress, Viceroy and Arduk were still pleased. They had to be, for the spirit gusts, coupled with snowy squalls, helped mask both sight and sound. While the storm certainly hindered their ability to locate and reach the carrier, it also impeded the enemy's ability to detect them. Difficult to fly in, yes. Perfect for stealth, absolutely! Fate had heard Viceroy's prayers and was with them.

When at long last they finally did find the carrier, they dropped low to skim the surface and steered their mounts around to the stern. There they found the porthole windows the squawkers had spoken about.

One window in particular caught their attention. It was cut square and was larger than the other windows. A pale glow emanated from behind it. Of much greater importance, the sash was popped slightly ajar. Could it be left unlatched?

The pair could hardly believe their good fortune, for now there might be no need to break a pane and risk sound. They could also conceal any evidence of their entry by simply closing the window behind them. It almost seemed too easy?

They steered their mounts to hover just slightly below the sill, where Viceroy carefully stood atop Redzag's saddle and reached to open the window. Yet the sash would not budge?

Having unclipped his safety straps, Arduk stood atop Whitezig's saddle. He was well aware of the wetrollers far below. If he were to plunge beneath them now, his bones would be chilled past forever. Assuming he didn't meet Morgue?

Arduk grunted as he tried to force the window to open. Again, it refused to budge. So he reached inside his cloak and unsheathed his dagger. Taking care to nix noise, he gently wedged the blade between sash and frame and struggled to pry the window further ajar. Again, to no avail.

Viceroy moved to help out. He carefully unslung his cudgel and began gently tapping the butt of the dagger to drive in its blade. Once there was enough gap between sash and frame to insert his fingers, he re-slung his cudgel and gripped tight the sash. Then he tugged hard and...

"Viceroy," Arduk nearly shouted as the window suddenly popped wide open and his startled partner slipped off the saddle and nearly dropped into the drink.

For several tense breaths, Viceroy dangled from horn and pommel; until a small hand reached down and locked tight about his arm, pulling him back up onto his mount. Viceroy could not help but wonder, *'How does such strength hide within one so frail?'*

Arduk kept his blade chomped firmly between his teeth as he pulled himself in through the window. Exercising utmost caution and self-control, he slid softly down to the planks of the sole, before hastily pushing to his feet with his blade gripped to do battle. Noting no danger, he exhaled in relief. He was alone in the cabin.

He saw at once he had entered quarters befitting a commander of much importance, for the bulkheads of the room were covered with hide maps and charts. A narrow berth was bolted to one bulkhead, while an oval table was bolted down alongside another. More maps were spaced neatly about the tabletop, along with a brass spyglass and a wooden tankard.

Several purple capes hung slack from pegs, while a scabbard with cutlass swung ever so slightly from a peg on the cabin's main door. Nearby, a lone trident was racked on the bulkhead.

What most snagged Arduk's sights, however, was a portrait of a pudgy lizarma with peculiar pinkish eyes. It seemed almost as if the figure was staring back at him?

"Thud!"

"Dung!"

Arduk spun about to find one very embarrassed antema slowly pushing to his feet and rubbing his head. "Shhh…" the stable lad cautioned, pointing to the cabin door. "Me feets feels quivers in the planks. Somebody comes."

The antema merely nodded.

The anxious ladfolk ignored his bellybees and carefully reached to turn the door dog. He felt his guts sink when the latch clunked open. Then he gently eased the door ajar and peeked out into a passageway.

Almost too quickly, he pushed the door shut and latched it. His panic was evident when he motioned for Viceroy to hide.

Viceroy quickly squeezed underneath the berth, only poking his head out briefly to signal his snoopy aeront to cease gawking in through the window. The obedient beast was quick to obey.

Arduk pressed his frame tight against the bulkhead, hoping the open door would conceal his presence behind it. But what of his scent?

Soon voices could be heard, along with the stomping of feet.

"Viceroy," Arduk blurted out in a forced whisper. "Me sights ye cudgel."

Instantly, a bony hand whisked the weapon from sight.

Arduk might have exhaled in relief, except the voices and stomping suddenly ceased just beyond the door. Had they heard him? Could they smell him?

When the voices resumed, Arduk's lungs slowly voided their relief. Then they gasped with a start as the dog turned and slid open the latch.

"Waken me at the peek of dawn," instructed a hoarse voice, followed at once by a loud sniffle. "Not before. I need rest to beat down this bug."

Arduk was quick to recognize the ancient continental language, having learned it from nobles who frequented the stables. He and Chaps had often mocked them in jest. It always made them both feel just a little less, less than.

"Yes, Prod Commander," a gruff voice replied, before more stomping moved away from the door.

Then the door swung open and a pudgy shape waddled into the cabin. Arduk saw at once it was the lizarma from the portrait, clad in a serpent skin skirt with like-coloured vest. A purple cape hung from his shoulders. In his hand he held a burning oil lamp. It was clear he was a prod commander of very high rank. Perhaps of the entire fleet? Or even of the whole invasion force? Could it be so? Would Viceroy's deity Fate be this generous?

Neglecting to turn about, the unsuspecting prod sniffled and waddled away from Arduk. He sniffled again as he set the lamp down on the tabletop, before turning and stepping across the sole to his berth. After tossing his cape onto the mattress, he began unbuttoning his tough serpent skin vest...

"Ughh..." the prod grunted as the blade stuck through his vest and struck bone. Yet somehow he still managed to spin about and confront his attacker.

Arduk was caught agape by his adversary's strength as they fell to the planks. Again and again he stuck the blade into bone and flesh. And again and again the stubborn lizarma refused to yield, grappling the smaller ladfolk chest to chest so as to weaken the blows.

The frantic combatants rolled over and over towards the bulkhead, before banging hard into the table. The spyglass and lamp crashed to the deck.

The lizarma choked up blood as strong fingers found his throat. Swiping at the lamp, he intentionally batted it noisily across the floor. Thus he began digging his claws into Arduk's shoulder and arm.

"Smack!"

Suddenly, the pudgy prod laxed his hold on Arduk and slacked limp. An eerie moan seeped out from between his quivering lips. His peculiar pinkish eyes blinked blankly at naught.

"Smack!!"

Arduk felt his gut squirm as the prod's skull was crushed by the cudgel. Rolling onto his side, the exhausted ladfolk spewed clean his belly. His cloak and tunic were torn where sharp claws had dug into his flesh. A sticky warmth trickled down his shoulder and arm.

Flames engulfed the lamp and spilled onto the planks. Viceroy scorched his hands on the hot handle. In one unbroken movement, he swifted across the cabin and punched the window wide open. Mere bits later found the flaming object plunging into the drink. Burning oil still floated on the surface.

Viceroy hoped only the aeronts had witnessed the spectacle as he whipped a hide cover from the bunk and hastened to smother the flames. Next, he tactlessly ripped the flight sack from Arduk's back. Retrieving the skin costrel, he quickly popped free the stopper and splashed its contents across the smoldering planks. When he was satisfied the flames were doused, he lunged across the room and latched shut the door. Only then did he pucker his lips and squirt a healing mucous onto his hands. Chitin hung loose from some of his digits, and yellow goo oozed from a nasty gash in one palm.

"V-Viceroy," Arduk puffed, somehow pulling himself up into a sit and shaking the mush from his mind. He paused to fill his aching lungs before resuming his speech. "Me be sorry. Me not be true on the stab. Me…"

The antema pressed his unscathed palm to Arduk's mouth and touched a blistered forefinger to his own. "Shhhh…"

"Thump. Thump. Thump. Thump…"

Both stiffed in silence as their ears snagged the distinct sound of footsteps approaching the door. Then all became quiet.

"Boom! Boom! Boom!"

"Dung!" Viceroy cussed. "What do we do now?"

"Prod Sergon?" a deep voice barked from the other side. "All is well?"

"All is well," Arduk replied, perfectly mimicking Sergon's hoarse voice. "Just a small spill of burn oil is all. Smells much worse than it is. Now leave me to nap."

Viceroy was astonished by the likeness in tone, especially the way Arduk made the fake voice sound hoarse.

They readied their weapons and tensed for the outcome. Neither dared stir so much as a twitch. It seemed like forever had already come and gone before there came a response.

"Very well, Prod Commander. There be throat syrup and schnozz rags in the infirmary if ye be ill with the bug? Shall I fetch some?"

"No. Snff. I have plenty of both."

Another tense forever came and went before heavy footsteps began stomping away down the corridor.

"That was close," Viceroy whispered as the echo of footsteps waned in the distance.

303

Arduk merely nodded in reply, while licking to cleanse his own wounds.

Viceroy carefully crept across the deck towards the door, pausing with gritted teeth whenever a plank creaked out in protest. He carefully reached for the dog.

Both gasped as the latch slid open with a clunk. The nervous antema slowly opened the door. When a quick peek out into the passageway revealed no lizarme, Viceroy stepped from the cabin and beckoned his young partner to follow.

Arduk made extra certain the door was shut tight behind them before following Viceroy along the narrow passageway. Bracketed oil lamps swung from iron hooks and cast eerie shadows about the bulkheads. Closed doors kept each cabin's contents a mystery? Whenever the pair stealthed past a ladder, a smelly stench wafted up from the monster's bowels.

They settled on a secondary ladder; reason dictating that the crew might be less apt to use it. So began their descent into the ship's hold. As they descended the ladder, the hot reek goaded them to gag. Yet regardless of the foul stench, they kept on. After all, what other options were open to them?

After some time, they emerged from a narrow passageway into the main galley. Messy chopping benches spoke to such. An open bulkhead led to the scullery.

An adjacent mess was rowed with tables and stools. Metal ladles hung from the rims of common quench barrels, and buckets were filled to the brim with discarded fat and scales and feathers. The stench from an open head proved almost unbearable, moving Arduk to pinch a sleeve tight to his nostrils lest he should spew.

"Down," Viceroy blurted, yanking Arduk to the deck.

Both crawled behind a pile of grain sacks, where they crouched with weapons at the ready. Each was primed for a fight as a door creaked open in the scullery and footsteps started shuffling towards the mess.

A tug on Arduk's sleeve heeded his notice, and he followed Viceroy in behind a stack of traps filled with clawed crawlers. There they waited with needled nerves as they watched a plump lizarma in a stained apron fling one of the heavy sacks up onto his shoulder.

The lizarma braced his legs and bounced to adjust the weight of his hefty load, before turning to shuffle from view. A door creaked shut behind him.

"Come on," Viceroy said, striding across the mess towards another passageway. "Darkness will pass quickly enough. We must keep on."

Arduk would have responded, but a slight movement near one of the buckets snagged his sights. With his blade at the ready, he crept up to the bucket and yanked it aside.

"What is it?" Viceroy inquired with rare impatience.

Arduk merely pointed.

"A squeaker? We've no time for this, Arduk. Let's go."

"No, wait. Let me ask him if he can take us to the oil?"

Before the impatient antema could reply, Arduk bent low to take in the trembling rodent. He tactfully whispered in squeak to calm its nerves.

Soon the wee squeaker ceased to shake. It even grew gutsy and actually hopped atop Arduk's outstretched arm, where it proceeded to rant and point with purpose. It was obvious the wee fellow was quite excited and most willing to help.

"Squeaker will help us if we pledge to take him away with us. Him says much barrels be stacked with crates and sacks beneath Big Claws."

"Big Claws? Who is Big Claws?"

Arduk turned and whispered back to the squeaker.

At once, the wee squeaker became quite excited and rapidly spilled forth so many words that Arduk had to motion for him to slow down.

"What did he say?" Viceroy inquired once the tiny rodent had finally ceased with his squawble.

Arduk shrugged. "Him says sometimes Big Claws catches crates and lifts them up to top deck. And sometimes Big Claws lowers crates back down into the cargo hold."

"Good to know. But does he know how to get to the cargo hold?"

"He does," Arduk replied. "But he says we must take him with us. Him not likes smelly boat. Or smelly scaleez."

"Tell him I promise we'll take him with us. Also, tell him we are wasting time when we have precious little of it as is."

Arduk nodded that he understood, then turned and whispered to the squeaker.

The wee squeaker also nodded that he understood, before scrambling down Arduk's cloak and leaping to the planks. He pointed and beckoned for them to follow him back across the mess.

After pausing briefly to make sure his new friends were close behind, the squeaker led them towards a narrow passageway that did not enjoy the glow from any lanterns. This instantly put all three at ease, for each knew lizarme could not sight near so well as they in the dark; it always being to one's advantage to see those who cannot see you.

A short time later they emerged into a well-organized factory. It even had a forge, complete with furnaces and bellows for casting metal into moulds. There was a powerful trip hammer to pound impurities out of iron blooms and shape them into ingots. A smaller trip hammer would then shape those ingots into flat plates for making armour, shields and helmets. Blocks of metal ingots were stacked neatly by the furnace doors. Anvils were fastened to the deck, set for hammering out tools or weapons; while nearby, whetstone grinding wheels waited to sharpen blades and points. A sturdy tool board was bolted to a bulkhead; displaying tongs, hammers, punches and drifts. Everything in its place.

Blackened hide aprons hung from pegs. Gauntlet gloves drooped over anvils. All along one of the bulkheads, freshly forged tridents were rowed prongs-up in special holding racks. Newly shaped scimitars were laid out atop a long workbench, each awaiting the grinding wheel. Beneath the workbench, small buckets brimmed with arrow tips, while larger baskets were packed tight with arrow shafts still waiting to be nocked and fletched.

Across from the forge, there was a well-equipped carpentry shop. Axes, saws, hammers, mallets, chisels, adzes, awls and an assortment of marking gauges hung neatly on the tool boards behind more workbenches. Again, everything in its place. The table for an ingenious treadle-powered spinning saw ran alongside a bulkhead. Various pump drills and bow drills were well designed for boring holes and even starting fires. Ample straw brooms saw to it that not a single wood shaving littered the deck.

Beside the carpentry shop, there was a generous cooperage. Bended hardwood staves were stacked for notching before the ship's coopers could assemble them into barrels. Shorter staves were stacked to make barrel heads. Metal hoops were stacked about posts in three different sizes; head hoop, quarter hoop and bilge hoop. Finished barrels were strapped to wooden skids, ready for transport. Assorted mallets, axes, adzes and shaving tools were hung neatly against the backing boards of workbenches. As with the carpentry shop, not a single wood shaving littered the deck.

In addition to the forges, carpentry shop and cooperage, there was also a sizeable weaver's stall, complete with spinning wheels and a loom. There were similar stalls for tailors, cobblers, tanners, chandlers, dye makers and various other trades. They even had a seers stall, complete with an orb of fine crystal. And of all things, a brewery!

Viceroy and Arduk could not help but admire their enemy's skill in the crafts. Regardless of the trade at hand, it was quite clear lizarme guilds demanded nothing less than the very highest of quality standards. Nor had the pair foreseen the enemy's penchant for planning and logistics. In fact, sneaking about the carrier was quickly dispelling many myths about lizarme intellect. Contrary to long held racist beliefs, the lizarme were not only sound of sense, they were in many ways brilliant. Who knew?

"This big boat be liken to a city at sea," Arduk noted.

"A city soon to burn."

Both were much relieved when the squeaker led them down a main passageway along the port side of the factory. Sneaking past the stalls had put them at great risk of being seen. Just one lizarma toiling at night could sound the alarm.

Subsequently, they would be forced to abort and escape. Assuming they could?

"Whew," Arduk whispered, wiping beads of sweat from his brow. "Boat's aura sure is fuggy hot."

"Just be thankful the furnaces are idle and the crafters are all at nap," Viceroy noted.

The new passageway was wider than those prior. Fortunately, there were countless compartments the trio could duck into whenever they heard approaching footsteps. They even slew a scrawny youth who came upon them hiding in a head, where they conveniently stuffed his limp body down the chute.

"That should mask the stench of his rotting flesh," Viceroy quipped.

Arduk merely soured face in disgust.

At one point they entered an enormous mess, filled with rows of snoring green forms that were swinging from hammocks or curled up on the planks. Here they stealthed softly on the spry, actually stepping directly over some of the forms that blocked their path.

They passed through three such mess in total. Each time they sneaked through undetected, except by curious rodents peeking from their holes or staring down from their perch atop beams. Their hearts pounded near to burst when Viceroy lost his balance and accidently stepped on a lizarma who napped with one eye partially open. Fortunately, the lizarma merely muttered a cuss and rolled over onto his side.

Viceroy silently thanked Fate for the jug of jabber juice the napping drunkard hugged tight with both arms. He pledged to give thanks even more in the future.

Next, they entered into a berth with racks in place of hammocks. Hanging capes and a boxy close stool suggested they were now inside a low commanders quarters. It was here where they had their worst fright.

They were barely halfway across the berth when a restless lizarma suddenly awakened and pulled himself up into a sit. The lizarma's eyes near popped from their sockets when he saw an unwelcome bug-like being stilting past his rack. But before he could call out, a swift slice from Arduk's blade severed his speech. The lizarma was rudely shoved to the mattress and a pillow quickly pressed to smother blood and gurgles; all while Viceroy's strong hands restrained the frantic kicks from clawed feet.

Viceroy and Arduk steered their sights about the berth until the kicks waned and their victim surrendered his struggle. Even at that, they held the unfortunate lizarma down until both were certain he had spent his last breath. Only then did they relax.

Arduk quietly exhaled in relief as he watched Viceroy calmly roll their victim's breathless form onto his belly and arranged the bedding so as to best mask the evidence. With that done, they were off again.

Neither knew exactly how long they spent sneaking about passageways and climbing down ladders into the bowels of the beast. What they did know was they were running out of time, that they had best locate the oil barrels before the crew awakened and discovered the bodies they'd left in their wake.

Arduk spoke to the squeaker about their ordeal, only to be offered up a shrug. It was now apparent the wee fellow was hopelessly lost.

Viceroy watched in stunned silence as an argument ensued, with both parties raising their voices dangerously above a whisper until the squeaker grew angry and turned his back with folded limbs.

"Squeaker be mad we not trust him to find barrels," Arduk explained. "But I know he be lost."

"Wonderful," Viceroy remarked with full sarcasm. "Soon the crew will be up and about. Every pinch of this carrier will be searched from stem to…"

Suddenly, the squeaker spun about and began frantically jumping and pointing.

"Whatever is he on about?" Viceroy asked, appearing quite perplexed.

Arduk stretched a smile. "Him says he remembers now. We take that passageway over there. Him pledges barrels be close by."

Viceroy's lack of confidence in their tiny guide followed them into the passageway and about a bend, but it was quickly replaced with hope as they swifted softly down a long ramp towards a growing glow of light.

Near to the end of the ramp, they slowed their pace to a creep. They could hear deep voices now and knew they could ill afford to utter so much as a peep. Just one errant step could cause the creak that betrays them.

Peeking out from the passageway, they found themselves staring into a cavernous cargo hold which was packed high with sacks and crates and barrels and casks. Five crew were standing beside a pile of bound hides, all looking up at a skid laden with casks and ingots being hoisted to the main deck. The metal cables stretched and creaked when the heavy skid started to spin and swing in mid hang.

Arduk felt a slight tug on his tunic as the squeaker scurried up his back and onto his shoulder. "Big Claws?" he asked, pointing up at the hoist.

The wee squeaker proudly nodded that it was.

"Then Big Claws will become our lift out of here," Viceroy whispered, shifting his sights back and forth about the cavernous chamber. "For now we must locate the oil barrels without being seen. Then we must work quickly to set them on fire. Time now favours the enemy."

Arduk nodded and patted his cloak pocket. "The wicks be waiting."

"All to the good, Arduk. Still, we must find the oil barrels and this cargo hold is immense. There must be hundreds of casks and barrels in this place. Maybe even thousands? And we are almost out of time."

"Me will find them," Arduk assured the anxious antema as they watched the hoist lift the skid clear of the main deck and swing it from view. "Burn oil stinks."

Arduk dropped to all fours and crawled from the passageway and on into the cargo hold. He beckoned for Viceroy to follow while he crawled and sniffed his way about the sacks and crates and casks and barrels.

Day's early light was already upon them when Arduk finally ceased his search and pointed across a wide aisle to a long row of barrels that were stacked and lashed together with strong strapping. Up above, the hoist was now swinging about to lower an empty skid back down into the hull. Voices could be heard barking orders down from the upper deck. With all the activity, there was no safe way to sneak across the aisle without the risk of exposing themselves to the five lizarme crew.

"There them be," Arduk said, retrieving his blade. "Me will cut some cork from the bung holes to leak some oil out. Then me will light the wicks."

"There they are," Viceroy corrected. "And it's 'I' will cut... Fearless Fate, Arduk, learning you proper speech is going to be a chore."

"Huh?"

"Oh, nothing. Now how do we get to the barrels? Those five crew shall surely see us."

Arduk briefly closed his eyes in thought, before his face lit up with the solution. He immediately turned to his furry friend and started squeaking in whisper.

The little fellow nodded that he understood and hopped from Arduk's shoulder. Next, he scurried across the planks and vanished behind a stack of sacks.

Viceroy appeared confused.

"Wait and see," Arduk explained, pointing to the lizarme.

Five pairs of crimson eyes stared up at the skid as it was slowly lowered into the hold. One of the lizarme reached out with a long hook and snagged a cable to steady the skid for landing. Another shouted and hand signaled to topside that all was well, while the remaining three started to remove the lifting hooks.

None of the crew even noticed the tiny rodent scurrying across the deck until he had actually climbed atop the skid and began squeaking in a rant. At least not until one of them chortled and pointed at the wee squeaker. Five bellies burst out laughter at the silly little squeaker who just didn't seem to know his proper size and place.

"Now," Arduk said, scampering across the aisle and rolling behind the barrels.

Viceroy was quick to respond. He too rolled behind the barrels before pulling himself up into a crouch and peeking out at the lizarme. All five crew were still laughing at the little rodent, who was now scurrying across the planks.

Laughter echoed about the cavern as a black slinker suddenly pounced out of nowhere upon its wee prey, catching it with its claws before carrying it off between its pointy teeth. A thin tail dangled limp from its mouth.

Arduk felt his heart weep as he watched the lizarme happily slapping each other on the back. Then he lowered his head with saddened eyes.

A firm hand came to rest on his shoulder, and he found himself staring up into sympathetic holoptic eyes. "One never gets used to losing an ally," Viceroy whispered. "No matter their size, it always feels the same. Nevertheless, you must mourn another time. By now the enemy has surely found the prod we slew."

Turning his thoughts back to the task at hand, Arduk began cutting away at the corks plugging the bung holes until a small amount of oil was leaking from several barrels. He hoped the smell would not attract the lizarme.

"Hurry," Viceroy prodded, nodding towards the lizarme. It was apparent the five crew working together would soon have the bundles of hide stacked onto the skid for hoisting.

Arduk carefully stuck the fibre wicks in to partially plug the holes, while still allowing some oil to leak out. He began blowing across each wick while expertly striking the flint. Sparks started to bite at the frays and tiny wisps of smoke soon curled up about each barrel. While he and Viceroy blew to feed the tiny flames, both hoped the smoke would not alert the crew as the leaking oil was now smoldering to burn.

Being satisfied the flames would take, Viceroy latched onto the startled ladfolk's arm and yanked him rudely to his feet. "We must sprint on the swift, Arduk. The oil will burn and the skid begins its lift. We must make our escape now."

Five lizarme stood like stunned statues as two intruders suddenly appeared and leapt atop the skid in mid-hoist. By the time they finally untangled their tongues, the skid was well up into its lift and beyond their reach.

Now many more lizarme began pouring forth from the same passageway that had brought the intruders into the cargo hold. They were led by snaping rexids, held back only by their chain tethers.

Upon spotting the escaping pair rising to topside, one of the handlers unleashed a rexid and sicked the vicious beast into charging across the deck. Foam frothed from its fangs as it used its powerful hind legs to lunge atop the skid. It was only denied by the blow from a cudgel, which broke off a fang and sent the squealing lizard crashing back down onto the deck.

"I must summon the aeronts!" Viceroy shouted.

"Me already did! They come!"

Viceroy chose to call the aeronts anyway. He placed a thumb and middle finger between his lips and blew his lungs void. Rexids promptly took to snarling and snapping at air. "Look there, Arduk – my whistle pains the rexids ears, but the lizarme cannot hear it."

Arduk would have responded, except his eyes snagged sight of several greenish faces with crimson eyes staring down at them. One of them was signaling to somebody beyond the lip of the deck.

Suddenly, the skid came to an abrupt halt. While it dangled and swung in mid-air, more greenish faces began poking over rim.

"Dung! We be trapped!"

Viceroy did not respond, but kept blowing on his whistle.

Smoke was beginning to scratch into the ladfolk's eyes. He began to choke. Shifting his sights back down into the hull, he spotted a panicky lizarma flailing about with one arm while pointing towards some burning barrels with the other. Greedy flames were already licking at many more barrels.

"There!" Viceroy shouted as the skid began to lower.

Straining to sight through the thickening smoke, Arduk became aware of two segmented blurs with dangling legs zipping down from above. He instantly dove from skid to aeront.

Mistimed!

Arduk felt the sensation of falling, yet he could not sight through the smoke. He simply shut his eyes and awaited his meeting with Morgue...

However, no such meeting would happen this day. Powerful mandibles snagged Arduk by his arm and whisked him violently upward. Pain screamed through his shoulder as he dangled in mid flight. He shivered as a trident whizzed between his legs. Another flew just wide of his belly. Angry shouts rang out everywhere the instant Whitezig and Arduk cleared the main deck.

Whitezig clenched Arduk's arm tightly as she zipped past the carrier's gunnel and out over the wetrollers. Viceroy's plan had actually worked, and now they need make good their escape!

Reaching above his head, the dangling ladfolk managed to clench his free fingers about the saddle horn. With a great grunted effort, he pulled himself atop the saddle and started choking his lungs clean. Somehow his feet found the stirrup straps. Beside him, a most welcome figure pointed his cudgel to the south.

"Dact's!" Viceroy shouted, snapping his reins for a fast shift to the northeast. "Follow me and hang on tight!"

The gagging ladfolk clung on for his very being as his own mount spun into a dive. His stomach sank as the feisty beast leveled off to zip just slightly atop the wetrollers.

Viceroy was ecstatic. "We did it, Arduk! They shan't catch us now! Look back! Whooweee!"

Glancing back over his throbbing shoulder, Arduk was unable to contain his joy. A thick plume of black smoke rolled skyward like an eruption. Famished flames were marching across the carrier's deck and lapping out from many of its scuttles. Tiny figures could be seen leaping from gunnel to sea.

A beaming smile spanned the elated ladfolk's face as he fumbled to clip his safety straps to his belt. He even welcomed the aches and throbs and cuts and bruises. Pain had never felt so good.

"KAABBOOOOOMM!!!!!!"

The force of the blast nearly drove both aeronts into the drink. They clipped the whitecaps and flipped over and over, while their terrified riders clung tight to their saddles. Neither expected to make it to shore.

Then it was over. Even the wind whistled a cheer as four horns listed farewell and sank beneath the sea. The floating monster was no more!

"Whooweee!!" Viceroy screamed. "Arduk, we did it!"

Arduk wanted to speak, but no words would come. Instead, the pair hovered silently in place and stared for some time at the empty sea where the carrier had been. All that remained was smoldering debris bobbing about the surface. And the bite of the wind.

Finally, the exhausted pair exhaled sighs of relief. True, there were more battles yet to be fought. More tears yet to shed. But the fortunes of war had flipped. News of the sinking would shock all of Cracow. A message had been sent: *The allies are still very much in this fight. Pid has won nothing.* Arduk and Viceroy could not mask their smiles as they reined their mounts about and bid them to zip northeast. Smiles well earned.

Below them, mobs of lizarme soldiers were rushing down to the shore all about Capital. A small unit of dacts flapped in place to the south, posing no threat to the much swifter aeronts.

"What you float, so shall we sink!" Viceroy sneered in a jab, unable to contain his sarcasm. He cared not that the enemy was too far away to hear.

Their flight back to the Upcoast Forests proved no less dangerous than their flight to Capital. Chilly gusts bit incessantly at their flesh and their digits were always numbed by the reins. On many occasions, they were forced to shiver while they hid out from dacts.

At one point they were delayed by three days due to a raging storm that spilled more than two stands worth of heavy snow onto the plains. It forced them to seek shelter amongst a pack of howlers, who eagerly welcomed them into their den. By the time they finally dug their way free of the drifts and zipped back into the above, more than eight days had passed since the combat carrier had sunk. Despite the passage of time, their elation had ebbed but little.

Several lesser storms further delayed their return to the point where Viceroy quipped they might as well put up with the howlers until the wet quarter. "Helenia can surely use the rest," he'd added. A jest that did not go over well with the ladfolk, as they were both beginning to needle one another's nerves.

Even so, and despite enemy patrols and severe storms, they at last managed to reach the Upcoast Forests. Its distant outline became a most welcome sight.

Night had fully retreated by the time they dipped to zip amongst the foliage of the forest fringe, and for a change there were no flurries or flocks of ugly skysheep charging pell-mell across the above. The sun smiled warmly upon the forest, bringing to a sparkle the beads dripping down wetspikes. Many more beads glistened atop the melting blanket of white.

It should have been the end of their adventure. And it may well have been, had Arduk not chanced a quick glance to the east.

Not more than half a kilopace away, a large flock of dacts was closing ranks into parallel formation; coming in pair after pair and dropping into a dive. It took no deep thought to realize a humanfolk patrol had been caught out in the open.

"Viceroy!" Arduk shouted, pointing at the flock.

"I've sighted them!" Viceroy replied, already steering his mount to change course for a fight.

As they closed in on the battle, Arduk withdrew his hurling dagger and clenched the blade tight between his teeth. He could see many galfolk trying to trudge through the drifts in a desperate dash for the forest. Others stood their ground and slung an onslaught of arrows at their screeching assailants.

Fury filled his thoughts when he watched a young galfolk spit through by a lance, the impact tearing her almost in half. A tapered onslaught from above cut down several archers as they turned and dove to the drifts.

Snapping the reins to his right, Arduk steered Whitezig into an angled descent. Unwary lizarme now flapped in place directly below him, struggling to get their wounded dact to cease snapping at naught. Blood gushed from a nasty gash in the beast's throat, while the shaft of a second arrow slapped against its haunch.

Sensing a shadow passing over him, Arduk instinctively flung his torso sideways to make Whitezig whirl in zip just as an arrow whizzed by his head. While spinning his speedy aeront into a dive he took the blade from his teeth. His arm instinctively cocked back to throw.

The lancer snapped back in his saddle as the dagger found its mark in his neck. He dropped his own weapon and reached back to pull the blade from his wound. But a solid smack from a zipping abdomen knocked him clear off his mount.

"Up, Whitezig!" Arduk yelled, snapping back the reins. The aeront responded instantly, soaring near to another unsuspecting dact.

The startled dact reared back to avoid a collision, nearly tossing both riders from its back. But the skilled flighter kept control and, by the time Whitezig looped around to attack, he was able to hurl his trident at the determined ladfolk.

Both flighter and lancer stared with popped eyes as the frail ladfolk snatched the weapon in mid-flight and steered his aeront to attack. Neither lizarme could imagine reflexes so swift?

Now the flighter reined the dact to flee, while the lancer wavered his tip in warning. The hunters were now the hunted. They swooped low on the turn, hoping to shake the aeront.

Noting the pair no longer posed any threat to the galfolk, Arduk opted to break off the chase and steered his mount back into the fray. With the trident couched in position to thrust, he picked out another dact and zipped on a line for its riders.

Sparks spit as steel prongs glanced off a steel tip, deflecting trident and lance aside. Spasms numbed arms and pain bit deep into shoulders. Somehow, both combatants managed to keep hold of their weapon? Only by Destiny's grace did neither get spit from his saddle.

Arduk would have reined Whitezig about for another go at the lancer, except for what next snagged his sights. Just slightly atop the canopy, Viceroy was trapped and battling three dacts!

Instructing Whitezig to hurry, Arduk dove to his friend's aid. *'Will me be there in time?'*

Alas, he was not. He watched in horror as one of the lancers found his mark, splitting Redzag on the spit. The aeront's breathless body crashed down through a gauntlet of needles and boughs.

All three dacts scattered to flee as many more aeronts suddenly burst free from the forest and swarmed at full zip into the fray. Thus, the flow of battle was reversed in a wink.

However, the horrified ladfolk no longer cared for the battle. With swirling thoughts and a sinking stomach, he steered his mount to touch down on the drifts. Frantic for time, he unclipped the safety straps and swiftly swung from saddle to snow.

He found Viceroy at the base of the needler, his body bent and broken amongst a pile of broken boughs. His friend was still of breath, but his legs were so badly broken the muscles had burst through the chitin. Redzag dangled in tatters above him, having broken the brunt of Viceroy's fall.

Arduk wasted no time in biting off two strands of Viceroy's grass skirt. He started screaming frantically for help as he tied off the flow of yellow goo gushing from his friend's legs.

After inserting sticks to twist tight the strands, the ladfolk took note of some humanfolk soldiers in snowshoes kicking high atop the drifts. Most diverged to assist in routing the enemy, while several made directly for him.

"Ye unit got a healer?" Arduk demanded to know.

"No units do," replied an able galfolk as she hastened to pull off her mittens.

A wounded aeront touched down to the drifts. Taking note of Viceroy, the dismounting antema somberly shook his head.

Arduk became angry. "Do ye got a saw and wound tar?" he snapped on the rude. "Him be the antemi ambassador!"

Being no stranger to pain or panic, the galfolk calmly ignored the out-of-sorts ladfolk whilst she kicked free of her snowshoes. She kneeled beside the wounded antema and took hold of one of the sticks. Another galfolk hastened to help with the other.

"I asked, be ye got…"

"Yes!" she snapped back at him, while motioning to some of the other soldiers. "You three, fetch the pot and the saw. You and you, collect dry sticks and broken boughs. You there, you will feed the flames to boil the tar. Quickly now. On the swift. This is the antemi ambassador."

Viceroy started to shake and foam at the mouth. With great effort, he reached up and grabbed hold of Arduk's tunic.

The ladfolk hugged his friend's head tight into his chest and kissed his burning brow. "One can breathe without limbs, Viceroy. We must clot the flow from ye wounds."

The writhing antema tensed to pull Arduk near to his mouth. "No Arduk – I do not wish to dwell on such as this… Allow me to meet Perish…ahhhhh…ahhhhh…"

"Make haste with that tar!" somebody screamed.

Arduk squeezed his friend ever tighter and started gently rocking him back and forth. "Such will be ye choice after ye learn me proper speech and stand witness at me wedding. Now it be me choice to saw."

Viceroy was no longer able to respond. His spirit was trapped between Morgue's maze and Fate's grace.

A Pact for Peace?

Doyen Commander Kryle's serious black eyes stared west as he rubbed his hands together and stomped his boots to help warm his digits. Aside from the cold, he had much to occupy his mind.

The coldest quarter in memory had been spent in savage claw to fist combat in deep snow and numbing cold. Allied troops had slogged and battled their way through the western foothills, before pushing on into the Great Forests. Now they were camped just east of their first great prize, the ancient lizarme port of Dega Doom. Moreover, messengers had arrived from Apel with news that the antemi had retaken Muga Terro. The allies were finally winning the war.

Yet Kryle's spirits were not on the gloat, for he knew no war was won until the final blade was thrust. *'How many more youth must perish in battle before Morgue's maze has reaped its fill?'*

The distinct sound of a slugging gulp needled at Kryle's nerves. He did not need to turn about, he already knew. Prince Torak was already well into his jabber juice and the pensive doyen commander had no desire to take in the white ape's bleary eyes and unkempt appearance, his patience with his friend being long spent.

"Ahhhh…" Torak sighed, before belching a burp.

Kryle looked to his right, where a thin ladfolk with golden locks and alert blue eyes stood staring down a slope. A frozen basin at the bottom was ringed with the nasty thistles and tall burdock bushes that were so common in The Great Forests.

A rumbling deep down in his gut moved Kryle to think, *'We have all burned far too much fat from our frames. After this war is over, I shall never again carp about the taste of any meal, no matter how bland. Or bleat on about the cold.'*

Sensing he was being watched, Aytik turned and offered his cully a brief nod before stomping some slush from the tops of his boots and sighting back down into the basin.

"Perhaps he notth' come," Prince Torak slurred.

"He will come," Kryle snapped. "Sickly is not one to break his word."

"Should we trust him, Doyen Commander?"

"We've already been through this, Doyen Zira. We will hear what he has to say."

"We are routing Pid's forces without his aid," Zira pressed.

"As is he without ours," Aytik cut in. "It is best we hear him out. Our troops are exhausted and we needn't gain a new enemy if we can woo a new ally. His favour could help end this war shy of block by block battles in the cities. Their cities. Cities where they know every nook and cranny and tunnel and arrow loop. Where rubble always works to the defenders advantage. It would mean a bloodbath for both sides. Perhaps such can be avoided? Let Sickly keep the peace in his lands. Let us return home to ours."

Kryle failed to check a slight grin. He thought, *'War has gifted you with wisdom, my cully. You will make a good king.'*

"There!" one of the doyens exclaimed while pointing. "Movement in the brush!"

It was true. Many of the burdock bushes were shaking as unseen legs walked amongst them.

"Ah!" Kryle exclaimed when a ragged troop of gaunt lizarme finally emerged from the brush and started to climb the slope.

They were led by an elderly lizarma who was clad in worn boots and torn trousers. A hide cape, lined with fur, was wrapped about his upper body. His movements were slow and laboured, and a walking stick was needed to help propel his hunched body forward. Misty breath gave evidence of heavy panting as he struggled to drag his mangled limb along behind him.

As he drew near, the elderly lizarma's solitary eye never strayed from Kryle. He was clearly sizing up his counterpart.

321

Black teeth smiled between his cracked and swollen lips as he extended his fist in greeting. "Ah, at last I meet the unstoppable Doyen Kryle. 'Tis a fine day for a fight, won't you agree?"

"'Tis always a fine day for a fight," Kryle replied, neglecting to bump fists.

"And always a fine night too," Aytik added.

"Hiccup..."

Ignoring the drunken prince, Kryle kept his attention focused fully onto their guest. "My compliments, Prod Sickly. Your hungry ones have fought well. They are to be admired."

"Would we be so admired were it not for our shared enemy? Or would we be but more scaleez to slay?" Sickly stated flatly.

"You have spine to come here," Kryle noted.

Aytik and Torak both nodded to agree.

"Your wisdom and moral character are well known to us, Doyen Commander. Were it not so, I would never have come. Yes, it is true Supreme Pid forced this horrible war upon us. But be that as it may, your troops still stand on lizarme soil. If this war is to end, you must agree to withdraw your troops east of the Divides – after Pid's regime has been crushed, of course."

Torak again moved to speak, but serious black eyes stared him mute. Clearly, Kryle was taking no chances. Not with so much at stake.

"We also have options, Prod Sickly," Aytik said sternly. "You know we are winning this war. Should we decide..."

"Winning with our help," Sickly cut in. "Our rebellion has kept legions of Pid's troops away from The Wall and Muga Terro – plus we've stretched Prod Gila's silence squads near to snap. All of which has taken a tidy toll on our common enemy and diluted the pressure put on yourselves and the antemi. So do not discount our worth as an ally, Prince. We hungry ones have been fighting Pid's regime and paying our own toll in pain and blood since long before your war even began."

"Yes, with your help," Aytik conceded, softening his tone. He knew Sickly's words rang true.

"It was lizarme who attacked us," Kryle proclaimed. "We had no option save to respond."

The frail lizarma reached up and gently patted Kryle on the arm. "Pid and his deep state cronies started this war, Doyen Commander. Those very same lizarme against whom we hungry ones have battled for cycles. Our quarrel has never been with apes or humanfolk. Our fight has always been with Pid and the likes of Gila and Dorak. I can assure you none have suffered more under their tyranny than our own. This is why I have come to offer you terms for an alliance. Terms to build a lasting peace between us. We hungry ones do not seek a new enemy. Nor will we dwell in the past. No good ever came of such folly.

"Surely, you can see how such an alliance will hasten an end to this war – how a lasting peace would bring great benefits to all of us. We have now fought two bloody continental wars. Both have wrought nothing but devastation and despair. Both have caused even more bad blood between us. Better we should learn to talk to each other and trade with each other than it is to fight each other. From now on we must always make an honest effort to coexist – to defy segregation – to settle disputes peacefully. We at least owe that much to our youth and to posterity. Would you not agree?"

Sickly's passion and logic were met with silence.

Noting their hesitation, Sickly cut to the meat of the matter. "History will judge us all quite harshly should we squander this opportunity to shorten a war and prevent another. There can be no healing as long as we occupy each other's lands. There must be a pact of peace so fair it bests vengeance – lest the future shall become a circle which leads us back to the past."

"And should we decline your terms?" Kryle asked, folding his arms across his chest.

Sickly toned serious. "That would deeply sadden me, Doyen Commander. Instead of peace, we will all have new enemies to battle. Make no mistake of it, we hungry ones will never surrender our freedom. Not to Pid, Not to you. Not to anyone. Ever. Nor will we accept foreign troops garrisoned on our land. Would you?

"Are we all so daft we would give the wrongs from the past over to posterity? I should hope not. Surely, we can solve disputes with speech over spears? Surely, the passage of time mated with humility can teach us forgiveness? True, time alone heals nothing – but forgiveness and a willingness to change do. And we can begin the healing this very day, right atop this very hill. We must at least try. We must, or two horrific wars will have taught us nothing. And there will someday be a third.

"So once more I ask that you consider our terms and allow we hungry ones to defeat Pid and his kind on our own. Such an act will sow seeds of trust in all our plots – seeds which in time will reap peace. And who of sense does not wish to dwell in peace? Is peace not what all save the merciless and the mad desire? As leaders are we not bound by our conscience to pursue peace at all cost – to make every effort? Am I not right with my words?"

A chorus of murmurs wafted across the hilltop as apes and humanfolk and lizarme all nodded in support of Sickly's words. Once the murmurs had waned, an uncomfortable stillness settled over the hilltop and all eyes stared hopefully to Kryle and Aytik and Torak. All knew one of history's defining moments now hinged on their choices.

"What precisely do you propose?" Kryle asked at last. It was apparent by his tone he was still cautious. *But hopeful.*

Sickly leaned forth on his stick. "These are our terms. You may keep the eastern foothills as your own. We cede all claim to any land east of the Divides. We will also negotiate in good faith for a settled border through the mountains. Properly mapped out and secured by written pact, should you so desire."

"We should," Aytik stated quite clearly.

"Also, all lizarme naval forces shall be recalled home without delay the very moment we hungry ones take power – although it pains me to confess that many lizarme youth have been schooled by the state and are thus incapable of critical thinking. They do not believe in freedom of thought for others – just those who agree with them. They only mimic the ideals they were taught by the state's educators. All other voices are to be silenced. Sadly, some will battle on to the bitter end. After all, we are dealing with closed minds. Closed and locked. Indoctrination of youth has long been a favourite tool of tyrants."

"My Father will deal with them," Aytik interjected. "We shall not hold you liable for rogue lizarme."

Sickly paused to collect his thoughts. "I thank you for that, Prince Aytik. As to Empress Antraha's interests, all claims to Muga Terro and Oasis Lake will be ceded back to her at once."

"And what must we cede in return?" Kryle asked, his tone still bearing a dash of doubt. Prod Sickly's terms seemed almost too good?

"After Pid has been deposed, all allied troops must be marched back behind our pre-war borders. We also propose a special tribunal be established to discuss and settle disputes between nations. Yes, there will be crises and setbacks – of that we can all be certain. No system will ever be perfect. But anything is preferable to repeating the senseless slaughters of history."

Kryle stroked his beard and nodded his consideration. "Hmmm? Who would oversee such a tribunal? Who appoints the judges? How would it enforce rulings should one nation decide to ignore the court? Where would this court be?"

"Those are matters for our best minds to discuss once all troops have been withdrawn back behind their own borders. But first we must bring an end to this cruel war."

"Prod Sickly, our troops have fought valiantly for their victory. Our nation has been ravaged by lizarme soldiers. Our crops have been burned. Our beloved Capital lies in rubble. The survivors deserve to see Pid's head stuck on a pike – and promptly. It is a matter of justice, not vengeance."

"Prince Aytik, I assure you justice will be swift once the supreme has been condemned by a proper court. Not before."

A silent standoff quickly ensued. All along the hilltop, weary soldiers exchanged worried glances. Could it all fall apart over this?

At last, it was Kryle's voice that tempered the tension. "We must discuss this matter amongst ourselves, Prod Sickly. My troops shall tend to your every need. Doyen Goorth!"

"Yes, Doyen Commander!"

"Our guests are to be given food and drink. Also, scrounge up some warm capes for their backs."

"Ah, just some cold water shall suffice," Sickly said. "We won't be a burden."

Kryle took no offence to Sickly's refusal. "As you wish. See to it, Goorth."

"At once, Doyen Commander!"

"And have all these guards deployed back to their units. We have no need of them here."

"Yes, Doyen Commander!"

Aytik and Torak and several of the most senior knights and doyens followed Kryle until they were all safely out of earshot beyond the far slope of the hill. There they began debating Sickly's offer, while Torak looked on with his jug.

"Why do we even need this Sickly?" one of the knights asked."

Torak squinted and scrunched face as drunkards do when they think they just missed something?

Aytik spoke straight to the crux. "To bring a swift end to this war. Just imagine trying to pacify the hungry ones. Look at that battle hardened lot. Sickly would mock Morgue himself to defend lizarme territory. This war would never end. Never. Posterity would know no peace – only more spilled blood. And we would be rightly cursed for it. No, Sir Brog, we very much need to end this war. And Sickly feels it too."

"But why does he offer such generous terms if he believes he could beat us in battle?" asked one of the doyens.

Kryle and Aytik simply shrugged.

"Perhapth heesth just weary of war?" Torak suggested.

Kryle and Aytik looked to their unkempt friend, then back to each other.

"Prince Torak speaks with sense, Kryle. I too am weary of war. And the hungry ones have been at war far longer than us."

The white ape beamed proud as all drunkards do whenever they think they've proved their wit.

"What say you?" Aytik pressed, speaking directly to Kryle.

"Antraha must be consulted and agree to Sickly's terms," Kryle noted. "There will be no separate peace. We shan't betray our antemi allies a second time."

"No, of course not. But if she should agree?"

"Hmmm…?"

"Kryle?"

"I'm still thinking, Aytik."

Night's skytwinklers were beginning to advance atop the eastern peaks when the eastern allies finally reached a consensus. They strided with purpose back across the hilltop to where Sickly and his entourage stood waiting. A tipsy white ape teetered along behind them.

"Empress Antraha must agree to the terms," Kryle stated. "We owe her that much and more."

"Agreed!" Sickly concurred with complete confidence, speaking as if he knew something.

"I hope she does," Kryle added.

"I do as well," Aytik put in.

"Antraha is quite sound of sense," Sickly reasoned, offering his hand to shake. A lone tear trickled from his eye. "With Oasis Lake and Muga Terro back under her rule, I am confident the empress shall opt for peace. Even antemi queens love their pupae. Moreover, no parent with sense wishes to see their youth wasted on battlefields – which is why we must always take heed never to rip scabs off old wounds and make each other bleed all over again. Bigotry can be patient. All too often it takes just one careless remark to raise the wrath of Morgue."

Aytik also felt his eyes wetting over. He wondered if it could really be true? Could the war finally be nearing its end? Would he soon be with Shyamala? With Olob? Would he soon see his sister? Perhaps he could even make peace with his father? Somehow, he sensed Sickly was a lizarma they could trust. A lizarma with honour.

As Kryle moved to shake Sickly's outstretched hand, Aytik noted the other commanders and knights were likewise making peace with Sickly's fighters. Thus, he also moved to shake Sickly's hand. If only for a moment, they locked sights and smiled in good faith. To the young prince, the touch of dirty claws never felt so good.

Tarawa's Choice

A lean and lanky figure sat at the edge of a steep cliff, high atop the crashing wetrollers far below. His weary face was a map of battles fought. An especially ugly scar spread across his brow.

"Ah!" he huffed, tossing a stone over the edge. He watched until it splashed down amongst a shiver of sharks. "Dung! It is utterly useless to fight on. Our youth are meeting Morgue for naught."

For most of the day, Tarawa had sat pondering his army's plight. He bore no illusions, their situation being beyond desperate. Dawn after dusk after dawn after dusk the tenacious allies had repeatedly launched daring attacks against his soldiers, and time after time after time his troops had fallen back in beaten disarray.

They now found themselves encamped on the shore of The Great Forests, just a short march from the ancient seaport of Dega Doom; a city now fully controlled by Prod Sickly's hungry ones, the local garrison having been defeated after countless days and nights of savage hand to hand combat. Reports confirmed casualties on both sides had been horrific, with neither giving quarter or taking prisoners. Civil war always spawns an especially spiteful form of hatred.

All attempts to stem the allied advance and regroup his own scattered forces had failed, due in no small part to the skill and tenacity of the enemy's capable doyen commander. Tarawa cursed in admiration as he thought of Kryle. Only a fool would have attacked with thoroughly exhausted troops immediately following the brutal battle at The Wall. A bold and brilliant fool! Even he had to admit Kryle's brazen assault had caught him completely unawares. It had since proved to be a turning point in the war as it put the lizarme army permanently on the defensive. Momentum now sided completely with the enemy.

To rub salt into open wounds, he could get neither
Supreme Pid nor Prime Prod Dorak to accept reality. As with
most tyrant's who become potted with power, Pid was void of
all sober perspective. As was Dorak. Both held tight to the
surreal belief they were still in control and winning the war.
This in spite of transparent truths to the contrary; their main
army had been pushed westward all the way back to the
outskirts of Dega Doom, and what remained of a once proud
fighting force was now depleted and exhausted, mere skeletons
of their former bulk.

Making matters even worse, humanfolk partisans had
proved themselves a hardy match for Sergon's occupation
forces who were currently bogged down in the east. As well,
Muga Terro and all lands surrounding Oasis Lake had recently
fallen to the antemi. Even the hungry ones had become a
formidable force, taking control of village after town after city
all throughout the realm. But most telling of all, fighting was
now raging in the very streets of Cracow itself!

Despite all the glaring realities, Pid spent his time snorting
powder and ordering imaginary armies into battle. Armies that
had long since been decimated in battle. All of it made Tarawa
sick to his stomach.

Thinking briefly of Sergon, Tarawa wondered why his friend
had not sent him any letters for some time? It was not in his friend's
nature to neglect such things. If nothing else, Sergon was meticulous
about keeping in contact. *'He always writes me... Very strange?'*

Shifting his thoughts to the past, Tarawa's mind settled on
young Gekar. His son would have been eight cycles aged now.
How he missed Gekar's rebellious nature. His laugh. His hugs.
His obsession with dacts. Although Tarawa himself had
survived the ambush, his heart and spirit had passed on with his
family. Now every day was darkness.

Tears trickled down scarred cheeks as Tarawa thought of
his mate. Not a single day passed without him praying the
deities should return her to him. If only for one embrace. Just
one kiss. He'd give anything to gaze into her beautiful blue eyes
and feel her smooth flesh pressed tight against his. To caress

her. To see her white smile as she teased him for speaking aloud to himself. If only he could reverse time, how different he would have acted during that fateful carriage ride back from the palace. If only he'd been more vigilant. If only he'd been more aware of his surroundings. If only… If only… If only… There seemed no end to his regrets…

Such thoughts proved too painful for his mind to bear, so Tarawa quickly steered his thinking back to the situation at hand. His army was nearly encircled; by the allies to the east and south, by the hungry ones to the west. Trapped between one rapidly advancing army and another that refused to budge. Only the swells of the sea kept his own army from being completely surrounded.

His troops had fought valiantly. That much at least made him proud. Few of his soldiers or commanders had proper cause for shame. Until quite recently, very few had deserted. He could not blame those who did so now. Why meet Morgue for naught, especially with young tots of their own to feed? What if he still had Gekar? Would he not himself desert? At least he hoped he would.

Mistakes had been made, the most costly by himself. He had badly underestimated Doyen Kryle; a mistake which had thereafter kept his army fighting a defensive war against an adept and determined enemy who simply refused to rest. An enemy who just kept on coming. And coming… Yes, he had completely misjudged Kryle's character. Not once had he considered the black ape would toss the bones to risk it all; that the usually cautious and calculated doyen would recklessly attack westward in such great numbers. Or that he would be so relentless in pushing an offensive war so deep into lizarme territory. Vanguard over rearguard. And for all of that, Tarawa knew the blame weighed fully on his own shoulders.

'Strange,' he thought, 'Pid has not yet relieved me of my command. Perhaps his powdered mind has him spun completely round-the-twist?'

Tarawa would have welcomed such. Putting aside Pid's rants and Dorak's ridiculous orders to attack, was it not enough his army also had to battle four foes all at once? Six if one mixed in hunger and cold, for the frigid quarter had been more biting than most. Far too many soldiers had lost digits to the freeze. Plus he could no longer bide the spectacle of his soldiers struggling to survive. On too many occasions he had witnessed his gaunt troops gnawing on roots and the gummy under bark of trees, or digging deep beneath frozen ground to catch dormant wigglers.

The recent onset of the wet quarter was granting little reprieve, as the damp chill of constant skyshowers was inflicting many with the spewing sickness. Many soldiers had also succumbed to the hack, for there were few healers to mix elixirs. Others had taken to the shivers, with only boiled water to warm their innards. In fact, Tarawa was now losing more soldiers to sickness and desertion than to enemy attacks!

A flighter had offered to have his dact flap him away to safety, but Tarawa had refused. Abandoning his army and fleeing was not an option. Nor would it ever be. His loyal troops deserved better. No, he must stay and do whatever he could to help those soldiers who had so bravely followed him into battle. He must try to spare them. To see them safely home to their families. To their mates. To their Gekars. But how?

Shifting his position on the slippery slab, he took in his options. All of his best thinking had found but two. He could order his army to fight to the last lizarma, or he could surrender and throw his troops at the mercy of their enemies. Baring Destiny's divine intervention, there was no third option open to him.

Would his old adversary seek revenge and put all lizarme troops to the noose and the spit? Tarawa doubted it. All evidence thus far shouted to the contrary. In fact, the great ape himself had sent two scribed notes pledging that any lizarme who surrendered would be treated with dignity as befits all beings of Destiny. Prince Aytik and Prince Torak had also stamped their seals to both documents.

Sickly had likewise sent a scribed message pledging that any prisoners of war would be given food and apothecary care as best his forces could provide. The rebel prod also swore a personal oath before Morgue that there would be no reprisals taken against any troops who laid down their weapons and surrendered, regardless of rank; Prod Gila's silence squads excepted, of course. Fair terms, to be sure. But could he trust the hungry ones? Then again, could he afford not to? True, there was no guarantee Sickly would keep his word. Alas, it was equally true that should he not forfeit the fight his own troops would soon starve or be taken by illness.

To fight on was futile. Absurd even. Only Morgue could approve of such madness. More battles make for more orphans. Had the war not already made too many widows? Would it not please Destiny for him to spare his defeated army to return home to their families? Was it not best his final order should be one of honour over one of duty, an order to preserve life rather than take it? Surely Seed would agree?

Tarawa would have kept on with his debate of conscience, were it not for a brouhaha erupting amongst his commanders. He twisted about to find them all shouting and pointing at a lone dact, which was flapping up the escarpment towards them. The beast's awkward efforts to stay aloft showed it to be quite weary on the wing. It also neglected to screech upon its arrival; always a telltale sign of dact fatigue.

The dact's flighter steered the beast to touch down amongst the excited commanders, all of whom hastened to crowd around the welcome messenger. Even before he dismounted, the young flighter was forced to field a barrage of questions. Eventually, he turned from the impatient mob and retrieved two mail sacks from his beast's back. Upon opening one of them, he pulled out a small scroll and asked something of the growing crowd. Several responded by pointing to the cliff's edge.

After nodding his gratitude, the flighter handed both sacks over to the melee of outstretched arms before pushing his way through the mob. His small purple eyes were fixed firmly upon Tarawa.

Ignoring the sacks, many of the commanders started following the flighter. Common soldiers likewise hastened to join in. They too took note of the scroll and sensed it might be a document of much importance.

"Prod Commander Tarawa?" the flighter asked as he approached.

"I am he," Tarawa said, pushing to his feet.

All stared with wided eyes and muted tongues while Tarawa took the scroll and walked away. Upon reaching the edge of the cliff, he stopped and carefully slid the ribbon from the scroll and broke open the seal. Then he hastily read the message:

PROD COMMANDER TARAWA:

Prime Prod Dorak dispatched in ambush. Prod Commander Sergon burned at sea. Hungry ones attack in great numbers. Civil war imminent. Abandon The Wall at once. Quick march army west to defend Cracow. By order of Supreme PID III.

"Hmpff," Tarawa muttered. He knew not whether to howl or weep. *'Yes,'* he mused, *'Pid has spun completely round the twist. Madder than a shiver of sharks in a tide of blood. The fool's mind thinks we are still attacking The Wall. Ha! Destiny so punishes the wicked.'*

Tarawa turned to address the messenger. "Are you certain Prod Dorak and Prod Sergon have both breathed their last? That they have already met Morgue?"

The flighter nodded. "Yes, Prod Commander. The message came direct from Capital. About Prod Sergon, I mean. I saw Prod Dorak's bloat with mine own eyes. Not much left of his face, but I know his long body. It was he, I am sure. Bashed near into goo he was. A right fine splotch…"

"I get it," Tarawa interrupted, raising his hand for silence.

Tarawa clasped both hands behind his back and took to pacing back and forth in deepest thought. Initially, only the seaside breeze cut through the silence, until a soft pattering of light skyshowers also spoke its piece. Far to the northwest, booming skybangers echoed after flashbolts.

Tarawa raised his eyes to the dreary above. The cold drizzle felt fresh against his face. Briefly, he peered down at the shiver of sharks thrashing about the swells in search of a meal. *'If only the purpose for being could be so simple for all,'* he mused.

Things had not been all bad, he reasoned. Not really. He had risen from an unlettered nobody to become Prod Commander of Land Troops. More importantly, he had known love in its purest form. He winced at the thought of Anole and Gekar lost in the maze. Alone? Frightened? "Be it Morgue's will, I will soon embrace you both."

"Prod Commander?"

The disruption to his thoughts caused Tarawa to turn about with a scowl. He caught himself and stretched a fake smile for the benefit of his troops. Many anxious faces now looked to him for an answer. He fully intended to give them one.

"My loyal troops!" Tarawa shouted to top the wind. "Hear my words well! I am proud to have fought alongside all of you! We thought victory would be ours! But Destiny decided it was not to be! Yet here you stand, willing to fight on! You need carry no shame!

"Enough widows have been made! Enough orphans! Too many tears have been shed! Too much blood has been spilled! Too many hearts brim with sorrow! Too many dreams have been dashed!"

Tarawa paused to let his words sink in. More tears came as he saw a hint of hope in his soldiers' eyes. *'They too are weary of war. They too miss their loved ones. Their mates. Their tots. Their Anoles and their Gekars. They just want to go home. To be with their families. To grow old and play with their grandtots...'*

Brandishing the scroll high atop his head for all to see, Tarawa worded his lie carefully. "This scroll comes to me direct from the hand of Supreme Pid himself! You all see it! It states I am hereby ordered to accept all allied terms of surrender! Envoys will be dispatched at once under flags of truce to both Doyen Kryle and Prod Sickly in order to make terms for an orderly cessation of hostilities! All weapons are to be heaped high in piles and ceded to the allies on demand! The war is over!"

Tarawa's words were met with shock and silence. None could imagine their supreme ever suing for peace. Yet Pid had done just that. Prod Tarawa held the proof in his hand. At first, not a single commander dared to speak. All were muted by fear mixed with relief. Peace was welcome, yes. But what should become of them now?

At last, one of the high commanders asked what all were thinking. "Prod Tarawa, what pledge do we have our enemies will show mercy in their terms? Are we and our loved ones bound to become their villeins and serfs?"

A murmur floated about the crowd as many lizarme shook their heads in defiance.

"We'll battle on, Prod Commander!"

"We're still fit for a fight!"

Tarawa paused with pride as he took in his army. Even now, they would fight until their final breath for him. He thought, *'Perhaps they fear the peace more than they fear the war?'*

Regardless of their reasons, on this day he would choose honour over duty. Duty counts for naught when a cause is unjust. He saw such so clearly now. Honour is never about loyalty to any prod. To any ruler. To any kingdom. To any nation. To any deity. Honour is about loyalty to that which is just. And to meet Morgue without honour is to never know peace. *'Is it too late for me? Has my fate been sealed? Oh, well – I shall know soon enough?'*

Looking out over his loyal troops, Tarawa couldn't help but wonder how many had mates? How many young Gekars were waiting back home in their cribs? How many young apes? How many young humanfolk? How many antlings? How long must these senseless slaughters go on? How many more wars will need numbers? Could he make a difference? Perhaps? At least he must try. For the future Gekars.

Donning his most scary of scowls, Tarawa rolled and tied the scroll. Next, he flung it over his shoulder and into the sea. "Who amongst you dares question our Supreme!? Well, speak up! Speak up, I say!"

335

Only a whisper of wind and the soft patter of drops replied.

"Very well then! Now still your wavering tongues! This war ends today! Our enemies are mortal! As are we! Our enemies desire peace! As do we! Our enemies have shown honour! As shall we! Should we accept their terms of surrender, you will be spared to return home to your families! As I shall soon seek out mine! Mercy shall shine! Prod Sickly has sworn an oath before Morgue!

"Surrender and there will be no revenge or reprisals against any of you! Sickly and the allies have pledged such in ink! Now go, do as I order! All high commanders will act as envoys and approach under flags of truce! Some to Sickly! Some to the allies! All mid and low commanders will see to the piling of weapons! Every trident! Every scimitar! Every lance! Every shield! All of it is to be sorted and piled. Such is written into our pact for peace! Now go! Tend to your tasks! I wish to be alone with my thoughts!"

Most commanders hesitated, until the ranking high commander shouted, "Ye all heerd thy prod commander! Now move ye lazy butts and make ready to pile thine weapons! Commander Tagus, see to it! Commander Draco, ready a peace contingent to approach Prod Sickly! Commander Skink, muster a second to approach Doyen Kryle! Commander Volans, dispatch messengers to spread the terms of surrender. All units are to stand down at once! We are at peace!"

Tarawa could barely suppress a smile of satisfaction when all of his commanders and soldiers began scrambling down the grade to capitulate. That is, all but one.

The lone flighter who had delivered Pid's message stopped partway to his dact and turned about to sight in Tarawa. At first he moved to speak, but decided better of it and simply smiled knowingly. After offering a sincere nod of gratitude, he hastened to mount the weary beast.

The Prod Commander of Land Troops stood with wetted eyes as he watched his soldiers vanish off into the foliage. For some time he found himself unable to move. His entire body felt numb. At last, the terrible conflict was coming to a close. There was now little left to ponder?

Tarawa savoured the pleasant sensation of cold water cooling his flesh, yet his insides felt warm. Destiny's reward for doing what is morally just? Perhaps? For the first time in a very long while, he felt free from his fears. Free from his pain. Everything was now exactly as it should be. He had played out his part.

Tarawa knew eventually the true nature of Pid's message would become known. His place in history would then become that of a traitor. There would be no future for traitors in the new order – lizarme soldiers would never forgive him. Treason is never deemed a virtue by either side. He thought, '*How very lonely it feels to do that which is just*'.

Turning to face the sea, Tarawa stepped up to the edge of the cliff and deliberately unsheathed his scimitar. Closing his eyes tight to dull the pain, he deliberately drew the blade across his wrist.

A sticky warmth trickled down his hand and dripped from his digits as he prayed of Destiny to pity him and judge his heart alongside his deeds. He confessed he should have always placed honour above duty. Anole had encouraged such, but he did not always listen. Ambition had driven his success, and led to his failures. As soldiers so often do, he had confused duty with honour. He'd seen both as the same. And for such he was sorry.

As his mind waned, he begged of Morgue to unite him with his family in Utopia – and to let him become a better mate and father in the afterlife. Shifting his sights to the dreary above, he thought briefly of Sergon. Would they meet again in Morgue's chilly maze? Or would they both be pardoned into Utopia? He whispered one final prayer for his old friend before closing his eyes to cleanse his mind and heart of all hate.

Satisfied he could do no more, he thought once more of Gekar and Anole. There had been much happiness after all. Reaching inside his vest, he pulled out the most prized of his chattels. A crystal vial filled with ashes and bone dangled from a gilded snake-chain. Tears seeped from his eyes as he lovingly kissed the object, before placing it back against his chest.

"I've always kept both of you next to my heart. Be it Morgue's will, I shall soon hold each of you in my arms."

And with that, Prod Commander Tarawa simply spread his arms and fell to meet Morgue.

Pid and Gila

A tongueless toiler with purple eyes and amber flesh honed his ears for sound as he polished the legs of an enormous hardwood table. As he buffed the smooth surface to a fine shine, dancing particles of dust waltzed about within the warm beams that penetrated down from the dyed-glass windows in the library's domed ceiling.

Shifting his eyes upward, he stared past the brazier and the windows to take in the clear above. A flock of dacts flapped across the blue sky, each bearing a flighter and a lancer, while clenching spears and bashing-balls in their sharp talons.

The toiler would have favoured skyshowers on this day, for such conditions always made it difficult for flighters to sight in their targets. They would be forced to swoop in low, exposing their beasts to barbed bolts and arrows. Still, in spite of the clear sky above, the toiler had good reason for hope. Earlier in the day, word had been passed along to him that the battle for Cracow was finally going well for his side. Quite well in fact, as most of the populace had at long last broken free from their fears and now openly sided with the rebels. After thirty cycles of abuse and struggle, the winds of war finally blew at their backs.

Ever the actor, the toiler knew nothing could seem amiss in the discharge of his duties. All must appear routine and normal to the palace guards, lest he should raise their suspicion. His role as a witless toiler lacking in pluck must be played out a bit longer. Too much was at stake. Besides, he had nursed his revenge for far too long to spill its spoils now. *'First one – then the other. Patience... Focus... No mistakes...'*

With his cleaning rag and bucket in hand, he limped from the table over to where fine hardwood chairs were rowed neatly along a study counter. Snuffed candles in various stages of melt were positioned in front of each seat.

The toiler paused to scan the library. Three walls were fitted ceiling high with cubbyholes for scrolls. Wooden ladders were clamped to metal slides for quick ease of movement. Brass sconces were fastened to the panels beside each cubby so the scrolls could be visually verified before removal for further study. Some of the lower cubbies were packed full with stone or wooden tablets, and a few even contained the latest items for sharing information; bound sheets of calf vellum called books. Along the fourth wall, a row of padded chairs were lined up facing a long counter. A candlestick was placed in front of each chair, with each candle snuffed until next it was needed. Yes, everything was in its proper place.

A subtle grin stretched across the toiler's bruised face. He thought, *'How furious Pid's Prods would have been had they discovered I was aiding the rebels from within this very palace – that I have long been smuggling out detailed copies of their battle plans. Our rebel commanders, especially, benefited from my pilfering of writings on military tactics, all taken straight out of the Royal Library! And they were mercifully spared much anguish thanks to Gila's foolish boasting beforehand of his planned raids on their hideouts. Gila's big mouth has always been one of our greatest assets. Well worth every beating. Ha!'*

'Wait – the shuffle of approaching feet!' Dragging his clubbed foot on the swift, the toiler hastened back over to the table and began washing the tabletop. Sunbeams warmed its smooth surface.

His heart raced as a heavy hardwood door squeaked open. Exercising extreme caution, he positioned his eyes to sneak a subtle peek. Yes! Pid was alone.

The supreme appeared shrunken as he shuffled along in a stoop. His purple robe hung loose about his frame. His mien was unkempt. He suffered from powder nose. His eyes were weary and glazed. Drool dripped from his mouth. Flesh sagged on his face.

His sceptre aided his movements. A crown of white gold was cocked sideways on his head. A vial of white powder swung from his neck chain.

The tongueless toiler thought of the many times he had tampered with the vial's contents. Not that the powder alone wasn't poison enough, but he had often mixed in another powder of the type used to rid the palace of rodents. He still could not believe that the Palace Guard had not once questioned his access to the royal bed chambers. They simply ignored him. Such were the benefits of being seen as nothing more than a servile simp, as Prod Gila was so keen to call him.

"Slerf, fetch my guards," Pid ordered in his strained and raspy voice.

Slerf bowed and plopped his rag into the bucket. Then he turned and limped from the library, returning moments later with two guards in tow.

"Fetch me Dorak!" Pid ordered. "I must speak with him!"

Both guards exchanged bewildered stares before shifting their sights back onto their Supreme.

"Are your ears sewn?" Pid snapped. "Or do my own guards also slight their supreme's commands?"

A tense pause ensued before one of the pair finally got up the courage to speak. "Sire, Prod Dorak was dispatched in an ambush two phases past. He was…"

"Why was I not informed of this?"

Again, both guards exchanged bewildered stares. This time neither dared to speak.

"Very well," Pid huffed at last, "I always knew he would abandon me. Just like all the others. Tarawa, Sergon, my soldiers. Traitors, I tell you! Traitors, every one of them! Were they still of breath, I'd have them all put to the spit! To the spit, you hear me! To the spit!"

Tension ruled as Pid made mute and closed his eyes. He began rocking back and forth on his sceptre, while softly humming a burial lament.

Both guards looked to Slerf, who merely offered up a shrug.

"Gila!" Pid suddenly blurted, popping open his eyes. "Fetch me Gila at once! Dorak and Sergon as well! They must ready a ship for my escape!"

341

This time the guards did not hesitate. With quick bows of respect, they turned and fled from the room. Both clearly concluded this was a matter for others to deal with. Neither wished to be part of their supreme's madness any longer.

Pid smiled giddy as he uncorked the stopper to his vial and then snorted in the contents.

"Ahhhh…" he sighed, sealing his eyes and savouring the rush as it passed through his body. Satisfied, he replaced the stopper and gazed vacantly about the room. He was visibly lost in his surroundings.

"Slerf? Where are – Ughh…"

Panic gripped Pid's mind as the blade plunged repeatedly into his chest. His throat was being squeezed in the crux of a thin, yet determined, arm.

In panicky confusion, Pid tried to shake off his assassin. He spun around and around, flailing about with his sceptre, trying to fling or knock Slerf from his back. His crown fell from his head. Garbled gurgles spit royal blood across the tabletop as he tried to call out; but his voice would not respond. The determined toiler had his throat crooked too tight in a squeeze.

With all strength sapping from his limbs, Pid slid from the table and dropped to his knees. Glazed eyes near popped from their sockets as he pitched forward to meet Morgue.

Slerf paused in mid pant and honed his ears to snag sound. They heard only the beat of his pounding heart. And silence. Beautiful, welcome silence. The guards had not…

"Uhhh…"

Slerf near scat from his skin as an evil spirit fled from Pid's throat. So he plunged deep his blade just to make sure.

There was no more time to waste. Mustering up all of his courage, Slerf calmly re-sheathed his dagger and dragged Pid's limp body behind the table. Next, he retrieved his rag and bucket to sop up the mess.

Once the telltale blood had been sopped clean, he tossed the rag back into the bucket and hid it beside Pid. He then drew his blade and hobbled on the swift to wait by the door from the anteroom. His heart pounded on the sprint. Revenge was so very close. He whispered, "Destiny, I beg of you, do not deny me now."

There was no more pause for prayers as unseen knuckles rapped from behind a cubbyhole, warning Slerf to make ready. An unseen guard greeted a grumbling voice from somewhere within the anteroom. A screaming silence preceded the distinct clunk of a latch locking into place. Slerf knew at once Gila was in the library.

Suddenly, Slerf caught sight of Pid's crown laying on the floor. *'Dearest Destiny! How could I be so remiss?'*

With no time to fetch it, Slerf re-sheathed his weapon and stepped out into Gila's path. The War Criminal stood directly before him; clad, as always, in his black cloak and matching skullcap. His cruel purple eyes glared daggers through the mute little toiler who dared block his way.

Slerf feigned complete surprise as he bumped into the irate prod, knocking Gila's spectacles from his hand. A glassy *crunch* confirmed that the clumsy toiler had *accidentally* stepped on the fragile object.

"You servile simp!" Gila screamed, grabbing Slerf by the jaw and slamming him up against the wall. His facial scar seemed to swell with his rage. Spit sprayed from his mouth. His brandished fist revealed the all too familiar ring in the shape of a skull.

Even as he squirmed and struggled to gulp in a breath, Slerf simply could not resist. In his first open act of defiance against the cruel prod, he spat forth with a gob of his own and kicked out hard at his tormenter.

Gila was fleetingly frozen. He stared in disbelief at the insolent toiler, completely uncertain of what to do next? Until next his anger exploded into open rage. His claws dug deep into his victim's throat, cutting into the flesh. With his free hand, he reached to draw his blade.

"I'll gut you from groin to – Ughh…"

Gila grunted in agony as a blade stabbed his belly. Barely a nick later a well targeted slash severed his speech. He released his grip on the toiler and grabbed his own throat. In their frenzy and fear, legs became tangled and both fell to the floor.

Slerf lay atop the cold marble, writhing to draw breath. He thought, *'Must keep Gila from alerting the guards.'*

Somehow, throat still in hands, Gila managed to stagger to his feet and stumble for the door. Until thin arms tackled his legs.

Slerf gasped for air as he crawled atop his abuser. It was now a battle for his being as well. He gripped the hilt with both hands and lunged forward to finish the deed. For far too long he had wanted this moment. Ever since Gila had severed his tongue, revenge had filled all of his waking moments and much of his dreams as well. He would not be denied his revenge now. No matter the cost.

"Ughh..." Slerf grunted as the blade stuck into bone. Pain shot up his arm and found his shoulder. Wrapping his free arm about Gila's neck, Slerf drew power from pain and plunged blade to the hilt. Over and over and over...

"Ahhhh..." the crawling war criminal moaned as he dragged his much smaller assailant along with him towards the door. Just a bit further...

"Crack!"

Gila froze in mid fight as two hands cupped tight about his chin and snapped his head rudely to the side. He found himself staring up into laughing purple eyes.

Despite his lack of a tongue, the muted toiler still managed to gurgle in glee. Making certain Gila was fully aware of his joy, he retrieved his blade from the cruel prod's ribs and sank it deep into his heart.

Gila's body quivered, before slowly slacking still. His grip waning along with his breath.

The grateful toiler sat choking for breath. Only Destiny's grace had prevented Gila's claws from gouging out the fatal cut. Sticky warmth trickled from the gouges in his face and throat. His limbs felt heavy, his vigor drained.

With much effort, Slerf pushed up to his feet. He thought briefly of Pid and Gila. *'Enjoy the chilly depths of Morgue's maze. Ye both earned your place.'*

Slerf next scooped up Pid's crown. Once melted, it would fetch its worth in coin. Easily enough to buy medicine for his ailing mate. *'Spoils of war,'* he reasoned.

Reaching down into the bucket, he squished damp the rag and started washing the blood from his throat and face. He must not leave a trail. With that thought foremost in mind, he dipped his hand inside his robe and retrieved a small pouch.

While leaving the library, he opened the pouch and spread its contents about the floor. *'Peppercorn always puts rexids off a scent.'*

While passing back through the anteroom, Slerf could not resist a glance back at the motionless heap on the marble. He then glanced in the mirror and gave a thumbs up. Unseen knuckles rapped back from behind the glass.

Slerf spread the remaining spice all about the anteroom. Satisfied it was sufficient, he pushed his way past a red curtain and limped on into a narrow servants' corridor. Partway down the corridor, he paused to scan about. Being certain only friendly eyes could be watching him, he reached out and slid a panel aside to reveal a small cubby hole. Inside it were a chamber pot, a pillow, a basket of biscuits and a full costrel of good wine.

Having quickly glanced about one last time, Slerf bent down and squeezed into the cubby. He carefully slid the panel back into place and sat in silence upon his pillow. He thought, *'Soon the guards will find the corpses and begin rounding up toilers. I just hope all are in hiding?'*

Yet Slerf reasoned the guards best take revenge on the swift, for advance units of rebels were already battling to reach the palace walls. And once they did that, his palace spies would sneak some of them in through secret sally ports. After which, total victory should be theirs in a matter of days. Perhaps even sooner?

Until then, the Prod Commander of Cracow's Hungry Ones was quite content to wait out the war all alone in his cubby. And to savour his wine and his biscuits.

Liberation

King Myro stood still and silent while taking in the devastation along the harbour of his once vibrant city. Charred remnants of cranes littered the piers. The blackened ties of the boardwalk were still mostly in place, but virtually all of the warehouses had been gutted, their insides reduced to charred heaps of ash and timber. Every shop and the entire rookery had been razed to the ground.

Olob stood beside his king, long of face and torn of heart. His white hair and beard were thick with dirt and his hooded blue frock was worn and in dire need of a brushing. Yet despite his dishevelled appearance, the old historian's quick blue eyes were as alert as the dawn he was birthed. Wisdom still etched deep into his face.

Next to Olob, a weary galfolk in a worn cloak and tattered blue gown stood staring out over the carnage. Her palm was slapped tight over her mouth, yet her sobs seeped through.

Myro thought, *'Shyamala weeps for those whose homes have been burned. While I must cede she has shown ample courage during the war, is it wise to choose such a benevolent queen to raise a royal heir? Perhaps my grandtots should be placed in the charge of worthy knights for their upbringing, lest they become spoiled and weak? I must remember to raise the matter with my son.'*

Standing next to Shyamala, Princess Helenia shifted her tired eyes back and forth across the shore. Her tunic stretched to cover her growing belly.

'It shan't be long now,' Myro thought, as his daughter noted his stare and returned him a smile. He patted his own belly. She patted hers and nodded all was well. It was a gesture that brought relief to his worried heart, for he had not wanted her to make the journey south from the Upcoast Forests. Nor had

young Sir Arduk for that matter. Of course, Helenia being Helenia, she had flatly refused to stay behind while their army attacked and liberated Capital.

However, none had expected to find the city all but abandoned. Most lizarme had simply boarded their vessels and sailed home. Others had surrendered without giving battle. Save for a few skirmishes with lizarme zealots and looters, the liberators were met with no real resistance.

The king hoped such conditions would prevail, for messengers had recently arrived with news that both Cracow and Dega Doom were now firmly under control of the hungry ones, and that Supreme Pid was with Morgue. Dispatched by his very own toiler was the rumour. But no matter the cause of Pid's demise, there was no sense in either side prolonging the slaughter. It was finally over.

Myro shifted his eyes onto the frail lad with a freckled face who stood beside his aeront. "Sir Arduk, are you certain the city has been abandoned?"

Arduk bowed in reply. "Yes, sire. We seeked for the enemy, but there just be some prisoners who gived up."

A knight banneret of the Royal Guard stepped forward to elaborated. "It is true, sire. We have collected several hundred starving enemy soldiers who surrendered without a fight. My knights were hard pressed not to put them to the spit right off, but by Sir Arduk's appeal we spared the scaleez their due. What would your grace have us do with them?"

"Feed them," Myro replied quite curtly. "What else is there to do?"

"Sire?"

"I said feed them. And have their ranking officer brought to me."

The bewildered knight paused for his tongue to fetch words. "Sire, we have barely enough food for our own? Surely, you..."

"Share with them what we do have," Myro snapped. "The war is over. They are no longer our enemy and we shall show them mercy."

"But, sire, what if there should be others. I mean, more scaleez may still be in hiding…"

Olob scowled serious and cut in. "If they attack, slay them. If they surrender, feed them. Such is your king's command. Why do you question it? Are your ears sewn?"

"As you wish, sire." The knight bowed to Myro, before turning and swifting up the slope.

"And refrain from calling them scaleez!" Olob shouted after him. "They are lizarme!"

"Father, might we approach our castle now?" Helenia inquired.

Myro shook his head. "Patience, my dear. We must wait until the entire castle has been searched from keep to curtain wall. If there are enemy troops still spoiling for a fight, it is there where they will rally their defence."

"We've waited thus far, Princess," Olob added. "A little bit longer shan't matter for much."

"Ye father and Olob be wise," Arduk added, moving to embrace Helenia. He gently placed a hand upon her belly, smiling as he exchanged thoughts with his tots.

Helenia snuggled into his arms and buried her brow in his shoulder, wrapping her arms tightly about his waist.

Shyamala and Olob exchanged sneaky smiles, while Myro rolled his eyes. Both knew their king had developed quite a fondness for the *'scrappy little runt'*, as he privately referred to Sir Arduk. In fact, ever since the ladfolk had returned from sinking the enemy carrier, all of nobility had adopted him as one of their own. But it was the king himself who seemed most eager to welcome him into their class. Naturally, he insisted Arduk learn his letters. And proper manners. A knight must always conduct himself in keeping with his rank. Especially one destined to someday become an earl. Possibly even a duke?

Some bachelor knights arrived with a shackled lizarme in tow. Before their captive was brought before King Myro, the knight banneret caught up to them and lashed out with his tongue.

"A low commander!" he ranted. "You bring to our king a low commander! Sire, my apologies for…"

"Sire, I am our highest ranking commander," the shaken lizarma informed Myro. "All above me have fled or met Morgue."

A charged silence followed, with neither knight certain what to do next.

"Dearest Destiny, bring the youth here," Olob scolded at last.

"Why is he in shackles? Release him at once."

"Yes, sire."

Myro and the others waited impatiently for the guards to remove their prisoner's irons. All felt some pity as they looked into the youth's pleading purple eyes. A tattered skirt-of-battle was all that clothed his emaciated body. Amber flesh hung in folds from his frame.

The youth mustered up a grateful smile as he bowed low before Myro. He had clearly been expecting the noose or the spit.

"Rise," Myro ordered in his strictest tone. "Commander, should you and your soldiers keep the peace in my kingdom, then you need not fear reprisals. I have pledged mercy to all who surrender. The war is over. Tell us, what is your name?"

"Relief spread across the young commander's face. He eagerly pushed up to his feet and effected another bow. "Most merciful, King Myro – my name is Tagu."

"From where do you hail, Tagu?" Myro pressed.

"My clan are desert traders, sire. Our tents are our homes. Sire, my soldiers wish only to surrender and return home to their families – there to dwell quietly in peace. You shall bear no further bother from us. This I pledge upon my very soul – lest Morgue should banish me to the deepest depths of the maze."

"Stand up straight," Myro commanded. "You need not bow every single time you speak. It's rather trying. We accept your surrender, Tagu. My Royal Guard has been charged with your protection and your health. Unfortunately, we are somewhat short of healers and apothecaries, given the fortunes of war. You may, however, have your wounded and sick brought to our infirmary. We will do for them what we can until our navy can escort you to the foothills west of the Divides. Once put ashore, you must find your own way home.

"Sir Arduk will see to matters. He also has ken of the ancient language. You may raise any concerns directly with him. Sir Arduk, escort Commander Tagu back to his troops – and make certain they are fed."

"Yes, Me King." Arduk gently tugged on Whitezig's reins and beckoned for Tagu to follow.

After effecting yet another bow, Tagu started to turn away. Then he paused and fixed his wetted eyes upon Myro. His tone was sincere. "We are grateful for your mercy, sire."

"Just see we have no further trouble from your kind," Myro stated flatly. "Now be off with you."

Myro turned to speak with Olob, but was interrupted by an approaching guard.

The elderly grandfolk panted forth his message. "M-Me King – thine castle is secure."

"Are you certain?" Olob pressed.

The winded guard merely nodded.

Myro looked lovingly at his daughter. "Very well, then. Shall we go and reclaim our home?"

Helenia smiled and took hold of her father's arm as they began the long ascent up the escarpment towards the castle. She could not help but note how bony and fleshless the limb felt.

As they slowly wound their way up about the rubble, the aged king took note of several tough-looking galfolk lazing about the broken debris, chewing the blabble and puffing on gagweed. Stretching a slight smile, the grateful ruler silently praised Destiny for sparing his subjects a battle to retake the city. He thought, *'It is proper the war should end this way. Too many fine young galfolk have been lost to Morgue already.'*

Soon the entire entourage was plodding along on the pant. Wind and unseen spirits whispered from amongst the burned-out boxes that were once home to prosperous guild workers and artists. Scorched clay slabs littered the cobblestone roads.

Noting the sorrow in her father's eyes, Helenia gently patted his hand. It felt cold to the touch. Such seemed strange to her, given they were now well into the hot quarter and the sun's rays warmed the flesh. "It's all good, Father. We will rebuild."

Myro nodded and smiled at his daughter. "In time you and your brother will restore Cracow well beyond its former glory. Alas, I shan't breathe to see it."

Helenia thought to respond, but tiny feet kicked within her womb. "Ahhh…"

"My dear?" Myro inquired, grabbing hold of her arm.

Shyamala also moved to steady the woozy princess. "Helenia, is it time?"

"N-Not right now," Helenia managed, shaking her head. "But soon."

"I will send for a midwife?" Olob stated, gesturing to a young guard.

"No," Helenia replied, noting the worry on her father's face. "I am well, father. Truly, I am. They kick like mules is all. Arduk says they grow restless within my belly as they are eager to meet with family. He has told them so much about us. But he won't tell me if they are sons or daughters. I swear it gives him great pleasure to torment me so."

All those about the princess shared suspect looks. It was clear they were anxious over Helenia's mind as well as her body.

Olob and Myro especially exchanged troubled stares. Had not the realms ranking midwives assured them Helenia's belly grew but one tot? Yet Arduk asserted her belly grew two? Could he be right? Possibly? But as to his claims he could surmise both tots gender from their mother's scent and that he'd been linking thoughts with the siblings for some time now – ABSURD!!

"Come on," Helenia said, smiling and tugging on her father's arm. "We still have quite a climb before us."

In due course the roads widened and the burned out boxes were replaced by the stone manors of wealthy merchants and money lenders. Their gates and curtain walls remained fairly intact, although lizarme writings and drawings defaced much of the stone. The manors' walls themselves stood much as before, except all of their ornate panes and doors had been pilfered. As a result, their interiors had been both looted and ravaged by

weather. Weeds were now taking root in some of their foyers.
Broken statues littered the properties, clearly the work of vandals.

Above the manors, the faux castles of the nobles had fared
much worse. Curtain walls still stood much as before, although
with gates swung open. Every manor had been torched from the
inside and its thin walls had been knocked down. Piles of
broken stone mixed with pan tiles were all that remained where
magnificent homes had stood for generations. Even so, many
courtyards and gardens had been meticulously maintained?
Very strange?

"Sergon's high commanders likely dwelled in these manors
until they withdrew from our lands," Olob reasoned. "They had
them torched and pounded into rubble out of pure spite, I'll
wager."

"A wager you would most likely win," Myro concurred.

As the entourage drew near to the castle, they could not
help but note a stark contrast between the scorched shingles of
some roofs and those the flames had passed by. Even from some
distance, they could see that all of the keep's dyed-glass panes
had been pilfered. Without them, the tower bore a much
harsher side to its soul.

The cobblestone drive widened as they approached the
barbican protecting the main gate leading to the lower bailey. A
pair of somber guards stood still as statues outside the main
barbican as their king passed beneath the portcullis and into the
tunnel.

While grass still grew in tufts about the lower bailey, all of
its gardens had been trampled under. Only charred ruins
remained of the stables and barn and other wooden structures.
A blackened stone shell was all that endured of Knight's Hall,
it's wooden roof having burned and collapsed into its center.
One lonely anvil squatted amongst the ashes and rubble of the
blacksmith forge. Nary a creature was seen or heard, neither
domestic or wild; not even a bird.

After crossing the ward, King Myro and his entourage took
a brief rest before starting up the winding steps to the barbican
and the drawbridge. The stench of moat and waste grew

stronger with each step, moving weaker stomachs to spew. As they approached the barbican, soldiers of the king's Royal Guard peered down from the bretèche.

Most wondered, *'However can they stand the smell?'*

The drawbridge had been lowered in anticipation of the king, hence his entourage wasted little time in crossing over the smelly moat towards the gate to the upper bailey, where the heavy iron portcullis was dropped to the ground.

"Sire!" a soldier shouted down from the bretèche, " The portcullis will not raise! The windlass drum is cracked! There is only the wicket!"

Myro simply waved to the youngster.

After the entourage had filed through the walker's wicket, it was but a short amble past the cisterns to the castle keep with its great hall. Myro led the way, using his sceptre as a walking stick while panting to scale the same narrow stairwell he had so often raced up and down as a lad. Once the aging king had finally struggled and puffed his way to the top, a burly guard strained to open the heavy oaken door.

Myro shuffled down the acrid and puddled corridor towards the great hall. Once again, tears flowed down his cheeks. His tongue could taste the brine on his lips. He seemed indifferent to a guard holding the door open for him, as well to the marble fragments crunching beneath his worn out slipperboots.

"Thank Destiny it is just one broken statue," Helenia muttered beneath her breath. *'It pains me to think of what these primitive lizarme will have done to our kingdom's cherished works of art? Just look at how they pilfered the panes.'*

Upon entering the great hall, all were stumped by how the keep's interior had been spared the flames? Clearly, someone had battled hard to confine the blaze? But who? Surely, not the lizarme? Whyever would raw savages put themselves at risk to save humanfolk art? Or any art for that matter? Lizarme and culture were two words never spoken together.

Even more baffling, the lizarme had neither pilfered or destroyed the many fine works of art to begin with. Fortunately, not a single tapestry or painting seemed out of place. Unfortunately, every work had suffered some smoke damage. They were all coated with a thin film of soot, while a musty odour came from the tapestries. Nevertheless, no work seemed beyond mending. If used properly, vinegar and lye could work wonders.

"The scaleez left our most precious works hanging in their proper place," one noble noted.

"Maybe the scaleez are more civilized than they let on," another suggested.

"I thought I made it clear we are not to address them as scaleez," Olob scolded. "At this moment vulgarity rests not with the lizarme."

Both nobles simply bit their tongues and lowered their eyes. They knew full well who the old historian cited.

It was but a short stroll from the great hall to the adjacent throne room, and soon the entourage was shuffling down a short corridor towards a charred door. Statues hid behind soot and tapestries reeked of mould. Discarded buckets lay in puddles. It was evident flames did battle with swash in here as well.

More guards toting pikes and shields stood rigid with respect as their ailing king shuffled past.

A hunched and aged archer in a flat cap stepped forward and creaked open the door. His free hand cupped a puffing pipe. He nodded and stretched both galfolk a gloating grin, exposing blackened teeth through white whiskers.

Now recognizing Rufus Tindal from the battle at the forest fringe, Helenia and Shyamala smiled and returned him nods of respect. They both wondered, *'From what well does that grandfolk draw his spit and sass?'*

Upon entering the throne room, the entourage spread out along the walls to take in its condition. Again, all were surprised the enemy had seen fit to care for the room's décor and artwork. The king's throne was kept in its proper place, although one of his purple cushions had been torn. His favourite jewelled goblet was also in its place. Quite puzzling, really. Why had no lizarma seen fit to at least pilfer that?

"Perhaps we have wrongly condemned all lizarme with the same verdict," one of the elder witan suggested.

"Some seem to possess a penchant for decency," added another.

"It appears so," Olob agreed.

All eyes locked upon their king as he shuffled his aged body across the room as though looking at something?

"Sire?" Olob asked.

Setting his eyes upon his historian, Myro stretched a satisfied smile. "The floor," he added.

His words were met with silent stares.

"The floor," he explained. "Can you not see it? How can you not see it? Look here, our enemy has hand painted a floral scene directly onto the marble and sealed their work with some sort of wax coating before polishing it. See there, those yellow sunflowers look almost real. So do those honey bees gathering nectar. Look over there, those purple coneflowers are home to ladybugs and butterflies. They even included hummingbirds. Hummingbirds of all things. Did you know hummingbirds were my dear wife's favourite? She often said they were sent by Seed to remind us laughter was life's most precious gift. It has been too long since we have laughed our cares away. We must all learn to laugh again. We must laugh, or life is not life – but just death in waiting.

"You know, I understand all this. Artists do what artists do – whoever they are and wherever they are. They cannot help but do it. Creativity is baked into their soul. Fantasy flows through their veins. Art is the one true labour of love – a passion for passion. It connects spirits who otherwise would not mix. How bland life would be without artists. And the lizarme clearly love art. I never imagined beings I deemed barren of culture could create such wondrous works as these. Works as beautiful as any I... Ughh..."

"Father!" Helenia screamed as she dashed to catch the king before he slumped to the floor.

With Olob and Shyamala's help, they lowered Myro gently onto the painting. He clenched his left arm as he stared up at them with blinking eyes. Sweat coated his brow. His laboured breaths filled the room as he struggled to speak.

"Don't just stand there and gawk – fetch a healer!" Olob screamed at some of the guards. "Swift on the sprint!"

"H-Helenia…" Myro somehow managed at last. "My… my… I love you…"

The trembling princess sat upon the cold marble and gently lifted her father's head into her lap. She kissed his burning brow. "Keep silent, Father. The guards are fetching a healer."

"Ughh…" Myro groaned, squirming about in Helenia's lap. With great effort he twisted his head to face Olob. His determined eyes revealed he had something more to say.

"Old Friend, what is it?" Olob asked, bending his ear close to his dying king's mouth.

Myro reached up and grabbed Olob's frock by the scruff and tactlessly yanked the startled historian's ear down to touch his quivering lips.

Olob nodded to show he understood Myro's whispers. Then the weeping historian reached inside his king's robe and retrieved a tiny hide pouch.

"Such will be done, old friend," Olob promised, holding up the pouch for Myro to see.

The king nodded his gratitude before shifting his eyes to gaze up at his only daughter; to whom he gifted his final smile…

"No!" Helenia shouted as her father's body sank limp and his eyes stared only to Morgue. Tears poured freely down her face as she cradled his head and began rocking him back and forth in her arms.

Silence ruled the room for the longest time as every subject stared down with wetted eyes. In Myro they had lost not just a king, but a just king. A king who truly loved his subjects. He had led them in battle against the invaders, and stayed of breath long enough to share in their victory. Now he was gone. For each journey must end, even a king's. It is Destiny's design that none breathe forever. And that none ever will.

Helenia wept openly and rocked her father's still form back and forth in her lap, fully unaware of two familiar forms entering the throne room. Both were filthy and weary, yet beaming with joy.

One was a bulky figure with hair as black as his eyes. He had a broken upper fang. His wrinkled skin was worn tough by the winds. A braided beard draped down between his pecs. A battle-axe was strapped across his back. Fists dangled like clubs from his thick arms and he bore spiked wristlets of rank.

The second figure was a handsome ladfolk with long golden locks and alert blue eyes. His sturdy legs supported his lean torso with broad shoulders. Dried muck was caked about his boots. Sweat stained his trousers and tunic. A broadsword was slung across his back.

"My King," one of the nobles stated as he bowed low before Aytik.

"My King," echoed all others, mimicking the gesture.

Aytik instantly took in the sitch and charged across the room to be with Helenia and Shyamala. Joy and sorrow battled mixed feelings while he stared down at his father. Tears began to seep from his lids and trickle trails down his cheeks. He had arrived too late.

While Aytik began rocking both galfolk back and forth to comfort them, Olob struggled to a stand and stuffed the pouch into his frock. He then moved to stride away.

However, a hairy hand grasped him firm about the shoulder. He turned to find himself staring up into two bothered black eyes.

"Olob, where is Princess Tianga?"

The pity in the aged historian's eyes answered Kryle's question for him. And for the only time since he had first learned to walk, he felt his legs weaken.

A New Beginning

King Aytik donned his regal robe and matching red slipperboots as he sat at the king's table overlooking the festivities. A gemmed circlet kept his long hair in check. In one hand he clenched his gold ruler's sceptre, in the other a tankard of small beer. His alert eyes scanned the many spectacles occurring all about the upper bailey.

The sight of such a merry crowd warmed the king's heart, for it was not long past when these very same subjects had little to cheer about. Now they were feasting and laughing and cheering and dancing and clapping out cadence. There were jesters and jugglers and minstrels and poets from every corner of the realm. To add sugar on sweet, Destiny had blessed their wedding day with a windless blue sky.

The realm's wine casks still sat empty, yet there was plenty of mead and ale to liven one's spirits. Pandemain and wastel were also in short supply, but there were ample loaves of clap cakes and horse bread made from legumes and bran and acorns. And while meat was still scant, the war having claimed most of the livestock, for today the pipkins bubbled over with mutton potage while seven prize hogs spun on spits. Yes, the feast and festivities were going quite well despite the lack of many staples. Should any guests leave without a full belly they would have only themselves to blame.

A satisfied smile stretched across Aytik's face. Since dawn he had gained both a queen and a brother-in-law. Also, he had never seen his sister so happy. Helenia's face beamed like the moon.

It had been Queen Shyamala's selfless design for her and the king to share their wedding day with the younger couple. Aytik had quickly agreed, although not because he thought it a fine notion. King or not, he knew there were just some things a

358

groom dare not do. One was to trespass on *her* wedding day. Like all grooms before him, he was barely a bit player in her show. A living prop of sorts. And King Aytik knew it unwise to interfere in *her* event. A wise king he might be, but a wise husband he must be.

Seated side by side were a black ape with a broken fang and a gaunt old lizarma with one eye. Aytik smiled and nodded to both ambassadors before steering his attentions back to the merrymaking.

Aytik laughed aloud as he observed Prince Arduk and Princess Helenia in dance. The circle dance had started out slow, with each dancer moving sideways to their left. They began each step with their left foot, next sliding their right foot to strike it. The entire circle spinning slowly in time. Courtly... Polished... Graceful...

When suddenly, Arduk broke from tradition. He squatted low with folded arms, wildly kicking out with his legs.

The talented minstrels quickly adapted and upped the tempo. Then a loud cheer erupted and the revelers began clapping out cadence, while Helenia laughed aloud and whirled in circles around her freckled young groom.

Somewhere beyond the curtain wall, the prince's howlers began baying out their approval.

The new king shifted his sights to lock eyes with his queen, who looked six tiers above striking in her flowing blue gown. She offered him a pleading grin as she held both of their nieces. Beside her, Ambassador Viceroy made faces, which caused the blanketed bundles to coo with delight.

Aytik smiled as he recalled how he and Arduk and Viceroy had been present that stormy, moonless night when Princess Helenia had birthed the tiny pair into the queen's waiting hands. He smiled as he remembered how he and Arduk had steadied their legless friend, and then caught him in mid-drop. He still found it highly amusing how such a brave and battle-hardened antema had swooned at the sight of a birthing; neglecting, of course, to remind himself he had also felt quite light-of-head; selective memory being every king's privilege.

Suddenly, Aytik's smile slacked into a frown. How he wished his own father had breathed long enough to meet his grandtots. How he wished he had told his father how much he loved him while the old king was alive. Not a single day passed that the new king did not wish he could have swallowed back his parting remarks that final eve before he set off to war. If only he'd written… If only he had the power to roll back time… If only…

The young king wondered what his father would think of his efforts to rebuild Capital? Mathematicians and builders were already drawing up plans for an even bigger city, complete with a modern system of sewers and cisterns to keep spoiled water from fouling the pure. New Capital will have a modern hospital where healers can treat the infirm and help stem the spread of pestilence. There will be much wider roads and proper schools. The realm's youth will learn their numbers and letters. Aytik also wanted them to have proper clothing. To provide such, he had decreed all subjects under fourteen cycles aged were to be provided with free school uniforms, including boots and capes to keep them dry and warm through wet and cold. Under his rule, no youth under fourteen cycles aged would be permitted to toil in the mills or the mines. Nor would any galfolk be forced into a loveless marriage. Or any marriage.

To be sure, these many changes could not fully find their place until after the realm had recovered from the devastation of war; but find their place they shall. Aytik often pondered over whether his father would approve?

Aytik watched with unspoken admiration as the antemi ambassador ceased his play, bowed his respect to the new queen, and then arm-swung on crutches over towards the other ambassadors. He thought, '*I think I should join them.*'

"A lack of legs certainly poses no hurdle to his happiness," Sickly remarked.

"Does your mangled limb pose any barrier to yours?" Kryle asked.

Sickly shook his head. "No, it does not. Whatever lot we must bear, I believe we will be as happy or sad as we mentor our mind to be. I seem to recall a famous humanfolk speaking such words, although the name escapes me? It's an age thing, you see."

Kryle smiled at his friend's quip. "Don't I know it. I'm not that far behind..."

"Sire," Sickly cut in, bowing before the king.

"Sire," Kryle followed.

"Yes," King Aytik assured him, nodding at Viceroy. "The ambassador does have a knack for the positive. In fact, just this very day he was telling me how he successfully petitioned Empress Antraha for resources and workers to build an Academy for Peace in Muga Terro. Quite admirable, to be sure. Scholars shall debate in the ancient continental language and its doors shall be open to all students – not just antemi. He thinks bringing together scholars and students from afar to discuss their ideas freely will help cultivate a better understanding of each other's cultures and in turn prevent future wars. He is of the radical idea that allowing students to disagree and even shout at one another is still communication; that real trouble begins when we deny those we disagree with a right to their voice. Naturally, he will offer his services as provost – at least until the institute has taken root."

"Which it no doubt will," Sickly affirmed.

"The ambassador will make an exceptional leader for the cause of peace," Kryle added."

Viceroy nodded to acknowledge the compliments. "I am hopeful for a chance is all. If the position is offered, I shall take it. The decision rests solely with the empress."

Aytik thought about his admiration for all three ambassadors. He had grown to like Sickly, who had refused the lizarme offer to become their absolute monarch. Instead, Sickly had put in place a ruling council similar to that of the Black Ape Federation, before accepting his current post in the diplomatic corps. A position he had much coveted, for diplomacy often clasps the keys to peace.

Aytik next steered his sights and his thoughts onto Kryle. He was quite worried about his cully, for the great ape had greyed and thinned terribly since learning of Tianga's ugly meeting with Morgue. In fact, Kryle barely ate at all. He had even declined a seat on the Federation Council, which had been his ambition ever since he was a young lad.

Aytik also thought about the effect the war had taken upon his other friend, Prince Torak. The white ape had failed to show up as promised. Again. The king mused over what his slurring friend's excuse might be this time. Regardless, he owed Torak for having his back during countless battles and he had no intention of abandoning his friend now. Or ever. Torak's obsession with jabber juice had the realm's best medical minds completely baffled? None knew what could be done with him? Or with the many others so afflicted? All of the realm's finest healers expected such sots to meet Morgue well before their time and agreed there was nothing more to be done for them. Such a prognosis left Aytik broken of heart. *'Alas, there are some things even a king cannot fix...?'*

As if reading King Aytik's thoughts, Kryle suddenly spat out, "The sting of war can be especially painful, sire. It not only claims lives and limbs, but maims minds as well."

"It does at that," Sickly agreed. "But at least the sting hurts a mite less when you win."

Kryle nodded. "This is true, ambassador. Albeit barely a mite of a mite. Let us hope going forward peace will rule over this land we must all learn to share."

Sickly sighed heavy before responding. "I also hope for such. But alas, forever is a very long time." The wise lizarma paused briefly before adding, "Should our scions forget the lessons of this age and allow a Third Continental War, then perhaps we do deserve to languish inside Morgue's chilly maze."

The others all nodded in solemn agreement.

"To peace then!" Kryle exclaimed, lifting his tankard.

"To peace!" added the others.

Aytik could not help but note Olob shuffling up to Shyamala. The king was intrigued as he watched the aged historian whisper something into his new queen's ear. Shyamala responded with an affirmative nod before gently handing her nieces over to their wet nurse. She then pushed up to her feet and walked alongside Olob as they approached Aytik and the ambassadors.

Olob bowed before his king. "My apologies, sire. Might I have a word with you and her majesty in private? It shan't take much time."

Aytik returned his mentor a loving smile. "Certainly, old friend. My ears never tire of your wisdom."

"It is not wisdom I bring you this day, sire."

The aged historian led them from the bailey and into the keep. Aytik and Shyamala exchanged curious glances as Olob slowly led them down the corridor leading to the great hall. Shadows from statues seemed to dance along the walls.

They startled three inattentive guards who were busy throwing cubes. Upon sighting their king, they tripped over one another's feet in their haste to stand and draw open the new oaken door. Olob scowled his displeasure as they passed between the anxious trio, each of whom knew they had not heard the last of it.

"Let it pass, Olob. A king must always be gracious on his wedding day. Besides, everyone else is making merry. Perhaps you could have some hot food brought up to them? And some small beer. We don't want them getting too tipsy."

"As you wish, sire. Their laxity will be excused – this time."

Queen Shyamala smiled and hugged Aytik's arm. She was clearly proud of him.

Once they had entered the hall, Olob led the curious pair across the polished tiles until they stood beside the king's table. There the old historian paused briefly to catch his breath. He patted Aytik on the upper arms and smiled. "It has been a fine day for a wedding, won't you agree?"

"A very fine day," Aytik agreed.

"For two weddings," Shyamala noted.

"Ah, yes. For two weddings. My apologies to her majesty."

"No apology is due me, Olob" Shyamala assured him, feeling somewhat awkward in her new role as queen.

I always knew someday you two would become king and queen of this realm," Olob said, dipping a wrinkled hand inside his frock. "I believe Destiny desires it. It warms my heart to see it is now so."

"Thank you for such kind words, Olob."

"You're most welcome, My Queen."

"It is sad my father could never share your feelings on this matter," Aytik said. "Still, I would have very much enjoyed his presence here on this day."

"I would very much enjoy your father's presence anywhere on any day," Olob replied with the sincere smile of one fondly remembering a departed friend. "Alas, we must settle for his spirit. Can you not feel his spirit's presence?"

"I can't say that I do," Aytik replied.

"I do," Shyamala said, nodding in sympathy at the old historian. "I know you miss the king something terrible, Olob."

"More than words can say, Your Majesty."

Aytik sucked back his own tears. "I think of him every day, Olob. I do and it pains me. I did not mean those cruel words I spoke. If I could roll back time…"

"The king knew you didn't mean it," Olob interrupted. "In fact, we often drank wine and enjoyed many a chortle over your stubborn manner."

"You did?" Aytik asked, suddenly hinting at a smile.

"We did," Olob assured him, removing his hand from his frock and offering the new king a tiny pouch. "I would present this to you on bended knee, sire. But alas, at my age I may not get back up."

Aytik passed on the jest and looked blankly at Olob.

"A gift from your father," Olob explained.

Taking the pouch from Olob's hand, Aytik loosened its string and spilled out the contents. A gold band on a silver chain dropped into his palm.

Again, Aytik looked to Olob. Then to Shyamala. Then back to Olob.

"I do not understand?" Aytik managed at last.

With the love of a mentor burning in his eyes, Olob moved to explain. "Aytik, this ring belonged to your mother. Your father carried it on a chain next to his heart from the very moment she met Morgue. He never parted with it, not even while bathing. He

364

said it reminded him her spirit was well and watching over him – and over you. He drew strength from it. Aside from you and Helenia, it was the most precious possession he ever had. He would have sacrificed his throne to keep it."

"Olob, I never knew…"

"Sire, there are a great many things during our life's journey we will never understand. One is a father's love for his son. I must confess, it is a love of which I have had no acquaintance. I have no sons or daughters of my own. No siblings. No family whatsoever. My father abandoned my mother and myself when I was still feeding from her breast. Perhaps that is why I have long suffered the pangs of envy while hearing your father speak so proudly of you. Oh, how he loved you. He always knew you loved him too, in spite of your mulish nature. It is past time you forgave yourself for your tactless tongue. As best I know, there is no decree banning acts of forgiveness to one's self. In fact, if memory serves me well, somebody once told me a king must always be gracious on his wedding day."

Aytik's smile began to stretch. "Clever. Trapped by my own words."

"No, not trapped. You are free to choose. Forgiveness or bitterness? Sire, the choice is seldom painless – but it is always our own."

"I hear you, Olob. But how does one forgive without feeling less than?"

"Perhaps it will help if I add one last piece to the puzzle. The final piece. For without all of the pieces one can never see the full picture. Sire, your father also bore regrets. And more than anything, he wanted your forgiveness."

"Olob, how could you know what was in my father's heart?"

'I know because it was his final request I should give your mother's wedding ring over to you – and because, with his passing breath, he said to tell you he hopes it fits Shyamala…"

THE END

About The Author

When I was a young boy growing up in Canada, I loved to read fantasy stories that took me to faraway places in distant times. As an adult my interests strayed from fantasy stories to nonfiction books about medieval life. The historical events of that often-misunderstood era intrigue me to this day.

Some years ago I moved far from home and away from my family and friends. Very quickly my biggest struggles in life became boredom and loneliness. To deal with these issues, I decided to try writing a story, thinking that a creative mind was no doubt healthier than a stagnant mind.

Since then I have combined my love of fantasy and history to produce three novels which are currently available in either print or eBook format through Amazon. My only goal is to be read. If readers can escape into my books and laugh and weep over my words, then I have done my job as a writer. And hopefully my stories will leave some of you feeling all nice and warm inside. Hugs.

Message from the Author...

Thank you for reading my book.
I hope you enjoyed this story,
Please help guide future readers by
leaving a review on Amazon.com
If you have comments or questions,
feel free to contact me at:
rennickderon@gmail.com

Read another novel by Deron Rennick...

Chasing the Staff
The Webscroll